NEW SILK ROAD

BROOKS TENNEY

Order this book online at www.trafford.com/07-0246
or email orders@trafford.com

Most Trafford titles are also available at major online book retailers.

© Copyright 2007 Brooks Tenney.

All rights reserved. No part of this publication may be reproduced, stored in a retrieval system, or transmitted, in any form or by any means, electronic, mechanical, photocopying, recording, or otherwise, without the written prior permission of the author.

Note for Librarians: A cataloguing record for this book is available from Library and Archives Canada at www.collectionscanada.ca/amicus/index-e.html

Printed in Victoria, BC, Canada.

ISBN: 978-1-4251-1836-5

We at Trafford believe that it is the responsibility of us all, as both individuals and corporations, to make choices that are environmentally and socially sound. You, in turn, are supporting this responsible conduct each time you purchase a Trafford book, or make use of our publishing services. To find out how you are helping, please visit www.trafford.com/responsiblepublishing.html

Our mission is to efficiently provide the world's finest, most comprehensive book publishing service, enabling every author to experience success. To find out how to publish your book, your way, and have it available worldwide, visit us online at www.trafford.com/10510

Trafford
PUBLISHING

www.trafford.com

North America & international
toll-free: 1 888 232 4444 (USA & Canada)
phone: 250 383 6864 ♦ fax: 250 383 6804
email: info@trafford.com

The United Kingdom & Europe
phone: +44 (0)1865 722 113 ♦ local rate: 0845 230 9601
facsimile: +44 (0)1865 722 868 ♦ email: info.uk@trafford.com

10 9 8 7 6 5 4 3 2

Table of Contents

	Note to Readers	5
	PROLOGUE	8
PART 1	CENTRAL ASIA	
Chapter 1	New Silk Road	14
Chapter 2	Astana, Kazakhstan—1995	17
Chapter 3	A Visit to Walter Reed	20
Chapter 4	2001, Pre-9/11; Naval War College—Newport, R.I.	28
Chapter 5	Valentin—The Systems Architect	32
Chapter 6	Homeland Security Facility, Northern Virginia	38
Chapter 7	After the Education	42
Chapter 8	Valentin Adds Value	46
Chapter 9	Why Walt Loves The Silk Road	54
Chapter 10	Planning the Silk Road Tour	61
Chapter 11	Arkady Explains His Code	65
PART 2	VISITING THE SILK ROAD	
Chapter 12	2002—Scouting the Silk Road	72
Chapter 13	2003—Flo Expresses Displeasure	76
Chapter 14	Turkmenistan, 2003	79
Chapter 15	Kutchka—The Mighty Handful	85
Chapter 16	2004—Trouble in the City of Love	88
Chapter 17	Undisclosed Location, Northern Virginia	101
Chapter 18	Lawn Party	104
Chapter 19	2004—A Tale From Bukhara	107
Chapter 20	Valentin, The Enforcer	114
Chapter 21	Val Proposes a Solution	119
Chapter 22	Shanghai Skyscraper, 42nd Floor	124
Chapter 23	CHOCO's Plans for Turkmenistan	128
Chapter 24	Packaging	131
Chapter 25	2005—Summoned From Washington	134
Chapter 26	Mr. Wu's Movie	138
Chapter 27	Valentin's Little Sister	145

PART 3	HERDING CATS	
Chapter 28	Notes from Walt's Briefing	150
Chapter 29	Dreaming of Somewhere Else	154
Chapter 30	Cats Across Central Asia	160
Chapter 31	Gina Santorini	164
Chapter 32	Hong Kong Film Studio	168
Chapter 33	Mira in Ashkhabad	173
Chapter 34	Dialogue	176
Chapter 35	Chinese Fire Drill	178
Chapter 36	Arkady's Criminal Empire	180
Chapter 37	On Location in Turkmenistan	182
Chapter 38	The Mighty Handful Go To The Movies	184
Chapter 39	Valentin's Unexpected Orders	192
Chapter 40	Mira Finds Help	198
Chapter 41	Gina Follows a Hunch	202
Chapter 42	Mira's Debriefing	206
Chapter 43	Visiting Khiva	213
Chapter 44	Feedback From Mira's Trip	218
PART 4	CONFUSION	
Chapter 45	Trouble in River City	224
Chapter 46	Off the Beaten Path	229
Chapter 47	In Vino Veritas	233
PART 5	FLIGHT	
Chapter 48	Flight	236
Chapter 49	Train Ride Across Turkmenistan	242
Chapter 50	Val Changes Direction	248
Chapter 51	Snatch and Grab, Russian Style	260
Chapter 52	Arkady's Punishment For Val	263
Chapter 53	The Movie	276
Chapter 54	Mira	280
PART 6	THE CARAVAN RETURNS	
Chapter 55	Florence Returns	286
Chapter 56	End of the Line	293
	EPILOGUE	306

Note to Readers

In consulting multiple sources of information about the Silk Road, one encounters many alternate spellings for the same personal names or place names. Thus: Bukhara, Bokhara; Samarkand, Samarcand; Turkmen, Toorkmun, Kirgizstan, Kirghizstan, Kyrgizstan, Genghis, Chingiz, etc. These alternates present no difficulties for an attentive reader and there is no pressing need to select a uniform spelling. Furthermore, in real life, many individuals will spell the same word differently at different times, depending upon—possibly?—phases of the moon. Who can say?

Bearing in mind Emerson's description of the hobgoblin of consistency, I have chosen to spell these words as I, or my fictional companions, have encountered them. If one doesn't encounter consistent spellings in daily life, why expect it in fiction? Any other spelling problems are, of course, chargeable to me.

The poem "On a Blind Girl" was written by Baha Ad-din Zuhayr (Arabic) who died in 1258. It was translated by E. H. Palmer.

The poem "Black Marigolds" was written by Bilhana (Sanskrit) sometime in the 11th century. It was translated by E. Powys Mathers.

The fragment from the untitled Chinese poem quoted by Mr. Wu in Chapter 51 was written by Yen Chi Tao sometime during the Sung Dynasty (960-1279). It was translated by Duncan Mackintosh and Cheng Hsi, and rendered into verse by Alan Aying.

The untitled Chinese poem quoted by actress Li Ju Zhang in Chapter 51 was written by P'u – I Ho Chu (937-978 A.D.). It was translated by Duncan Mackintosh and Cheng Hsi, and rendered into verse by Alan Aying.

I am grateful to helpers in Central Asia. Uzbek guides Yuri Kim, Larisa Dumchova and Zahir showed me around Tashkent, Samarkand, Bukhara and Khiva, aided by driver Andre and many friendly Uzbeks. *Katta Rahmat* also to Alexandra "Sasha" Kim. *Spaseeba* to Turkmen guide Mayya and driver Volodya who navigated me around amazing Ashkhabad.

Several individuals read early versions of the manuscript and contributed suggestions and corrections for which I am indebted. I appreciate the comments provided by Bob Fischer, Bethany Haswell, Wilma Young, Linda Stevenson and Carol Countryman (who caught everything I missed), and especially the assistance provided by my best proofreader, editor and critic, my wife, Hope.

PROLOGUE

Prologue

> "Over and again, the chronicles state in just a few words: 'He seized the town, it was plundered and burned, and all its inhabitants killed or taken into slavery.' Capturing a town was first of all a punishment for not having surrendered immediately. Even if it did surrender, it could still be plundered, on the slightest pretext, as occurred in Rome at the time of the Germanic invasions. This was a way of demonstrating one's strength, of setting an example, in order to terrify the adversary."
>
> SILK ROAD; (MONKS, WARRIORS & MERCHANTS)
> LUCE BOULNOIS
> TRANSLATED BY HELEN LOVEDAY

September 9th was a national holiday in Tajikistan, but Arkady wasn't celebrating and he was in a foul mood. On the day before, he and five of his "associates" had flown from Astana in Kazakhstan to Dushanbe, Tajikistan's capital, and today they had driven just under a hundred dusty miles to the border town of Poyon. The road facing east led toward the mined border with Afghanistan, giving them long, magnificent views of the foothills that stretched into the distance, brown and undulating, like the flanks of old cattle; worn by weather, time and hard use.

Poyon had little to offer in the way of entertainment but Arkady did not plan on staying longer than it took to complete the business that had summoned him.

He and his companions had paid for the use of a small roadside tavern outside the town. The simple, mud-walled building was set back some distance from the road leading to a military checkpoint at the border. A temporary barricade had been set up at the entrance to the tavern. One of Arkady's companions was parked near the barrier in case the infrequent visitor needed to be reminded that the place was closed to normal business.

Arkady and the remaining four companions were seated around a table when a vehicle was admitted around the barricade and motored up to the tavern complex. In the mild, sunny September weather, the men from the north were sitting outside, under an arbor of vines that had only recently been harvested of several bushels of grapes.

The vehicle stopped and two men stepped out. They opened the back of the van and dragged out a third man, securely bound and gagged. Their prisoner was bloody, dirty and disheveled, but most of the blood was old and dried. His face was haggard and worn from lack of sleep. He made an impossible attempt to walk unassisted and the two men guided him to the trestle table where Arkady and his men were drinking vodka. The driver remained with the vehicle. The bound man, ungagged, was led to stand before Arkady.

"Well Vartan, what do you have to say for yourself?"

"You see me, Arkady. What can I say?" It was painful for the man to speak because his lips were split and scabbed. He said the words slowly and carefully.

"Vartan, Vartan. I expected much better from you. I have come such a long way to see you."

"I think we both know why you have come."

"Perhaps. But then again … we could both be mistaken. This is a curious world we live in. And one can never be certain exactly how things might play out."

"As you say." The man, Vartan, hung his head.

"There are questions, Vartan. To which you know the answer. And we have come so far. This place where you live is a true shit hole."

"It is not Astana."

"Astana's asshole is more like it. Listen, Vartan. Give them up. You have a wife. You have, I am told, two sons. Why should they suffer because you are stubborn?"

"Why can't you believe I acted alone, Arkady? Does it hurt your pride to know that someone can act alone? I thought I could help my miserable family. I was wrong."

"You did not act alone."

"I acted alone. There are some dealers in China who work for cash. You don't know them all. But, I admit … I was foolish. I was wrong. And I am paying."

"You know, of course, that I can make you tell me their names."

"I know that you can make me scream, and curse God and say names. But you can never make me give up the names of those who helped me because they do not exist. And if I give you a thousand names, they will all be lies. There is no one."

Arkady sensed a defiant spirit in Vartan that he could abuse, dismember and eventually kill, but never subdue and it angered him to be confronted by such an individual in front of his men. This bastard had dared to purchase RPGs from the Chinese and add them to a shipment of his own weapons that were destined for the ethnic Tajiks that lived in Afghanistan, across the border.

In reality, no significant loss had been incurred but Arkady could not permit independent operators to be muscling in on the lucrative weapons trade with Afghan tribes, many of whom were enriched by infusions of uncirculated cash from America's CIA.

Arkady sensed that if he continued to talk with this man, things would only look worse for him. He had known such men in prison, men who could be destroyed slowly, bit by bit, but who would remain defiant as long as they had breath to speak. Some of these casehardened bastards could literally be taken apart without yielding. Most folded easily, but it was sometimes hard to predict how a man might behave. Vartan, he was sure, would never yield.

He beckoned to one of his minions and whispered something into his ear. The man left, headed for the owner's residence in the rear of the mud walled tavern. Vartan, exhausted, slumped to his knees in front of Arkady.

"When I was in prison," Arkady said, "I was, for a time, in a cell with a teacher of history. From him I learned much of the history of Central Asia. This place, as you must certainly know, was overrun by the Mongol hordes under Genghis Khan."

The man's head slumped and he looked to the side, as if to suggest that he was not paying attention. This infuriated Arkady but he continued to speak in a calm voice.

"By the time the great Khan's grandson came into power, the empire had grown so immense that it could not possibly be governed by a single ruler. Kublai Khan, the grandson, broke it up into pieces. He kept the easternmost chunk for himself. Mongolia and China were his, the Khanate of the Great Khan. The westernmost segment was designated the realm of the Golden Horde, the Khanate of the Kipchaks, today's Russia. Tartars. To the southwest, the Khanate of Persia was ruled out of Baghdad. This region, where we are now, was the Khanate of Chagadai and it was ruled from Samarkand. Do you not find this remarkable?" Arkady's question was addressed not just to Vartan alone, but to the entire group. No one knew how to answer.

"No one had even discovered the United States, a wilderness of red savages. But in Asia a vast empire extended from the Pacific Ocean to Vienna. Not remarkable? No? How about you, Vartan? Not remarkable? You haven't heard of Kublai Khan?"

The man who had left a few minutes ago returned with a large, rolled carpet over his shoulder. Behind him, a young son of the tavern owner carried a second carpet. The boy returned to the house and the man unrolled one of the carpets on the packed earth under the arbor.

Vartan had never said a word since Arkady began speaking, but when the carpet was unrolled his eyes widened with interest—quickly changing to fear.

"Put him in the center, lads." Two men grasped Vartan under the arms and dragged him to the carpet's center.

"Shoot me, Arkady," Vartan said. He turned to the men holding him. "Please. Just shoot me."

"Shall we tape his mouth, Arkady?"

"It doesn't matter. As you choose," said Arkady, examining something from his pocket. "Just center him up."

He turned to his other two men. "The second carpet, lads. On top." The men unrolled the second carpet over the prostrate man who was beginning to make desperate sounds. The carpets were old and worn but the owner had been persuaded to part with them for a generous amount of cash and they would be easy to replace.

Muffled sounds were coming from under the carpet.

"Now the table, lads. Upside down. Get it centered." The flat top of the heavy trestle table was placed on top of the covered man. Sounds could still be heard.

"Now, lads. The other tables. Move them so that one end of each table rests on a side" For the next minute or two the tables under the arbor were rearranged so that the legs of four tables were pinning the inverted table resting on top of Vartan. Arkady had them shuffle the tables until the arrangement satisfied some aesthetic sense of symmetry.

"So then. It is done. Yuri! Step inside and ask the owner for two bottles of vodka. And glasses for all of us. Nine of us. Three bottles, maybe that would be better? However you feel. Ask if he has Ochotnichiya. Even better—ask for Pertsovka. Otherwise, as you like. We will sit here awhile and we will drink."

He seated his men at each of the four tables, near the end that was pressing the doomed man. The three men who had accompanied Vartan looked shaken and uncomfortable but they drank the fiery vodka. They had nothing to say and when the vodka circulated they filled and downed their tumblers.

Arkady's men sat and talked aimlessly for an hour. They spoke of women and girls they had enjoyed. Of experiences—largely criminal in nature—that had loomed large in their lives. At the end of an hour, Arkady rose and signified his intention to leave. Before returning to his vehicle, he walked to the center of the inverted table and made a few test bounces, as if testing the springiness of a diving board. But he still wasn't finished.

"Well, lads. This is the real Central Asia. I learned this from Kublai Khan."

One of his men moved close to whisper something.

"No, let them all go. This, they will not forget and they will take this information back. And they will think twice next time." He reached inside his jacket.

"Fold it up, boys. Then drag it down toward the creek and soak everything in gasoline. He flipped a pocket lighter through the air. "Leave it to burn." He turned and walked toward the van.

Three men moved to carry out their boss's orders.

"Next time," one of them said to his companions, "we're taping the son-of-a-bitch's mouth shut."

PART 1

CENTRAL ASIA

Chapter 1

New Silk Road

"One might be able to define it in this fashion: a network of transcontinental commercial routes, leading from China to the coasts of the eastern Mediterranean through Central Asia in its widest sense, and Iran, as well as a complete network of maritime routes to which it connected; routes through which, since the second century BC, the exchange of merchandise has been conducted (of which silk was the principal Chinese export) and through which was diffused scientific knowledge and techniques, religion and arts."

SILK ROAD; (MONKS, WARRIORS & MERCHANTS)
LUCE BOULNOIS
TRANSLATED BY HELEN LOVEDAY

Some of the first visitors to carry Chinese silk from Central Asia to the land mass known as Europe were the Parthian soldiers who defeated the Roman legions under Crassus at the battle of Carrhae in 53 B.C. Accounts by Plutarch, and other writers describing this engagement years later, referred to Parthian 'standards, shining with gold and silk.'

By the time the Roman Empire split and gave way to Byzantium, the trade route known as the Silk Road was in full swing. The trade that probably began as nation states exchanging gifts or submitting tribute gradually morphed into more conventional business deals. Merchants carried silk and other high value items—pearls, coral, ceramics, and bronzes—across the entire continent of Asia, traversing, in stages, the rugged regions known as *the roof of the world*.

The caravans that plodded across Central Asia created a web of trails that left chains of caravanserais; caravan "palaces"—actually walled inns—which often grew into cities. Where an oasis would permit agriculture to flourish, the *serai* became a collection of mud huts. After the arrival of Islam, mosques would be added to the shops, grocers, bakers, saddle makers and animal drivers who congregated around water sources: oases, wells, rivers. Caravans were instrumental in creating the series of cities that we associate with Central Asia; places like Samarkand, Tashkent, Bukhara, Merv.

As travel routes became safer and more reliable, these highways for humanity became avenues for exchanges: of art, culture, religion, language, and technology as well as commerce. The span of the Silk Road was not limited to Central Asia. In the Far East it began deep inside silk-producing China, usually following the northern and southern fringes of the terrifying desert known as the Takla Makan. To the west of Central Asia, the road ducked down to pass the southern margins of the Caspian Sea to continue across the Caucasus region into Turkey. Goods continued to travel westward toward Constantinople—today's Istanbul—eventually reaching Rome. Even beyond.

In its broadest sense, the Silk Road was also dependent on sea travel to carry its primary product to the limits of Rome's empire in the west. From the Black Sea coast, materials could be transported by land or by sea. Greek merchants had been visiting every corner of that body of water long before the indistinct beginnings of Silk Road commerce.

Central Asia underwent a millennium of turmoil and conflict as its mountains, steppes, deserts and riverine green belts were swept by successive waves of invaders and conquerors—including Persians, Greeks, Romans, Parthians, Arabs, Turks and Mongols. For decades it was the scene of a titanic standoff between the British Empire and Imperial Russia. The histories of the Silk Road and Central Asia fill entire libraries.

After the collapse of the former Soviet Union the Russian Mafia moved quickly to gain control of some of the most lucrative segments of their impaired economy: alcohol, weapons, drugs, sex trade. Their leaders were frequently men who had survived in—and been hardened by—Soviet gulags. Some who rose in the hierarchy were recruited from the discredited KGB, or from hardened military leaders who had been blooded in places like Afghanistan, Chechniya or Ossetia.

Valentin Mihailovich Kuriatin satisfied two of these criteria. The native of Kazakhstan had graduated from the Soviet Military Academy and served in Afghanistan. He was an excellent linguist, a competent mathematician and a skilled systems analyst.

After returning from Afghanistan, Valentin joined the KGB and spent several years in India learning how India developed an internationally recognized capability in computer software design and in the management of service bureaus. When the KGB imploded, Valentin found that his services were in demand by Mafia leaders. In particular, he pioneered the establishment of a complex web of drug smugglers transporting heroin and opium from growing fields in Afghanistan, Tajikistan and Kirghizstan into Europe and the Western Hemisphere.

His major contribution was the creation of a tracking system, using satellite communication and cell phones, linked with service bureaus in India. Drugs were packaged and shipped with documentation not unlike that used by UPS to track parcels in the United States. With this system in place, members of Russia's crime syndicate could devote their entire attention to the ruthless enforcement of efficient package handling. Whenever a uniquely identified parcel disappeared between two well-defined "nodes" it was a straightforward matter for "enforcers" to find the source of the discrepancy and deal with the problem.

As a senior member of the crime syndicate, Valentin sometimes traveled with violent men whose job was to ensure that drugs flowed in steady, unending passages from Central Asia to consumers around the world. At the direction of his criminal overlord, the Kazakh native spent much of his time in enforcing the flow of goods from their points-of-origin to Istanbul, gateway to the West. Across the western portion of Central Asia, the route employed to transport drugs from Afghanistan's poppy fields corresponded—in large measure—to the path of the ancient Silk Road.

Chapter 2

Astana, Kazakhstan— 1995

"Already growing poppy plants that supply nearly 90 percent of the world's heroin, Afghanistan now also ranks as a pot superpower. The United Nations Office for Drug Control is preparing to report that it has identified between 116 and 135 square miles of Afghan marijuana plants—over six times the cultivation in Mexico. It's a figure that startled investigators, since most of the attention has gone to Afghanistan's poppy fields. Most Afghan-produced drugs are sold in Europe and Asia, but investigators fear the expanding production will end up in the world's biggest pot market, the United States."

"AFGHAN FIELDS ARE GOING TO POT"
U.S. NEWS AND WORLD REPORT, NOVEMBER 14, 2005

In Kazakhstan's capital, Astana, members of the Russian Mafia meet to decide a strategy for the next five years. Principal activities are to include plans for building a secure route that will guarantee the steady flow of drugs, chiefly opium products and hashish, from growers and producers to consumers. It will require some technical expertise to track and monitor goods in transit. Over the longer term they would also like to obtain a choke hold on pipelines that the Chinese are seeking to build for oil and gas across the "stans"—Pakistan and Afghanistan.

Near-term needs? Enough cash to acquire computer systems for monitoring drug flow along New Silk Road to Istanbul. To avoid passage through Iran, one route would involve carrying drug products to ports on the Caspian Sea and crossing by ferry to any of several independent countries or semi-autonomous regions of Russia. One route, for example, might cross the Caspian from the Turkmenistan port of Turkmenbashi to Baku in Azerbaijan. From Azerbaijan, material would transit Armenia or Georgia to enter Turkey. Once in Turkey, material could travel by land or sea to Istanbul and the rest of the world.

These complex requirements are not easily treated by a convention of men who have spent the greater portion of their lives in Russian prisons for violent crimes, augmented by former KGB agents whose specialty was 'wet work,' assassination, torture or deep-cover espionage.

The problem is basically one requiring a broad understanding of the shipping practices and the systems used to manage this business. Career criminals are inured to practices such as extortion, intimidation or bribery. Their immediate reaction to a poorly understood business problem is to find someone capable of doing the work, someone they can intimidate, bully and control.

In the case of shipping volumes of opium-based drugs and hashish, one of the pivotal countries is considered to be Turkmenistan, nominally an independent republic but actually a dictatorship under a curious, crackpot leader. He is the self-styled Turkmenbashi, a self-anointed president-for-life, whose real name is Saparmurat Niyazov; and he needs to be bought.

The criminal cartel plans to get an initial infusion of cash by investing profits from other criminal enterprises, or extortion from oil corporations with interests in the region.

Seven members of the Russian Mafia have been meeting in an expensive hotel for a week. For the first three days of their meeting they focused on aspects of the financial arrangements that have bought them together. The last four days have been spent in drinking, whoring and gambling. Little has been accomplished.

At the end of their stay, their leader, Arkady Volkevich Fedorov, asks the group, "Who picked Astana for the meeting?"

Nobody is in a hurry to answer.

"I am just wondering why we have been wasting time here in Astana, when we should have been closer to the action. I was hoping someone would step up and take the blame so I could have someone to punish."

It is not a complete jest. If anyone had ventured to step forward as the organizer of this get-together to arrange the logistics of a complex drug operation, it is not inconceivable that Arkady would have felled him on the spot—with a blow.

Arkady is a creature from central casting for Russian Mafia types. His face is weathered and brutal, the result of long years in prison, and his tattoos, like service ribbons on soldiers, reveal to those in the know a great deal about where he has been and what he has done. His hands are hard and callused, reflecting years of hard labor, reinforced in recent years by his addiction to rowing machines. He usually spends an hour a day on these machines, and for most normal males a handshake with Arkady is a painful experience.

But his question to the group is asked after he has consumed approximately 500 milliliters of vodka since breakfast and consequently he forgets that the Astana meeting was his proposal.

Their work during the last week made it clear that they should have met in Almaty, far to the south, near the border with Kirghizstan. Much of the criminal activity with which they are concerned is managed from Almaty, the former capital of Kazakhstan, and still its *de facto* business capital. Nothing exciting is happening in Astana, where bureaucrats focus on the administration of the vast, young Kazakh republic.

The men remain silent and unresponsive, involving themselves with their food and drink, the last shared meal before they depart for their respective cities.

Penetrating an alcoholic fog, the truth breaks through to Arkady and he is quick to fix the problem. He pushes away a scantily clad Mongolian girl who is trying to refill his tumbler with vodka.

"Go home. Go home everyone and take care of your regular work. For two weeks. Take two weeks and make sure everything is running smoothly. Then we will meet again after two weeks. Next time we will meet in Almaty. I will have my assistant make the flight arrangements and contact you. If there are problems, maybe three weeks is better."

Chapter 3

A Visit to Walter Reed

> "The government of Uzbekistan has given America 180 days to vacate its Karshi-Khanabad airbase, which has been at the heart of American military operations into Afghanistan from Central Asia. The eviction notice was delivered on July 29th to America's embassy in the Uzbek capital, Tashkent, seemingly in retaliation for a UN airlift to Romania that day of 439 Uzbek refugees from Kirghizstan, to which they had fled after a massacre in the eastern city of Andijan in May. America was closely involved in the airlift."
>
> THE ECONOMIST
AUGUST 6TH, 2005

The forward base was perched on the edge of Afghanistan's nowhere. Three CIA agents who were in contact with CENTCOM headquarters were briefing the Special Forces team of thirteen on their intended mission. They were supported by four Sikorsky UH 60s, the model known to the public as Black Hawk. While not the latest model in the field, they were dependable and could serve equally well for transporting troops, carrying cargo or evacuating wounded.

The coded message was received about two hours before darkness. A renegade warlord believed to possess a significant cache of weapons, including stinger missiles and RPGs, was holed up in a tiny village north of Spin Buldak. The GPS coordinates were provided by a team of three Army Rangers who were operating with Afghanis.

Paul Chapman, the senior spook in charge of briefing the Special Forces team, was dressed in Afghan clothing, and he was starting to smell pretty strong.

"Here's what we know," he said spreading the map across the top of several cartons of MREs. "The village complex has about fifteen structures. Actually, there are more, but the main cluster has fifteen or so. They're joined together with an enclosed court and it's hard to guess exactly what we'll find when we get inside. HQ would like to have this guy alive, but he's not the highest priority. My instructions are to tell you to bring him out alive. I would never tell you to shoot the son-of-a-bitch if he offers the least difficulty. No. Certainly not. But your number one priority is coming out alive. They tell us he probably doesn't have more than thirty men."

"So how do we recognize our man?" The speaker was Walt Roberts, a young 1st Lieutenant out of Fort Bragg, who spoke Turkish and a little bit of some Turkic languages used in Afghanistan.

"Easy part. His left hand has only two fingers...and a thumb. White beard. Down to his chest. He's in his 70's and he may have been wounded in an earlier attack. They aren't certain about that part."

A gust of wind rattled an unsecured tent flap and lifted the corner of the topographic map off the cartons. Sergeant Spencer took a couple of clips out of his patch pockets and placed them on the map.

Chapman continued. "All of you want to take a good look at this and form a mental picture. We're gonna come in about three miles north. Go in the rest of the way on foot. It's supposed to be level but you know how that goes. Ninety minutes should get us there unless it turns out to be real dogshit. Thing to remember if we have to bug out is to head due north from the complex. OK? With me? In case of big fuck up? Head north. Due north. Magnetic. By the compass. I'm sure you boy scouts all know how to use a compass."

"Fuck you, civvie," someone muttered.

Chapman smiled. "Stick with me now. We'll go in as a group, then break into two teams of seven. One team provides a base of covering fire. The other makes the assault. Two guys stay back and protect the choppers. Hopefully. OK, here's how it's going down."

The operative word in this military operation turned out to be *dogshit*. It was like a movie. The choppers landed. Two teams deployed rapidly. The supporting fire spread out and looked for anything that moved. The assault team, lead by Walt Roberts, stormed in bravely. That far, everything was textbook. There was a small amount of fire based on nerves, but dern, darn, dang, drat and dadgumit, there were no frigging targets. The compounds were empty. Totally empty. Even the old men and women and children were gone. So there must have been a leak somewhere. The whole thing was a bust. After the adrenalin rush of going in, the whole team was still running on self-secreted chemicals as Walt radioed back that the village was completely empty.

Chapman, tsar of the spooks in the whole province, came in for a look see. He ended up taking away some documents in Arabic and some other languages Walt couldn't recognize. The whole team was heading back toward the choppers when Lt. Roberts got unlucky and stepped on some type of crude improvised explosive device at the edge of a footpath. Apparently it was a real Rube Goldberg gadget. It made a lot of noise and the flash blinded Walt for an instant. But the inconvenient thing about it was that it blew off his right foot—above the ankle. A chunk of something came up and struck his cheekbone making an unsightly flesh wound, but mercifully hitting him hard enough to render him unconscious. He didn't come to until he was almost back to the aid station where they could get some new lines started so he could be transferred back to the base at Karshi-Khanabad in Uzbekistan. He was plenty unhappy.

After the injury but before Walt was medevac'd from Afghanistan, one of his comrades found the part of his foot that had been blown away and placed it on the stretcher between his legs. It went with him all the way to the airbase in Uzbekistan, but it was always clear that there wasn't much to be reattached.

The trip back to the military hospital in Germany was a blur; he was coasting on pain medication. The first days in Germany were like a dream. He was a boy again, in Turkey. He was with his Turkish friend, Ekrem, and they had taken French leave for a couple of days to visit Nemrud Dagi, the monuments on top of Mount Nemrud. Floating in a drugged haze, Walt was conscious of the surgeons who were discussing his leg as they were preparing to go to work. What was the use of worrying? He was in good hands. When he closed his eyes he was back on a hillside in Turkey with Ekrem.

He and Ekrem were the same age. Ekrem's father was a Turkish officer assigned to liaison duties at the U.S. Air Base in Injirlik. Ekrem's family lived in the town outside the base, but their big home was in Antalya, on the south coast. Ekrem spoke some English and he was helping Walt learn Turkish. Learning from being with Ekrem was nothing like learning in school. With Ekrem, out on the streets, language was fun.

Walt's dad was always busy with work at the base, and his mom played tennis with base wives. His parents gave him a lot of freedom to roam and they both knew Ekrem's father and mother.

In his dream the boys were riding in the back of a Turkish Army truck. The Turkish officer's son had talked to the driver and finagled a ride partway to their destination. Then they hitched two different rides that got them to Tatvan where they spent the night in an inexpensive hotel with great food. From there they managed to get into a convoy of three vans carrying Italian tourists to the mountain, a popular destination.

The road wound around spectacular views of the surrounding countryside, with tiny farms perched precariously all the way to the top. Full of enthusiasm, he and Ekrem had clambered up the rough path to the top of the mountain. Both boys had been unprepared for the mysterious, awe-inspiring monuments that looked out over the countryside. The stone heads of seated gods had been toppled by time and weather, but they were still impressive. Headless torsos remained in their stone seats, while their heads, Apollo, Zeus, Hercules and others neither of the boys knew, stared out, sightless, looking at eternity. Walt was astonished by the nude figure of the Greek hero Hercules shaking hands with the strangely garbed eastern king Mithridates. He had been curious to know more about the motive behind this bizarre monument.

Ekrem had known little or nothing about the stone heads, but Walt promised himself he would find out all he could about this unforgettable hilltop location. They stayed for hours before bounding down to the visitor center for hot tea and something to eat. The day was wearing on, but they decided to climb up again to watch the sun go down. It was dark when they descended the rough path of shale and loose rock. All the vans carrying Italians had left, and the boys weren't sure how they would get off the mountain. Then they learned that one party of Italians had also stayed for the sunset and were slowly descending behind them.

In Walt's hospital haze he relived the adventure on the mountain. Then the dream ended and he was awake in a ward with several other wounded soldiers. The nurses were mostly young and pretty. He remembered that he ate, drank, was helped to the toilet. But war seemed far away and he wanted to get back into his dream of the mountain.

He tried to make his dream of the mountain return, but his attempts were unsuccessful. Once, however, he did dream back to another adventure with Ekrem. The boys had described their adventures to their fathers, both of whom supported their independence on the road. Encouraged by the adults, they had planned another excursion.

This time it took the combination of hitching rides and buying bus tickets to get from Injirlik to Kars in the north, not far from the border with Armenia. After spending the night in Kars, they cadged a ride with a German tourist group to their destination, the ancient ruined city.

The walled city of Ani had once been a thriving Armenian city before the birth of Christ. After Christianity overtook the Armenians this city was reputed to be the site of 1000 churches. Turkish raiders overran the Armenians and the Byzantines who supplanted them. Then Arabs. Then Mongols.

The two teen-aged boys, traveling alone, arrived at Ani to find it guarded by Turkish soldiers assigned to keep watch on Armenian outposts on the opposite site of the border; in this case a deep gorge formed by the Aras River.

The ruins at Ani were almost as impressive as those at Nemrud Dagi. Most of the city's buildings had been looted for materials or had weathered away. But the ruins of ten Christian churches remained. Like young goats, the boys scampered over the tumbled ruins. Scattered everywhere they found inscriptions in Greek or in blocks of Armenian text of which they could not recognize a single character.

Nothing was cordoned off, nothing protected by barriers, interpreted by signs or improved in any fashion. The only visitors were the small group of Germans who had paid an admission fee to the military guards. The site was so big that once inside the walls they were unaware of the Germans. Everything was overgrown with weeds and thistles; the haunt of owls and ravens. Both boys loved the eerie quiet of the ruins.

Back at the gate they bargained with the soldiers, to obtain permission to spend the night so they could reenter the site early the next morning. That night, after drinking tea with guards, they slept under a Turkish army truck on a piece of canvas provided by the friendly soldiers.

Walt dreamed of Ani. He and Ekrem were climbing down a steep slope to the river separating Turkey from Armenia. He could hear the distant sound of a bulldozer, occasionally visible on the other side.

There was no path to the place they were visiting by the river, the Ipek Yolu Köprüsü, the Silk Road Bridge. All that remained of the bridge across the river were the two buttressing towers on either side. The arch itself had tumbled into the river and been swept away long ago. The two boys sat near the abutments on the Turkish side and talked of the camel caravans that had crossed this road in the past.

Both boys had visited museums in Istanbul and Ankara, and they were aware that goods from the distant east had once traveled across Turkey to find buyers as far away as Rome. But the bridge in this lonely, forgotten place made the Silk Road become real.

Walt dreamed of the bridge. He dreamed of fording the river at the ruined bridge site to view the city from the east, a crossing that was forbidden and could have cost him his life. They could see watch towers on the Armenian side. It seemed strange, but all too real. Turks watching Armenians, Armenians watching Turks. *Cross the river. Cross the river.* His boyish enthusiasm was urging him to see things from the other side.

Some of his dreams during his hospital stay never left him completely. They were locked in his memory with an unforgettable clarity that made them more real than reality. But though he tried many times to revisit those places in his dreams, they could never be commanded to return.

His youthful companion, Ekrem, had a younger sister. She was just a little girl of twelve when Walt and Ekrem were having their adventures. She was a twig of a girl. Slender arms and legs with no shape to her stick body. When they swam at the pool on the base he had the feeling that his hands might meet around her body. But her black eyes were enormous and Walt could see that she would be a beauty. Though he could never express this to his friend, or, in fact, to another human soul, his boyish heart conceived the notion that he would come back for her some day. Her name was Ipek. Not the word as written here, but with the second I employed in the Turkish language, a capital I with a dot. When she was older—old enough for a boyfriend—

he would come back and find her. Ipek. It was a curious name but it came to hold a special magic for him.

Then, while he and Ekrem were clambering around in the ruins of Ani, he became aware that the ruined span across the river separating them from Armenia was called the Ipek Yolu Köprüsü. Yolu, he knew, meant "road" or "route." Köprüsü meant "bridge." But Ipek? That was the name of a little girl who would grow in a handful of years to become a great beauty. Then it came to him in a stunning flash that Ipek was the Turkish word for "silk."

The object of his secret affection was named "silk." It was a magical discovery, one he had made for himself and it made him so happy to have this secret knowledge buried deep in his heart. Silk. Silk. What a perfect name for such a pretty dark-eyed girl. He could remember exactly where he was standing at Ani when the meaning for Ipek's name hit him like a bucket of cool water.

He woke up to discover that his foot was hurting. But he remembered that the foot was gone. He would wait for a while. Try to deal with the pain. The phenomenon of phantom pain had been explained to him. He'd wait. See what he could take. Then call a nurse.

From Germany he was flown to the Walter Reed Hospital in Washington. Walt's memories of the days spent at Walter Reed faded faster than he expected. In his mind he could recall that it was a painful time, and yet, there was no memory of the pain. The strongest memories were of the nurses who tended him in the earliest days while his wounds were healing, and of the PTs—physical therapists—who pushed him to walk and to become accustomed to his prosthesis. Probably no PT was the subject of more fantasies than Anne French.

The first attempts to walk with the prosthetic leg were more painful than he had expected. At first, he would have been willing to reconcile himself to using a crutch for a long time. But the PTs knew all this. They worked with guys just like him every day.

Within a couple of days of arriving the technicians had made a temporary cast of his stump and had him walking. Annie explained every step of the way. "The problem we're concerned about is edema. Bandaging is important and nobody will be able to do it better that you. So stick with me. I want you to be the best. You're pretty lucky, you know."

"Lucky? Yeah, sure. How do you figure?"

"Not lucky to be injured, hon. But lucky that your trans-tibial is about halfway down. If it had been higher it would have been harder to get a good fitting. A very long stump would be more prone to circulation problems. You're just about perfect."

"Annie. Annie. You need to get out more."

"Pay attention to what I'm doing, hon. I'm going to have you doing the tango when you get out of here. You are going to be so … hot." She leaned in to complete wrapping the figure eight around his stump and he inhaled as deeply as he could. She smelled like strawberries.

Pain from the healing stump made him break out in sweat the first time he stood up and took a few steps using the preparatory prosthesis. He could reach the bars from the chair.

"This hurts like hell," he said. "Maybe it needs a few more days to heal."

The PT was silent, helping him onto the bars.

"Did you hear me? It hurts. I don't think I can do it."

"You're doing fine. Just keep moving."

"It hurts. It hurts up in my fucking hip."

"Tell me about it, soldier. Of course it hurts. It's supposed to hurt."

"Jesus. Aren't you supposed to be on my side?"

"Look at you. You're almost to the end."

"And it's killing me."

"I doubt it. If you hadn't been complaining so much you could already be halfway back on lap two."

Each day got better. And each day he looked at his PT a bit more closely. What was it about nurses and PTs? The white uniforms or lab coats? She usually had on a loose scrub top that was blue or green. Short reddish hair. When she bent over to help him adjust the leg, he couldn't help looking down the front of her top. Small breasts. Freckles part of the way down.

She always had the smell of strawberries. Or something close to strawberries. It was faint, but it was her signature. Honestly, he couldn't say if she was pretty or not. But he came to love her. She worked with him most of the time. Each time she came close, he made it a point to inhale deeply, but not so she would notice.

Annie was bandaging his stump. "Watch me carefully, sweetie pie," she said. "Tomorrow you're gonna do this all by your lonesome." He took a deep breath. "I know you're sniffing me," she laughed. "It's not supposed to be noticeable."

"It's true," he said. "I am."

She was pulling the elastic tight. "Pay attention, soldier," she laughed. "There. Now, you do the rest."

While Walt was fumbling to place the exo-leg, she pushed her chair back and looked at him.

"What are you gonna do when you get home?" she asked.

"Probably go back to college. Get an advanced degree. I want to teach. In a college. Then have a couple of kids. Two. At least. No only child. It's too lonely growing up."

"Your wife is very pretty."

"She is. Yes."

"This ward frightens her, Walt. This room scares the hell out of her. You should think about that. It's going to be just as hard for her to get used to this as for you. Maybe harder."

"I am thinking about it."

"Talk to your counselor about your concerns. Don't put it off. Ask questions. I want you to do well, hon. You are doing well."

"What are my options?"

At first Flo came every day, but it was clear that the place made her uncomfortable. She was wound tight from the moment she came on the floor, and although she tried to be cheerful and upbeat, it was too much for her. Her smiles were forced and it showed. She hated it. After a while she came every other day and Walt stopped looking forward to her visits.

There were therapists. All nice, all equally capable, all equally demanding. Two black guys. Another white woman. Heavy set. But Anne French was the one who stayed in his mind.

When he was finally released to go home, he could have walked out. They rolled him in a wheel chair, but he could have done it. It was Annie who came and kissed him on the cheek. He might have preferred something more.

Flo walked beside the wheelchair as an orderly wheeled him out to the waiting car. Anne was somewhere else, maybe off the floor when he left his room, but she knew it was his last day and she came running to catch them before they reached the door.

"Take care of yourself, soldier," she said. "You've graduated." Then, a handshake, the briefest kiss, and she was gone.

"Well, well!", Flo said as Annie disappeared around a corner.

His graduation present was the expensive new leg he would get to keep. For the first couple of weeks, every time he put on his leg he missed Annie bending over to help—or just to check that he was doing everything correctly. He missed looking down the front of her blouse at the freckles between her breasts. Then, like his memory of the pain, his picture of her gradually faded and disappeared.

Chapter 4

2001, Pre-9/11; Naval War College— Newport, R.I.

> *"China and India have recently tried to bribe, bully or buy their way into 'equity oil': in Latin America, Canada, Russia and Africa. And yet, the billions they are spending on this quest for energy and security could well be wasted. Thanks to the spectacular rise of futures trading, oil has become a fungible global commodity. The conventional notion that stakes in oil fields add up to energy security no longer holds up: if there is an oil shock, then the market price of every barrel of oil in the world will shoot up past $100 a barrel."*
>
> THE REAL TROUBLE WITH OIL
> THE ECONOMIST, APRIL 30, 2005

The meeting was arranged at the request of Admiral Barker from the Naval War College at Newport, Rhode Island. The Admiral flew down with two senior strategists from the College: one a senior Captain, the other a high level civilian.

Six other men were in the room, three from Homeland Security and three from the CIA. Each agency had sent men equivalent in rank to the Navy's representatives. The senior men from each of the two agencies were Deputy Assistants, and everyone in the room had experience in Central Asian Affairs.

It had taken Admiral Barker nearly a month to set up the meeting to meet his demands, which were: no more than three men from each agency, deep knowledge of affairs in Central Asia, and the ability to make binding decisions at the meeting—decisions that would result in a concrete plan of action to address the Admiral's concerns.

At the Admiral's express request, the meeting started at 7:00 a.m. and this meant that the men had been in the room drinking coffee and nibbling around a tray laden with fruit and pastries for a half hour before the doors were closed. Outside, half a dozen administrative aides were poised to perform whatever task was asked, but once the minute hand hit the hour, the doors were shut and the Admiral took the floor. Since he called the meeting, he was the first to speak.

"As most of you are aware, the next big threat that the U.S. will face militarily will come from China. We are already facing a threat in the economic and political area but this is not the immediate concern of the Navy. The problem we face is the growing threat that will be posed by a Chinese Navy whose presence in the Pacific can only be expected to grow as rapidly as their economy.

Even as we speak, the Chinese are strengthening their fleet of conventional and nuclear submarines. And though their navy is no match for our own, they have demonstrated the capability to expand rapidly."

As he spoke, the room lights dimmed and his prepared charts were projected on the big screen at the end of the table.

"The charts speak for themselves and I don't expect them to hold a lot of interest for all of you. Just now, our fleet of carriers is superior to the combined carrier forces of the world. The tonnage figures shown for today are not expected to alter exponentially over the next two decades. Of course, things could change, but these projections have also been made with a confidence band, showing the predicted best case that the rest of the world could accomplish. You can see that our expectation is that we will retain carrier superiority for the next two decades.

Now in the case of projections for submarines and for small, missile-carrying vessels—light cruisers, for example—the situation appears to be quite different. Look at our projections for China's submarine fleet. Now look at the band showing their 'best case' scenario. Note the similarity between these curves and those for a fast missile fleet.

Gentlemen, our intention in exposing you to these figures is to encourage you to think about the energy source that allow these projections to become a frightening reality. That energy source is oil. The bulk of the Chinese fleet we envision will rely on oil. They are producing some nuclear submarines, but oil will power their surface fleet.

The Chinese are looking at potential sources of oil in the world with the same mindset that led the Japanese to head for the former Dutch East Indies. Today's Indonesia. In particular, they are looking at sources of oil that have not already been preempted by western nations.

It's clear that China won't profit much from any oil that comes from Alaska's North Slope. Likewise, oil in the North Sea may not make it to China. But Central

Asia…? That's another matter.

I know that all of you are specialists in this region. That why I requested you to take part in today's meeting. Some of what we will tell you today, you may already know. Some facts, will, I have no doubt, be new to you. All of this information is extremely sensitive and must be treated with the highest security priority."

The last of the slides came off, the room lights came up and the projector shut down. The civilian from the War College ejected the disk from his laptop and locked it in his briefcase.

Admiral Barker, whose unofficial nickname was "Iron Jaw," screwed the top off a half-liter water bottle and drank most of it without pausing. Then he leaned forward with both hands on the table and waited to insure that all eyes were focused on him.

"We have recently received intelligence that the Chinese have initiated a program intended to develop a pipeline corridor linking the oil and gas fields of Turkmenistan with the Indian Ocean. They have determined to bypass Iran and concentrate on traversing Western Afghanistan and Pakistan. They apparently feel more secure dealing with Afghans and Pakis than with Iranis and they currently have high level delegations working on the political details. At the same time, numerous survey parties are moving from half a dozen nations—to lay out a route that will be both economical and secure."

The lights dimmed again and the giant screen filled with a large map of Turkmenistan and Uzbekistan. It appeared to overlay the details of a topographic survey map with satellite photography.

"No doubt this is familiar territory to all of you. So you will be aware that these ugly duckling nations spawned following the breakup of the old Soviet system have considerable amounts of oil and natural gas that is difficult to get to markets in the west." The Admiral paused for a second and Chester Kennedy, an old Asia hand from the CIA, broke the Admiral's monologue.

"Admiral, the old Soviet establishment has made it virtually impossible for western oil companies to get into the region. Which I'm sure you realize. After the breakup, the new rulers weren't too anxious to lose autonomy, but they all needed cash. So they let some Europeans and at least one U.S. firm in to make surveys. But that was before Iran got to be so difficult. As far as I know, all the earlier surveys were through Iran into the Persian Gulf."

"Thanks, Chet. Yes. Aramco, Dutch Shell and one other outfit made surveys for a route across Iran. But nothing ever came of it. For a lot of reasons. Now, we believe the Chinese are prepared to go hell for leather. They'll throw a lot of government money at it. And they'll make it sweet for the Pakis by offering them help with terminal facilities—probably including LPG terminals. The west will be frozen out if China gets her way.

Gentlemen, I don't intend to do all the talking. We need to have a clear understanding of what the Chinese are doing in Turkmenistan, Uzbekistan and probably Tajikistan as well. Kazakhstan? Well, that's really not much different than dealing with Russia at this time. But that could change.

We know that each of your agencies is interested in this region—possibly for different reasons. Probably because a lot of the heroin from Afghanistan is traveling over the old Silk Road to reach the rest of the world. We also know that residual chemical WMD from Soviet stockpiles in Uzbekistan and elsewhere must flow through this region. What we'd like to do is collaborate with you in some way. To put a team in that area. Maybe for a month or so. And to look at things on the ground. It may sound like wishful thinking… but if we put our heads together I believe we can do something that is mutually beneficial."

Lights came back up. The group took a pee break. More coffee came in. And several phone calls were returned. Fifteen minutes later, the group reconvened and this time some notepads came out. No monologues. Everyone in the room was a quick study and they had all done plenty of homework in advance of the meeting.

They broke every ninety minutes or so to get rid of accumulated coffee or to order stuff from aides… to be sent in by encrypted e-mail. Lunch was brought in and the group ate in the room.

The meeting continued all afternoon and past their usual cocktail hour. It was after seven when participants broke for the night—after receiving their homework assignments. Pleased with the progress that had been made and the cooperative participation of his team, the Admiral toyed with the idea of changing tomorrow's starting time from 7:00 a.m. until an hour later—and taking everyone out for a drink. But he had his reputation as a hardass to consider and the notion came and went. Time enough to socialize after they had agreed on a plan.

On the following day, the schedule was much the same, but they ended an hour earlier. And on the third day their draft plan for collaborative action was completed by noon. Once more, lunch was brought in and then the entire assemblage, joined by half a dozen staffers who had been working outside the room, reconvened at a private club operated for senior officers of the CIA. This time the Admiral did buy the drinks.

Not one of their recommendations was implemented. Nothing ever happened as a result of this meeting.

Chapter 5

Valentin—
The Systems Architect

"Hulagu desired then that all persons in the harem be counted. Seven hundred women and slave girls were found there, and one thousand eunuchs. The Kalif begged to have those women given him who had never been under sunlight or moonlight directly. The conqueror gave him one hundred. Mostassim chose relatives and they were led forth from the palace. All the best treasures were taken to Hulagu's camp ground. Around the immense tent of Jinghis Khan's grandson were piled up great masses of wealth...."

THE MONGOLS; A HISTORY
JEREMIAH CURTIN

Valentin Mihailovich Kuriatin, at age 46, has an MBA from Harvard and comfortable apartments in London, Istanbul, Moscow and Almaty, business capital of the Republic of Kazakhstan. From time to time the young Russian also has access to nice apartments in Miami, Houston and Marseilles, where his work occasionally requires him to spend time. Val, as his friends call him, is a handsome man, with dark hair and wide Slavic cheekbones. His teeth are one of his best features, and when he smiles, which is not often, his close acquaintances are surprised all over again. His mustache is dark. If you picture someone along the lines of Omar Sharif, you won't be far off the mark.

Val is highly intelligent, an observation which will not strike you as surprising, considering that they don't give MBAs away at Harvard. You don't have to be an absolute genius to finish their program, but you do need drive, the desire to succeed and the determination to do whatever it takes to get the job done. Those qualities Val possesses in spades. Val Kuriatin is not a man who is easily thwarted when facing a challenging assignment.

In this regard, his self-assigned goal is to be numbered among the world's richest men and to enjoy a lifestyle that will allow him to travel freely while enjoying a lavish life style. The world is viewed as a big, delicious apple—to be eaten slowly, savoring every bite. Val is also an ardent womanizer.

After graduating from Moscow's Technical University with a degree in computer science, Val served as a junior officer in the Russian Army at the tail end of the Afghanistan War. After the war he was assigned to the Baikonur Cosmodrome near Leninsk in Kazakhstan, Russia's principal space center.

Upon leaving the Army, Val spent several years in Bangalore before applying to Harvard. While in India, he honed his computer skills and learned to speak fairly good English. He also learned several things about women that appeared to be useful across cultural and language differences. But the most important lesson—well internalized—was that the world he was living in was considerably different from the world he was born into. Moreover, only a handful of people understood these differences, and of those who did, an even smaller number knew how to profit from it. Since his desire to become fabulously wealthy had been formed at an early age, all of the experience picked up in India was brought to bear on achieving this goal.

Some of the most important concepts absorbed in India could be summarized in a few, brief words: dissect, deconstruct, and outsource. Simple enough.

There were colossal profits to be made in drugs, easily grown in Kazakhstan, Afghanistan, or any of the 'stans' where fields could be watered by melted snow from the world's roof. From what he knew of Turkmenistan, the irrigated desert regions where cotton culture prevails could be converted to poppies with little difficulty. Although no agronomist, he knew that poppies also had a long history in Kazakhstan.

After things became quieter in Afghanistan, poppy cultivation immediately began to flourish. Opium production was already starting to build even before the Americans arrived. Improved roads and an increasingly stable environment enabled the drug trade to grow explosively.

So, Val concluded, most of the world's demand for opium-based products could easily be satisfied by the capacity existing in Central Asia. There was no problem in obtaining the product. Likewise, there was no lack of demand. "If you build it, they will come," the movie star had said in a popular American film. *If you offer it, they will buy.*

The problem was in getting product into the hands of distributors and from distributors to individual consumers. This is where dissection and deconstruction helped him to understand the problem.

"Don't think about this shit as drugs, Antonin. Think of it as packages. Pick a size. Let's say a package weighing ten kilos. We want to get a ten-kilo cardboard box from, let's say Shymkent to—you pick a place... no, don't bother—say to Orlando in Florida. It doesn't matter where. The box has got to be delivered safely, within reasonable time limits, at low cost, with absolute security." His listener was leaning forward over a column of three small, inverted tumblers that once contained vodka.

Val continued. "We need to be able to track each package, to know where it is, on which leg of its journey, who are the carriers and who has responsibility. These are all problems easily handled for our hypothetical box. It doesn't take a lot of skill to track this information. Same with collecting the money. Only a few elements to decompose. Payment received? Who got it? What did they do with money? Transferred to a safe place? Once the goods are delivered and we have the money, we would also prefer that traces of this transaction cease to exist. But only after we have the money. Are you with me, Antosha? Or have you had too much vodka?"

"Fuck you, my friend."

"Don't be offended. I just want to know if you are following me."

"You make it sound too easy. It is, of course, as you know, much more difficult. Much."

"Yes, of course! But managing the steps from node to node in the process is easy and cheap to accomplish. Easy, that is, if we don't depend on fucking Russians to track the packages. The difficult parts will be setting up reliable transportation between nodes. And placing reliable operators at each node. Many details must be worked out, but we can learn quickly and profit even as we make our initial mistakes.

The world is connected by the Internet, by cell phones and satellite phones. I am looking at your face, Uncle. You are ready to go to sleep. Bah! Why didn't you stop me?"

One of the problems Val had to get used to was the fact that most of his high-level business associates really understood very little that he was talking about. Understood little and cared less. Most of the moneyed thugs with whom he mingled at the higher levels were hardened criminals, great at extortion, murder, robbery and simple crimes that were, for the most part, almost mindless. Find the money. Go take it.

Valentin Kuriatin had visions of a higher order of criminality. He aspired to drugs, oil fields, shipping lines, arms sales. There was easy money to be made in any of these fields. Drugs held the greatest promise for the immediate future. Later, he would need a large bankroll to build infrastructure for the empire he envisioned.

Once in place, a drug network would be a self-sustaining fountain, allowing him to play in the undeveloped oil fields of Central Asia. That was his dream!

First things first, he reminded himself. *To build my drug web, I will need money.* His associates would provide plenty of muscle once he gave them clear directions. Weapons sales were a possibility, but in the near term, rising petroleum prices in world markets were increasing the whole world's interest in access to fields in Turkmenistan and Uzbekistan. But first, build a drug empire.

Val looked at the fresh tumblers of vodka that tawny Li had just set before them.

Fucking Antosha appeared to be going to sleep sitting up. The girl stood waiting for further orders; a pretty piece of woman, that. Under the silk dress she was wearing he could count her ribs. *She looks as if she might have Uighur blood on both sides. I would like to taste her*, he thought He poured his vodka into Anton's tumbler and held up his hand to the girl who returned his smile.

"Nyet! Hayir! Enough! Bring me chai! Hot tea!" Their eyes remained locked during the exchange. The girl nodded languidly and moved away taking the first several steps backwards so that their eyes stayed in contact. Turning, she moved away swiftly.

Val looked at his watch. It was just after nine. Three hours. Four. *I should probably be in bed by one in order to get an early start tomorrow. That should be enough time for Li.*

It had taken Val four years of continuous travel and hard work to get enough money to begin building the drug network that would push his wealth into the stratosphere. Some of the easiest start-up cash to be found was in surplus weapons sales. The Middle East and Central Asia was awash in military weaponry, and factories of the industrialized nations just kept cranking out equipment that was better, more lethal and, ultimately, more appealing to buyers. But there were warehouses full of usable hardware—last year's models—waiting to be converted into cash.

Early on, it became clear to Val that there was some complex relationship between big weapons and sex for a certain class of male. Occasionally he would run into a woman who seemed to get turned on by military weapons, but this was very rare; maybe because not many women were involved in the international arms game. The women who responded to weapons were easy to spot. Just watch their eyes as they handled an M203 of American manufacture. Or a Chinese knock-off of the same item. *Be thankful that they don't have access to a sackful of grenades or your Slavic ass might be in trouble.* It wasn't a reaction he could understand, but he could recognize it wherever he found it.

There wasn't much money to be made with Kalashnikovs. *Paagh! Almost everyone already has one hidden away somewhere.* Some American military weapons were appealing to customers; lightweight items like newer models of the M60 had many of the qualities buyers liked. The MP4 used by American Seals was also a popular model, probably because of its ability to perform well after immersion in water. But it was hard to obtain in quantities that would earn any real hard currency. Nine millimeter automatics—particularly the smaller models—were easy to move. Also hard to find in quantity.

Grenade launchers. They could have been money makers, but they were also somewhat difficult to obtain for reasons that were hard to understand. They looked like cheap pieces of shit the way they were made. Not many floating around. Unless he wanted to spend more time in eastern Europe.

Rocket propelled grenades, RPGs, were big cash generators. As were Stingers. Available from many nations now that the American technology had been copied. He could have found buyers for every one he could get his hands on. Mines were cash generators, too. They were made everywhere. Brazil, China, Czechoslovakia, France, Germany, the U.S. For a while there was some concern that international treaties banning land mine use would slow down production. As far as he could see, there were just as many as ever, although, admittedly they were not being employed to the extent as in the past.

Weapons sales to tribal leaders in Afghanistan, Iran and Iraq accounted for much of the initial fortune he was able to amass. That first pile, earned by travel to places like Yemen, Somalia and Syria, enabled him to begin building his drug empire. Usually his bigger weapons—like Oerlikons—were shipped in groups of four or five, with arrangements staggered so they weren't all on the same plane.

Nikolai Volkevich Dunyenko had been Valentin Kuriatin's Russian mentor. He was born in Almaty, a city in Kazakhstan, where he had lived for six years until his father, an officer in the Soviet Army, was reassigned to Moscow. Niki, who had from early childhood demonstrated precocity in mathematics, got an appointment to the Military Academy where he graduated with honors and received his commission.

He had spent several years in Afghanistan where he devoted much of his energy to untangling the complex logistical system that delivered supplies to the soldiers who were struggling with the unconventional tactics employed by Afghanis—exacerbated by rugged terrain and the absence of a decent road network.

Nikolai's analytical capabilities came to the attention of his superiors and before long he was called back to Moscow to be interviewed by the KGB. The work they proposed for him had a complex theoretical aspect that appealed to him. More importantly, it got him out of Afghanistan where there was a real lack of available, attractive females to bed. It also offered substantially higher wages. He was unable to compare the risks inherent in his new job with the dangers of life in Afghanistan, but he was willing to run any risks that would give him an opportunity to rise. In any case, his new bosses proposed to send him to India. They didn't spring that on him until the third interview.

"India? Why India? What interests do we have in India?"

"We have interests everywhere, Nikolai Volkevich. Are we to understand that you would not be happy to be given this assignment?"

"No. Certainly not," he backpedaled smoothly. "But I am, of course, interested to learn something of the nature of any specific assignment that I might be given."

"And in time, we expect that will become much clearer to you than we could possibly explain fully if we talked all night."

Well before the United States discovered that India was an inexpensive source of technologically capable labor, the Russians, spearheaded by the technology arm of the KGB, had recognized the possibilities. Nikolai Volkevich was, one might say, on the tip of the spear.

Unfortunately, the Russians did little more than recognize the latent capability in India. They did not have sufficient business applications to fully utilize what India had to offer, and, in years following the Soviet Union's collapse, the intelligence activities envisioned by the KGB were no longer supported by a seemingly inexhaustible supply of unallocated funds.

Nikolai was in India—on the scene. He came to know the players, and his assessment of their capabilities was on the mark. When Valentin arrived, the older man took the younger man under his wing. The two men could hardly have been more different. Val was youthful in appearance, of medium build, muscular, robust and healthy looking. He was a dedicated sensualist. Women played an important part in his life; or perhaps it would be more accurate to say that he devoted a great deal of his energy to sexual gratification. The actual companionship of women usually bored him. With the exception of the differences in their bodies, he frequently found them dull and uninteresting.

Nikolai, in contrast, was slender, pale and wiry, with sunken cheeks and an overall haggard appearance. He was given to months of abstinence followed by short periods of heavy drinking, accompanied by deep depression. Nevertheless, the two men formed some type of incomprehensible bond and Nikolai Dunyenko shared his knowledge of managing software development processes with Valentin Kuriatin. The pursuit of flesh was also an interest held in common and it became an accepted practice for them to share—and compare—the same female.

Val's background and training had equipped him to recognize an exceptional teacher, and he reveled in the chance to learn as much as he could about the methods for doing business in India. Nikolai introduced him to key people, to multi-national entrepreneurs, and to the financial people who were putting up their start-up money in India. Niki was also envious of Val's effortless style of womanizing. He may even have been a bit jealous of the casual, offhand way in which Val began his liaisons. It was not uncommon for Val to manage concurrent relations with three handsome Indian women, each of whom felt that she was his only partner.

Nikolai was in India for the whole time that Val was assigned there. The lessons that Val learned from Nikolai convinced him that he could build and manage a drug network that could serve the world. When Val returned to Russia, Nikolai remained and for a year they maintained contact by periodic phone calls. Val was surprised to learn that Niki had died suddenly, apparently from a stroke.

The younger man realized that his time spent with his mentor had been a fortunate gift and he was sorry to lose such a good friend. The problem was, as it always is in these cases, that one can never be certain how Nikolai really died.

Chapter 6

Homeland Security Facility, Northern Virginia

"Securing China's energy need does not simply entail obtaining resources; it also requires getting them home. Transport is no easy feat for a country that still has no cross-border pipeline. The China National Petroleum Corporation struck a deal for a major pipeline with the Russian oil giant Yukos in 2003, but the plan fell apart after the Russian government first dismantled Yukos and then accepted Japan's high bid on the project. Negotiations for a pipeline that would transport Caspian Sea oil to China through Kazakhstan are slowly moving forward, but China remains heavily dependent on international sea-lanes...."

CHINA'S GLOBAL HUNT FOR ENERGY
DAVID ZWEIG AND BI JIANBAI
FOREIGN AFFAIRS, SEPT/OCT 2005

After the hectic, unfocused years following 9-11, Government officials connected with Homeland Security gradually woke up to the fact that quantities of heroin from Central Asia were arriving in the U.S. at a disturbingly steady rate. While this problem wasn't number one on the Agency's hit parade, it was a matter of concern, because it took little imagination to replace heroin with plastic explosives, a shift that put a completely different face on the matter.

Within the CIA, a former Special Forces officer who had been in Afghanistan would eventually remember a soldier who once communicated with members of the Northern Alliance without the use of interpreters. He remembered, too, that this veteran had maintained an intense interest in the history and lore of Central Asia and had led tours into all of the "stans" that came into being following the breakup of the Soviet Union. The summons from Washington would come right at the time when the soldier's marriage was disintegrating.

One man inside the Agency would envision a mission inside Central Asia between Turkmenistan and Kirghizstan, ostensibly designed as a cultural visit by academics and graduate students, but actually a fact-finding probe intended to shed light on the techniques used to funnel material along the route of the Old Silk Road.

The meeting took place at an undisclosed location in northern Virginia. Six senior officials took part in the initial planning. They represented Homeland Security, CIA, FBI and DEA. Homeland Security and the CIA were each represented by two people.

Carter Thatcher was the senior representative from Homeland Security and he kicked things off by displaying a map of central Asia, from Afghanistan to the Black Sea Coast.

"Let me start things off by painting the big picture. You are all aware that since our involvement in Afghanistan—and despite our efforts to stop poppy cultivation—opium or its derivatives have become that country's number one export. Hashish is gaining ground every day. It's not just Afghanistan. Other opportunists are trying to horn in on the easy money. Now we're seeing record acreage devoted to poppies in the eastern corners of Uzbekistan and in Tajikistan. As you are also aware, in the past these countries have been synonyms for *remote*. Back during the Cold War days it was difficult for visitors to get in and out. Today, it's a lot easier. Still not easy. But much easier." He scanned his audience; paused to unscrew the cap off a bottle of water and took a long, noisy swig.

"Getting large quantities of drugs out of these countries appears to have attracted some high-class talent. Our intelligence says that most of the drug traffic coming out of these places has been taken over by the Russian Mafia. One of the reasons they have been successful is that many of their members are former KGB agents. The top guys in their Mafia are frequently out of the prisons and gulags. Some starting to get along in years, but very tough customers. Ruthless. But what they have done is recruit heavily from former KGB personnel, many of whom were bureaucrats and administrative types. It's these guys who appear to have masterminded the drug networks."

Pete O'Meara from the DEA broke in. "Can we ask questions as you go?"

"Give me a couple more minutes. Then we're open for questions and discussion. I'm almost there." He flipped out the laser pointer on his key ring and pointed to the area near Almaty in Kazakhstan. The laser spot danced slowly west toward the border with Iran and the Caspian Sea.

"Some drugs undoubtedly leave the region by air. This is relatively easy to monitor when we put our minds to it. The hard part is tracking the stuff that goes across by other means. Somehow they've found a way to make it work. We think a lot of the stuff that originates deep in Asia makes its way to Istanbul and from there... to the rest of the world. Once it makes it to the Black Sea, it's on the way into Central Europe and from there it's almost impossible to track.

What we need to do is to come up with a way to get a handle on exactly how the Mafia guys are making this distribution system hum. Until we understand how they're doing it, it'll be hard to come up with a counterstrategy. I'm hoping this will be a brainstorming session. We'll have a few proposals, but so far nothing has gelled. We're open for ideas."

O'Meara pushed back his chair. "Why are we looking at heroin right now? The problem that's eating us up here at home is meth. Most of it made right under our noses. But as it becomes more of a money maker it's gonna get industrialized and start coming in from god knows where."

"Stick with me here," Thatcher said. "What you say is true. But the meth isn't coming from Central Asia. The area that's sending us heroin is as much of a powder keg now as it has ever been. And that's saying a lot. Heroin is coming from an area that grows poppies, cotton and grass. Hashish. It also contains a significant amount of the world's total gas and oil reserves. And within a few years it is likely to have a major water shortage. The whole area is a tinder box. That's a trite phrase, I know, but in this case, it's accurate. That entire region could become unstable at the drop of a hat. It's quiet now and may stay that way for a few more years. But it's basically unstable."

Freihofer from the FBI cleared his throat to speak. "That's what our analysts tell us. Plus we hear that the Chinese are making a push to cultivate these former SSRs. We know that they're itching to get a pipeline that will carry gas and oil to ports that are accessible by their tanker fleet. The Navy is scared shitless that China will get the rights to run a pipeline into a port on the Indian Ocean."

"Exactly." Thatcher waved his pointer down the map to the Indian Ocean. "And that means that they'll need to get across Afghanistan and Pakistan. Or possibly Iran. They're already trying to buy their way in. One of the best ways for them to do that is... what would you expect?"

Captain Cliquennoi spoke up. "Weapons. Heavy industrial machines. Aircraft."

"Any and all of them is the right answer," Thatcher said. "Right now most of those countries would like to stock up on RPGs and shoulder-fired surface-to-air missiles."

O'Meara stood up and walked to the far end of the room, stretched his shoulders and touched his toes. "This is like world hunger. It's like you're talking about sticking your dick out the window and fucking the world. It's too much. What's actionable here? This thing is bigger than evil. With a capital E."

"That's the wrong response," said Thatcher. "We need to send in a team to cover the ground and make an estimate of how the drugs are crossing Central Asia. We have a handle on the flow from Afghanistan to the Pakistani coast... But how stuff gets across Central Asia reliably is still a mystery."

The meeting broke for lunch and continued in the afternoon. There was agreement to meet again to consider ways to address the problem.

Six weeks later, at a secure facility outside Washington in the vicinity of Langley, a similar meeting was conducted. The meeting room held thirteen high-level people representing five government agencies. Each of the seats at the table was provided with laptops that were all linked to the presentation of each speaker. The CIA had five people in the room and each of the other agencies, Homeland Security, DOD, NSA and DEA, had two participants.

To get things going, a tall, cadaverous Section Chief from the Central Asia desk set the objectives.

"There is a lot going on in Central Asia that requires our close attention. Afghanistan is getting a lot of exposure … as is Pakistan. But the other 'stans' are coming into their own as trouble spots. Or maybe potential trouble spots."

This was one of a score of such meetings where there was much hand-wringing but little in the way of concrete action.

Chapter 7

After the Education

"… *southward bound*
For the warm Persian seaboard—so they streamed.
The Tartars of the Oxus, the King's guard,
First, with black sheepskin caps and with long spears;
Large men, large steeds; who from Bokhara come
And Khiva, and ferment the milk of mares.
Next, the more temperate Toorkmuns of the south,
The Tukas, and the lances of Salore,
And those from Attruck and the Caspian sands;
Light men and on light steeds, who only drink
The acrid milk of camels, and their wells."

FROM "SOHRAB AND RUSTUM"
MATTHEW ARNOLD

Back home, the one-legged soldier decides to pursue a lifetime interest in history, archaeology and anthropology. His tour in Afghanistan exposed him to the history and culture of Central Asia. After the death of his grandparents, the sale of their family farm provides him with enough resources to attend Princeton where he gets an advanced degree in Asian History. He aspires to teach, but after graduating with a master's degree and realizing that a career in academia will be significantly enhanced by the Ph.D., he returns to university, bolstered by a wife who sells real estate and the legacy from his family. After graduation he finds employment, and moves to a small town in Pennsylvania. His wife hates life in a small college town and her simmering dissatisfaction wrecks their relationship.

The graduation ceremonies were barely over when the couple began to argue over job prospects. The offers didn't come pouring in. One of the promising responses came from James Buchanan University near Mercersburg, Pennsylvania.

"Mercersburg?" Flo sputtered as he slipped the letter back into its envelope. "Mercersburg? Pennsylvania? Where the hell is Mercersburg? Is that a place you just made up?"

"It's where James Buchanan was born, Flo. It's close to Hagerstown. Maryland. We went there once. In the mountains. Springtime is beautiful there. It has four great seasons. We're going to love it." What he meant was—*I hope you can learn to accept it.* Part of him knew for certain that she would never learn to love it.

"Why couldn't you take a job at some decent school? Where there's a city with some decent attractions? What can you do in Mercersburg? Watch cows graze?" She put the casserole on the table with a bit more force than was necessary—just in case there was any doubt in his mind that she was miffed.

"I spoke to the head of the Department. They want to expand their program in Asian Studies and I'm the first who will be offering courses focusing on Central Asia. In the past the emphasis has been on Japan, China, Southeast Asia. If there's a good response, it could grow into something interesting."

"Interesting to who?"

It would be useless to attempt converting these exchanges into conversation. He ate his food in silence and took his plate to the dishwasher when he was finished.

"I rinse them in the sink first before I load them," she said. Still cross. Still angry.

He dropped everything in the sink and left the kitchen.

By the weekend she had calmed down a bit. He suggested that they take a trip to Pennsylvania and look things over.

"We can take our time. Make a vacation out of it. The Poconos. Or angle north and go through the Finger Lakes Region. Take in some back roads and see the country."

"If that's what you'd like," she answered. She was determined to be sulky and sullen. *To hell with it*, he thought; and the following day they left on a five-day excursion that was miserable for both of them. He was delighted with the look and feel of the countryside around Mercersburg; just as he knew he would be—but she was miserable to think that she would have to live there—just as she had determined she would be.

Two weeks later they loaded the contents of their small apartment into a van and headed west for the Kittatinny Mountains. They settled into an old farmhouse that they had arranged to rent on an earlier visit. Walt began an entirely new life as an academic with little idea of what the coming year might hold.

The new professor had just wrapped up his final lecture of the term on "The Legacy of the Silk Road." Many graduating JBU students were already loading their possessions for the mass exodus from the campus. He had arranged his color slide lecture to include intervals when the lights went up. *Too much darkness and they snooze.*

Light. Dark. Light. Dark. Don't let 'em get comfy. His students, like the others at Buchanan, were itchy to wind up the term, and many had been partying hard the previous night. Walt was happy to have the class over. This wasn't his favorite part of the year. As the last student disappeared out the door, he disconnected the slide projector and stowed his equipment on the cart.

When he looked up from the slide tray he saw that one of his grad students had come back and was waiting for him to put things up. Katya. She was from Russia... no... wrong. Get it right! She was from Kazakhstan and had grown up on a horse ranch. Ekaterina Kalashvili.

He usually thought of names with 'vili' as denoting Azeri. Someone from Georgia—Azerbaijan, or one of those Trans-Caspian countries he was just beginning to study. Hard to keep all the countries—republics and semi-autonomous regions—straight in that melting pot region. But one time when they had been talking, he had come out and asked her if the Kalashvili name was common in Kazakhstan.

"No," she had told him. "My father was conscripted into a labor battalion during the Stalin Era and was sent to work on the railroads in the region around Astana. Back then it was nowhere, but subsequently—after the breakup of the Soviet Union—the city became the capital of the new Republic of Kazakhstan." After her father had been released from his term of service he decided to stay in Astana and he began working with horses. It was a skill he had picked up in Georgia as a boy.

"He did well, my father. Married my mother who was born in Kazakhstan and tells me she is descended from Genghis Khan. That's where I got these eyes," she said with a laugh.

She looked like a girl who had grown up around horses. For that matter, she looked like she could have ridden along with Genghis Khan, or Timur, or Alp Arslan or any of the semi-mythical figures who influenced the history of Central Asia and the world—but are so little known in this country.

He bit back a response that included mention of her eyes. She had come to him to get some recommendations for reading material about the culture of the Scyths. She had accumulated a small list from the Internet, but she wanted to know the three or four that were, as she put it, "seminal." Katya was very smart and she had a better vocabulary than most of his other students. Her choice of words made him slightly uncomfortable, but surely a young woman this attractive wasn't getting flirty with a one-legged guy with an ugly scar on one side of his face. He changed the subject, but inwardly he was laughing at himself. *Hey, maybe she doesn't know I've only got one leg. The limp is hardly noticeable these days.*

"What are you going to do when the term ends, Katya? Got any plans for travel, going back home? What's on your calendar?"

She smiled enigmatically. "Why are you asking me, Professor? Are you offering me..."

"Whoa," he sputtered. "It was just a conversational question. I just figured you weren't planning on spending the summer reading about the Scyths, and I wondered if you had found a job." She seemed to be taken aback by his response.

"My student visa will let me take jobs here until I finish my degree. Even then, I can probably have it extended. My father died last year. You might remember when I was gone for a while as you covered the Culture of Afghanistan. I went back for the funeral. No, I won't go back. My two brothers are managing the horse farm and they both have young wives. Three women in the same compound? No, I don't think so." She was getting a faraway look in her eyes that he hadn't seen before. So he sat back, tacitly inviting her to continue, and she took the hint.

"I've considered going out west for the summer. I know of ranches in Colorado, Idaho and Wyoming where they would take me in a heartbeat. It's pretty easy for someone with my experience with horses to find work at a dude ranch." She paused, and looked at the floor, laughing modestly. "To tell the truth it helps a lot that I'm a woman....

But the work is boring, and—I almost hate to say this—many of the guests, clients, whatever, seem to be rude in proportion to their wealth. Kids are rude, women are rude and men are rude... unless, of course, they're trying to get in my pants." She looked him square in the face to see his response, but his face was still.

"No, I think I might spend the summer doing computer programming. Did I mention that a lot of places in the west remind me of Kazakhstan? Especially, Montana. Yes, I have three solid job offers in the Philadelphia area. Wouldn't be as scenic but it pays better and it's a skill that seems to be transferable."

"How about anthropological field work?" he asked. "Not that I'm selling anything. But if you have any intention of following academia as a career.... There are a number of opportunities to work in some pretty exciting locations. You'd be a great addition to any program."

She smiled. "Thanks for the vote of confidence, Prof. I've thought about it. I'd like to go on your next Central Asia trip."

Chapter 8

Valentin Adds Value

"Ogulmush, a Turk general who had subdued Persian Irak and then rendered fealty to Mohammed, was murdered at the direction of the Kalif, under whose control a number of Assassins had been placed by their chieftain at Alamut. In Persian Irak the name of the Shah was dropped from public prayers, after the slaying of Ogulmush."

THE MONGOLS, A HISTORY
JEREMIAH CURTIN

Valentin's understanding of the package tracking system used to transport drugs from sources in several countries was comprehensive and technical. He understood how the system worked and he had an understanding of the software that made it work. Enforcement of an existing system was merely drudge work for criminal muscle that had little appeal for him. But, unfortunately, his boss had little feeling for what he did, or what he added to the process, and Arkady wanted to shape him to more closely resemble other career criminals in the organization. Basically, his boss couldn't understand him, or what he did, so the boss wanted to remodel Val into something he could understand.

Naturally, this led to conflicts. In order to avoid some of the unpleasant tasks connected with enforcing discipline in a criminal network, Val turned his thoughts to ways to improve the existing system.

In the days of the old Silk Road, goods traveled across Central Asia by camels, in large processions moving slowly in single file. They moved together, stopped together and arrived together—unless, of course, they were attacked. Or perished en route. Camels. Close together. Traveling in a group and arriving at one destination. Now the goods he wanted shipped were carried by truck, bus or van; occasionally by train.

There was no advantage in dispatching many trucks in a convoy.

To the contrary. It was better to have many different trucks leaving on different schedules, by different routes, arriving at different destinations. This, of course, led to complexity and made management more difficult, so this was where the use of computers could manage the welter of details.

For most of the shipments, the finished product, usually some form of heroin, was concealed within other legitimate products which provided cover. Increasingly, the product of interest was coming to be hashish, which, being bulkier, was more difficult to conceal.

Now, Valentin had a flash of insight that would make his product easier to conceal, harder to detect. If his raw product arrived at a shop or factory making any legitimate product for subsequent shipment, the packaging for that product could conceal his drugs. Rugs and kilims sprang to mind immediately. Flattened packages could be concealed in rugs rolled for shipment. Easy to package, but easily detected. Any canned goods could easily contain coded cans with drugs. Anything with an opaque container would be a potential candidate. The criteria? Inexpensive to accomplish. Easy to conceal. Difficult and time-consuming to intercept. Then, suddenly, he thought of watermelons. Melons of every type could become natural containers for properly packaged goods.

The trick would be to select several products which could provide natural cover, and then determine the best way to penetrate the product at its source. This would require careful planning, and in some cases, a technical understanding of methods.

Another flash of insight. Packaging engineers! Like programmers, they could be contracted from India. Indian contract engineers would be unlikely to question the legality of any procedures they were asked to analyze. When a sequence of concealment was selected, another group of specialists would be required to determine the best way to corrupt existing processes. The fewer people involved, the better.

If the volume of drugs crossing any given border was dispersed in many different products, traveling by many modes of transportation, arriving at all hours of the day and night, to different destinations, by different routes, complete interdiction would become statistically impossible, and in any case, too expensive to contemplate.

Hashish was more difficult to handle than heroin because it was bulkier. It could be concealed within cotton bales or sacks, but marking it for recovery might present some challenges. Other types of food products shipped in bulk might present opportunities. Leblebi—chickpeas—were shipped in a variety of containers that might present opportunities. Same for pistachios. The sacks could be marked for identification using the bar code scanners commonly found in every American grocery store.

While he was at Harvard, he had examined everything he could find about Wal-Mart's processes for inventory management. Their supply chains extended from thousands of suppliers in China, across the ocean to collection nodes, followed by managed distribution to a large number of retail centers. The entire process was handled by low-wage people, most of whom were simply cogs in a vast machine. How did this differ from the problem he was trying to manage? At the time it had not been clear to him how he might apply the knowledge he was collecting, but he was confident that it could be put to profitable use across the vast distances of Central Asia.

Actually, he found himself thinking of his drug management requirements as his "Wal-Mart" problem, but he realized that the use of this term to his Russian colleagues would be meaningless because they couldn't share his understanding of what the concept encompassed.

And the internet—it was God's gift to those wishing to transmit covert information. Every web site could conceal a million messages in a million codes that could be discarded and renewed. Ever-changing, ever-growing, the messages could almost be sent in the open if they changed with sufficient rapidity. This could be tried out almost immediately. He could begin an experiment with Raj and his team within a few days. They could communicate on a daily basis. Not that it was needed right now. But it was good to anticipate problems and solve them before they occurred.

He was excited by the ideas that were forming and tumbling in his brain, and he made several pages of rough notes to capture some of the concepts that he wanted to test immediately.

Zinaida had been waiting for him for some time. For a while she was doing something to her toenails that occupied her time, but—that task completed—she was now beginning to reveal her impatience, and Zinaida in a pout was a disappointing fuck. He wanted to make sure that he had enough notes on paper so that he could begin putting some of his ideas into practice. It would take some modifications to existing software, but it should be straightforward.

He was pleased with the progress he had made, and was already beginning to look forward to the next day when he could begin to get down to work in earnest. But, as he began pulling his notes together before turning his attention to the young woman, he realized that he was drunk.

At one of the meetings that Arkady called from time to time—for rewards and punishments—Valentin was summoned for a private audience. Arkady had received a call from a former Red Army colonel, now part of the armed forces of Tajikistan, assigned to border duty in the region between that country and Afghanistan. It was across this border that the poppy-based drugs and hashish poured in an endless torrent. The colonel was complaining that Valentin had cut the payments to army officials after threatening to stop them completely.

Arkady was angry at receiving the complaint, but he wasn't particularly interested in understanding the problem. He just wanted it to go away. Complaints of any type were anathema to him. One solution that sometimes worked for him? Kill the complainer.

But sometimes that just caused more problems.

Val labored to explain the situation.

"The soldiers at the border add nothing of value. They contribute nothing and they are greedy. Our trucks come through with produce of several types. We have regular routes for trucks carrying produce from several of Afghanistan's most productive provinces: Kunar, Takhar, Kunduz, Badakhshan. We work with produce merchants shipping melons, vegetables and animal carcasses; mostly sheep. A few other products. The raw opium is packaged to avoid contamination and concealed.

The border guards can't search every vehicle. We did an analysis based upon the number of searches they could reasonably conduct, and we concluded that it would be cheaper to lose those drugs than to pay the extortionate fees asked by the army guard commanders."

"You did a fucking analysis? *An analysis?* We are criminals. Fucking criminals! We do not analyze what we do!"

"Let me explain it another way. Which would you prefer to have, Arkady? A hundred roubles or a thousand roubles?"

"Do not make me angry, my friend."

"You see? Exactly. It is a question of money. We keep more if we do not pay the guards. Let them try to intercept what we are shipping. Anyway, we can often buy it back after they have confiscated it. Their officers would rather see them sell it back to us than to try peddling it to their comrades. They don't want the problems associated with use in their barracks."

"Why do they call me to complain? I am a busy man and I do not like to hear complaints."

"Naturally they are unhappy when I do not pay them cash. But it makes no sense. In Tajikistan we have several plants for processing the raw material into forms more suitable for shipment across Asia. There is no sense in paying exorbitant transit fees when they can easily be avoided."

"You are telling me that my friend, the colonel, should just go fuck himself?"

"Arkady, why would I tell a friend of yours to fuck himself? But neither would I give your money away to him. If this is what you wish, I can do it. But it will be because of your instructions. You may, of course, give away anything you wish."

"I do not want to argue about this, Valentin. Let's have a drink. I have some Starka that has been flavored with pears and a hint of apricot. This is only 43 percent alcohol, but I think you will like it. Drink with me. We will try it your way. I will think of some lie to tell my friend. No more of business for today."

How does it happen that an intelligent, educated man like Valentin Kuriatin finds himself working for a monster like Arkady? He has wondered about that, too. It still has the quality of a bad dream.

After the death of his friend and teacher, Nikolai, Valentin was compelled to rethink his ambitious plans for the future. He had harbored the notion that if he could obtain sufficient start-up capital, it would be a relatively straightforward process to get started in the drug business. In his problem-solving brain, it was just a question of either finding a way to make a quick killing in the arms trade or else find a silent investor who would put up the money with the promise of a substantial return. Val's ideas were technically sound, but they were extremely naive and failed to reflect an understanding of the scope and power of Russia's Mafia.

Many of the key figures at the top of the Mafia pyramid were career criminals who had spent time in Russian prisons and were hardened by years of violence and brutality beyond the comprehension of most normal individuals. Arkady Volkevich Fedorov was one such crime boss whose empire had begun modestly with a single vodka distillery outside Moscow. This ex-jailbird quickly expanded his vodka empire to include a score of distilleries, all producing a product that was not only legal in Russia but was widely exported around the world. People who crossed Arkady frequently ended up with life-altering disabilities and more than a handful passed on to the next world.

In the same way that many executives cultivate negotiating skills, Arkady cultivated techniques of violent behavior and terror. He used fear as an important tool in conducting business. This is how he "recruited" Valentin Kuriatin.

Valentin was in Moscow when he received the summons from Arkady. Arkady's name was familiar to him, and—in his ignorance and naivete—he thought that he could approach this powerful, wealthy man for a loan. The two men who knocked at the door of Val's Moscow hotel did not wait to be invited inside.

"We were sent to bring you to see the boss, Arkady Volkevich." Val recognized the name immediately.

"I am eager to meet with Arkady Volkevich," Val replied pleasantly. "Unfortunately, today is not a good day for me, since I have several other appointments this afternoon. If you can tell me the address and number, I will..."

"Maybe you are stupid. Today is a good day. And for this meeting, it is the only day. Get your coat. We have a car waiting."

"Pardon me, but it is out of the question—since...."

One of the man took a sap from his pocket and tapped it menacingly. The other man did the talking.

"Unless you want to be carried out with a crack in your skull, you will put on your coat and follow us quietly. More talking will not take place. We are leaving now. You may walk out. Or be carried." They spoke convincingly and Valentin was not anxious to have his skull cracked—or even dented.

In the car he was not pushed or threatened again and there was little talking during the ride to an office complex off Uspenskaya Avenue where Arkady Volkevich had one of his several Moscow suites.

The building appeared to predate the revolution and may have been a private mansion when it was first built. It looked like a residence out of Tolstoy, with a patterned marble floor fronting an impressive central staircase that split in two directions. Arkady's suite appeared to occupy most of the second floor but there were two additional floors whose purpose Val never learned.

On the second level he was led into a large, marble-floored anteroom where a secretary-receptionist sat behind an enormous antique desk of wood with two incongruous computers, their cables snaking across the floor before disappearing into what appeared to be a small, unlit closet. An attractive woman of about forty asked him if he would care for tea while he waited.

As soon as Val was seated his two escorts disappeared, although Val doubted that they had strayed very far.

Val waited for about ten or fifteen minutes before the woman behind the desk said, "You may go in now, Valentin Mihailovich. Just open the door and enter. He's expecting you."

Val opened the heavy wooden door and stepped inside. The door appeared to have been carved from one massive block of wood. Inside, Arkady was seated behind a desk fronting a floor-to-ceiling window that looked out over Uspenskaya Park and its skating pond. He was facing the window, but although the door opened without the least sound, he spoke as soon as Val entered. "Come in. Come in and take a seat. I'll be with you in a moment."

As far as Val could determine, he was doing absolutely nothing. Val sat and watched as Arkady gazed into the distance of a Moscow winter day. The wind was down and, though a few flakes were swirling lazily, it was a fine day for ice skating. On the frozen pond before the window a score of skaters were gliding and swooping, individually and in pairs.

They sat in total silence for several minutes, long enough for Val to become acutely uncomfortable. He was considering some move to break the silence, when Arkady stood, still facing the window, and it was then that Val noticed he was holding a cell phone. The connection was open.

"Yes, Emilian, I have been waiting. Once more, tell me. You have a view of the entire skating area? Yes? Good. I will call you."

The big man pushed the button on his phone and turned to face Val. "Valentin Mihailovich. I have been waiting for the right time to sit down with you." Val rose and extended his hand, but the big man did not take it.

"Sit. Sit. I know you are busy so I'll come to the point."

"Arkady Volkevich, I too have been hoping to meet with you. I have a plan for..."

"Be quiet and listen to me. I know what you have a plan for. I know what you have done in the past, and I know what you are trying to do. You have been involved in some weapons arrangements that took money out of my pocket and now you are attempting to do something even worse with drugs. But this will not happen."

"Arkady Volkevich, I have not...." The big man slammed the table with his open palm, causing Val to stop in mid-sentence.

"Keep silent and listen. As of this moment you are working for me. When we finish our discussion I will introduce you to several of my financial managers so you can learn how we will work together. I will provide you with the money you need to begin operating out of the city of your choice. My strong recommendation is for Almaty."

"Arkady Volkevich, we have not even said a word about..." This time a fist came down and Arkady's face grew dark.

"I will not say this again. Do not speak until I direct you." Val did not want to attempt staring this man down.

"You are working for me. You will be paid very well, and you will receive a portion of the profits your enterprise earns. It will be enough to make you very wealthy and should supply you with enough money for you to keep your dick wet for as long as you wish. Valentin Mihailovich, listen carefully, for I will not repeat. I know who you are. I know what you do, and I understand much more that you can imagine. When we talk again it will be after my financial people report to me on your progress." He paused, but Val held his tongue, thoroughly baffled.

"Now, Valentin! You are thinking, who is this son-of-a-bitch to think that he can own me. So I will tell you that, as of this moment, you remain alive at my pleasure. It is true, even though you may not, at this instant, believe it. So I must show you how lucky you are to breathe our Moscow air. Come to the window."

Val rose and walked to the window.

"Look at the skaters on the pond and choose one who stands out among the rest. Select carefully, for it will be a fateful choice for you both. Take your time before you speak."

Among the skaters there were several who appeared to be quite accomplished as amateurs, and there were occasional axels and camels to make casual watching by unsophisticated viewers a pleasure. One young woman, in particular, stood out, in part because the shell above her down jacket was a vivid shade of hot pink.

"You choose a female? Not surprising. And she is the only one in pink. Yes. Very well. Yes, she skates well." Arkady lifted the cell phone and pressed in a number. "Yes, Emilian? You see the young woman in pink? Yes. Very well." Arkady turned to face Val, his back toward the window. "Now, Valentin Mihailovich. Watch closely and picture yourself on a frozen pond."

Val kept his eye on the skater. Several seconds passed as Arkady remained facing away from the window with the phone to his ear. "Emilian! You are ready? No? Yes? Yes. Then.... Now, Emil!" he spoke into the phone. The woman dropped and there was a commotion among the other skaters on the pond. Had she been shot? Fallen? What had happened?

Arkady never looked back at the pond. He kept his eyes fixed on Valentin who was attempting to control his expression. Arkady was watching him like a hawk.

"Now, Valentin Mihailovich, as you are very intelligent, your clever mind will think of many ways to explain what you have just witnessed. So... ." He reached into a drawer and handed Val a small pair of field glasses. Val took the glasses, noticing that they were Zeiss 6 X 30's with a German eagle and swastika, a captured souvenir from Russia's great victory over the Nazi invaders. He looked through the glasses and was sickened. The girl had been shot, apparently in the head, judging by the amount of blood easily visible even at this distance and by the reaction of horrified skaters. A crowd was gathering and they were milling like insects.

He wanted to shout at Arkady, or to curse him, but some instinct told him to be very careful with this man. Arkady had never taken his eyes off Val since he spoke into the phone.

"So, you see, Valya, how thin the thread by which we all are hanging. At any moment.... In any place.... We can never be completely safe. It is always a relative thing. So. Now. You are working for me. I know it will be distasteful for you, but you must learn to like it. Not merely to accept it. To like it. Or you will be killed. Fucked first. Do not think of us as czar and peasant, or as boss and employee. Think of us as partners. Not equal, it is true. But partners with a common goal of making money and living the lives we choose. So. Now. You know how it must be. Partners. Both of us alive." He stretched out his hand to Val, and Val, despising himself, took it.

"Now, Valentin Mihailovich, Valya, Val, we can have a drink, and good vodka will help you to accept our new partnership. Then, when we are slightly drunk, I will introduce you to the wizards who collect our money. And now you may speak." The big man was already at the cabinet, beginning to pour Ochotnichiya into two tumblers

But Val, his brain still whirling from what he had just witnessed, could think of nothing that would be safe to say. His brain was racing to find something he hoped would not trigger wrath.

"Why do you recommend Almaty as a base of operations?"

Chapter 9

Why Walt Loves The Silk Road

"... he started telling me about his life, while I tried to remember what I knew about the Silk Road, the old commercial route that connected Europe with the countries of the East. The traditional route started in Beirut, passed through Antioch and went all the way to the shores of the Yangtze in China; but in Central Asia it became a kind of web, with roads heading off in all directions, which allowed for the establishment of trading posts, which, in time, became towns, which were later destroyed in battles between rival tribes, rebuilt by inhabitants; destroyed, and rebuilt again. Although almost everything passed along that route—gold, strange animals, ivory, seeds, political ideas, refugees from civil wars, armed bandits, private armies to protect the caravans—silk was the rarest and most coveted item. It was thanks to one of these branch roads that Buddhism traveled from China to India."

THE ZAHIR
PAOLO COELHO

Walter Roberts was born in Willow Grove, Pa., and moved with his parents to Injirlik in Turkey before he entered high school. His father, a career Air Force officer, relocated his young wife and son to the U.S. Air Force base where he was stationed for six years. Walter grew up exposed to the culture and language of Turkey. By a stroke of good fortune, when he returned to the U.S. he was essentially bilingual.

Walter's interests ran in the direction of history and archaeology, and the years he spent in Turkey sharpened this fascination. To Walt, Timur and Genghis Khan had become as real and as interesting as Mad Anthony Wayne or George Armstrong Custer. At Penn State he majored in history and stayed for a Master's degree, contemplating a career in academia. He married Florence, a polished sorority girl who captured his heart and dangled him cruelly before finally accepting his proposal for a post-graduation marriage. But after his father was killed in an unexplained plane crash, he was motivated to join the Army, a move that he felt compelled to make based on conditions in the world, but one which was, to Florence and to several of his young friends, incomprehensible.

When it became known that he could speak Turkish, he was steered toward the Special Forces, eventually winding up in Afghanistan. There, in a skirmish lacking military significance, he encountered a crudely made box mine, or improvised explosive device, and lost his right leg below the knee.

Back in the states he was fitted with a prosthetic leg, learned to cope and resumed the academic pursuits that had been disrupted by his father's death. Married, wounded, and rehabilitated, he managed to get into Princeton where he earned his Ph.D. His wife was a tremendous asset during his Princeton years. Intelligent, hard working and uncommonly attractive, she found work for a local realtor and by the time Walt graduated she had earned her broker's license.

Hired by a small, prestigious university in Pennsylvania, Walt contemplated a quiet life where he could concentrate on topics that had fascinated him ever since he had visited Topkapi Palace in Istanbul. There, he had seen large Chinese plates—gifts to the Turkish sultan—said to have been delivered by caravans on the Silk Road, across the roof of the world. Since his boyhood days in Turkey he had been fired to know more about the cities and oases that had existed along this ancient route across Central Asia.

As a member of the Asiatic Studies Department at James Buchanan University, Walter designed several courses on Central Asia that proved to be popular with students and with university administrators. Three of his courses quickly attracted students from other departments and were filled every time they were offered. One was on "The Life and Times of Alexander the Great." Another was "Genghis Khan: His Impact on Asia and Europe." A third winner was titled, simply, "The Silk Road." It focused on the history and culture of the trade route that once linked China with the West. He was working to develop another unit on Tamerlane. Timur the Lame. This one would be harder to research, but it too promised to be well received. Other courses were in the works. His study was filled with folders and he had already begun assembling material for *Manichaeism and Nestorian Christianity*.

Encouraged by the rapid acceptance of topics that interested him, he decided to float a radical new idea with the administration. His department head, Dr. Li, was moderately supportive, but because of the unusual nature of the proposal Li insisted that they review the concept with the president, the provost and a few others.

Walter's plan involved a "for credit" tour of Asia that visited ancient cities along this historic route: Ashkhabad, Merv, Bukhara, Samarkand and Tashkent. The idea would be to offer a two-week tour of ancient sites in the late August, early September time frame before fall classes had resumed. The course would offer three credits and would require a detailed trip report at the end of the tour. Participation in the two-week program would be graded in the same way as a conventional three-hour course. Unfortunately, Walter's wife found his interests and career aspirations to be lacking in stimulation of the type she felt she deserved, and she sought entertainment in other directions.

Wong Fong Li, his department head, kicked off their presidential review meeting with a lukewarm endorsement. Cautious Li was testing the wind direction and his face was totally unreadable. President Carson was skeptical and non-committal.

"What about the safety and legal aspects? Am I to understand that you'd be herding your students through five or six different countries? Former Soviet republics? Primarily Islamic…?"

"We would visit five countries," Walt interrupted. "But only if we could get the necessary travel visas in advance. Or in some cases—at the border. But the trip is safe. I have been twice, as a member of small groups. And I never had the slightest problem." He hesitated. "Some inconveniences, of course."

"How many students would you propose to take? My God. These are college students. Free in Central Asia? Think of the liability."

"Most international tour groups require customers to sign waivers. Some type of "hold harmless" agreement. Also, before anyone went anywhere they'd have to spend a couple of days with me. Getting indoctrinated. Parental consent—of course. How many? Probably ten to twelve max."

Dr. Farrington, the provost, leaned forward in his leather chair—which unfortunately made an embarrassing squeal that everyone pretended not to notice. "Tell us again. What countries would you propose to visit?"

"The countries lying along the ancient Silk Road in the region once lumped together as Western Turkistan. I would propose to begin in Turkmenistan, cross into Uzbekistan, then move into Tajikistan and Kirghizstan. End up in Kazakhstan. Fly out of Almaty to Moscow and come home. Two weeks. Maybe sixteen days. The Silk Road would become a real place. With a real geography. Like courses on the Erie Canal, maybe. Or maybe, more like Lewis and Clark. Only a bit longer."

Walter offered to show a carousel filled with 35 mm slides showing some of the sites he proposed to visit. "Most of the students will never even have heard of Afrosiab. We'll visit the ruins and…"

"Pardon me," Carson cut in. "Did you say *Afrosiab*? What the dickens is *Afrosiab*?"

"Ah, excuse me. Yes. Afrosiab. Perhaps if we looked at the slides…"

"I'm going to have to beg off until another time, " the president said, with a theatrical glance at his watch. "I'm scheduled to meet with some representatives of the Alumni Association at eleven-thirty. Perhaps we can get together another time. Meanwhile, we can be thinking this over. I'll be seeing Dr. Li early next week at our faculty meeting."

If 'twere done, 'twere done quickly, Walter thought, biting his tongue. He was thinking about the details that would require his attention if they were to make a trip this year.

What carried the day for his program probably had little to do with his meeting with the president. It had everything to do with six enthusiastic letters from the parents whose names were well known in connection with alumni contributions. Their kids were eager to visit Central Asia for an array of reasons varying from not very intelligent to stupid; from the desire for an adventure on the parental ticket, to the possibility for scoring cheap drugs while under the protective blanket of a university-endorsed activity. Only a few, he knew, would have legitimate academic interests.

It was about eight weeks after the initial meeting that Dr. Li called him into the office to say that the President had given his approval. There was no fanfare, no conditions. Walt was surprised by the absence of academic restrictions. They were giving him a free hand. Not much help, but no hindrance either. It sounds like a fine idea, Dr. Farrington had said. "Write up the details for inclusion in the next catalog. And, oh yes, don't forget to include a mention of the 'hold-harmless' agreement. Check with the Business Office to see what they recommend relative to speaking with a lawyer." It seemed they were giving him plenty of rope.

Approval from the front office came—so it seemed—in the form of a yawn and a hand wave.

Walter was pleased with the response despite the lukewarm enthusiasm—pleased but not surprised. He had been confident that the idea was sound. He was also confident that once word got around, his program would become a popular favorite, at least as long as Central Asia didn't blow up with civil strife, terrorist confrontations, or god knows what other events he had purposely neglected to catalog.

After 9-11 and Iraq, a trip into Central Asia was not for the faint-hearted. But most of the kids who would be interested in going were too young and dumb to be scared. Actually, Walt believed it would be safe.

What the hell, it's a chancy world. Some of these young people run a higher risk of dying from binge drinking at fraternity or sorority initiations than from some mishap in the mind-boggling vastness of Central Asia. Where most people are friendly.

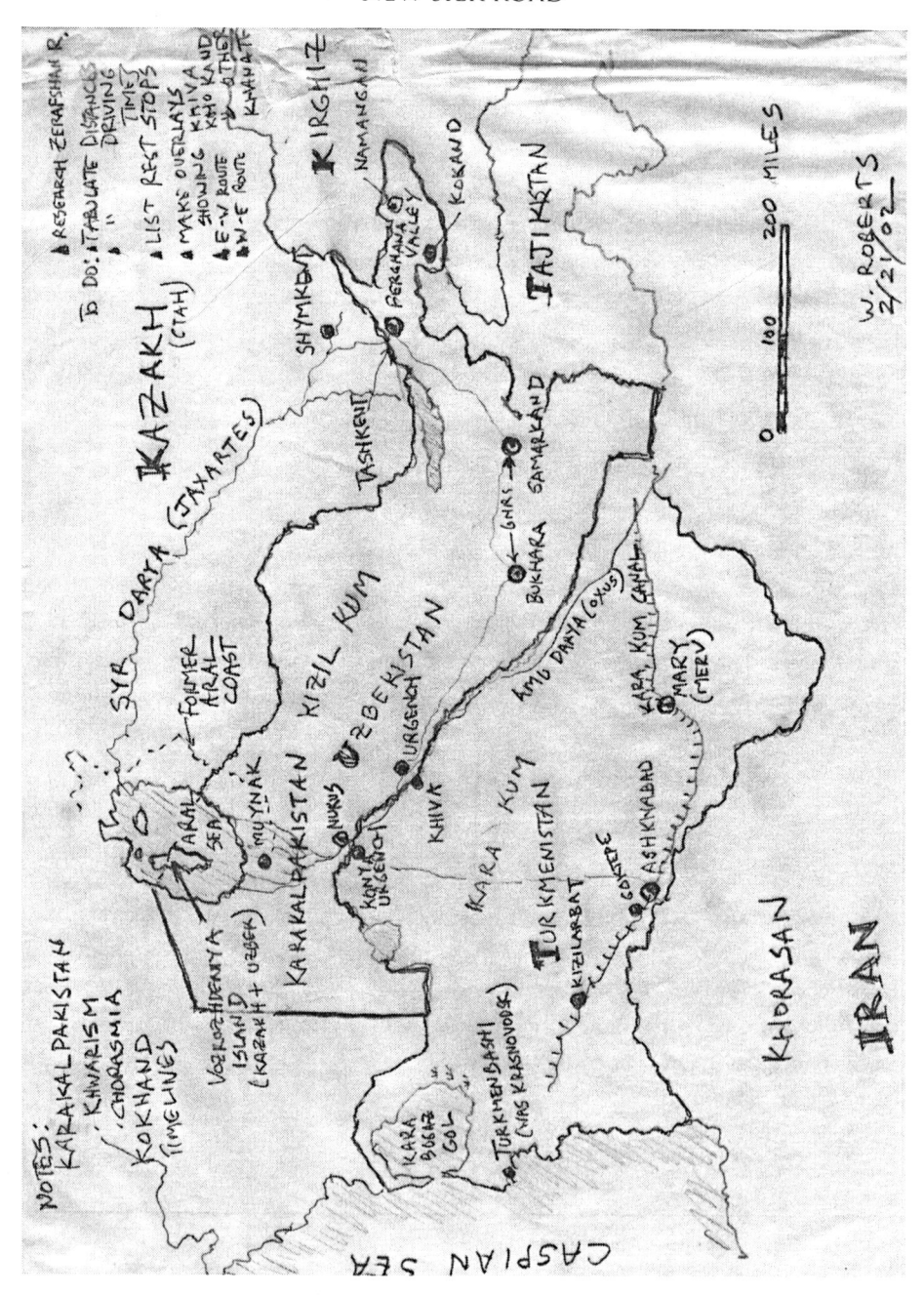

The sad note in the whole business was Flo's response. She had no interest at all in accompanying him, either alone, as part of another group, or as a companion on a trip where he would be the leader. The Bahamas? Aboard a cruise ship? That would have been OK with Flo. But not Central Asia.

"Cruise ships have toilet paper. And it's good paper, too."

"Well, thannnnnk you for sharing!"

"You're not a woman."

"Praise God!"

"Oh yeah, that's cute. Just why would you think I might want to go to a place with... what's the name of those deserts? The Kizil...? Whatever! Deserts? No. I don't think so. I don't complain if you want to go, Walt. Go! Do whatever you do out there. But it's a part of the world I just can't relate to."

"I've got the message. We've done this before."

"Then why do you keep bringing it up again and again?" She was starting to shift into warm-up mode and was clearly willing to stretch it out for a bit.

"Point well made," he capitulated, wishing he was out of the house.

"I mean—I don't like the food. I don't like the climate. I don't like the scenery and I can't stand the people. It's hot, dirty, dusty and unsafe. And now? After what's just happened in the world? Crazy! What could be pleasant about...."

"I'm going for a walk."

Things were going sour. Early in the first years of their marriage they had talked about children and for a time she had gone off the pill. But nothing had happened, and ever since he had come back from Afghanistan, she had used contraceptives regularly. During the years when he was back in school it had made sense. She was the big earner and it had seemed important for her to help him finish school and get settled in a good situation. Sometimes Walt had the feeling that Flo believed that if they had a child, it would be born with one leg.

Now, it seemed to him that he had found the good situation he had sought, but her attitude toward children seemed to have changed. The reality, hard as it was to admit, was that her attitude had changed since he lost his leg. It had really been deteriorating ever since he took the job at JBU. She hated Mercersburg. But it was more than that.

Jesus Christ, can it really be my leg? That's the only thing I can really think of that's different. From the day I came out of Walter Reed and moved back home, things really never got back to the way they were at the beginning.

Analyzing his situation, he had to admit that for the past several years his head had been buried in his work. He was trying to compensate for his... what? Handicap? For his loss? What?

He was trying to put the two of them in a position where they could look forward to a comfortable life. They had a decent house, a relaxed life style, jobs they both enjoyed and were proficient at. Now was the time when they could step back, start a family, enjoy the American dream.

She still excited him. Just the look of her. Slim hips, a small waist, eye-popping breasts, perfect teeth, golden hair that seemed to take care of itself and always made him want to touch it. *She could smile more.* But, he had to acknowledge to himself, he didn't seem to work on her the same way. *Maybe it's the scar. But it doesn't seem that bad.* This was an admission that didn't come easily. He had to walk around it for months. But once he allowed the idea to express itself… there it was. A big ugly fact. Like cancer or HIV.

Once he allowed the idea to take shape and form itself into words, it took on a life of its own. Events of the years since his return now seemed to fall into place in a different way. *She doesn't love me. The leg may be part of it. Or it may be all of it. But there it is. She never even looks at my stump. How can I live with someone who's repelled by me?*

Chapter 10

Planning the Silk Road Tour

"We entered the desert which is between Khwarizm and Bukhara, an eighteen days' journey through sands, with no settlements on the way except the small town of Kat, which we reached after four days march. We encamped beside it, by a lake which was frozen over and on which the boys were playing and sliding. The qadi came out to greet us, followed an hour later by the governor and his suite, who pressed us to stay and gave a banquet in our honour. In this desert there is a journey of six nights without water, after which we reached the town of Wabkana. Thence we traveled for a whole day through a continuous series of orchards, streams, trees and buildings, and reached the city of Bukhara."

IBN BATUTA; TRAVELS IN ASIA AND AFRICA, 1325-1354
TRANSLATED BY H. A. R. GIBB

The trip he planned at the desk in his study was the trip he always wanted to take. East to west, or west to east, depending on the season and the political climate. *The countries? Always unpredictable.* That much geography is always likely to include hot spots.

Starting in the west he would begin in Ashkhabad. Then Merv, known today by the improbable name of Mary. From there to Urgench which could be used as a base for exploring the ancient oasis town of Khiva. Traveling east from Urgench he would follow the line of the historic Amu Darya River to visit Charjew before heading on to world-famous Bukhara.

The route east from Bukhara would lead to Khokand and Samarkand. A detour to the south would take them to Dushanbe in Tajikistan. A detour to the north would lead to Tashkent, in the northeastern claw of Uzbekistan. From Tashkent it might be feasible to make a sortie out to the oasis kingdom of Khokand, an empire once on a par with Khiva and Bukhara.

He envisioned his tour ending in the Kazakhstan city of Almaty, mostly because he did not believe he could successfully plan a scheduled tour that would go as far east as Urumchi. Extending the trip to Urumchi—or maybe Turfan—in China's Uighur region would be a project for a later time. For now, he believed that a trip from the shores of the Caspian to the very heart of Central Asia would stimulate his students to want more.

With the broad strokes of his tour laid out, he began the weeks of work necessary to build a program that would be interesting, challenging and inspirational. As he began to work, he found that his difficulties had more to do with what to leave out than with what to put in.

One of his first problems came when he put down the words, "from the shores of the Caspian." How would he treat the Kara Bogaz Gol? Was it sufficiently important in the scheme of his program to include a detour to the Caspian port city of Turkmenbashi? Maybe the wonders of the Kara Bogaz Gol would have to be omitted?

He made a list of the cities and sites he would like to visit in his perfect tour. Ashkhabad. Merv. Khiva. Charjew. For each of the places he would like to visit, he listed the sites that would merit a stop. Clearly there were many that he would not know. But at the same time, several of the places on the "must visit" list were World Heritage sites. Bukhara. Samarkand.

Gradually he filled his notebook with jumbled ideas and suggestions that could later be worked into lecture notes.

In Samarkand the Shah-i-Zinda necropolis is worth a half-day visit for the variety of Islamic architecture and the spectacular tile work that decorated the mausoleums of holy men and leaders. Samarkand, known at various times as the "Pearl of the East" or the "Mirror of the World," was visited by Alexander and Genghis Khan. Built by Tamurlane, the Registan, Samarkand's great square, is considered one of Central Asia's splendors, meriting comparison with the much better known Taj Mahal.

Khokand was the third of the three great khanates separating Imperial Russia from Afghanistan, Iran and the British Empire in India. Much of the struggle known to history as "The Great Game" took place in the regions that once belonged to the Khans and Emirs who added color and romance as compensation for tyranny and oppression. When Arab invaders swept across the region bringing Islam, they matched the Khans in violence. But neither the original inhabitants nor their Arab conquerors could match the ferocity of Mongol warriors—beginning with Genghis Khan—who swept in from the east. The Mongols extended their empire until it spanned the breadth of Asia, from eastern Europe to the seas beyond China.

With the fall of Tsarist Russia, Bolshevik armies moved in to conquer and occupy these territories and, in time, they became part of the Soviet Union. Usually they were designated semi-autonomous regions or SSRs. Khokand, located along the ancient Silk Road, had existed as a major city mentioned in Chinese records as early as the 5th century A.D. At one time it was part of the vast empire known as Parthia.

The ancient oasis city was built mostly of mud. Its prosperity was due in large measure to the availability of water for irrigation. The fertile pocket known as Ferghana enabled Khokand to recover following the pillage and plunder of Arabs and Mongol conquerors, but these invaders lacked the modern explosives available after World War I. It took modern explosives to finally level the mud wall fortifications. Today, little is left of this ancient capital.

Ancient Tashkent of Silk Road fame is the capital of Uzbekistan, a metropolis of over two million inhabitants who speak Russian and Tajik in addition to Uzbek, the official language. During the middle of the 19th century, the heart of Central Asia was under the control of three khanates: Khiva, Bokhara and Khokand. *The easternmost of these warring khanates was Khokand, a geological valley "island" surrounded by the formidable barrier of the Pamir Range. Penjikent? Can this be visited comfortably as a day trip from Tashkent?* He underlined this sentence with a highlighter and continued capturing his random thoughts as they tumbled out.

After the fall of Imperial Russia, Bolshevik forces occupied all of these once-independent khanates and the ruling emirs were deposed, killed or made to disappear. Likewise, the atheistic Soviet occupiers attempted to suppress the dominant Muslim religion. With the fall of Soviet Russia, Uzbekistan became an independent republic and Islam reasserted itself. Notes and ideas came to Walt in a rush.

One consequence of Uzbek independence has been a mass exodus of Russian citizens which some have compared to the French departure from Algeria. The botanical gardens in Tashkent are home to the wide variety of plants and trees found in Central Asia.

Issyk Kul. The lake in the mountains. Need more details about the travel routes around this lake.

Dushanbe. Capital city of Tajikstan, site of cruel fighting during the Bolshevik conquest of the region. Ruins nearby? Check it out.

Almaty. Once the capital of Kazakhstan, this city was renamed by the Russians from its original Turkish name, Alma Ata. Apple Father. Father of Apples. Horticulturists from around the world still visit Kazakhstan to study the wild trees that grow on mountainsides.

By the time Walt finished making notes he had filled half a legal pad with ideas for follow-up and material to begin the detailed research and planning needed for his program notes. It was well after one a.m. and he was tired, but he had made a good start and the ideas were still bubbling. He made a couple of additional notes for the next day's research. *Check out Kwarizm.* To hell with it, he concluded. *Enough for tonight.*

The FM radio station had just begun playing playing Moussorgsky's "Pictures at an Exhibition," music that seemed curiously appropriate. He switched off the light at his desk and put his head down to listen to the end. With his head on the desk, the smell from the highlighter pen was overwhelming. No wonder. He had used a dry erase marker. *I'll start again in the morning.* Flo had already gone to bed and he didn't want to wake her. He sat on the couch in his study, took off his pants and shirt and then unfastened his leg, placing it where it was within arm's reach. The wool blanket was by his legs. Then, stretching back, he reached over his head to turn out the light.

Chapter 11

Arkady Explains His Code

"When Alim Khan of the Manghit dynasty assumed power as emir of Bukhara in 1910, the Russians had already controlled his homeland for two generations, and he ruled more as a pampered puppet than did his ancestors of earlier centuries. Seven hundred thirty-one years after the first tribal **khuriltai** *met on the shores of the Blue Lake by Black-Heart-Shaped Mountain in 1189, a much different group, also calling itself a* **khuriltai** *but consisting of the delegates of the Bukhara Communist Party, met to depose his last descendant.*

In the final week of August, he fled Bukhara, and after a brief attempt to mount a resistance from Tajikistan, he found refuge under British protection in Afghanistan, where he lived for the remainder of his life. As the emir departed, Bolshevik forces under Mikhail Vasilyevich Frunze attacked the citadel in Bukhara, the same fortress where, precisely seven centuries earlier, the Spirit Banner of Genghis Khan had led the Mongols to their first victory in Central Asia."

GENGHIS KHAN AND THE MAKING OF THE MODERN WORLD
JACK WEATHERFORD

The Big Boss had come to Almaty to tour Valentin's set-up and to get a briefing on how things were working out. Val's complex occupied two floors of a ten-story office building. The top floor and roof were a restaurant and bar. Val's "business"—which was listed as a vodka wholesaler—occupied the fifth and sixth floors.

About 35 people were employed in the "business," and all but a handful manned computers where they sat with phone headsets talking to people all over the world in half a dozen languages.

A small handful of trusted associates was involved with the software used to manage the system. From scores of locations in half a dozen nations of Central Asia, a steady stream of heroin, hashish and raw opium flowed in containers designed to carry everything from flavored cigarettes to caviar to auto parts.

In setting up his system, Val had drawn on the experience and expertise of many businesses in the West. One that had been particularly useful had been the maker of a hot pepper sauce produced in southern Louisiana. To control the quality of the peppers used in their products this manufacturer ended up working with growers in many countries of Central and South America. The company had to guide growers in all aspects of pepper culture in order to obtain the uniform quality they required for their product. Every step of the growing process had to be understood and controlled. Inspectors in the field advised growers of the precise time required to harvest their crops.

Val had met one of their managers while working in the MBA program at Harvard. The woman had been highly intelligent, but what had drawn Val to her at first had been her tawny skin color and her wild untamable hair. A few days after his pursuit had been suitably rewarded, he began to see a different side of her, and they spent several interesting weekends at Bed and Breakfast establishments at Gloucester, Plymouth and some other New England towns whose names he had forgotten. Once they even took the summer ferry from Boston to Provincetown on the Cape. From her he learned the importance of paying attention to every element of a process, since the smallest details, left unattended, could gum up the works in ways that were sometimes spectacular.

The business models he had found most helpful were Wal-Mart, and the major package shippers—notably Fed Ex and UPS—and that pepper sauce manufacturer in Louisiana. So far, he did not have a need to spend that much effort in controlling the uniformity of the product he was managing, but who knows? The time might come.

To prepare for Arkady's visit—planned to spread over two days—Val had made arrangements to have exclusive use of the restaurant, and one corner would be decorated with flowers. It was hard to know in advance if Arkady would be traveling with Ludmila, but it was better to err on the safe side. The bar was stocked with ample supplies of Arkady's vodka, and there was enough caviar on hand to enable Val to have enough left over to throw a party for his staff after Arkady had left. Val's capable staff managed the details and he controlled himself from trying to micromanage the process. Finally, the big day had arrived.

Arkady's flight was met by a limo arranged by Val's office. The crime boss traveled with an entourage that included two bodyguards, a personal secretary and his current mistress, who for some time now had been the former ballet dancer Ludmila

Kutsunov. They went first to their hotel and the limo arrived at Val's office shortly before noon. He would have an opportunity to welcome them in his office before escorting them up to lunch.

Val chose to have his boss find him in his office, busy with details, rather than free to greet him at the entrance. He had arranged to be on the phone to India when Arkady was led into the office. In retrospect, he wasn't sure if that had been a wise decision.

Lunch went smoothly. After lunch, as Val and Arkady were drinking, Ludmila, pleading fatigue, excused herself to return to the hotel for a nap. Val smiled inwardly. The woman, lithe and sinewy, could probably have run a marathon. Looking at her arms, legs and bony chest he concluded there was no part of her body that would float.

Val spent the balance of the day escorting Arkady past the desks of his operators, explaining their functions, showing him the details of the various displays managed by each, and guiding him through the complex printouts used to track problems whenever they arose. Toward the end of the afternoon he took Arkady inside the environmentally controlled area housing the old DEC mainframe he had purchased for a song from an American petrochemical company.

That night he had dinner with Arkady and Ludmila, drank too much, ate too little and had an ugly hangover the following day. He was angry with himself when he arrived at his office on the morning of the second day; angry and hung over, thus in a bad mood to listen to what Arkady had to say. The boss didn't waste any time getting down to business.

"Quite an operation you have here, Valentin. Everyone seems happy to be working for you."

"Spasseba. I believe we are making good progress. What does your accountant say about us?"

"There are no problems in that area. The money is flowing in. We scarcely know what to do with so much of it."

"Maybe before long, I can make some recommendations?"

"And if I want them, I will ask. Val, there is something that causes me concern that we must resolve."

Val waited without answering. This did not sound like anything he wanted to hear.

"Val, what am I?"

A trick question? Be careful about answering. Is he really expecting an answer? He strove for a thoughtful look. But it was rhetorical.

"A criminal! Right? I am a criminal. You know that. I know that! The world knows that. I am a criminal. I look like a criminal, I act like a criminal and I am a criminal. I am not ashamed to be a Russian criminal."

Val held back. There was nothing to be said.

"You? You think of yourself as a criminal? Do you? This is important! Because you are a criminal. Your life is based on committing crimes. Am I wrong? Tell me if you do not agree.

And yet, you do not behave like a criminal. You behave like the president of a bank. You behave like someone who sells vegetables in a vast market. You are moving numbers, shuffling people, pulling strings."

"That is true. I am managing a vast number of details."

"But!" Arkady's thick fist hammered the desktop. "This is not crime. Crime is violence. Crime is murder. Crime is blood. Robbery, Arson, Torture. This is crime. Rape. Pillage. This is what we do. This is who we are. Do you wish to become a criminal? Or do you wish to manage a bank?"

"Arkady, I wish to develop this network we are running until it becomes even more profitable."

"And then? What else do you aspire to?"

Val hesitated before answering, and with a supreme effort of will he avoided looking away. He maintained eye contact with the boss. *Is this man insane?*

"I aspire to rise in your organization. Which I see expanding. I see the promise of expanded weapons sales around the world. And I see the dynamic growth in gas and oil from the countries of Central Asia that were once part of the USSR. I see you at the head of a magnificent empire. Already it is great, but I see more growth. And I want to be part of it."

"But it must be the growth of criminal enterprise. I am not a businessman. I have killed businessmen. With my hands."

Val was at a loss to know how to respond to his boss. And he was keenly aware that it was definitely possible to say some words or phrases that could be misconstrued—deliberately or unintentionally—that would cause hell to break loose. He gritted his teeth. Finally he said, "What would you have of me, Arkady?"

"I would have you act like a criminal. Become a criminal. Actually, you are already a criminal and could go to prison in almost any nation of the world. Yet, you do not act like a criminal and your heart is not in crime. Valya, we are in Central Asia. We are the heirs of the Mongols, of Genghis Khan, of Timur, of the Scyths. We are killers and plunderers. We take what we want and we destroy those who oppose our will.

If you are to rise with me, we must be of the same blood."

"Arkady, I will do as you…"

"Val, shut up and listen to me. I know that you are intelligent and that you have an education. You are an intelligent, educated man. While I, I am a wild man. A criminal and a savage man. Ludmila has explained it to me very well, that I am a savage and little more than a beast. And yet. And yet. She stays with me. Why?"

"Arkady, I…"

"Shut up, you foolish bastard, and listen to me. You know of Alexander the Great? Correct? Just nod your head. You know that he marched his army of Macedonians all the way into Central Asia? Yes, you know this. He marched across this part of the world, past Samarkand and all the way into the Ferghana Valley. Yes? You have been into the Ferghana Valley? The country of flying horses? Yes? You know?

To the west, the Red Sands. On the other three sides, mountains. Except for those who can survive in the snowy peaks, it is a box. Yet Alexander marched in, and he marched out. And they say that he never lost a battle.

But what did he win? What is left to indicate the presence of the Macedonians? The Greeks? Or the Persian fucks he brought with him? He marched into today's Uzbekistan. Why? To what end? Could he stay there? No, the people were too fierce, and even if he could subdue their mud-walled towns, kill their men and rape their women, how could he subdue those who fled to the hills? In the end, he had nothing. Only what he stole, what he raped, and the memory of those he killed, the blood he spilled.

Was he a criminal? I say yes. He was a criminal. He stormed into places that were not his. He took whatever he wanted and he killed any who opposed him. Who has ever called Alexander the Great a murderer? Who has ever read the story of Alexander the Murderer? Alexander the Criminal? No! He is The Great! The history of the world is the history of crime. I am a criminal and I am proud. If you wish to rise with me, Valentin, you must embrace your criminality. Otherwise…"

Arkady rose, and Val rose with him. He was about to speak, but Arkady, sensing it, held up his hand for silence.

"Nothing. Enough words. Think about what I have said. Do not take forever. We will meet again. Soon. Thank you for your hospitality. Ludmila enjoyed the flowers and she sends you her blessing. Enough. No words. I am gone."

He had left the office when he stopped abruptly, turned and stuck his head back in the doorway. "And Valentin. Just one more thing. Next time I come! You will have some Krepkaya on hand, OK? Something good!"

PART 2

VISITING THE SILK ROAD

Chapter 12

2002—
Scouting the Silk Road

"Northwards from Krasnovodsk, not a single patch of green breaks the monotony of gray hills and depressions that form the Caspian's coastal strip. The soil is too salty for plant-life and no stream interrupts the surrealistic patterns of salt flats dotting the barren earth. All this is evidence of how the Caspian has continued to shrink since parting company with her "husband": even the vast inflow of the Volga is unable to keep up with the combined effects of evaporation from the Caspian itself and the Kara-Bogaz."

SOVIET DESERTS AND MOUNTAINS
GEORGE ST. GEORGE
THE WORLD'S WILD PLACES/TIME-LIFE BOOKS

Looking back, he could see that his marriage began to crumble from the moment he made his first visit to Central Asia as a tourist. Flo declined to go with him, claiming that it was too dangerous, too primitive, too boring or some combination of the three.

He, on the other hand, had been eager to get out of the country for some time. His trip was scheduled for late August and early September. The tour company was from Canada and they had experience in guiding travelers along the route of the Silk Road. Their standard itinerary had attracted him and he was as anxious to critique the tour guides as he was to visit the sites on the route.

Destinations included Ashkhabad, Merv, Charjew, Bukhara, Samarkand and Tashkent. According to their itinerary, it was possible that they might be able to visit Lake Issyk-kul in Kirghizstan. But it would depend on conditions at the border. The trip would end at Almaty in Kazakhstan.

Flo hadn't argued with him, but she was immovably resistant.

"What kind of a trip do you think that would be for me?" she snapped at him as she poured his coffee.

"All well and good for you, Mister Silk Road, but my idea of an interesting dinner is not one that has been cooked over camel chips."

"The cities we'll be visiting are all large population centers. They have hotels. They have hot water. They even have good toilet paper. I'll promise you that if you come, you'll never see a sleeping bag or eat out of doors... unless it's on the terrace of...."

"Let's home in on the toilet paper. What are you going to promise me about the toilet paper in Uzbekistan?"

He sipped his coffee and turned back to the newspaper. It was no use trying. He could see that her mind was made up. Her question hung in the air, and for an instant he had a comic image of himself, standing on a windy hill, papered with streamers of white tissue.

'What will you do with yourself while I'm gone?" he asked, finally.

"Don't worry about me. I'll think of something to do. I can play a lot of tennis with Jeannie, and I won't need to worry about getting home to fix your lunch."

Ouch! That stung a little. But he couldn't tell for certain if it was just an honest response to the prospect of time alone, or if she was being deliberately waspish. He knew that she had enjoyed playing tennis with him in the past—before his leg. He knew that she had been pleased that they were fairly evenly matched, and that she could occasionally beat him, fair and square. Her serve had been as good as his.

Now, the way things were, there were no more tennis matches that could hold her interest. A couple of times they had gone out and swatted some balls across the net, but it was awkward for them both and they gave it up without discussion. She enjoyed playing with her neighbor, Jeannie, who gave her a good game, but who usually faded toward the end of a long match.

He packed for the trip carefully, trying to limit his luggage to stuff that could be carried easily and was readily washed and dried. Lightweight Gore-tex jacket and ski pants could stop sand, dust and—in unlikely circumstances—rain. If they made it to Issyk-kul it might be chilly in the evenings, and he had silk underwear for use in the high country.

From JFK his first flight was to Moscow. Two members of the tour were on the same flight. He met them briefly at the terminal but they didn't have much chance to talk. He watched the in-flight movie, *Sleepless in Seattle*, and chose the channel for Russian to listen to the spoken language. He couldn't understand a single word. Then he tried to sleep as much as possible.

In Moscow their two Canadian tour guides joined them before they switched to a flight to Ashkhabad in Turkmenistan. One was a young woman whose parents had emigrated from Ukraine. The second guide was a young Canadian male of Asiatic parentage. Walt was glad that he had rested because the view from the window was almost worth the price of the ticket. The flight path crossed the Caspian Sea and he was hoping to see the Kara Bogaz Gol from the air.

It was his good fortune to be seated beside a Russian geologist who was on his way to Ashkhabad to attend a conference on petroleum extraction. The geologist spoke English enabling them to converse with relative ease.

"This is the first time you have visited the Caspian region?" the geologist asked.

"Yes. And I'm anxious to see if we will fly over Kara Bogaz Gol. I've read about it—but it's hard to imagine."

"You may be in luck today, my friend. You are American, no? Permit me. I am Anton," he said, extending his hand.

Anton was the perfect companion for the flight over the Caspian.

"You have seen the gullet before?" Anton asked.

"Beg pardon? You said "gullet?""

"Ah, yes. The Bogaz Gol. Black Gullet Lake. It is like leak from the bag. A part of the east shore of the Caspian is like dike. Holding back the sea from a depression that is four meters—thirteen or fourteen feet—lower than sea level."

Walt laughed. He had interpreted the Turkic word *bogaz* as *strait*, but he liked Anton's *gullet* better.

"Turkmens have a legend. They believe that Caspian and Black Seas were once connected. The Black Sea was husband and Caspian, the wife. They couldn't agree and so they parted. Allah was angered by their breakup and so he determined, as punishment, that offspring, the Kara Bogaz, would never be able to sever its umbilical cord from the mother."

As Anton was finishing his story, the opening—perhaps a hundred feet across—slid into view. It was an impressive sight from the air. The barren rocky ridges enclosing the sea to the west was notched to allow water to drain into the western margin of the Kara Kum desert, a vast salt pond where the water simply evaporates to leave behind a white scum of salt. The white margin at basin's edge stretched away to disappear into the desert haze.

"Isn't all that salt valuable?" he asked Anton. "It looks like it's just there for the harvesting."

The geologist laughed. "No, my friend," he said. "That's not table salt. It is mineral called mirabilite. Sodium sulphate. Fish that are swept from the Caspian into that salt water are quickly killed. That entire vast body of water is poisonous."

"What about erosion?" Walt asked the geologist.

Anton laughed. "Sill is basalt. It has been running for centuries."

From the air, the Caspian Sea was pouring continuously through a narrow gap, the Black Gullet, to ooze into the vast evaporating pond. Its barrenness and desolation reminded Walt of a moonscape, except for the major difference that this one was shaped entirely by water. A sea was leaking into a blotter, to dry and be blown downwind.

Even from the air, the gulf had a dead, poisonous appearance.

He had remained glued to the window, studying this strange place until the pilot announced they were passing Turkmenbashi—formerly Krasnovodsk—on the right. Then he got up and climbed over Anton to take a fast squint at Turkmenbashi from the air. Afterward, unlike his remembered images of the Bogaz Gol, he could hardly remember any details of the city from the air.

A short time later they landed at Ashkhabad.

Walt was surprised that their guides hadn't briefed the travelers on the Bogaz Gol before the flight. After the plane landed in Ashkhabad and they were en route to their hotel, Walt told the Canadians about his conversation with Anton.

"A lot of what Anton told me I already knew. But he made a good travel guide. Luck really favored me on this flight because my window seat on the left side of the plane gave me a great seat for viewing what, for me, is one of the world's most interesting wonders."

There was little reaction from the pair. It didn't seem to interest them.

"Do you know the story of how it came into existence?" he asked the Canadian female. She shook her head. "You guys were sitting on the wrong side of the plane. And the pilot never said a thing as we flew over."

Alone in his hotel room, Walt made a couple of pages of notes about what he had seen as he tried to relive the flight from Moscow.

His first trip to sites on the Silk Road was, for all practical purposes, a success. He came home with a spiral notebook filled with notes pertinent to repeating the trip with a group of students.

In the weeks that followed, as he struggled to get a grip on his feelings regarding Flo's discontent with their marriage, he kept going back to the view of the Bogaz Gol from the air.

The Caspian and the Black. Together once. Now apart. After visiting the sights in Ashkhabad, Merv, Bukhara, Samarkand and Tashkent, the jeweled cities of the Silk Road, his most vivid memory remained the expanse of the Bogaz Gol, with the Caspian pouring endlessly into the desert. He also remembered Anton's story of The Gullet's origin, its umbilical cord to the Caspian. He and Flo had been together once. What form would their punishment take?

Chapter 13

2003—
Flo Expresses Displeasure

> "Every day I have to walk nearly an hour to the village where I go to school. I see the women going to fetch water, the endless steppes, the Russian soldiers driving past in long convoys, the snow-capped mountains which, I am told, conceal a vast country; China. The village I walk to each day has a museum dedicated to its one poet, a mosque, a school, and three or four streets. We are taught about the existence of a dream, an ideal; we must fight for the victory of Communism and for equality among all human beings. I do not believe this dream, because even in this wretchedly poor village, there are marked differences; the Party representatives are above everyone else; now and again, they visit the big city, Almaty, and return bearing packages of exotic food, presents for their children, expensive clothes."
>
> THE ZAHIR
PAOLO COELHO

Flo was on a tear. "Here's what I don't get," she said, setting down a mug of coffee in front of him a little harder than necessary.

"I don't get your need to go traipsing off to Central Asia again. Not France. Not Italy where tourists go to enjoy the scenery or the art or the culture... but Central Asia. Central fucking Asia. I don't get it."

"You haven't been listening. Can you remember what I do, what I..."

"Oh, I know what you do, all right. I'm married to what you do. Not much chance I'm likely to forget that."

"Flo, from the beginning I explained how my interests would lead me to specialize in...."

"From the beginning? In the beginning it wasn't apparent to me that you wanted to spend your life cooped up in a college town."

"I don't feel like we're...."

"From the beginning I never understood that I would be staying behind in some dinky burg while you jetted off to third world countries."

"To places of historic interest. Accompanied by students who wan..."

"To countries where the inhabitants have never even learned how to make decent toilet paper."

There it was again—predictably—the reference to toilet paper. Sometime in the past, maybe on an early foray to Greece or Turkey, some unfortunate experience had apparently left deep scars wherever toilet paper can reach to earn a permanent reputation. The TP bitch, he called it. It usually showed up in the first several minutes when she was in an argumentative mood, as now seemed to be the case. He had a pretty good idea of what was likely to follow and it made him sad to realize that it was coming.

She had poured herself a cup of coffee and slumped into the seat opposite with her elbows on the table. With her head resting in her hands the tension on her cheekbones gave her a slightly Asiatic look which he found appealing. But that hardly seemed to matter anymore. Her tirade seemed to have stopped for a moment.

"Be honest, Flo. Would you want to go with me if we were traveling to France? Or to Spain?"

"I'd be a whole lot more likely to want to go to Spain with you than to fucking... where? Turkmenistan? Uz-fuckistan? Wherever."

"You're cussing a lot. And that's not an answer to my question. You say 'fuck' as much as some of my students."

"Because it's not a real question. You're not going to Spain. You haven't asked me to go to Spain. You aren't really interested in Spain. And anyway, what's the point of going to college if you can't say 'fuck'?"

"It's true that I *am* more interested in the region I've spent a decade studying."

"And where you left part of your body."

There is was. Right on schedule. The bitch about the leg. *First the toilet paper; then the leg.* It hurt his feelings that it mattered so much to her when he was trying so hard to make it not matter to himself. But nothing was improved by getting mad, or by letting his feelings show. He tried to keep his face perfectly still.

"Flo. You know better than...."

"I know. I know. They took your leg back, considered an attempt to reattach it. But you lost it in Central Asia. It seems like to me that would be enough to keep you from wanting to go back."

He could see that this was going nowhere. It was the same old spiral. She was dissatisfied with him and she was dissatisfied with herself. It wasn't clear which was the biggest dissatisfier, or which came first. He had tied himself in more than one knot trying to figure that one out—until he recalled the story of Alexander and the Gordian knot. Sometimes the best solution to a knotty problem could be obtained with a sharp weapon.

When he was completely honest with himself, he had to admit that maybe he didn't love her as much as at the beginning. Their lives were comfortable and conventional—and perhaps a bit too predictable. Her concerns relative to his leg were a bit harder for him to understand and accommodate.

In the beginning, when he returned from Walter Reed, she had been supportive, loving, liable to tear up when he was having difficulties. But by the end of a year at home, when he was coping without complaint and accepting his new condition as normal, she wanted it to continue to be a handicap. He was determined to be a complete, whole person, and to pursue the interests he had chosen. As painful as it was, he was willing to accept it as a fact that he could not make her love him, support him, or share his interests, if she did not choose it on her own. But she was making him weary.

At Walter Reed, the PTs, including Anne French of the appealing freckles, had counseled him on dysmorphobia, the fear of changes to the body image. He had faced it squarely and tried to deal with it. Maybe even succeeded. Flo hadn't faced it and he didn't want it to be something they had to work on together. Goddammit! If he could handle it, why couldn't she?

"We're going in circles," he said.

"Do you get what it is that I don't get?" she asked.

"Oh, yeah. I got it a while back."

Chapter 14

Turkmenistan, 2003

"In the name of Allah, the most exalted Turkmen. My beloved people! My dear Nation,

This book, written with the help of inspiration sent to my heart by the God who created this wonderful universe I wrote this book containing the nation spirit, its morality, and historical immortality. My dear Turkmen nation, in order to urge your soul and mind to fulfill these duties and to raise a strong faith in your heart for self-confidence, and to be a support to you I have written this book, Ruhnama. You are the meaning of my life and source of my strength."

RUHNAMA—THE BOOK OF THE SPIRIT
SAPARMURAT NIYAZOV (PRESIDENT OF TURKMENISTAN)
FROM THE INTERNET; WWW.RUHNAMA.COM

On his second trip to the Silk Road—a trial run—Walt took three graduate students. In the air he had a sudden insight. His fascination with Central Asia would be a lifelong quest. The vastness, the complexity, the hugeness of the region could never be comprehended to any extent by a single individual. This country had too much of—what? Everything! Culture, art, architecture, history, warfare, agriculture, religion, languages. Any one of these topics easily consumed ten lifetimes. The deserts alone could command a lifetime of study. The mountains. The rivers.

It came to him as his plane was landing in Ashkhabad. During his first visit he had not realized how utterly strange and bizarre Turkmenistan really was. He had traveled in the country in the same way he had visited Turkey as a child. In comfort, but off the beaten path.

Turkmenistan was big. Two-thirds the size of Turkey, with less than six percent of Turkey's population. And it was 80 percent desert. About ten percent bigger than California. Complex. Strange. Challenging.

Now, as he returned to Turkmenistan with his group of students, he felt himself overwhelmed by the baffling incomprehensibility of the country. It could never be explained to westerners. Not in a single lifetime. It was too old, too complex. Too… strange!

The curious thing about this new sensation was that it was somehow liberating. He realized, perhaps for the first time in his teaching career, that there were no single, easy paths to knowledge. All one could do was to cough up the facts, try to stimulate interest and curiosity, and turn things loose.

On the plane from Moscow he had been reading a USIA briefing document on Turkmenistan. He was mildly chagrined to learn that previously he had been in the country for several days and had researched it carefully prior to this trip. And yet he had failed to get his hands on a copy of *Ruhnama*. It was like living in Utah and never having looked at the Book of Mormon.

The *Ruhnama* is a book written by the egomaniacal ruler of Turkmenistan, a chubby man named Saparmurat Niyazov, who has set himself up in the mode of Louis XIV, or perhaps The Emir of Bukhara, and renamed himself Turkmenbashi, The Ruler of the Turkmens.

The man was probably certifiable. A nut case. Aside from the *Ruhnama*, which was a mishmash of the Holy Quran, Dale Carnegie and Emily Post, there was his preoccupation with the amount of jewelry to be worn by proper Turkmen girls. According to this wacko, proper women wore heavy necklaces to protect their necks from attack by swords. Multiple heavy bracelets were intended to provide protection for wrists in case of attack and the length of necklaces in the front could also ward off vulnerability to spears and arrows.

According to their leader—Turkmenbashi means "father of all Turkmens"—the proper Turkmen woman should wear 36 kilos of jewelry. Silver and gold. There had to be a misprint somewhere. *Thirty-six kilos?*

But this was only the beginning of Turkmenbashi's bizarre instructions to his subjects.

Katya moved down the aisle and whispered something into the ear of the passenger in the seat next to Walt. The passenger mumbled something, coughed, and got up to move to another seat in the rear. Katya dropped into the seat next to Walt and offered him one of the four little bottles of vodka she had between her fingers.

Walt took one, even though he didn't particularly want a drink. "What? No ice?"

"You can handle it," she laughed, sliding down to place both knees on the seat back in front of her.

He wanted to get to know this young woman better. "Thanks! Katya, I need your opinion on something. What do you think is the right weight for the amount of jewelry a woman should wear?"

She laughed. "The right weight? I've never heard anyone ask about that."

"What's the most jewelry you ever wore?" he persisted.

"The right weight?" She snorted and took a swig out of one of her bottles. "A couple of bracelets maybe. I'm not that much into jewelry. Where is this coming from?"

"The president of Turkmenistan believes that a proper Turkmen woman should wear 36 kilos of jewelry. In precious metals."

"I never switched to metric."

"Thirty-six kilos." He tried to remember the relation between kilograms and pounds. *What was it? Two point two?* "Gee, that must be over, what, sixteen, seventeen pounds of jewelry. Something in that range. That can't be right."

"Well, professor, I just stopped by to tell you that I'm looking forward to this trip."

"No, wait. I did it backwards. A kilo is 2.2 pounds. That would be somewhere around eighty pounds. A bag of cement. Something's wrong somewhere. The 36 kilos must be a mistake. Yeah, Katya, I'm glad you came."

The Antonov hit a pocket of turbulence and commenced an alarming rattle in the overhead storage bins. Katya's eyes widened momentarily and she slugged down the rest of the tiny bottle's contents.

"Assuming we get there."

"You read all the stuff I sent you in advance?"

"All of it."

"You know we're going into a weird environment?"

"All set for it."

"You're not planning to wear that top tomorrow?"

"What's wrong with it?"

"Then you didn't read all the material I sent."

She pushed another small vodka toward him and he took it. Mostly so he wouldn't watch her drink it.

"I'm just kidding you, professor," she laughed. "No, I'll look different tomorrow. You won't have to worry about me. I'll be fine. Promise."

"Did you know this little country, just a bit bigger than California, has so damn much natural gas that every major oil company in the world is competing to build a pipeline? They want to cross Afghanistan and Pakistan to get to the Indian Ocean."

"Big money."

"Do you know how crazy that makes people behave?"

"Kinda, sorta."

"And that they have a canal that brings water all the way from the Tien Shan mountains in Central Asia? As far away as China?"

"That was in the stuff you sent me."

"So what is it you're looking to get out of this trip? What do you want to take home?"

She looked thoughtful for a moment, as if she was contemplating an answer. Then she slowly unscrewed the cap of the last little bottle of vodka, sucked out most of the contents in a way that bordered on obscenity.

"If this trip meets your wildest expectation, what would you go home with?"

She took her knees off the seat back and placed both feet on the floor, smoothing her skirt primly with both hands. The little bottle was held in her mouth and she was using her tongue as a stopper. Skirt smoothed, she drained the bottle, replaced the cap and stuck it in the seat pocket.

"It's the whole concept of the Silk Road. All the way across Europe, Turkey, all the countries in Central Asia. Across the roof of the world. Who wouldn't want to see these places? Bukhara, Samarkand, Tashkent. They're places wrapped in mystery and intrigue. Actually, professor, the place I'd really like to visit is all the way at the end of the line. Mongolia. Or even the Uighur region of China."

"Have you studied much about these regions?"

"Only a little. I read a book by a bunch of American students—four—who tried to get across the Takla Makan Desert."

"You can go in. But you can't come out. That's what it means in Turkic."

"Exactly."

Katya was a mystery from the time she showed up as a grad student. She was smart. She seemed to be very savvy about Central Asia, and she looked at the men and boys on the campus as if they were pond scum. She seemed to be smart and ambitious, but something about her seemed dark and hidden. That was it. She seemed to have some dark secrets. Maybe that was one of the factors in her drinking. She rarely seemed impaired, but she could drink with the big boys. On this trip he would make a point to draw her out a bit. No doubt about it. She was interesting. And whatever it was, it was much more interesting than just sex appeal. They talked for most of the remaining flight to Ashkhabad.

Half the people in his Central Asia grad seminars had never even heard of the Uighurs. Katya knew of the Uighurs, that they were Muslims living in northeastern China. They were of Central Asian origin, distinct from Mongols and from Chinese. They shunned pork, still used Arabic characters to write their Turkic language and very rarely intermarried with their Chinese neighbors. Walt was impressed by her knowledge of these remote people.

The second trip was successful and came off without a hitch. There were a couple of tense moments in Uzbekistan, but Walt's driver intervened and Walt pulled his most aggressive alpha male away for a stern lecture and a threat. Katya—older and more mature than the boys—was a real help in coordinating activities. Walt was glad to have her along. She was an attractive, independent female and there was never a moment when he wasn't aware of her as a desirable woman—but he wanted his marriage to Florence to work and he still harbored the hope that her dissatisfaction might go away if he became more successful. Still, he was male—and Katya was appealing, available and she appeared to like him. He had to work on his own head to keep from utilizing her more in the routine work of the trip.

All of his students were thrilled by the trip, even though they were disappointed by the care that needed to be taken with regard to the consumption of alcohol.

Back in Mercersburg, the fall term began and the campus paths buzzed with students. Walt's classes were all filled as the word got around. Many students from other disciplines took Walt's courses as electives and he paid special attention to making the course sufficiently challenging and difficult to keep its quality high. He knew it was important that none of his offerings ever have a reputation as an easy three credits. The word soon got around. *Interesting and stimulating, but you have to do the reading and there are a lot of papers to write. It's not a gimme. Don't take it if you aren't prepared to do the work.*

Winter came and for nearly three months the mountains were white with snow. To Walt, the setting was beautiful, but Flo's discontent intensified and colder weather didn't help. They slept in separate rooms. Sometime she would be gone for a weekend, and to avoid constant arguments Walt tried to immerse himself in work. He also tried to walk regularly, in all weathers. It was a matter of pride to him to walk in such a way that no one would detect his leg. It wasn't a matter of being ashamed; quite the contrary, he was proud of having served. He felt himself to have been one of the elite. But he held this pride close to his own heart. It was something not to be shared unless with someone who loved and was loved. It made him sad to realize that Florence was not this person.

And so, he disciplined himself to walk in a controlled, measured pace that could vary with terrain—and conditions—but which would be undetectable. Running was harder.

In spring he could work on his running. There were times, on weekends, when he could run on the cinder track at the stadium and time himself over a quarter mile. On one unbelieveable Sunday morning—early, before students began to stir from their dorms—he made the circuit in seventy-eight seconds. But—he knew—he was running to dispel unhappiness, and it was far from the best solution. As the lindens began to blossom again and the air filled with their unforgettable perfume, he began to immerse himself in work. And to plan for the next fall trip.

At graduation exercises he said goodbye to Katya who had finished out the year. Her thesis paper on *Scythian Metalworking—Practices and Techniques* was exceptionally good, and Walt was curious to know about her plans for work after graduation. She came to his office to say goodbye before she left the campus. "Your paper was excellent, Katya—as I've already told you. I think with those photos of the excavated tumuli you were able to get from your Russian contacts you could find a magazine or journal to publish parts of the thesis. Have you thought about that at all?"

"Thanks, professor. No, not really. But thanks for the vote of confidence. That's not why I came by."

"You haven't told me what you think you'll be doing after graduation."

"Yeah," she laughed. "I'm kinda secretive. Nothing personal. It's just how I am."

Walt pushed back in his chair and considered if a response was appropriate.

"Look, the reason I wanted to see you is … well, you have a great program going. But don't you think it's a bit dangerous? It's easy to imagine a scenario when you have a couple of the wrong kids along. Where you could have big problems. Visiting the mosques and all."

"I've thought of it a lot," he said. "Yes, there is some danger. But there's danger here on campus. I think if we come up against any organized terrorist types, I'll be singled out. The random stuff? Well, I'll keep trying to ride herd on any wild behavior. So far I haven't seen any reason to be overly concerned. Also, I'm starting to have a few university or museum contacts in all of the cities we visit. I'm not a total stranger any more."

"I probably shouldn't even have brought it up." They shook hands when she left. He was sorry to see her go.

Chapter 15

Kutchka— The Mighty Handful

> "Of the thousands of cities conquered by the Mongols, history only mentions one that Genghis Khan deigned to enter. Usually, when victory became assured, he withdrew with his court to a distant and more pleasant camp while his warriors completed their tasks. On a March day in 1220, the Year of the Dragon, the Mongol conqueror broke with his peculiar tradition by leading his cavalry into the center of the newly conquered city of Bukhara, one of the most important cities belonging to the sultan of Khwarizm in what is now Uzbekistan. Although neither the capital nor the major commercial city, Bukhara occupied an exalted emotional position throughout the Muslim world as Noble Bukhara, the center of religious piety known by the epithet 'the ornament and delight to all Islam.'"
>
> GENGHIS KHAN AND THE MAKING OF THE MODERN WORLD
> JACK WEATHERFORD

The Mighty Handful was a nickname Valentin gave to the sociopaths assigned to help him in his enforcement assignments. They were handpicked by Arkady who had known some of them in prison. Three of the five were hard core criminals, heavily tattooed from their years in Russian jails. Two others had been KGB agents assigned to work with soldiers in Afghanistan and had seen—and committed—the worst atrocities the human imagination can contemplate. None were married; or more accurately, none admitted that they were married.

Val named them the Mighty Handful or *Kutchka*, after the nickname for the famous group of Russian composers; Alexander Borodin, Modest Moussorgsky,

Nikolai Rimsky-Korsakov, César Cui and Mily Balakirev. None of the men ever got the joke, but—to Val's surprise—the brute Arkady, who had a former ballet dancer for his current mistress, caught on at once. He thought it was clever and afterwards always referred to the group as Kutchka, and he seemed to be reluctant to separate them. In time, Val came to regret his attempt to be funny.

Boris. Yuri. Anatoly. Vasily. Janos. Others—handpicked by Arkady—filled in for one of them on occasion. But Val never had to contend with more than five at a time.

The presence of these men in Val's orbit increased his resentment, especially at the beginning. He could not recall ever seeing five more violent, dangerous individuals seated around a single table. When they first showed up he was certain that they had been sent to spy on his operations or to check on his day-to-day activities. For a time he thought they may even have been sent to kill him. In fairness to Arkady, the boss had arranged for Kutchka to be paid from an office in Moscow, and their travel expenses were also paid out of the Moscow office. As time passed and Val remained alive, he accepted they were there for another reason. It quickly became apparent as his drug tracking system began to demonstrate its utility.

Using the system he had put in place, it was fairly straightforward to see where materials were being siphoned off by individuals tempted to put money in their own pockets. When these men could be identified individually, they could be punished. It was always desirable to recover the stolen money, but that was not always possible. It was, however, usually possible to punish an offender with sufficient severity that he would be unlikely to offend again, if he continued to be employed. Also, it was often desirable for the offender to provide a conspicuous example to others in the network.

This arena was the specialty of the Mighty Handful, experts at instilling fear and terror, administering pain or creating serious injuries. The easiest activities involved killings, but these took little time and presented little in the way of challenges to their sadistic imaginations.

In the beginning months of Val's operation, the group would travel to designated cities equipped only with a name and a business address and a verbal instruction as to whether the offender should continue after punishment, be severely punished as an example, or should be terminated. After a brief period, a system evolved in which Val had merely to indicate—with his fingers—one, two or three—the level of punishment to be administered. If the value of the stolen material exceeded a value of one thousand dollars American, Val made a point to show three fingers. Death. It was amazing how quickly word spread and things tightened up.

The Mighty Five did not always travel together. For most jobs at Level 1, two men would be adequate. The former KGB men liked to travel together, but the ex-convicts were indifferent. In Val's opinion they were even indifferent to whether their travel companions were human.

Because the former convicts were heavily tattooed, it was felt, by them and by others in Val's operation, that they could easily be spotted and identified by Interpol or even by members of rival gangs. For this reason, most of the ugly work that needed to be done in Spain, France or other western European nations was handled by the former KGB men who were less likely to stand out. But for Eastern European countries or Central Asia, the former prison inmates generated the same kind of feelings as those inspired by Genghis Khan or Timur.

Val was not opposed to the notion of employing a ruthless team of enforcers to see that his network was not compromised. But, for him, at the beginning, enforcement was something of an intellectual exercise. A problem was identified. The Mighty Handful were notified. *Vot!* The problem was fixed.

Initially, he did not dwell on what might actually be happening when the Kutchka was summoned. This situation did not last for long, because Arkady had other ideas. After profits from the drug enterprise began to roll in at a steady rate, Arkady's mental image of the enterprise was that it was now a steady business—like running a bakery. The bakers come in. They bake. The bread gets sold. Why does Valentin, who costs me a lot of money, need to continue traveling to India and to other countries around the world, when the business is running? He should be out with members of The Handful, insuring that offenders were duly punished. He made a few hints in this direction, but Valentin failed to respond and it was not Arkady's way to exhibit patience when he did not have his way.

So far, profits from the drug enterprise were so dramatic that Arkady purchased an apartment building in St. Petersburg for his mistress who enjoyed the art season in that city, and he replaced her vehicle with a later model that was customized and bullet proofed.

Like some members of their Mighty Five namesakes, Val's Kutchka had their own problems with alcohol. Physiologically, two or perhaps three of these inhuman bastards were ticking bombs. But this was of little consolation to their victims. And the Five themselves seemed indifferent to almost everything—including their own lives.

Chapter 16

2004—Trouble in the City of Love

*"The mystery does not get clearer by repeating the question,
nor is it bought with going to amazing places.
Until you've kept your eyes
and your wanting still for fifty years,
you don't begin to cross over from confusion."*

FROM "TATTOOING IN QAZWIN"
THE ESSENTIAL RUMI
TRANSLATED BY COLEMAN BARKS

A major problem came up during Walt's third trip to the Silk Road. For this trip he had rounded up five students. He arranged for his Turkmen driver and guide to go along with a slightly different arrangement. Instead of starting his trip at Ashkhabad in Turkmenistan and traveling from west to east, he decided to begin in Almaty in Kazakhstan and travel from east to west. There was no particular advantage in this arrangement, but he was trying to get the feel of the experience, to determine if it made any difference in the way his students perceived the Silk Road. After all, the silk was traveling from east to west.

He began in Almaty or, as he preferred to call it, Alma Ata. *Father of apples.* From there his caravan departed for the same destinations: Khokand, Samarkand, Bukhara, Urgench and Khiva and, finally, to Ashkhabad and Merv.

Hassan, his principal driver, brought his cousin along to take turns driving and to help with baggage and other chores. Jamil proved to be quiet and dependable. Walt decided he was a good choice and might be used again. If anything, he was even quieter and less obtrusive than Hassan.

The student group consisted of four seniors, two girls and two boys, and a female graduate student. The grad student, Tara Kuchenko, came from a Ukrainian family in Cleveland and could speak passable Ukrainian and a bit of Russian. She had majored in Middle Eastern Studies and in Fine Arts. Now she was pursuing an MFA at Buchanan but, despite her presence in two of Walt's three-hour courses, she had never made it clear what she planned to do after graduation.

As he expected, there were a few predictable problems along the route. Despite his pre-trip briefings, the girls didn't pick up on the need to dress carefully. While uncovered hair, scoop neck blouses, bare arms, and exposed legs could get by in Almaty, things were different in Tashkent and they didn't have to understand the language to guess at what was being said on some occasions when they appeared in public.

They quickly adapted to wearing jeans under their dresses and they developed an interest in imaginative ways to use head scarves. They picked up dark, long-sleeved pullovers in a bazaar, and by the time they got to Bukhara they were generally acceptable except to the occasional, unavoidable fanatics.

In Bukhara, the two boys got drunk in the hotel bar after Walt had turned in for the evening. The resulting hangovers delayed their morning departure by a couple of hours and threw the day's travel schedule slightly out of kilter.

Everyone probably had problems with diarrhea at some point in the trip, but they had all been briefed to carry medicines and everyone handled their own situation so that the group wasn't impacted.

The group was uniformly impressed with stops they made along the way. Walt made sure that they spent a full day at Khiva about which they knew little. Actually, they spent two nights in nearby Urgench, but the museum at Khiva generated almost as much interest as Bukhara.

From Urgench, they headed south across the spectacular Kara Kum desert to the last stop on their tour, the oasis town—now the capital city—of Ashkhabad. After a day in Ashkhabad they were scheduled to fly to Moscow for a transfer back to JFK.

Things were happening pretty much according to schedule as they careened across the sandy expanse to Ashkhabad, listening to Walt's stories about caravans that attempted to cross during winter storms. Tara was sitting directly behind him in the back seat, so he was less aware of her response until, while shifting his seat, he noticed that her eyes were closed and she seemed to be gritting her teeth.

"You OK, Tara?"

"I think something at breakfast may not have agreed with me."

"Stomach?"

"Yeah. I might have to call for an emergency stop. Sad to say."

"You got medicine?" Warren asked. He was directly behind her.

Warren started rummaging around in his day pack. "I've got some pink pills right here, Tara. You need a couple?"

"I think I'm OK," the girl said, but her voice sounded a bit strange and Walt made it a point to keep an eye on her for the balance of the day's ride.

The hotel at Ashkhabad was clean and modern and they had a decent meal after checking in, but Tara didn't join them and he went up at dinner time to check on her.

"Are you feeling better?" he said. "Are you going to be able to join us?"

"Not much. Probably better if I skipped."

"Shall I send up something? Tea maybe? Anything sound good?"

"Thanks, professor," she said, flopping back on the bed and curling into a ball. "I just want to rest. I've been crapping my brains out and it's made me feel weak. I need a good night's sleep."

"Dehydration?" Walt said. "Have you got plenty of bottled water?" He could see a liter bottle on the nightstand that was about half full. "That's probably not enough to get you through the night."

"I've got another liter in my day pack," the girl answered—without opening her eyes.

"I'll have someone drop off another liter before they turn in," he said.

As he went out the door he heard her say in a small voice, "You're sweet, professor."

Tara wasn't down for breakfast the next morning. "I don't think she's gonna be going with us today," said Brenda. "She said she didn't get much sleep last night." Like Walt, Tara had been booked into a room of her own. The other kids were sleeping two to a room.

This was the point at which Walt's worry mechanism began to shift into high gear. They didn't have a stressful day planned. Just visits to a couple of museums and brief swings past several architectural points of interest. He had also planned a short ride out of town so they could get a look at the Kara Kum Canal and visualize its impact on local agriculture, chiefly cotton farming. Alfalfa for horses. But on the following day they were scheduled for a 10 a.m. departure to Moscow. He finished his breakfast quickly and went up to look in on the girl.

Tara's room didn't smell all that good, and she had tried to knock down some of the odor with some of the scent she may have picked up in Bukhara or Almaty. It was a heavy rose aroma on top of sick and he was tempted to throw open a window, but he resisted the urge. Walt knew that Tara's signature scent was baby shampoo, so he could tell at once that she wasn't up to par.

"What can I do for you?" he offered. "I'm assuming you're gonna sit this one out."

"I'm bushed, professor," she said with a weak smile." I could do it if I had to, but I think it would be better if I just sat it out."

"That's probably a good idea. Just more of the same thing you've been seeing. Warren will have plenty of images in his digital, and I can fill you in on anything you might have missed. Either on the flight back or back on campus. You just try to get some rest."

"I'll be OK."

"What can I send up? What can you eat? Some fruit maybe? Watermelon? Grapes, cantaloupe?"

"Ugh! No, no. Nothing."

"How about a boiled egg? Or some toast?"

"Jesus, professor, you sound like my dad. Not to worry. I'll be OK. Get out. Go give your lectures."

But at the end of the day, when the group returned to the hotel, Tara was still in bed. Walt looked in again, and this time he took Brenda along. That was a wise move, because when they knocked at the door and Tara cracked it open, she wasn't wearing anything but a pair of cotton panties. Brenda slid in quickly and they found a pullover sweatshirt before Tara slumped back onto the bed.

"You didn't get up all day?" Brenda asked. "Jeez-o! You haven't eaten anything for over twenty-four hours?" Brenda was a zaftig type, comfortably sleek, who probably never went for that long without food in her entire life.

"I still feel like shit," Tara said. Walt felt the girl's head to see if she was feverish. She felt fine to him. Cheeks flushed. Maybe a little warm, but nothing alarming. Unbidden, a thought ran though his head as he examined the girl closely, in particular trying to determine if her pupils were dilated. *If this is how you look when you've been sick for a day, you ought to try being sick more often. They'd have to lock you up.*

"Tara, I'm worried about you getting on the plane tomorrow if you're still feeling this bad. I'm thinking we ought to rebook you for early next week."

"Professor, I really don't want to..."

"I'll change both of us. I couldn't go back and leave you alone. The other four can travel as a group. We've already been through Moscow together, so they know the drill. But I'm wondering if you need to be seen by a doctor."

"An Islamic doctor? In Turkmenistan? Pardon me, prof, but—pardon the expression—fuck that notion. I've heard about these guys and their interest in body cavities. I just need a good night's sleep. And I need to quit crapping."

Brenda giggled. "I could stay with you when the doctor comes."

"What have you been taking?" Walt asked. "Show me." The girl pointed to the foil packages on the nightstand. "I can probably find a doctor who's not Muslim," he offered.

"I've been taking two in the morning and two at night since this came on." Her tone was almost defiant.

Walt looked at the foil packet and examined the faded printing that had been mostly rubbed off by riding in a backpack across Central Asia. The pills appeared to be a remedy for stomach gas or flatulence.

"Jesus Christ," he muttered. "Don't take any more of these. Brenda, stay with her 'til I get back."

He went to his room and rummaged through his bag for a packet of Loperamide. Back in Tara's room he helped her sit up and gave her two pills. "These should help. But just in case, I'm going to change our flights tonight. Can you drink tea? Or eat some dry bread?"

"I don't think..."

"Never mind. Just stay in bed. C'mon, Brenda. Let's join the others. We've just had a change of plans."

Walt had to decide whether or not to notify Tara's parents that she was sick. It was a tough decision. But based on the fact that she had no fever, coupled with the fact that she took the wrong medicine, he gambled she would be fine once the Loperamide cut in. The 36-hour interval without food seemed to have hollowed— half a millimeter. perhaps?— and colored her cheeks, making the girl seem to glow from the inside. Walt was stunned by his own reactions to his student. He recalled reading about this type of change accompanying a mild illness. *Where? Maybe it was "The Tale of Genji?"*

Automatically, Walt wondered how Flo might react to the picture of this long-legged girl, with the glowing cheekbones. Already the two females had met at one of Walt's auditorium presentations at JBU. Flo's eyebrows had gone up after they were introduced.

When Walt mentioned a call to her parents, Tara talked him out of it. "They don't know exactly when I'm returning. You'll just scare them."

"Maybe you could stay with her for a while, Brenda. In case she needs anything."

It took over an hour for the necessary phone calls and to make the ticket changes. Tomorrow morning he would have to go to the airport at Ashkhabad to finalize the details, but finally it was done. He had all the information except seat assignments. When he went up to check on Tara, Carly had replaced Brenda and the sick girl was sleeping.

Next morning, after breakfast, the group said goodbye to Hassan and Jamil after tipping them for their service. The group trooped through Tara's room to hug the girl and say goodbye for a few days until she would rejoin them on campus. Walt reminded everyone of the idiosyncrasies they could expect at Moscow's airport. He made each one produce a passport, cautioned them about over-friendly strangers and the merits of an uncompromising buddy system when splitting up or using restrooms.

"Don't worry about us, professor," Peter said. "We're big boys. We can..."

"That's what I'm worried about. Big boys. You guys get these girls home safely. That's all I ask. And lay off the vodka, at least 'til you get back on campus."

A few hugs, a few handshakes and they were gone. He was alone at the hotel. Alone with a sick girl—in a foreign country. Hassan would return to the hotel once the group had been dropped off. But for the morning, Walt had nothing to do... and nowhere to go that had to be planned and scheduled. He was free.

He went back to his room and checked his bags. There wasn't much to pack because he never really unpacked. He was used to traveling light and living light. Each night he washed the special socks and elastic bandages he used over his stump, and he rotated them on a regular schedule. Yesterday's socks were already dry. When it came time to move out, three minutes would get the toothbrush back in his kit and everything zipped ready to boogie. Maybe it was a holdover from the military. Or maybe it was just him.

Stretching out on his bed he opened one of his reference books and read several pages. *Foreign Devils on the Silk Road*, by Peter Hopkirk. A good bit of the material he had incorporated into his lectures came from information he had first learned about from reading Hopkirk. He reread some of the passages about the Emir of Khiva.

Once, when the Emir of Khiva appeared before the court of Tsar Alexander with his two ministers, their beards had been dyed red for the occasion. The Tsar gave them heavy gold chains which showed off nicely against the red beards. Walt tried to picture the shade of red.

When Walt got around to looking at his watch, his charges were already in the air, winging their way back to Moscow. He hoped they'd be smart enough to go easy on the vodka until they were on their next, long leg. It was nearly time for lunch and he knew that he would have to look in on his sick charge. As he walked down the hall to her room, he suddenly wished he had kept Brenda back with him.

It was a thought that would come back to him again and again. Looking back, this was probably the point at which the wheels began to come off.

When he knocked at Tara's door, she answered at once. "Is that you, prof?" When she opened the door she was wearing panties and a semi-transparent camisole, a combo that looked like something from Frederick's of Hollywood.

"My god, Tara, how about putting some clothes on? Are you feeling better? You sure look better." Her nipples were trying to punch their way out of the thin material.

"I took three more of those pills this morning. Now I probably won't go to the john before we get home. But I'm feeling better and I just took a shower. Right now, I'm starving. Let's go eat." Now she smelled like baby shampoo.

It was easy to believe that she was feeling better because it would be hard to imagine her looking any better.

They ate in the hotel restaurant. She was ravenous. He sat back and enjoyed watching her wade into the food. The brief bout with diarrhea hadn't hurt her appetite. He was annoyed with himself for not being perceptive enough to check her medicine earlier. But, after all, he had been quite specific about the items they needed to bring on the trip, packed where they would be easily accessible when needed. If he had checked on her earlier, they could be on their way home now instead of here in Ashkhabad—with a couple of days to kill before the flight out.

"After you feed me," Tara said with a laugh, "what are you going to do to entertain me?"

He was used to getting off-the-wall questions from students, so the question didn't seem amiss. Until later.

"Hassan will probably be back in an hour or less. We could take the van and go for a short ride out into the Kara Kum desert. Any interest in seeing some of the wildlife that lives in the Kara Kum?"

"Not especially, prof. You know I'm a Fine Arts major. Take me to see some architectural wonders. Do they have any places here to compare with Khiva?"

"Khiva is remarkable, isn't it? That's a tough act to follow. But I think we can find some places to visit when Hassan returns."

To tell the truth, it was pleasant being alone with her now that the others were gone. When he was shepherding the group, he was always "on," always responsible to see they were fed, transported, housed, entertained, and that they were learning things. While en route he was, as a rule, providing a running commentary. And he had to talk so that he could be heard by everyone. He had to perform. Now, with her, he felt free. And alive.

With Tara, alone, it was just the two of them. It was just conversation. He had Hassan take them on a brief ride around the train station where he explained the significance of rail transportation in this once-isolated oasis. He told her how the Soviets had tried to introduce technology; how they had built the railroad, and the canal. And how the introduction of cotton monoculture had produced unintended consequences in other parts of Central Asia.

They visited the Kara Kum canal and explored the edge of vast fields of cotton stretching to the horizon. Back in town they went down Lenin Prospect, turning off from time to time to get a better look at any of the mosques that caught Tara's fancy.

"I don't have to tell you," he said as they passed through residential neighborhoods, walled and secretive, "that some of the gardens concealed behind these walls might compete with Charleston or Savannah. But unless you know someone, it's hard to get to see them. Even then...."

"I know. This has been just fine. And I thank you for the attention. Honest and truly. I just hope I can repay you."

Still, even then, the warning bells hadn't begun to sound.

They visited the Turkish mosque, built along the lines of Istanbul's blue mosque and they had chai at a small tree-shaded street café. Hassan found a place to park the van and he joined them. Tara took pictures of the mosque and the surrounding gardens with her digital camera. When she rejoined the two men she ordered apple tea. Then, while the waiter went to fetch it, she adjusted an adjacent table to support her camera and focused it for a shot of the three of them drinking tea. As soon as the waiter returned, she pushed the shutter for the timed shot and rejoined the group to smile at the lens. She took several pictures of the threesome drinking tea together.

Watching the laughing girl, Walt felt relief that she was completely recovered. He was anxious to finish the trip, eager to get home and begin dealing with his domestic problems and to get ready for the fall semester.

They rode through streets of Ashkhabad until it got dark. Then the three of them went back to the hotel and had dinner together. One of the dishes was a pilaf, made with rice and dried apricots. Tara's appetite had returned. At her request they split a bottle of local white wine. Hassan, a Muslim, abstained, as usual.

Afterwards, Hassan took off to get back with his family who lived some distance to the east. He had been away for the full two weeks of the tour. Walt and Tara sat at a table in the hotel's bar that seemed to be mostly empty except for a half a dozen Russians who were starting to get noisily drunk on vodka. The group of American oilmen who had been monopolizing the bar was somewhere else tonight.

"They're starting to make a lot of noise," Walt said. "But I can't really tell if they're having a good time."

"Well," said the girl, leaning toward him and lowering her voice. "Some of the things they are laughing about have to do with you and me. Especially me. My Russian isn't perfect, but it's good enough to know they are talking about us." She hesitated. "They're making me uncomfortable."

"Come on. Let's turn in and get up early. We can go for a walk before we eat breakfast. Hassan won't be here with the van until ten. I told him to eat with his family. We have the whole day to kill."

"Didn't we see everything today?" she said, rising to leave.

" I thought you might like to see the archaeological site at Nisa. It was once the capital of the Parthian Empire. You've heard of the Parthians?"

At the door of her room, she paused. "Come in and stay with me for a little bit. I put the rest of the wine in my day pack. We can have a sip together and you can tell me about Parthia."

"It's probably not a good idea."

He knew better. It was a very *bad* idea.

"Please, professor. Haven't I been a good student up 'til now? Except for getting the runs, did I give you a minute's problem? I've been good, and I've only been a nuisance since I've been sick. Be nice to me."

"One glass of wine. Then you go to bed and sleep 'til morning."

In the room he moved her canvas suitcase out of the corner chair and took a seat by the window. Just a few hundred yards from the hotel window they could see an amusement park with flashing neon lights and a variety of rides, including a carousel and a Ferris wheel.

Tara poured wine in two plastic cups from the bathroom. With the lights off in the room, they stood at the window, sipping wine and watching people in the park.

"Funny, isn't it. It has a Christmasy look. Cheerful."

"H'mmm," she said, sipping from her cup. "I didn't notice the park before. The lights are nice. I like it." Also he had just come to notice she had slipped out of her jeans and was standing beside him in her briefs and a Buchanan U. sweatshirt.

For a long moment they continued standing, saying nothing. He enjoyed the silence, but was apprehensive about what might come next. Finally he spoke.

"What would you like to know about Parthia?"

"OK, let me think. OK. If you and I were to find ourselves to be transported back to Parthia today—into the heart of the Parthian Empire—would you think I was pretty?"

"Jesus Christ," he said. "I thought you were being serious."

"I am serious, professor. This is as serious as I am ever likely to get. I am, what you might say, completely hanging out here."

He set his plastic cup on the window sill. "Look, Tara, I don't know what…"

"Yes, you do. You do know. Because you aren't stupid. And you have known it since before this trip. You know that I've got it bad for you. You knew it back in Pennsylvania. Before we left."

"Tara, look, I never…" *All he could honestly remember were several sessions where it was clear she didn't want to leave. But he had never done anything to encourage…*

"Just be quiet and listen for a minute." A long pause with a heavy sigh before she started again.

"You're an intelligent man. And you know that in this world, as they say, shit happens. You know that I have it bad. And you also know that I would be good for you. That I could understand you and help you and be a good lover. You know this."

"Tara, you don't even know…"

"Know what, professor? That you're married? Yes, I know. That you're not happy? Ever look at yourself in the mirror at the end of the day? When you're getting ready to go home? I know more than you might think."

"Tara, it's probably better for both of us if I just lea…"

"And I've met your wife. Remember? I've seen you two together. I know how she looks at you."

"I should leave."

"Leave? Run away is more like it." She lowered the blinds and drew the drapes. With only the bathroom light on, the room was dim. "Look at me," she said. "Don't you think I'm pretty? You damn well know I'm smart enough for you."

"Tara, you are smart enough for anyone. But you aren't pretty. You're beautiful. You could have your pick of any of the boys on campus."

"That's true. Boys. But you're a man. And I need a man. No! I need you."

She was still standing facing him, holding the cup in both hands, almost like she was a child…with a sippy cup.

"Tara, I…"

As he started to speak she suddenly threw the cup into the corner and peeled off her clothing. Stepping out of her panties she stood before him, naked.

"You say I'm beautiful. Don't you want me? Don't I even appeal to you a little bit?" But the tone of her voice had changed and she sounded as if she was close to tears.

"Tara. Tara. You are overwhelming. So beautiful. But I am not equal to you. You are so young. And so perfect. I am older. Damaged. Far from perfect. Not to mention the little fact that I'm married."

"You are perfect for me." She stretched out her arms to him and he could feel the changes taking place.

"Tara, thank you for your wonderful gift to me. You are a sweet and generous girl. And I will never forget this moment. You have a big heart. Mine is not so big. I could never repay your gift to me."

"Take off your clothes."

"Tara, please, this has gone far…"

"Take off your clothes. Or do you want me to scream?"

"Jesus, Tara, Do you know that I…."

"Know that you're missing a leg? Yes, of course I know. Everybody knows. What difference does that make? Do you think that matters to me? And for your information, I know a helluva lot more about you than you know about me. I guarantee that when you get to know me, you will like me a whole lot. Maybe even—it's possible—get to love me."

"Tara, I feel so inadequate for you. You are such a strong, beautiful, intelli…"

"Quit stalling. Cut the crap and take off your clothes. Look, I'll make this easy for you. You don't have to do me if that's so hard for you. Just take off your clothes and hold me for this one night. You don't have to do anything."

'My god, you don't have any idea…" He didn't know what he wanted to say. He knew he should leave but his feet would not respond.

"Nothing! You're stalling and it's making me frustrated. And angry. Take off your clothes. We'll get in bed. Side by side. Just barely touching. You don't have to handle me."

Later, when he thought back on it, the whole episode had a dream-like, fantasy feel. He remembered sitting on the side of her bed as she lay on the spread beside him, rigid and undemanding. He finally slipped off his dockers and folded them on the floor beside the bed. Then he unfastened the prosthesis. He put the leg beside the bed where he could reach it in the dark. His heart was beating rapidly and he remembered struggling to get it under control.

"Why me?" he whispered.

"Shut up," she said. "Just lie down. I want to feel you in the bed next to me. You don't have to talk if you don't want to. I can listen to your breathing." They were touching at hip and thigh. Why was his heart racing? It was beating faster than it had when he was in danger.

"I feel bad about my leg," he said. "Like I'm less than whole. And you…"

"Won't you just shut up?" she said. "And let me enjoy this… now. Now. This moment."

For a long time they were silent and his pulse finally went back to normal. So did his dick—gradually— for which he was grateful. She was his student. His charge. His responsibility.

Although she was silent he could hear her silence and electricity was flowing from her hip into his body. It was an interesting sensation and he couldn't recall the last time something similar had happened. She was as still as death. No, not quite. Not with the electricity.

When he spoke, it was in a whisper. "Would you like me to tell you a little about Parthia? That you might not already know?"

She answered in a whisper voice to match his own. "I would love it."

Sometime—he thought it must have been after midnight—he heard the sound of her breathing shift gears to tell him that she was asleep. He debated getting up and leaving, but decided against it. He pulled up a sheet to cover her body; *my god but she is a lovely creature*, and lay back down beside her. After a few minutes, she moved in her sleep, threw her left arm across his chest and snuggled her body close against him. Where her crotch touched his flank, she felt like an oven. It took him a long while to get to sleep as he lay savoring her heat.

In the morning she was up and dressed when he awoke. His first action was to fasten his leg and pull on his trousers. She bounced out of the bathroom with her toothbrush still in her mouth, and she kissed him on the lips with a mouth full of toothpaste. Like a child. There was the shampoo smell. "Good morning, professor. Thank you for last night."

"We didn't do anything," he reminded her.

"No, that's true. But we will. I put a spell on you last night and you are now, as they say, ensorcelled." And from the bathroom, she kicked out her leg.

"We will. We will. It's inevitable." She seemed to be a completely different girl from the grad student he had known in his classes and he wondered if, in fact, she might not know something about witchcraft. It was clear that his behavior had been completely out of character.

At breakfast, she was back to her normal self; no out-of-the-way behavior. Hassan came promptly at ten. They visited the site at Nisa, ate shashlik at a cafe chosen by Hassan and went to the carpet market in the late afternoon. She was such a pleasant companion that Walt began to think that he might actually *be* under a spell. It felt good to be with her. By the time they returned to their hotel and were ready to release

Hassan for the day it occurred to him that he had been happy. All day. Happy in his heart. It felt good.

At dinner he could hardly find words to express what was in his mind. For most of the meal they spoke of things they had done during the day, but finally the conversation lagged.

"You're wondering, aren't you," she said.

"Wondering what? Am I supposed to guess what I'm wondering?"

"C'mon, professor. No games between us—now. We know what each other's skin looks like. And you know where I stand. But tonight is our last night here. Our last night alone together in a corner of the world where no one knows us. Knows or gives a damn. You could do anything you choose. With me, that is. Anything."

"But—tonight—this last night…" She sighed. "No pressure. Sleep with me or not. As you choose."

He could feel his heart rate begin to increase and he struggled to find the right words. When he did speak, his words were so lame that he embarrassed himself. "You're feeling a lot better tonight."

She laughed. "That one won't count. You can try again. And I won't hold that one against you."

He had to laugh at himself. "That was pretty pathetic. wasn't it? Yes, Tara, I would like to spend the night in bed with you. Sleeping next to you. It gets lonely traveling by yourself and sleeping single in a single bed. You are a sweet, lovely companion, and I thank you from *my* heart for your companionship today."

"This was a taste, my lovely professor, of what life can hold for those who will take what they must have. But tonight, you must be careful in your choice. Like you, I am only human. And, like you, I can be hurt."

That night she slept close in his arms. They spoke little, but they touched each other tenderly, with care. And their voices never rose above a whisper.

Once, in the small hours of the night, she pulled his face close to hers and whispered. "I want you to make love to me." He groaned. "No!" she added. "I want you to *want to* do it whether you do or not. I want you to want me. And you will." Then she bit his mouth, hard enough so he could taste blood. Even with the small part of his brain that was still thinking clearly, he began to wonder what he had gotten into.

In the morning, he was groggy and it felt as if he had hardly slept at all. As they were going down to breakfast, it suddenly came to him. Ashkhabad. Ashk. Love. The city of love. *Lovely place.*

Hassan carried them to the airport and they said farewell to him with a few details about plans for their next tour. On the flight from Ashkhabad to Moscow they held hands like high school sweethearts, discovering other human skin for the first time. In Moscow, they still touched each other frequently, but by the time the reached JFK, the distance between them was being reestablished.

By the time they boarded their flight back to Harrisburg, they had, without a word being spoken, slipped back into their respective roles. What they could not hide, however, was the way their eyes met.

Back at the university, several weeks would pass before Walt learned about her photos. While he had slept, she had used the timer on her digital to take pictures of them in bed together, unclad, entwined, in compromising positions. She had at least a dozen of them. Souvenirs from the Silk Road, she called them. "Don't be worried," she told him later, after her secret had been revealed. "I would never do anything that would hurt you. These are just for me." But he wasn't sure he could believe her.

Chapter 17

Undisclosed Location, Northern Virginia

> "The good news is that one part of Afghanistan's economy is booming. The bad news: It's the opium business, which, by United Nations estimates accounts for more than half the nation's gross domestic product. Cultivation of opium poppies, which produce the raw material for heroin, is a record 379,650 acres this year, up 44 percent from 257,000 in 2005, according to preliminary crop projections. That indicates a major failure for U.S.-backed eradication efforts. Afghanistan last year provided nearly 90 percent of the world's heroin supply."
>
> THE LAND OF THE OPIUM POPPIES
FROM "U.S. NEWS & WORLD REPORT"
AUGUST 28, 2006

In a secret CIA facility somewhere in northern Virginia, seven senior analysts with responsibility for tracking affairs in Afghanistan were having a regular weekly conference to compare notes. Normally their meeting started at ten and lasted until noon. On this day they had started at seven-thirty, at the request of their section chief.

Harvey Leonard, a 15-year veteran of Central Asia affairs had brought in a manila folder filled with notes, data, reports and computer printouts. For the past two weeks one of their deep cover agents, operating on the border region where Afghanistan meets Turkmenistan and Uzbekistan, had failed to communicate. The agent nominally operated out of the ancient Afghan city of Balkh, but now he had gone strangely silent and even some of the top secret techniques that had been developed to warn of impending danger had not been activated. Two weeks and no "signs of life." There was cause for serious concern.

The agent's purpose was to keep an eye on illegal trafficking in drugs and weapons. The region was a hotbed of other forms of smuggling, including trade in electronic equipment, pornography, alcohol and slaves, primarily women and children, but the CIA's interest focused on weapons and drugs.

For several weeks the group had been considering alternative approaches to intelligence gathering in the area. Even before their contact went silent they realized the inadequacy of the information that was coming in. But Balkh was an area where it was virtually impossible for westerners to operate, and the language requirements made recruiting a constant problem.

After everyone had gotten coffee and found a seat around the table, Leonard pushed his chair away from the table and spoke while remaining seated.

"OK, let's get started. You all know why I called you in early. We may have a problem. Probably do have. The Camel is silent. Still no word. We need to send someone in to see what's happened. And we need some innovative ideas about how to do it. Who wants to start? Charley, you act as recorder and capture all the ideas. And remember, guys, nothing is off the table at this stage."

A few of the younger men were eager to put forward some ideas. One proposed contacting the Russians. "There must be retired KGB agents who could meet our criteria to go in and take a look."

Another idea proposed canvassing all Russian graduate students currently studying or visiting in the U.S. to determine if any originated from Turkmenistan or Uzbekistan. One of the builds off this idea was a canvass of former Soviet soldiers who had been in Afghanistan. "We'd need help from the Russians on this one."

Ex-KGB, ex-soldiers, ex-Russian Mafia, active Russian Mafia—hired for the job; it was an all-too-familiar laundry list of undesirables.

Paul Chapman, Leonard's deputy, sat quietly listening to these proposals while trying to keep his mind open to the practicality of the offerings in the complex world they inhabited. At the same time he was trying to keep one ear tuned to the silent rumblings coming from his guts.

Chapman, the oldest man in the section, had served in the field for six years as a contact with U.S. Army Rangers. While on duty in the early days of U.S. engagement in Afghanistan he had received a nasty shrapnel wound and, as a result, had been forced to give up a foot of his large intestine. Although he recovered fully, he retained—as a souvenir of Central Asia—an inability to control his bowel habits as precisely as he might have wished. Now, he was hearing a few familiar internal noises that he correctly interpreted as harbingers of things to come.

A whippersnapper with a master's degree in political science from some Ivy League school—he couldn't remember which one—was reminding them that Balkh had once been an important city along the ancient Silk Road, when Chapman recalled something he had been reading two days ago. *Balkh?* It had been the story of an early participant in the conflict between Britain and Russia for predominance in Central Asia once known by the euphemistic expression, "The Great Game."

Back in the 1820s and 30's an adventurous Briton, William Moorcroft, had wandered through the trackless wastes of Central Asia as an agent of the East India Company. Upon discovery, he was killed as an infidel and a spy. His body had been tossed into an unmarked grave outside the mud walls of Balkh. *That's where The Camel just went silent.*

Chapman made a sign to Leonard and slipped quietly out of the room to deal with his problem. On his way back from the toilet, he stopped at his cubicle to get a tea bag. Three cups of coffee already and it wasn't even ten o'clock. As he opened the desk he noticed a small blue glass bead in the drawer among the odds and ends, paper clips, extra staples, a bottle of white-out. The blue bead was about an inch and a half in diameter, made to resemble an eye. It was an evil eye, a Middle Eastern good luck charm, popular in Turkey, said to be effective in warding off bad luck.

He picked up the bead and examined it. It had a hole for a string. The string, like the eye, had been blue when it was new. Now, much of the string was a brown, rusty color. Stiff. It was, he knew, human blood. He stood for a long minute contemplating the amulet before slipping it into his pocket. Then he rejoined his colleagues.

The parade of ideas lasted until eleven and Leonard let everyone have the floor for as long as it took. Chapman remained silent until everyone had spoken. Finally everyone seemed to be out of ideas.

"How about you, Paul? You usually have something to throw into the pot."

Chapman stuck his hand into his pocket and fingered the charm. *Balkh!* he thought. *They were never even sure if the body recovered later belonged to Moorcroft. It could have been anyone. What a fucked up world we live in. The Silk Road. Still a breathtaking highway to hell.* Chapman, as crafty a fellow as one could want for this type of work, had anticipated this need months ago.

He looked Leonard squarely in the eye and held his gaze. "I think I may have a workable solution," he offered. "But it's kind of a long shot. I'd prefer to go over it in private."

Chapter 18

Lawn Party

"Alas, alas for the great city, the mighty city of Babylon! In a single hour your doom has struck!'

The merchants of the earth also will weep and mourn for her, because no one any longer buys their cargoes, cargoes of gold and silver, jewels and pearls, cloths of purple and scarlet, silks and fine linens; all kinds of scented woods, ivories, and every sort of thing made of costly woods, bronze, iron, or marble; cinnamon and spice, incense, perfumes and frankincense; wine, oil, flour and wheat, sheep and cattle, horses, chariots, slaves and the lives of men. 'The fruit you longed for,' they will say, 'is gone from you; all the glitter and glamour are lost, never to be yours again!'"

REVELATIONS 18:10-11

For a summer gathering of faculty families at the home of Walt's department head, Flo had dressed while nursing a snit that Walt could not understand. She looked like a million dollars in an off-white dress of textured silk, not too low in front, but low enough. The party, spent entirely out of doors on a sticky afternoon in early August, was unstructured and pleasant. Children were running and playing, while at one end of the lawn, croquet was keeping several adults occupied. A group of six or seven was making a half-hearted attempt at *bocce*. Intermittently, a couple or a foursome would take a turn at the badminton net.

There was plenty of gin and tonic. And ice. And a table filled with anything else. As the long, languid summer sunset slowly turned down the lights, the chorus of peepers began to be heard from surrounding wood lots. In the distance, toward the southwest, dark clouds on the horizon suggested that the temperature might drop when a late night shower knocked down the dust.

Here and there knots of people were conversing, but the talk was light; there was no business to be conducted, there were no hidden agendas. If department politics was afoot, Walt was unaware.

He walked from group to group, mingling and chatting, exchanging pleasantries. It was a summer evening we have all experienced—at least in our imaginations—and Walt, for a time, felt free.

As darkness fell slowly, there was no movement to go inside or to move to the terrace at the back of the house. Lightning bugs made their appearance and the children's voices rose after someone suggested catching them to make lanterns.

It was the kind of lawn party where nothing special happens, but which will linger in the memory as being near some type of perfection. What could be improved? Perhaps a French Impressionist painter to capture everything in oil on canvas.

Turning to look for Flo, Walt was surprised to see her seated alone in an Adirondack chair near the edge of the patio. Even in the gloom, she was stunning. She was facing straight ahead, smiling slightly, looking at nothing. He stood for a long interval just watching her.

Their problems had started when he took the position at JBU. She had wrinkled her nose when he went on the first trip with a female grad student, Katya.

Despite the fact that he had never felt an interest in another woman—and had made sure the two met socially before the trip—Flo had simply turned up the chill.

And recently there had been another student who seemed to enjoy his company and was working hard to get it; pretty, blond Tara. But he had never made the least comment, or given the least sign to encourage any of the females who, predictably, get crushes on professors they find interesting.

He went to Flo silently, then stooped to kiss her on the neck.

She turned her head away to avoid him.

"Are you OK?"

Her voice was cold. "I'm bored *itless*."

He paused to think of an appropriate response but nothing seemed to fit. He thought a long time before he spoke.

"Let's wait a few more minutes to see if anyone moves inside. Then we can leave."

Later—and ever after—ever after, ever after, he would remember that evening; the light coating of *sweet summer sweat*, the funky smell of lightning bugs on children's hands, the clink of ice in glasses, laughter, distant heat lightning, a faint whiff of Flo's perfume... and talcum powder. All over-poweringly sweet; all condensed into a single pseudo-word. *Itless*.

The next day he rose early and used his walker to move into the den. There he fitted his prosthesis and dressed silently so as not to disturb his wife. Leaving the house without eating or even having a cup of coffee, he walked four miles. His brain was racing.

I've got to face it.

She doesn't love me.

She's never going to love me. There is nothing I can ever do that will change that. She's miserable with me and it doesn't have anything to do with the conditions of her life. It just this simple. She doesn't want to live with me. God only knows who she does want to live with. Anyone but me.

But what will I do about it?

It was hard for him to believe his leg could bother her so much. A couple of hours later when he returned home, he was covered with sweat, but he was no nearer to having an answer to his *problem* than when he left.

Chapter 19

2004—A Tale From Bukhara

> "At the ancient caravan town of Bokhara, further along the Silk Road, the Bolsheviks were less fortunate. Under the Tsars this great stronghold of Islam had never been fully absorbed into the Russian Empire, but had been allowed to remain a protectorate under a hereditary Emir. The Bolsheviks were determined to liberate this backward, mediaeval society from its harsh and autocratic ruler."
>
> SETTING THE EAST ABLAZE
> PETER HOPKIRK

Tara accompanied Walt on his next visit to the Silk Road. This was his second trip in the same year, scheduled because he wanted to keep his groups small and most of all because things were miserable at home. It was a push for him, but he needed to get away from the grief of a split with Flo.

On the flight into Central Asia it had been fairly easy to keep Tara at arm's length. The first half of the trip she had watched him the way a cat watches a canary, but they had reached Bukhara, traveling west to east, before she bewitched him.

Bukhara. Their second day. They had an early breakfast and got on the road before the city was fully awake. He wanted his group to see the city as it might have looked several hundred years ago. They drove to the east, in the direction of the mountains. The horses and oxen of the past had been largely supplanted by Kubota tractors. Early morning traffic on roads leading from the city contained more Japanese trucks than horse-drawn wagons, but there were enough rickety farm carts to give the place a feel that Walt wanted to convey to his students.

In particular he wanted his students to see the open fields stretching into the distance, bounded by the ever-present rows of poplars that he had come to associate with Central Asia. The morning sun was still low enough for the trees to cast long shadows and his students seemed to respond with the mood he wanted. They were less talkative, more interested in taking pictures. As they continued to drive toward the distant purple mountains, there were plenty of postcard views to go around. Gradually they worked their way south over dusty roads, past cultivated fields, farmers working, and windbreaks stretching into the distance. The group was headed in the direction of the green belt corridor of farms, orchards and villages lining the fabled desert river, Zerafshan, "the Gold Strewer," stretching between Bukhara and Samarkand.

After an hour or so they turned back to Bukhara. All the museums were open by the time they arrived. The day was spent touring the town's scenic wonders. They visited the ancient fortress known as The Ark, once a residence of the ruling Emirs. They rested inside the impressive public square at the Registan, once the site of gruesome public executions.

Next they toured the Bolo Hauz Mosque before continuing on to the Poi Kalon Minaret. The Tower of Death. His students were impressed by this famous symbol of Bukhara, described in guidebooks as a "javelin thrust into the heart of the old town." Originally built in 919, the 155-foot tower was destroyed by a natural catastrophe in 1068. The replacement lasted until 1127 when it collapsed while in use, with substantial loss of life. Walt described the tower's history through —and past—the Soviet Era, to its last restoration in 1976 as a UNESCO World Heritage Site.

The Kalyan Mosque portal with its tile façade in blue and turquoise was a big favorite, as was the 9th century Mausoleum of Ismail the Samanid. Inexplicably, there were fewer visitors than usual and, to include people in the photos for scale, his students took turns posing for one another—in doorways and on park benches.

Another favorite site in their busy itinerary was the Khalif-Niyazkul Madrassa, dating from the early 1800's. Although it lacked the colorful tile façade and decorative calligraphy of some madrassas, its curious, clumsy shape—suggesting some type of industrial building—seemed to delight his students and they questioned him concerning the reason behind the building's four, lumpy towers.

It was a pleasant day, sunny and mild, with little dust in the air and no crowds of foreign tourists. They ate at a café he had visited before, a place serving Russian food as well as Uzbek dishes. Afterwards they visited the Nadir Divan Begi Madrassa dating from the 1500s but handsomely restored to emphasize the artistry of Bukhara's tile workers.

Despite the miles they had walked, Walt could not recall a day in which everything had gone smoother. They encountered no problems anywhere along the way and his group was obviously excited and stimulated by their exposure to another example of the culture of Central Asia.

At dinner, much of the conversation had to do with comparisons between the visits to Khiva and Bukhara. There were arguments on both sides, but all agreed that the tile work at Nadir Divan Begi was hard to surpass. After dinner, Walt was tired. He had been walking all day and was ready to lie down. His stump was painful and swollen with fluid after nearly eight hours of remaining upright. It had cost him some effort to keep his discomfort from showing by the end of their walk.

All during the tour Tara had kept some distance between them and both had tried to avoid any eye contact that might have been a tipoff.

Walt hung around the bar with the young people until shortly after nine when he called it a night. "Tomorrow," he reminded them, "you can sleep 'til eight when we'll meet for breakfast and then take off for Samarkand."

It was about 10:30 when he heard a tap at his door and hopped over to open it. She slipped in without a word, pushed him against the bathroom door frame and kissed him on the mouth. He had to grab the frame before she realized that he was standing on one leg.

"Tara, is this a good idea? I mean…"

"Shut up, professor. Just shut up. Wasn't I good today?"

"Yeah. Thanks for not blowing up my whole program."

"I'm not going to hurt your fucking program. In fact, I think I'm gonna help it. Come on, peg leg. Hop over here and get off your feet. I know you must be hurting."

He realized that talk was futile. *Peg leg? What a little brat!* That was something new. Her eyes were glittering and she hadn't been drinking. No drugs either. This was something natural that she was secreting from her own body and part of him was thrilled to think that he was the cause.

"Thank you for today, professor. It was wonderful. But then, you already knew that."

"It's nice for you to say it."

"And I know that you have very mixed feelings about me. That you think I'm much too pushy. Maybe even a little scary."

"Tara, you're not scary at all. You are a totally amazing girl. And I'm a bit awed by your interest…"

"Stop talking professor. You've been talking all day. And anyway, you look a little tired. You can just lie back and go to sleep. Or read. Or do whatever you were gonna do. I won't be a bother. I just want to be near you again. Near enough to touch you. And no, I don't want to make you fuck me."

"My god, Tara…"

"Unless you want to. Then it's different. Please, professor. I won't be a pest."

"More like a tornado."

She drew her knees under her on the bed and pulled him back gently.

"Just relax with me. I know you won't let me rub your back. So I won't even ask. I'll be gone in the morning. Come on. Tell me a story. Tell me a story about Bukhara."

"And if I tell you a story, you'll stop driving me crazy?"

"Promise."

They lay back on the bed and Tara pulled the sheet over him. She slithered across him to turn out the light. Then, under the sheet, she wriggled out of all her clothing and snuggled against him. Jaybird.

He seemed to be almost paralyzed until she laughed.

"I'm not going to eat you." That made him laugh. "I was hoping," he joked.

Then they were both laughing and after a few moments he relaxed.

"You want me to tell you a story?"

"Uh huh."

"About Bukhara?"

A pause. "You said."

"I'll need a minute to think of something." She moved her leg across his body and he could feel her heat.

"OK. I've got it. OK. Here it is." *Jesus Christ. What am I going to do with this girl?*

"We're going back to the time of World War I. Bukhara is a semi-autonomous nation. Ruled by a hereditary Emir who has absolute power over his people. They're mostly Muslims. The Emir had made some type of half-assed pledge of loyalty to the Tsar, but Russians weren't a major presence in the area. Yet. Bukhara was one of three Khanates. Khiva. Where we've been. Bukhara, where we are now. And Khokand. Near Tashkent. Where we're going."

She pulled his arm across her rear and placed his hand. "You can touch me while you're talking."

"Christ!" he gasped. "Are you even listening to me?"

"Khiva where we've been. Bukhara. Now. And Khokand, later. Yes. I'm listening. But you can still touch." And she bit his shoulder. Not hard enough to break the skin. It felt to him as if some trap door had just snapped. But instead of the door shutting him in, enclosing him somewhere, it snapped open and let him be free in the big world. "Keep going," she whispered.

"When the Russian Revolution took place, there was the potential for conflict in this region—between Britain who had vast interests in India, and Russia who had always wanted to control Central Asia. The Bolsheviks moved into all of the khanates and took over by a variety of means; subterfuge, deceit, spying, war. It was a harsh, violent time. Over time the Bolsheviks morphed into the Soviet Army. Now you have a Communist army moving into this city and the surrounding territory, to take over every aspect of government and to essentially abolish the practices of every religion."

"OK."

"Are you still listening?"

"Intently. Yes. That's nice." Her voice had dropped to a drowsy whisper and he thought she might be falling asleep.

"The Emir of Bukhara, the old guy who lived in that palace we saw, had a harem containing four hundred wives. All young. All pretty. All accustomed to an easy life in a sheltered environment."

"Four hundred? Not three ninety-seven? Four-oh-two?"

"Four hundred. Who knows? Don't mess with me. Maybe more. But with the dethroning of the Emir, his harem full of wives needed to be liberated. Naturally, as you might expect, these women weren't unhappy about getting shut of the old geezer, but neither were they anxious to leave the harem."

"Um! Could be some good things about harem life," she said. She sounded far away.

"Are you going to sleep in the middle of my story?"

"Oh, no."

"These were lovely young females, some from Central Asia, but others from different parts of the world. Selected for their beauty and grace. Cared for under the watchful eye of eunuchs and old women. In their sheltered lives, naturally—naturally—nat—tur—ra—ly—*maybe she is falling to sleep; she's very still*—they dreamed of the handsome strong males who might some day carry them away. Have you ever read any the love poetry of Persia? Or from Central Asia? Rumi, maybe?"

"I don't think I care to answer right now." *Dreamy voice. Is she really listening?*

"It can be intense. These women may have been wound up as tight as springs. They lounged around in soft filmy clothing, eating sweetmeats, telling each other stories, reading poetry, making themselves and each other beautiful. Just waiting to be summoned by an old bastard, older than their grandfather. Actually, Tara, I don't have a clue what harem life was like. But this really is a true story. Anyway—anyway—any—any—way—*her breathing is changing, maybe I'm hypnotizing her*—in the 12th Century an Arab poet wrote a poem to a blind girl. It went like this. Wait. Want to hear it?"

"Um."

"*They called my love a poor blind maid;*
I love her more for that, I said;
I love her, for she cannot see
These gray hairs which disfigure me.
We wonder not that wounds are made
By an unsheathed and naked blade;
The marvel is that swords should slay,
While yet within their sheaths they stay.
She is a garden fair, where I
Need fear no guardian's prying eye;
Where, though in beauty blooms the rose,
Narcissuses their eyelids close."

Her voice seemed to come from another place—far away. A whisper. "That's from Bukhara? Nice touch!"

"Anyway. One of the Communist leaders sent to Bukhara was a young Indian revolutionary who had come to the attention of Lenin and had developed a rapport with him. A wanna-be protege whose real interest was setting India on fire against the Brits. So Lenin assigns him to deal with the harem problem in Bukhara. The Indian recommended the issuance of a proclamation divorcing the women from the Emir and leaving them free to marry whomever they wished. And so they became free agents. But our Indian didn't stop there. He summoned a gathering of the troops who had invaded Bukhara and told them that any soldier who wanted to take one of the Emir's concubines as a wife—and settle on a farm in the region—would be given a plot of land and the cash needed to make a start. There was no lack of soldiers eager to accept this arrangement."

"I bet."

"You're still awake? The problem was that the women weren't eager to leave the shelter of the harem. They had gotten used to their pampered lifestyle. So the youthful Indian called another gathering of the soldiers that had responded and told them they could go in and choose for themselves. With the understanding that no violence would be tolerated."

"I hope they didn't turn loose 500 soldiers to get 400 women."

"Don't be troublesome. I don't know how they managed that part of it. Even the Soviets were smart enough not to do that. Remember, these women had lived much of their lives in seclusion. Many were just girls. Think about the sad way they spent their days: idle until summoned by the emir."

"Um!"

"In the 11th century, an Indian poet named Bilhana wrote a long poem in Sanskrit. Its title was *Black Marigolds* and it had fifty stanzas. It's about a young man who falls in love with a girl far above him. She loves him in return. But ultimately. Ultimately. Ultimately...."

"Um!"

"He pays with his life." His voice had dropped to a whisper.

"If you read the whole poem, it almost makes you dizzy. It's one of the few poems you can smell, and it's a smell that includes musk and sandalwood. Even translated it can make your head spin. Want a stanza?"

"Um!"

He waited for a long moment to begin; long enough that she jabbed him with her elbow. He spoke slowly, pausing after each line. Remembering the words.

"*Even now*
My thought is all of this gold-tinted king's daughter
With garlands tissue and golden buds,

Smoke tangles in her hair, and sleeping or waking
Feet trembling in love, full of pale languor;
My thought is clinging as to a lost learning
Slipped down out of the minds of men,
Laboring to bring her back into my soul."

He paused, to remember, and she jabbed him again.

"Even now
If I see in my soul the citron-breasted fair one
Still gold-tinted, her face like the night stars,
Drawing unto her; her body beaten about with flame,
Wounded by the flaring spear of love,
My first of all by reason of her fresh years,
Then is my heart buried alive in snow.

This is all I know. It goes on until your knees buckle.

Anyway, the soldiers entered the former Emir's harem, and according to the storyteller, handsome, rugged Russian soldiers walked off with beautiful, well-pleased Uzbek—or I should say Bukharan—wives. Wiiii—ves."

"Jesus Chrrriiiiiissstttt! Don't!"

"You don't like my story?"

"Please. Oh God. Don't stop. Do…nottt…" Her body was jerking. "…stoppppp!"

"That's it. Your story is over," he whispered.

"Oh, Jesus. I'm…am…com…Com………ing!
Oh! Oh!
Ohhhh.
Oh!"

After the fifth time she said Oh! it occurred to Walt to do something he had never done before. He began to count. She said Oh! twenty-seven times and no two successive times sounded exactly alike except the final three.

She pressed her face into the side of his neck and bit him again. On the collar bone. It was much harder this time, and it felt like she might have drawn blood. Then he felt her face wet with tears and he couldn't tell if she was laughing or crying.

But he wasn't crying. He was laughing and kissing the tears from her wet eyes.

"Sweet Tara. Sweet Tara. What have you done to me? What happens to me now?"

After that it was a whole different kind of trip.

Chapter 20

Valentin, The Enforcer

> "The discovery of the world's largest known natural gas fields in far-off Bukhara, in Central Asia, supplementing known sources in the Ukraine, the Volga area and the Caucasus, is reputed to have increased gas production tenfold in a decade. It is rapidly transforming the backward but historic Bukhara into a Russian city, the site of a huge projected chemical plant and other industries. Natural gas from Bukhara is already serving Tashkent and has been piped to the Urals. An extensive network of pipelines, expanding as fast as 40-inch pipe becomes available, carries gas and oil to many industrial centers in European Russia, the Urals and Siberia."
>
> AN INTRODUCTION TO RUSSIAN HISTORY AND CULTURE
> IVAR SPECTOR (1964)

Valentin sat in the hotel restaurant in Bukhara and sipped his tea. Two pale-faced Russian girls in western dress were sitting at the bar and showing him a lot of leg. They were drinking vodka and talking animatedly. The blond had pale gray eyes, slightly slanted—he had noticed them as they came in, walking next to his table— eyes that were unusual and very appealing. Val tried to undress her mentally even as he speculated. They might be prostitutes, but from their dress and demeanor it wasn't certain and they had never even looked his way once. Coming out of his reverie, he checked his watch. It was time to call Raj.

He took a leather-bound notebook from his pocket and opened to a page full of numbers. He flipped open his cell phone and dialed the international number. It rang four times before Raj picked it up. *Hello? Yes?* These Indians were nothing if not dependable. The connection was good.

"Yes, this is Valentin, yes? You are calling right on time. And how are you, my friend?"

"Good, thank you Raj. And you? Not eating too much of that hot curry?"

"You can't fool me with talk of curry, my friend. I know you too well. I know what you are missing that is hot."

"I'm calling from Uzbekistan, Raj. Yes, it would be nice to be back in Bangalore. You must give my regards to Neela."

"You may rely on it, my friend. What can I do for you today?"

Valentin checked his notebook and read off a fourteen-digit sequence of numbers. They were clustered, two digits, six, then six more.

"I am looking now," Raj answered. The answer came up in seconds.

"The carrier picked up 137 kilos packaged to specification in Tashkent. Truck transport across the standard route to Bukhara. Delivery time within specification, but the receiver in Bukhara only received 130 kilos. The driver from Tashkent was actually Turkmen. Name on our records is Murad Kolyazov. Age 35."

"What have you got on file for him?"

"His home is Ashkhabad. Married. Two daughters. One was ten. One thirteen. That was when we hired him two years ago. Twelve now. And fifteen."

"I have his name. What else in his record? Any problems in the past?"

"No, nothing, my friend."

"Okay, thank you, Raj. Don't forget to remember me to Neela."

The Indian laughed. "I do not think she is likely to forget you, my friend."

The girls at the bar were laughing loud enough to attract his attention as he switched off his cell and made a couple of notes in his book. Gray Eyes flashed him as she swiveled her legs around on the stool and—even though she had never even glanced his way—he took it to be a deliberate flash, and he wished he didn't have work to do. Damn! Those eyes were appealing. She looked as if she might have a trace of Mongol blood somewhere. Or maybe Uighur. She had Asia in those gray eyes. They had not once looked his way—even though she had deliberately shown him the color of her underpants.

Vasily and Janos were already out looking for Murad and they were making the round of truck stops. If they ran true to form, they'd have him this afternoon. The information on his daughters was new.

After the girls at the bar left, the room was nearly empty except for a few old men puffing on their hookahs. He debated tossing a few vodkas, but changed his mind and ordered more chai. Before the waitress returned, Janos came looking for him.

"In the van," Janos said.

"That was fast."

"Da, easy too. He didn't put up a fight. He is afraid. He has already wet his pants."

"That should speed things along."

Val fished out a few bills of Uzbekistan's crazy currency and slapped them on the table.

"Let's do it."

The three Russians drove the rented van out of town to the west. They drove beyond the train tracks linking Bukhara with Mary and continued on into the desert. When they were beyond any signs of habitation Vasily turned south and headed in the direction of the Amu Darya, out of sight, far in the distance. It lay across the border, in Turkmenistan.

Murad was bound and gagged, with a hood over his head. He wasn't struggling against his bonds and his face wasn't visible, but he had lost control of his bladder and the smell of urine was strong in the van... even with the windows open. When they reached an area of low dunes, Vasily pulled off next to a few sparse clumps of dune grass. Sand stretched into the distance.

They pulled the frightened man out of the van and dragged him a few yards away. Janos gave him a sharp punch in the stomach and pushed him to his knees, facing away from the van. When he removed Murad's hood there were no visible terrain features the man could recognize. Sand stretched as far away as one could see. Janos cuffed their wide-eyed victim on both sides of his head. "Look straight ahead," he barked.

Vasily busied himself with a small portable charcoal grill like a Japanese hibachi. Within a few minutes it was glowing.

Val dropped to one knee facing the visibly shaken man, addressing him in Uzbek. Val's Uzbek wasn't good, but it was adequate for the task.

"Well, Murad. It has come to this. That is your name isn't it? Murad?"

"I am Murad. I drive a truck."

"Yes, I know. You drive a truck for me. And what else is it that you do, Murad? Why are we all here? Why have you caused us all to interrupt our lives to come to this godforsaken place?"

"I don't know what you're..."

"Listen, Murad. You have a family, isn't that right. Two daughters?"

"What does my family have to do..."

"Two daughters. No? And the youngest one is pretty, is she not? We will see shortly. My men are hunting her as we speak."

Murad's face seemed to crumple. He didn't want to cry, but fear was turning to panic. He struggled to control his features and seemed at a loss for words.

"I'll bet you have never even imagined what it would be like to watch someone fuck your daughter."

"Tell me what you want from me." His voice sounded as if it was shredded.

"Can you imagine watching half a dozen grown men take turns fucking your daughter? You would probably want to help her. I imagine you would be very angry unless there was something you could do. But if there was nothing you could do, what would happen to that anger?"

"Tell me what you want to know."

"Six men, Murad. Big men. How will your little girl like that? Do you think it will be a life-changing event for her?"

"I will tell you what you want to know."

"Yes, I am certain of that."

"Please, please…"

"I am certain you will tell us. But listen, Murad. What will you tell us? You must know what our questions will be if you already know the answers."

"Please…"

"Murad, listen. You are getting boring. I think you know why we are here, and so we are in no mood to play games. I don't want to spend a lot of time asking questions. I want you to tell us a story about why we are here. Complete with all the details. We know you will do this for us. The only question is… when will you begin the story we wish to hear? How long will you make us wait?"

The acrid smell of heated metal registered on Murad's brain as soon as it reached his nostrils.

"I will tell you what happened. It was not my idea."

"You are beginning to understand, Murad, But you have wasted a lot of our time and we still have much to do so now you must stand up so we can take your trousers down."

Murad was openly crying now. Janos cuffed him about the head a couple of times and hauled him to his feet. Vasily took the red hot pry bar and branded the truck driver across both buttocks. The heated metal smell was overwhelmed by the stink of roasting flesh.

The scream was strangled in Murad's throat as Janos stepped in and clapped a vodka-soaked rag over his nose and mouth—stopping his breathing.

After thirty seconds he pushed the gasping, blubbering man back onto his knees. Valentin had never changed his position and his tone of voice was unchanged.

"And so you see, Murad, our afternoon's work has just begun. How long we will take depends on your ability to tell us a good story; one that we will like to hear and will be able to understand."

Murad was not an experienced criminal, and he had, indeed, been encouraged to steal six kilos of heroin from his last delivery without giving a great deal of thought to the consequences. That was stupid, but he was not completely stupid and—a chess player—he realized that he was probably playing an end game and he was not eager to prolong the game.

In the next thirty minutes he reconstructed his drive from Tashkent, and gave up the names of two confederates who had the one-kilo bricks of heroin. He described the men in detail, and he told his captors where they were likely to be found. His accomplices lived in Kattakurgan, on the highway to Samarkand.

Vasily burned him a second time when the story slowed down and Murad seemed to hesitate while describing his friends. This time he moved the bar a little lower. When Murad stopped choking and resumed blubbering, the details came easily.

"Do you think you have enough information to find these men by tomorrow?," Val asked his companions.

"Easily. If they have not left town we will not need much time."

"Then we are done."

"I will make him howl like an animal," Vasily said. Torture came easily to him and he enjoyed the opportunity to practice.

"No, we will go back."

Murad, beyond all hope, was crying softly, lost in his own thoughts.

"It will not take me long with this bar," Vasily protested.

Valentin opened the small backpack and took out a small automatic pistol. He tossed it to Janos.

"Shoot him," he ordered.

"This is a nice pistol. I have not seen it before."

"It's yours. A Vektor. From South Africa. Model CP-1, fairly new. Nine millimeter, thirteen rounds. The clip is loaded. Just jack one in."

"It's very nice. Small. I like it. I am to have it? Thank you." He chambered a round and shot Murad in the right ear.

"Can I see it?" said Vasily, slinging the heated bar out into the sand.

"Don't worry, Vasily Borisovich," Val told him. "I have one for you, but it's back at the hotel."

"There's still vodka left in this bottle," said Janos, taking a swig as the words left his mouth. He handed the bottle to Vasily who eyed it carefully and drank half of what remained.

"Why do we have to hurry back to that shithole town?" he said as he handed the bottle to Valentin. "It's not Moscow. There's not a whole lot going on."

Valentin laughed. He was thinking about the woman with the gray eyes who had shown him her underwear. She had to be somewhere in the city. *Track her down.* It would be interesting to look for her. He was laughing at Vasily and Janos. *Fucking Neanderthals. Siberians. They have no imagination.*

Chapter 21

Val Proposes a Solution

> "Alma-Ata (pronounced Alma a-TAH) sits between two rushing glacial streams, the Greater and Lesser Almatinka Rivers that have their headwaters high in the snow-packed peaks to the southeast and disappear into a haze in the vast, arid center of the country. The name Alma-Ata, which means "father of apples," was invented by the Russians after the revolution (and changed to Almaty in 1994, three years after Kazakh independence). It had been a trading center on the Silk Route at least since the time of Alexander the Great. Imperial Russia staked out a military post there midway through the nineteenth century and gradually imported Cossack forces to hold it in the name of the czar."
>
> APPLES
> FRANK BROWNING

At the next meeting called by Arkady, the crime boss summoned Val into his suite in a temporary office in Almaty. After passing through all the security checks, Val found himself in the large paneled office with no one but Arkady and his personal secretary who made notes and kept a recording of everything that was said. Arkady lived in a different world, a world without trust, honor or any of the normal attributes that make civilized life possible. He lived an interesting life, Val had to admit, but it was not a life to which he aspired.

Arkady got to the point. "A lot of money has been spent getting you into your own facility, and more has been spent on equipment to provide you with tools. But I need to understand—in simple terms for I am a simple man—how you propose to maintain control of the drug network that requires so much constant attention."

"My proposal is based upon..."

"Remember that I do not have your education."

"My proposal is based upon the lessons I learned in India."

"Explain!"

"In the United States, it is common practice to send parcels by private shippers. When such packages are sent, each container is measured, weighed and given an identification number. Afterwards the container—as simple as a cardboard box—is marked with a label containing this number. The number may contain several different codes that identify the points—the nodes—where packages may be handled again. By means of the codes the status of the container may be checked or verified along its route. At any time, whether in transit, or at a node awaiting transportation to its next destination, the package may be checked. Its existence can be verified, and if necessary, its condition checked."

"This is not different from the way we ship vodka." Arkady rose from behind the desk where he had been cleaning an antique automatic pistol. It appeared to be a classic German Luger, but it might have been a replica. More likely though it was the real thing.

"Speaking of which, how about if we drink," Arkady said. It was not a question. He had the bottle out and the liquor poured before Val could respond. They raised their glasses and tossed back the contents. The vodka had been lightly flavored with syrup made from some type of melon. "You like it? It is an experiment. Not like Starka. This is an idea of my own. Mild. It is good, no?"

"I like it. It is good."

"Not too mild?"

"No. It is good."

"Then you take a case back and try it on the Mighty Handful. This is my idea. It seems to fit with our part of the world. Fucking Ludmila can make a breakfast on three kinds of melon."

"I will take a case back to the hotel. But let me tell you what is different about my proposal. In many places in the United States the high cost of technical labor has led industrialists to vend out certain tasks to overseas companies. In particular, they can now hire computer programmers and technicians more cheaply in India. Technical education in India has become very good, comparable to the best that is available anywhere in the world. The same is becoming true of China, but India has a long head start."

"So we can hire Indians to help us track our shipments? Towelheads?"

"They can remain in India. And they know nothing about what we ship. They are tracking numbers. Thanks to technologies like satellite telephones and fiber optic cables, we can be in contact with a technical work force in India. I can sit here in my Almaty hotel room and communicate with a technician in India who can tell me the status of a shipment that is in transit across Turkey in a truck from Samsun to Istanbul. When the shipment arrives in Istanbul, if the contents are not identical with those that left the last node, then I and the Mighty Handful will know where to begin our little quality check. Usually this does not take too long, and there are few repeat offenders. Actually, so far, there have been no repeat offenders."

"You have this system in operation already?"

"Of course not, Arkady. Only a prototype. Not until it has been approved by you. But I do have a pilot program set up on my own initiative. Using connections that I made while I was working in India. Men of ability and discretion. And, by the way, I must stress that they have no awareness of what is being transported. I hinted that it might possibly be cultural artifacts so they are aware that they must reveal none of the details or our contract is immediately voided. But…" He pointed to the bottle of melon-flavored vodka and Arkady pushed it in his direction.

As he was pouring himself another drink, Arkady's cell phone rang.

"Yes. What? No, don't tell me more. I already know. What? No. Bring him here. This is for me." Then he returned the phone to his jacket pocket and turned back to Val. "We will have to interrupt our business for a few moments. I am going to need a new carpet."

Val glanced at the deep red carpet spread out across the floor in front of Arkady's massive desk. It didn't appear worn to him, but he knew that Arkady's whims and preferences were sometimes incomprehensible.

Arkady appeared to be preoccupied by some information from the phone call and he seemed to be searching through his desk drawers for something. Val was waiting for Arkady's attention before resuming when there was a knock at the door. The secretary opened the door and three men entered the room. At a nod from Arkady, the secretary left the room.

Two large rough men were supporting a third man whose hands were bound behind him. He was bleeding from the mouth and his upper lip was swollen and split. His eyes were wide with fear. Val couldn't recognize the man who appeared to be in his mid forties. He looked Russian and Val's guess was confirmed when Arkady addressed the man.

"Well, Dunya, it appears that your sins have caught up to you."

"Arkady, I can explain everything."

"No need, Dunyosha. I already know everything. And it saddens me."

"The launchers I sold were not part of the consignment you purchased. They were a gift to me from the Chinese. A commission."

"But I already pay you. Am I wrong? Do you draw a salary from my organization? Or not?"

"Of course. You pay me well. I have no complaints Arkady. But that batch of launchers was not included in the transaction. They were separate. They were shipped separately and sold separately. They were a gift to me from the Chinese manufacturer."

"They were part of the transaction. You stole from me."

For the first time Dunya noticed the pistol on the desk and he stepped forward to appeal to his boss.

"Don't shoot me, Arkady. It will never happen again. I swear."

"This is what hurts me, Dunya. The knowledge that this was not the first time. You have stolen from me before. I hoped that you would get it out of your system."

"A commission. It was a commission. Truly. Not a theft. I can prove it to you."

"This may have happened more times than I even know about."

"A commission. I swear. Arkady. Look at me. Please. Irina is about to have a baby. Please, Arkady. No."

"You are worried, my thieving friend, that there will be no one to fuck Irina? Do not worry, Dunya. Irina will be well fucked."

"Please, Arkady. Do not shoot me."

"Dunyosha, Dunyosha. I will promise you. I will not shoot you. You may rest easy on that. Also, do not worry for Irina.

"Thank you, Arkady."

"You are welcome, Dunya. The rug, boys. Put him in the rug."

Val saw that the front of the man's trousers were wet as he lost control of his bladder. The man on Dunya's left kicked him behind the knees and he fell to the floor on the carpet. They dragged him to the end and began to roll it up. When he arched his body to keep from being wrapped up, he received a vicious kick in the stomach and began to sob.

"In the middle, boys. Get him centered." Dunya, gasping, was dragged by the shirt until he was centered and they began to roll him in the carpet."

When he was completely rolled up, his muffled screams were still chilling and Val helped himself to another small tumbler of vodka.

Arkady walked to the center of the room whose floor was now bare. The man took up six feet of carpet and there were another six feet projecting at either end beyond the man. Val was unprepared for what happened next. Arkady hesitated at the edge of the rolled carpet as if trying to visualize the enclosed man. Then, at the spot where he gauged the man's head to be located, he began stomping the carpet. The first sound from the carpet was indescribably horrible. Neither a scream nor a groan, but something in between that was cut short. Arkady continued stomping, first with one foot, then with another. When he was satisfied that the man was gone, he stopped and went to the cabinet for two glasses.

"Would you boys wish to drink with me?" He poured the vodka all around and they raised their glasses.

"Boys, get this carpet out of here. And tell the woman outside that I need a new one."

The men drank the vodka in one smooth gulp and then folded each end of the carpet toward the center. It was too stiff and thick to stay folded, so they each picked up an end and manhandled their unwieldy burden out of the room.

"Where were we when I was interrupted?" Arkady asked. Valentin feared that his voice might thicken. He did not want to take another drink with Arkady, but likewise he did not want to refuse one.

"I was telling you that technicians in India can track our drug shipments from source to destination with considerable accuracy and precision, and it will be reliable and relatively inexpensive. Also it will facilitate the identification of thefts and losses en route. It could be set up fairly quickly, and I could coordinate the entire process with a relatively small group. Enforcement would take more men than managing the information."

"It sounds as if it is worth a try for a year or two. Why don't you go ahead and begin to set it up. You can make a written estimate of the costs and leave them with Sophronia for my accountants. By the way, you seemed to be anxious about my carpet. Don't worry, it was not an antique Bokhara. Just a modern copy from Pakistan. There are more in the warehouse."

Chapter 22

Shanghai Skyscraper, 42nd Floor

> "...fertile oases are found along the Tarim River which receives its water from the melting snow on surrounding mountains. Through these oases ran the ancient Silk Road to the Near East, and at one time camel-driving merchants risked their lives so that the Roman world could enjoy the luxuries of the East."
>
> THE AGELESS CHINESE: A HISTORY
> DUN J. LI

Six floors of Shanghai's dramatic Great Wall skyscraper are occupied by CHOCO, China Oil Company, a giant corporation with holdings in gas and oil all over the Far East. CHOCO, like several of its North American counterparts, has a policy of secrecy that prevents the public from knowing much about what it does or how it does it. Even the Chinese government, with tentacles into every aspect of daily life, does not know all of the secrets that are discussed within the six floors of executive suites that occupy floors 37 through 42.

The view from these floors is pleasant and even inspiring. Chinese expansion over recent decades has created a building boom that may be unsurpassed in any major world city. Even today, the skyline is punctuated with building cranes in constant motion. These constant reminders of Shanghai's booming economy serve to stimulate and inspire the top level managers who occupy CHOCO's offices.

Today's meeting has been called for the purpose of discussing the CHOCO strategy for gaining access to the oil reserves of Turkmenistan. This is not a new topic for the twelve men who have gathered. They have been working to cut a deal with the nations of Central Asia for more than five years. But they have been stymied by the intransigence of Turkmenistan's unpredictable leader, Saparmurat Niyazov.

The big lure for CHOCO is the possibility of access to Turkmenistan's estimated 100 trillion cubic feet of natural gas, one of the largest proven reserves in the world. Based on estimates by CHOCO geologists, this treasure is easily accessible in the flat, desert regions of southeastern Turkmenistan abutting Afghanistan.

To bring the gas to lucrative markets in China and South East Asia, all that is needed is a pipeline leading south to the Indian Ocean. After leaving Turkmenistan, this line could be routed across Iran—whose government has been noncommittal—or across Afghanistan and Pakistan, both of which have expressed willingness to permit a pipeline.

The opinion of top negotiators at CHOCO is that the latter two countries could become cooperative partners in the enterprise. Both nations have, in the past, permitted Chinese survey teams to map out proposed routes for a pipeline that would terminate at Gwadar on Pakistan's southern coast.

Turkmenistan has been—and still remains—the stumbling block, and all because of their weird, unpredictable president-for-life, Niyazov, who has given himself the name *Turkmenbashi*. The Leader of the Turkmens.

Venerable Wen Wu was presiding at the meeting. His wrinkled face looked like an Asiatic version of Yoda. The man could not have weighed much more than a hundred pounds. And yet, he radiated energy and decisiveness.

"This morning we will discuss a strategy for getting into Turkmenistan. We have been waiting for too long and it is unlikely that more waiting will pay any dividends. Today we will talk about a plan for getting our teams into the country for a detailed route map."

The remaining eleven men at the table were silent, hesitant to interrupt before they were invited to participate. Silence reigned for a moment as the projector threw a big image of Niyazov on the screen at the far end of the table.

"This face will be familiar to all of you. Who knows what takes place in the mind of this crazy person? He squanders the resources of his nation and yet refuses every offer we make. He cannot be bribed or bought with money, women or weapons. And, as most of you know, he has written a book which attempts to improve the morals of his countrymen. I have not seen it myself, but I have been told that it cannot be compared in any sense to the writing of our ancient sages. I have been told that it is largely foolishness."

More silence from around the table as a series of views depicted Niyazov at various parades, public events and television appearances. Interspersed with the photos of the man himself were several pictures of large-size, gold-plated statues in a series of heroic poses.

"This egomaniac, Niyazov, may never come to his senses and allow us to build the pipeline we seek. But he will not live forever. Likewise, it is not certain that he will remain in control forever. He could even change his mind. And in such an event, we must be prepared to move quickly. All the major oil and gas companies are considering the same strategy. Or some alternative which meets their own needs. They, too, have come up against this fool's obstinacy. So then, you are wondering. If we cannot get our survey teams into the country, how will we survey the route? Who will tell me how we can do it?"

"Mr. Wen Wu, sir, your memorandum has already circulated. We have all studied it carefully."

"And? What is the reaction?"

It was Zheng Yu-Wei who had spoken. At 43 he was the youngest man at the table. He had graduated from Tulane and Rice in the United States. After graduation he was hired by one of Houston's largest consulting firms in the field of exploration, and his seven-year stint with them had taken him from the gas and oil fields of Central Asia to the North Sea and the North Slope of Alaska. Zheng had been in Turkmenistan for eight weeks and he knew that the country was, indeed, bizarre.

"Your plan to send surveyors into the country camouflaged as a film crew making a movie could work. If the crew has approval from Turkmenbashi, they would be relatively free to circulate. Undoubtedly the ruler of this strange nation would send his own staff of investigators—possibly even soldiers—to accompany the film crew. It is also, I feel, possible that our surveyors, properly trained and equipped, could evade those sent to watch them. There is, however, one difficulty that could bring your scheme to naught."

"And that would be... what?"

"If we subsequently failed to produce a film, Turkmenbashi would know he had been deceived and this would prejudice him against us in any future attempt."

"Yes. And so...?"

"It would seem, Mister Wen, that once we begin this deception we would have no choice but to make the film."

"Aha! Mister Zheng, your years of studies among the Americans did not dull your wits. You have seen the correct solution. As I was confident you would."

Zheng took his seat. Wen Wu stood up and beamed a radiant smile and the slides on the projector were replaced by a video tape of Mongol horsemen galloping across a barren steppe. It was followed swiftly by images of a caravan of laden camels, plodding steadily across a sea of dunes.

All around the table, smiles were breaking out, and then... applause.

"We *are* making a film," Wen Wu laughed. "All that we must decide now is... what will be the topic of our film? Genghis Khan? The Silk Road? Or something else that will appeal to the ruler of the Turkmens."

Laughter around the table.

"In your package of information, you will find several pages of material on ideas that we might use to induce a major Chinese film producer to undertake such a project. Of course we can make such a project financially attractive. Also, if we send a large contingent of attractive Chinese females into this repressed nation, they may help to constitute a diversion. But, gentlemen, perhaps we should pause for some refreshment."

At a signal, his administrative assistant rose and stepped out to summon the caterers waiting beyond the doors.

As CHOCO executives visited the trays of food and the thermos containers of tea and coffee, Wen Wu summoned Zheng with a nod of his head.

"Tell me, Zheng—you have been to Turkmenistan, right?—is it true that these foreign devils never eat pork?"

Zheng could not help laughing aloud. "It is true, Mister Wu, sir. They believe that the pig is an unclean animal. That is what their religion teaches them."

Wen Wu smiled. "Only fools could believe that the Lord of Heaven would forbid the eating of pigs. I think it is only proper that we find a way to gain access to these fools' gas with our pipeline. And Zheng, I believe you are on friendly terms with a gentleman named Wendell Cho. This is correct? Yes?"

Chapter 23

CHOCO's Plans for Turkmenistan

> "*The significance of the Türk Empire was great. For a comparatively long time by Inner Asian standards, it created a* **Pax Turcica**, *uniting lands stretching the length of the network of trade routes commonly known as the silk routes, from China to Byzantium, with a multiethnic society that served as a medium for transmission of both goods and ideas.*"
>
> THE TURKS IN WORLD HISTORY
> CARTER VAUGHN FINDLEY

Mr. Wu's schemes were almost always unnecessarily complex. The Chinese plan for entering Turkmenistan with a large crew of pipeline technicians required that they continue with the deception by actually making a movie. The group of senior decision-makers at CHOCO initially decided that their best option would be to make the film about Genghis Khan. They gave serious consideration to stories about the Silk Road, and there were a few supporters for addressing the life of Timur the Lame. But after some discussion, in which they brought in a couple of carefully coached film producers, they settled on an epic about Genghis Khan. It was a tentative decision, subject to responses from script writers.

In order for the ruse to escape detection, they would need to ensure that the film was available for distribution in Turkmenistan and, in particular, to make certain that it came to the attention of President Niyazov, self-styled Turkmenbashi.

A team of liaison personnel was assigned to work with the chosen film producer, and work was begun on a script. Within the roster of CHOCO people, the survey team would be drawn from a pool of competent field workers, carefully selected and specially trained for this assignment. All this work had to be carefully planned and coordinated but, for a major oil and gas producer, organizing a complex program involving hundreds of people and millions of dollars was all part of a day's work.

The route to be selected inside the borders of Turkmenistan would probably consist of fewer than 200 miles of possible pipeline, from the Dauletabad gas fields south of Mary, ancient Marv, to the border with Afghanistan. From Afghanistan the proposed pipeline would run south to Pakistan. It would then cross Pakistan to the coastal city of Gwadar.

No problems were expected from Afghan or Pakistani governments, both of whom were eager for the revenues to be gained from transit fees and from the creation of good-paying jobs. Still, it was clear that transiting the region around places like Herat in Afghanistan—where the influence of Iranian trouble-makers was strong—would probably create problems.

Competition for permission to construct the first gas pipeline was intense, and it was increasing steadily. American, European and South American companies were all making the same overtures to the same countries. Argentina was pushing hard, and they came with less ideological baggage than the Americans. Turkmenistan was a major sticking point. The ruler of this former SSR, now an independent republic, was still under the influence of Moscow, the legacy of his long years of service in that country.

Mr. Wu knew that the Russians had an agenda of their own. Their state-run firm, Gazprom, has a lock on all the gas flowing into Europe. With lucrative markets already served by existing lines to the west, they would naturally wish to control Turkmen gas flowing north into their system. They wish to retain this control at all costs.

The situation in the Turkmen capital of Ashkhabad is volatile, with large delegations of representatives from the world's major gas producers occupying hotel suites and office complexes. From beachheads in Turkmenistan they conduct strategies of flattery, cajolery, chicanery, bribery, business manipulation and other tricks or techniques intended to win approval from the single man who holds power: Saparmurat Niyazov. Turkmenbashi. Modern-day Emir of Ashkhabad.

Mr. Wu had already selected the man he wanted to head up the movie-pipeline project. But he wanted the selection to be made by someone else. This would be the role of Zheng Yu-Wei. Wu did not want his prints on every detail of the Turkmen survey. Weeks ago he had made a decision to approach Wendell Cho, a man who had studied in the United States and had many friends in the American oil business, as the man for the job. That wasn't the only reason for his selection. Cho was a capable project manager who knew how to handle complex assignments while keeping a close eye on spending rates. Cho was a known quantity.

Mr. Wu would also ask him to see that proper attention was paid to one of his favorite actresses, one who had been an occasional guest at the Wu complex in

Shanghai. Wu had already hinted to the actress that he might be considering producing a film as a personal investment if he could count on her support as an artist.

In the first confused weeks after the decision was made to proceed with this bizarre project, many of those involved were surprised to find that the roles they had envisioned did not, in fact, exist. Others found that although they had expected to have minimal involvement, they were being asked to pack up and get their passports and visas in order for stays in Turkmenistan and Uzbekistan.

Zhi Shu-Bian, the Chinese actress slated to have a lead role in the proposed film, was not especially pleased at the idea of spending several weeks on location in Turkmenistan.

Wendell Cho laughed when he received a call from Zhi's manager. He made a few notes during the call. And after the phone was back in the receiver he put his head on his desk and laughed. *That damned Wu. What has he gotten me into?* Already he was thinking of three different ways to bring Zhi into line.

The pipeline surveyors would be the least of his problems.

Chapter 24

Packaging

> *"In a couple of generations the Mongols as a whole became Buddhists in the East and Moslems in the West; and in the West the true Mongols gradually disappeared, being lost among the Turkish tribes they had conquered and led to victory. It was these Turkish tribes, known as Tartars, who for over two centuries kept Russia in a servitude so terrible, so bloody, so abject, as to leave deep permanent marks on the national character."*
>
> **FOREWORD TO *THE MONGOLS—A HISTORY*, (JEREMIAH CURTIN)**
> **THEODORE ROOSEVELT**

At a meeting in Tashkent, Valentin was explaining recent advances to Arkady and three accountants employed by the Russian boss to keep track of the tangled finances of his crime syndicate. There were questions concerning the labor costs at one of Val's warehouses at Andijan in Uzbekistan.

"The three engineers are experts in packaging, all Indians from technical schools. They all have advanced degrees from universities in the U.S. and could easily find work there. But they have Indian wives and children and they don't want to live there."

"You pay them a living allowance?"

"Of course. Their homes are in India. We pay them to share a small apartment in Tashkent. And there is another in Namangan where they spend considerable time. Two people share the apartment. They rotate assignments so that one person is back in India at all times."

"We hire three to get two?"

"We hire three, period. But they need time away from work. When they are here they work whatever hours are needed to get the job done. And, it is not too much to say that they are virtually interchangeable."

"Meaning what?"

"Meaning that I never need to worry or check up on them. We simply tell them what products will be used to conceal the drug shipments and they work with our suppliers to repackage the processed heroin into containers that are safe, secure from leaks or contamination, and which bear distinctive codes permitting them to be scanned and tracked."

"For this simple task you need three foreign engineers?"

"No, I could probably accomplish the same thing with a dozen Russians if you prefer."

This answer was annoying to Arkady and he was not a man who could conceal the slightest displeasure.

"I want to know if we are being taken for fools by these idol-worshipping sons of bitches. Give me straight answers."

Val knew he was on solid ground.

"Consider this," he said calmly. "The last time I checked, which was last week, the drugs that depart from our processing centers in Uzbekistan leave in shipments of one hundred and seven different, legitimate products. They are concealed in bags, boxes, cans, crates, cartons, sacks, bales and bundles. That makes it hard for police to detect and easy for us to track and recover. This does not happen without work. Our success rate is high. Or put it this way. Our loss rate in transit is very low. And why? Because we have good engineers who think about every likely step in the process. We pay them because they are experts."

"And they are irreplaceable?"

"Arkady, you want to rebuke me. But how much of this questioning must I tolerate? God damn it! No. They are not irreplaceable. Neither am I. Nor, for that matter are any of you. We can all be replaced. But what does that mean?"

"I am trying to underst…"

"I have hired the best men to do this particular job. Our system works reasonably well. As I am sure the receipts at the end of the line will attest. If you have someone else in mind for this job, tell me and I will find other work."

Although Arkady was not totally pleased with Val's approach to work, he was not ready to make a change. He slapped both palms on his desk in a way that indicated he was ready to end the day's session.

"Enough. We want to remain friends and there is one sure way to guarantee that." He opened the drawer of his desk and took out a bottle of Pertskovka, the paprika-flavored vodka he preferred. It usually brought tears to Val's eyes, but Arkady could gulp it down without a blink.

After three vodkas, Arkady's personality began to undergo a change that Val had come to recognize and anticipate. The third vodka, especially when they were drinking Pertskovka, was a signal to try to find a way out of his presence. Not always an easy task.

"The point you must remember, Valentin, is that we are criminals, and at all times we must behave in a way that lets the world know we are criminals."

"I understand, Arkady. I am a criminal and I never forget it."

"But you do not always behave as a criminal must. That is why I have assigned the Mighty Handful to assist you."

"We have worked together many times. As you know. They are very capable." Val hated to be hounded by these bastards, throwbacks from the days of the Tartar hordes that slammed up against the gates of Kiev.

"They are capable because they know how to instill fear in people."

"They do."

"And you, Valentin?" It was a question that Val was not anxious to answer because... *Where the hell was he going with this? A few minutes ago he seemed so friendly.* The ugly son of a whore was totally unpredictable. He was always dangerous but the vodka only made conditions worse.

"Do you know why I assigned the Mighty Handful to work with you?"

"Because they are good at what they do."

"And what is that, Valentin, my lad? Do you know?"

"They punish the..."

"That's not the point. Those who are punished have brought it on themselves. The Mighty Handful create fear of punishment."

"Yes, well, so you say. But usually when they create this fear they are so thorough that the wrongdoer will never experience fear again. I might call that punishment."

"Because you are not a criminal. The fear applies to others who see the example. We have differed over this in the past. Do you think you will ever become a criminal? Like the Mighty Handful? Or like me?"

"I don't know. I am trying to learn."

"I will choose to believe you, Valentin. So we will have a drink together. Then, tomorrow, or maybe next week, you will show me by committing a crime. You will think of Genghis Khan or Timur or Uzbek, and you will do something that would make any of them open their eyes. Am I correct?"

"As always, Arkady, you are correct. What are you pouring for me? I do not recognize that bottle." It was Ochonitchaya, another favorite, also flavored with pepper, cloves and ginger. It would be a long afternoon and they would both be drunk before Val could leave. Hopefully, nothing would set Arkady off.

Chapter 25

2005—Summoned From Washington

> "Nearly a hundred years ago, on August 31, 1907, the first Great Game ended when Russian foreign minister Count Alexander Izvolsky and the British ambassador Sir Arthur Nicholson signed a secret treaty in St. Petersburg in which both countries defined their imperial interests in Central Asia. The Russian government accepted that Afghanistan lay in the British sphere of influence. In turn, London pledged never to challenge the Tsar's rule over the rest of Central Asia."
>
> THE NEW GREAT GAME, BLOOD AND OIL IN CENTRAL ASIA
> LUTZ KLEVEMAN

The call to Walt from the CIA—or whatever agency was really behind the request—came at a time of personal turmoil and uncertainty. For the last half dozen years he had been working to secure a position that would provide some security for him and Flo. There had been plenty of indications of her unhappiness, but he had chosen to ignore the warning signs. Now ... she had left him for her two-legged lover.

Just as he was beginning to feel that he could be a good provider and they might start a family, she had made it clear that she wanted out. At first he didn't want to admit that she could have found somebody else. When he realized who had, as she put it, "captured my heart," and realized that it was that cocksucker Fred Waasdorp, he thought for a while that he'd blow a gasket.

He confided—a mistake—in his department head, who, predictably, recommended a shrink. For nearly six months he had been seeing the shrink once a week for an hour, and it was expensive. Part of the cure, as they say.

He was taking pills for depression and he managed to teach and work though his turmoil, but nothing seemed to make sense. The plans he had made were falling apart.

I'm nothing but a character in a soap opera. Or a cheap novel. In his despair he told the shrink about his leg. The shrink had not realized that he wore a prosthetic leg. It made him feel good to think that he was walking so well that it wasn't evident, but it pissed him off that the shrink had never firked it out of him, had never been perceptive enough to question him about the details of his military service. The guy was useless. In fairness, Walt had to admit to himself that he should have told the shrink that his wife didn't like to see his stump.

The medication made his mouth dry, caused constipation and he seemed to itch more than he could remember, even during the nights when he had slept with fleas.

During this time he and Flo had been sleeping in separate bedrooms. "It will be better until we come to some agreement on the next steps," she had said.

"What next steps? I'm stepping every day. What steps are you talking about?"

"We both need some time apart," she said, making him slightly crazy. How much more apart could they get?

"What is it you want from me, Flo? Tell me what I'm not doing to please you and I'll change." Even to himself it was hard to admit that his stump repelled her, that she did not wish to be married to a man with an injury she considered disabling.

He couldn't admit that his Flo, the girl he had fallen in love with and loved even yet … *maybe* … could find that slick weasel fuck Waasdorp more of a man. True, he wasn't a bad tennis player, and he was a good dancer. But he was married. Married—with two children—and as if that wasn't enough, the frat boy had probably been seduced by his wife. Otherwise …

At some gut level, he knew that Flo and Fred could never make it work for long. Maybe for a couple of years—at most—their screwing might pull them through. But in the long run … ? *Never. They'll never make it.* He knew it in his bones.

As summer began, Walt began to walk two or three miles every morning. Some days he walked a few miles in the evening, just around dusk. His town had plenty of quiet, shady streets, and two miles down the road could get him into dairy farm country. Unless it was raining hard he tried to be regular and walk on a timetable, but that proved to be too much like work.

Gradually he found his rhythm. In the beginning, after he began going several miles each day, it was painful. His leg would get chafed and sore, and he used a shelf full of emollients and antibiotics to avoid an infection and to ease the discomfort. For a while he tried using benzoin to harden the skin on his stump, but that tended to be too sticky and he gave it up after few weeks. One of the best things he used was aloe vera. Amazing stuff. Sometimes it fixed the raw spots overnight.

It was interesting the way that his pain moved around. On some days the pressure on his stump would cause pain at every footfall. Then, as he began to favor that side, the pain would move to the knee—above the stump. It was hard to maintain an even stride and pace without the body responding unconsciously. The pain would move from the right knee to the left hip. It hurt, but it could be tolerated. Gradually it would move to the left knee. Then back to the right knee. His stump was getting tough. It hurt, but it felt good to be able to deal with it—without needing to deal with therapists or shrinks.

During his walks he thought about Flo, considered a thousand options, plotted vendettas against Waasdorp, schemed at ways to win his wife back—to the way she had been at the beginning. But it was hard to hold these things in his head as he was walking. And in June the smell of the linden trees—*basswood*—never failed to distract him. As the days passed the flowers fell, lining the neighborhood sidewalks and adding the perfume that always filled him, inexplicably, with a yearning to travel.

Toward mid-summer of that first pivotal year he realized that he was walking the distance with no noticeable limp at the end. And he felt pretty good at the end of three miles. He decided that walking was better therapy than talking to the shrink. Walking provided no answers, but then, neither did the shrink. And when he walked there was no one to annoy him with those eternal standby questions favored by shrinks … *How do you feel about that? What do you think you should do about it?*

Now, just when things with Flo were headed for the dumpster, the call from Washington came at him from out of the blue. He was beginning to think about the new term in September, but his plans were knocked askew by what the future might hold for him and Flo. Increasingly, he was coming to the discouraging conclusion that no offer he could hold out was likely to change her mind.

Then came the unexpected call from the CIA.

"Walt. Good morning. This is an old friend from the past. I'll bet you're not going to recognize my voice."

True enough. He didn't. It was the voice of Paul Chapman, the head spook when he had been with the Special Forces Team in Afghanistan. He remembered Chapman well enough. They had been through some harrowing times together. Chapman had been there when he lost his leg. On the medivac flight out, Walt had given him the glass evil eye he had carried as a talisman. It was a souvenir from his boyhood days in Turkey. During the flight, it had been deep in his pocket where it was pressing his hip—in contact with one of the metal pipes in the litter. The pressure was irritating despite the painkillers and Walt was depressed; frightened at what the future was going to hold, angry at the world. Obviously the fucking evil eye charm hadn't warded off anything. He fumbled in his pocket, pulled it out, flipped it to Chapman who was beside him in the medevac chopper. "Keep this for me," he had said.

Chapman's voice over the phone sounded much the same as he remembered. For a minute or two they exchanged polite inquiries about health and old friends. Paul

Chapman got down to business soon enough.

"Walt, it came to my attention a while ago that every year for the past several years you've been spending some time in Central Asia. I'm still working for the government. In an advisory capacity now. Advising several agencies you might say. All with ongoing activities in Central Asia. It seems like some of your interests could coincide with ours. So we would like to set up a meeting. At your convenience, of course. To explore the possibilities. To see if there are any tasks that could be mutually beneficial." He hesitated, waiting for a response from Walt, but when there was none, he continued.

"Actually, I think I might be understating the seriousness of the situation. I think. We—or I should say your country—needs your help." Walt still held off, not knowing what to expect.

"Since I know you at first hand, and since I know your accomplishments in the past, I feel confident that you could be of great service to the country. But everything depends on how our needs would match to your current interests and experience. If you could come to Washington for a day or two...." He let it hang.

"Major, one question comes to..." Walt had always called him Major after finding that was his equivalent grade in the CIA hierarchy.

"Just call me Paul, Walt. I'm a civilian now."

"Paul, would this assignment, by any chance, involve what you guys sometimes call "wet work?"

"Good heavens, Walt. Absolutely not. We...."

"Because all that is in the past and buried. I'm a teacher now."

"Let me put your mind at rest on that score, Walt. We're looking for someone with an academic background. Someone with your credentials. Plus someone who has some ability to communicate in Turkic languages. As I recall you could make yourself understood pretty well when we were over there."

"I'm a little better now. Not much. Just a little."

"Listen, Walt. I don't want to take up a lot of your time on the phone. But if you could find your way clear to come down for a couple of days, we'll send a plane. Or even a limo. Whichever you prefer. You can bring your wife. We'll book a hotel and she can shop or visit the museums during the day. I can assign someone to escort her anywhere she'd like to go. But we'd really like to talk with you. I think you would find it worth your while."

"Paul, our fall term starts the second week in September."

"Don't invent obstacles, Walt. We can help with that. You would be on paid leave from the university. No break in service. This would count with JBU just like your other programs. Trust me. I can guarantee you that this assignment—if you accept—would only help you with your career goals and would almost guarantee that you would get tenure. Come down for a few days and we can talk. Believe me, it will be fine with your university. I can't say any more now."

Chapter 26

Mr. Wu's Movie

"The Chinese surely hope... that our chilly attitude toward the brutal Uzbek dictator, Islam Karimov, becomes even chillier; this would open up the possibility of more pipeline and other deals with him, and might persuade him to deny us the use of the air base at Karshi-Khanabad. Were Karimov to be toppled in an uprising like the one in Kyrgyzstan, we would immediately have to stabilize the new regime or risk losing sections of the country to Chinese influence."

THE ATLANTIC MONTHLY, JUNE 2005

Wendell Cho is a Chinese citizen and a graduate of Rice University—in Houston. He spent nearly a decade in the U.S. and is a fan of American action movies. In his role as special projects manager for CHOCO's Wen Wu, he is called upon to do a wide variety of management tasks. Wendell's years in the Houston area not only gave him a lot of friends in the oil industry, but also enabled him to develop close associations with many NASA officials. Because he attended a large Baptist church in Houston, he could move in certain circles that would otherwise have been closed to him.

Wendell is a personable man somewhere around fifty. Strangely, he is unmarried. His friends in America and China have frequently wondered at this because he isn't bad looking, with regular features that are hard to remember or describe. He likes women well enough and has never been at a loss for an attractive female companion for a party or a celebration of any type. But nothing ever develops, and the women who have been out with him have never said anything that would hurt his reputation as a gentleman. Some of his business acquaintances speculated that he might be gay, but there has never been any sign.

To Wen Wu—who Wendell secretly thinks of as Yoda—Wendell is the perfect man to have at one's disposal. He understands arcane methodologies of systems analysis and program management that help him tackle any assignment. This is hardly an exaggeration.

A few years ago when CHOCO was considering whether to lease several new supertankers from a Malaysian consortium, or to spend a staggering sum to build and operate tankers of their own through a subsidiary corporation, Wen Wu and members of his board were having trouble sorting through mounds of conflicting economic data and cost analyses that were making them tear their hair. Mr. Wu called in Wendell Cho and gave him carte blanche to select a team of experts to make the decision process understandable while putting the board in possession of all relevant factors.

Cho put together a team of thirteen people, including—to everyone's surprise—five non-Chinese. The results took a three-day board presentation to be comprehensible. As a result of his work, CHOCO is now committed to a fleet of five supertankers, two of which have already been completed and are operating between the Persian Gulf and various Chinese refineries. Three more are currently under construction in Japanese shipyards. Numerous other examples could be cited of Wendell Cho's ability to tackle complex problems.

When Wen Wu conceived his idea for surveying gas and oil pipelines across Turkmenistan, the first person who came to mind was Wendell Cho. Cho, of course, knew little about the detailed work of pipeline surveys, but he was a quick study and he understood how to get a handle on the key cost elements of most projects.

Wu summoned Wendell Cho into his office weeks before the board meeting at which the chairman planned to float the concept of his movie project. He explained to Cho how efforts to survey a route across eastern Turkmenistan had been thwarted by the unpredictable behavior of Turkmenistan's president, Saparmurat Niyazov. When Wu suggested that a survey team might travel within a company of film makers he was watching Cho's face very carefully. Not a muscle flickered. By the time Wu had finished explaining his proposal, Cho was already beginning to formulate a plan of action to get his arms around the challenge.

"I have a friend in Hong Kong. Kenny Jiao. Perhaps you have heard of him. He makes films. He studied film making at UCLA and has many friends in the movie industry. He and I go way back. He will like this idea, and he can be trusted."

"This is not something that needs publicity," said Wu.

"No. Of course not. I understand. But you can trust me to know my man. Kenny is something of a prankster. This will appeal to him and he knows the importance of silence when it is required. Trust me, Mr. Wu."

"I do trust you, Wendell. That is why you are here."

"But, Mr. Wu. This will not be cheap. Film making is expensive and the returns are never certain. And I am sure you know that you will probably be compelled to follow the movie to its end."

"I would expect so. But I want a survey. I want a good survey and time is of the essence. The movie, if it returns its cost ... well, that is just something extra. Otherwise, its the cost of doing business. So, Mr. Cho. Will you wish to take some tea?" He hit the button to summon his assistant.

Six weeks after beginning his assignment, Wendell Cho was beginning to get a glimmer of the complexities in the arcane craft of movie making. He was having fun on this assignment which had already taken him to studios in Shanghai, Hong Kong and Bollywood in India. The Indians, he knew, had a reputation for making historic epics on low budgets. Not very good films, to be sure, but they earned money and they were put in the can for relatively small sums compared to American films. China's films were somewhere in the middle, although the ever-increasing Chinese penchant for elaborate special effects was driving up costs. And the salaries for big-name Chinese stars were rising rapidly.

Wendell spent a week in Los Angeles learning about movie making first hand. He was accompanied by Kenny Jiao who had many contacts with film company executives, agents, producers and directors. It was an education in predicting the unpredictable.

While they were traveling together, the two friends, Cho and Jiao, had engaged a team of Chinese scriptwriters to put together a film script for the life of a Mongol hero, like Genghis Khan or Timur the Lame, following the recommendations of Wen Wu. But Wu had given Cho extraordinary latitude to depart from his script idea if it proved to be impracticable. Cho was deferring judgment until he took a look at what the writers came up with. Even then, such was the nature of this capable man, that he would not make the final decision on the script's validity on his own. Instead he would depend upon recommendation from Jiao and others. This, of course, he did not need to cover in detail with Mister Wu.

Out of discussions with American studio officials, Cho formulated a few ground rules that would serve him well.

Mr. Wu had indicated that the presence of a large number of gorgeous Chinese film actresses would draw media attention in the country and in the world, and would distract attention from any work by survey teams. But major film stars tended to be prima donnas, requiring a great deal of care and attention. Some of the bigger stars, like their American counterparts, even insisted on having special trailers shipped ahead for themselves and their assistants. To avoid this, studio officials made it clear that it was easier to work with second-tier actresses—and actors—who were equally attractive and frequently just as talented as their better-known colleagues.

With very little effort, the casting directors brought forward by Kenny Jiao came up with more than a hundred of some of the most gorgeous females in China, or for that matter, the world. When Cho examined the photos of the women who had been identified as candidates for participation, he crossed that concern off his long list of activities requiring personal follow-up. Casting would not be a problem.

Cho came back from Los Angeles with a wealth of information and a few new friends in high places. One of the outcomes of his visit was the extension of an open invitation for several of his new West Coast friends to visit Shanghai. Some were interested in the city as a site for possible thrillers currently being cooked up in Hollywood studios. Others were simply interested in visiting China. One exec was anxious to visit the Terracotta Army at Xi'an. In any case, within four weeks of his return Wendell received calls from two different studio execs wanting to set up visits. It was easy to schedule these trips and the attractions of Shanghai's megalopolis were sufficient to keep his guests busy. When his visitors were not enjoying Chinese night life, or Chinese female companionship, they were more than willing to continue educating Cho in behind-the-scene details of movie making.

Wu was delighted to know that Wendell's visit to Los Angeles had borne fruit so quickly and it increased his confidence in his subordinate. Meanwhile, both men watched the constantly-changing situation in Central Asia to detect changes which might tip the scales in favor of multinational corporations based in other countries.

While writers in Hong Kong worked to produce a screen play for review by Kenny Jiao, the film maker visited Shanghai and met with Mr. Wu. Despite differences in their ages the two men got along famously. Over a long dinner, lubricated by quantities of rice wine, they discovered a shared interest in the poetry of the Shi King—known as the Odes of Confucius.

The older man, usually emotionless, expressed open surprise. "You know these works?" Wu asked.

"Ah, yes," said Kenny Jiao. "From my uncle. I can thank him. Shall I recite one?"

Mr. Wu clapped his hands with delight. "Please. By all means."

Kenny finished the wine in his cup and cleared his throat. "*Woman.*"

"*A clever man builds a city,*
A clever woman lays one low;
With all her qualifications, that clever woman
Is but an ill-omened bird.
A woman with a long tongue
Is a flight of steps leading to calamity;
For disorder does not come from heaven,
But is brought about by women.
Among those who cannot be trained or taught
Are women and eunuchs."

Mr. Wu clapped his hands and it looked as if his eyes were watering. Cho believed that he had never seen Mr. Wu so animated. There were three other company officers in their party and these men did not know how to react. But Mr. Wu was in the moment.

"And have you ever learned the one by Li T'ai Po called *'Drinking Alone in the Moonlight'*?" Wu asked.

"Not to recite it, Mr. Wu."

"But you have noticed that we can now see the moon from this comfortable place high above Shanghai?"

"I have noticed."

"I can't remember it all. Only a fragment."

"Please," said Kenny Jiao.

Mr. Wu took a sip of his wine and cleared his throat.

"'If Heaven did not love wine,
There would be no Wine Star in Heaven.
If Earth did not love wine,
There should be no Wine Springs on Earth.
Why then be ashamed before heaven to love wine?'

But…" he paused before finishing his lines, "…everyone should be drinking. Fill these cups again and I will continue.

'I have heard it said that thick wine is like the Virtous Worthies.
Wherefore it appears that we have swallowed both Sages and Worthies.
Why should we strive to be Gods and Immortals?
Three cups, and one can perfectly understand the Great Tao;
A gallon and all is in accord with nature.'"

In the hour that followed, more wine was poured and the fragments of more poems were recalled, and by the time the party broke up Mr. Wu and Mr. Jiao were good friends, both moderately drunk and emotional. They had agreed that when the movie was being filmed at an interesting location, Mr. Wu would be a guest at the site of shooting and Jiao would show him how the action looked through the lens of a camera.

Wendell Cho was well pleased at the shape his project was taking, but the film's cost estimate was still a matter of concern. To get a feel for what his film crew would experience in the field, Wendell Cho, accompanied by Kenny Jiao, two technical people and a budget expert hired from a film company in Hong Kong, visited Turkmenistan and made side trips into Uzbekistan and Tajikistan. They began in Ashkhabad, with excursions to Mary and Charjew. They traveled between Ashkhabad and Charjew by train. It was gritty and uncomfortable but it provided Cho with a feel for the desert that was missing in an air-conditioned van.

Back in Ashkhabad, they flew up to Urgench and motored across to Bukhara.

Uzbekistan was only slightly less weird than Turkmenistan. Cho was impressed by some of the ruins at Khiva, especially the portions of the old walls that remained. But he was unsure of the beautifully tiled minarets and towers. They looked too modern, too well cared for.

"Don't worry about that," Kenny Jiao told him with a laugh. "A lot of that can be taken care of in the studio. You will be surprised. It's just a matter of saying exactly what you want."

Bukhara was a promising location as were Samarkand and Tashkent—both in Uzbekistan. But the real focus would remain in Turkmenistan.

The trips to these cities were just window dressing in case anyone was paying attention. The scouting trips were interesting but the Chinese contingent complained of the lack of pork dishes in Islamic countries.

Usually they ate in restaurants specializing in Russian food, as preferable to ethnic Turkmen food. They also developed a fondness for Russian vodka that was available in several varieties not especially popular in Shanghai. At dinner, over a few drinks, the budget expert, who, like Kenny Jiao, had also attended UCLA's school of filmmaking, gave Wendell Cho some pointers on the economics of film-making.

"In most cases," he said, "the makers of indie films have trouble finding financing. That's what you are in this case. An independent. But unlike most one-time film makers you can pay for your own project. Thus, you will avoid the need for bonding."

"Explain bonding," Cho said.

"When a small filmmaker borrows money from several sources, they need to be assured that the film will be made. As a guarantee that they will at least have some chance of recouping their investment, they require a bonding. This insures that in the event the film process collapses, they will recover their investment. It's not inexpensive. To bond most independent films, the cost is roughly 20 percent of the total."

"Not unreasonable, I suppose," Cho yawned. It had been a long day.

"Basically, it's insurance," Mr. Tang, the budget expert, explained. "Stated differently, after a company raises the amount of money required, they sometimes find that they only have 80 percent of what they need. I know. It sounds like they are incompetent. Nevertheless, that's a typical experience."

"But we won't require it," Cho said. "That won't apply to us." *What's wrong with this guy? He's flogging a dead horse.* "So what are the elements of cost are we most likely to overrun? In your opinion?"

"Weather can always be a factor. Storms. I don't know if this area is vulnerable to earthquakes. Also you always have to pay close attention to the costs for leasing of animals. Horses mostly. Some camels. We still don't have all the estimates in. If we are able to hold fast to a shooting schedule we should be able to keep the costs of catering and lodging within our budgetary estimates. I intend to identify a contingency allowance for schedule slips as a line item." Cho was revising his opinion. Maybe Mr.

Tang was a good addition to the team.

"Now for the hard question," said Cho, stifling another yawn. "Do you think we can break even on sales of a film after it has been completed?"

Kenny Jiao was sipping his drink. He laughed so hard while he was drinking that it snorted from his nose. He looked for a napkin, and finding none, wiped his nose on the edge of the tablecloth. "The screenplay hasn't even been completed," he gasped.

Mr. Tang, the cost expert, never even smiled. "I have seen the roster of Chinese women being considered for roles in your film. If you use these girls, any film you complete will find some market in the United States. I don't believe you will stand to lose a great deal, no matter what you produce. Just let these girls walk around in tight silk and people will pay to watch."

Wendell Cho turned to Kenny Jiao. "So Mr. Wu is no fool. Do you think he counted on this result?"

Jiao laughed again. "There is no logic. Bad films can succeed. Good films can fail. Wen Tang may be on the mark. I think you will be surprised at how we may fare. At least, I hope so."

Cho signaled to the waiter to bring their check. "Let's go to the bar and have one more drink." He was beginning to feel optimistic. "Maybe we should go into the filmmaking business. Full time."

Chapter 27

Valentin's Little Sister

"I think everyone born in my country feels what the land felt, because every Kazakh carries his land in his blood. For forty years, the plains were shaken by nuclear or thermonuclear bombs, a total of 456 in 1989. Of those tests, 116 were carried out in the open, which amounts to a bomb twenty-five hundred times more powerful than the one that was dropped on Hiroshima during the Second World War. As a result, thousands of people were contaminated by radioactivity and subsequently contracted lung cancer, while thousands of children were born with motor deficiencies, missing limbs or mental problems."

THE ZAHIR
PAOLO COELHO

Valentin, now the brains behind Russia's most powerful drug distribution network, was not an only child. He had a younger sister. Her name was Tatiana and she was six years younger, not close enough for them to be tightly bonded. They didn't grow up playing together because of the age difference—and the fact that she was a slight, delicate child.

Tatiana had blonde hair and blue eyes. They hardly looked like brother and sister. But that was a whole other story. As the proverb goes, "It's a wise child that knows its own father." And although they weren't playmates, Valentin did have protective feelings for his little sister.

During the years when he was assigned to the Cosmodrome at Baikonur, he had a chance to see her from time to time. She had married a mining engineer who had worked for a time at various locations in Siberia, and—a year into their marriage—he provided her with a comfortable apartment in the Kazakhstan capital of Astana. The air connections between Astana and Baikonur were good and Val visited on several occasions.

Astana wasn't a bad town. To visit. But no one should spend a lifetime there. Same latitude as Kursk. Cold as hell in winter. Then, her husband's business turned sour for reasons Val could never understand. The engineer found himself unemployed after three years into the marriage. They gave up the nice apartment and moved into something substantially less comfortable.

The husband began to drink around the time that Tatiana discovered she was pregnant. There was little money for the bare essentials of life, and Valentin did not want to dwell for too long on what Tatiana may have had to do in order to continue eating. She cropped her long hair into a short bob, and with her enormous blue eyes, slender body and tiny breasts she was certain to be appealing to a certain type of man. Val continued to visit even after their circumstances became reduced, and each time he would leave money with her. But her husband, Evgeny, was too proud to remain at home whenever Val visited his sister. So he stopped the visits believing they did more harm than good. For a while he sent money in the form of cheques. But after six months some of his letters had been returned and he lost contact with his sister.

He never knew what happened to the child she was carrying . Was it born and died soon afterward? Did she lose it late in her pregnancy? He never learned with any degree of certainty. But he was able to find out that when she died she wasn't acting as a mother to any living children. He wondered. Somewhere in Russia—or anywhere in the world—might he have a living niece or nephew?

He was able to track down some of the events in her life. After her husband's descent into alcoholism, Tatiana struggled for a time to get help for him. But from where? After wrestling with poverty and despair for a time, the young woman turned to the only trade she was qualified for. From there, her decline was swift. She was frail and sensitive, and some street denizens found the perfect victim to ply with drugs. She became addicted to heroin and drifted away from her husband who was, by now, too badly impaired by alcohol to do anything about it.

Tatiana toward the end had been accustomed to frequent public spaces, bus terminals, railway stations and, on occasion, the airport, because they offered a degree of warmth, access to public toilets with potable water and, from time to time, clients with money.

It was a descent into the lower circles of hell, and that was where she was living when she was found by an American evangelist preacher outside an Astana bus terminal. The 37-year-old preacher, from some Baptist denomination in Arkansas, had been in Russia for six years and his "soul count" was dramatically below the target he had set for himself. He was moved by the sight of the shivering woman and by something indefinable in her enormous blue eyes. The preacher, whose name was Bob, took her home to the small apartment where he lived with his wife, Vanessa, and gave the half-starved Russian woman the first meal she had enjoyed in three days. Both Christian workers who by now knew enough Russian to carry on a moderate conversation, were filled with compassion for the woman. In her secret heart of hearts Vanessa wished that the skinny woman was not quite so uncommonly attractive, but she looked as if she was on the edge of starvation. Her concealed feelings were something Vanessa could never share with Bob.

When Vanessa helped her clean up in their tiny bathroom, she was secretly pleased to see that Tatiana was almost completely flat-chested. That was good. Bob liked big ones. When they were alone together, he called them her "twin fawns," from the Song of Solomon. *Say what you will about this good man; he knows his Scripture.*

Tatiana was covered with bruises. Every part of her body had dark contusions, some in places where one might never expect to receive a blow. Vanessa wanted to ask her about them, but it seemed inappropriate. Maybe later. After they got to know each other better. She asked Tatiana if she wanted to stay overnight in their apartment and Tatiana said yes. The following day was a Sunday and Bob was preaching a sermon in the storefront church whose low rent was being paid by contributions from the congregation in Arkansas.

It was easy for the impoverished woman to say yes. The building would be heated and there would be hot tea and food after the service, if not at the church then at home with Bob and Vanessa. The church meeting was small. There were only a dozen people in all, counting the three of them.

Tatiana stayed with her American hosts for the better part of a week before she disappeared. They told Valentin's investigators they had not seen her for more than three weeks when they learned from others that she had been found in the doorway of an unused building by the railroad tracks. The brief announcement in the Almaty newspaper described her as a heroin addict, and it was believed that she might have died from exposure. The nighttime temperature was well below zero on the night before her body was found.

Val learned this after he made a concerted effort to locate her. After a long interval of no contact, he was hoping to see her again. When he learned the circumstances of her death, he left his office for the rest of the day and diverted himself with alcohol and flesh, two dependable anodynes.

Several times in the evening an image of Tatiana formed in his head. For reasons he could not understand, she always appeared to him as she had looked in her teens, long blond hair below her shoulders. He saw her as if she was a creature from a story by Turgenev, in a soft, flowing dress of flowered cotton, rows of poplars in the background, golden leaves on the ground, and an old country house somewhere in the distance. It was a place he had never been before. And yet it seemed to be real, as if they had been there together.

Each time she appeared, he dispelled the image by squeezing harder on the object nearest to hand, glass or flesh. *She would get it from somewhere,* he thought. *Whether it came from me or not. The blame rests with her.*

Blame? This was not a term he could use comfortably. It nagged at him that he had been unable to learn where she was buried.

PART 3

HERDING CATS

Chapter 28

Notes from Walt's Briefing

"Yes, and thou must learn how to make pictures of roads and mountains and rivers—to carry these pictures in thine eye till a suitable time comes to set them down upon paper. Perhaps some day, when thou are a chain-man (surveyor's assistant), I may say to thee when we are working together: 'Go across those hills and see what lies beyond.'"

KIM
RUDYARD KIPLING

In describing Kellogg to Walt, Chapman had added this bit of information. "Kellogg is the go-to guy if for any reason the shit hits the fan. Between Gina Santorini and Paul Kellogg, you have two very capable resources on the off chance that anything gets sticky."

"That should make me feel good, I suppose. But somehow, it doesn't seem to be doing the job."

"The last person is someone you already know."

"Someone I know?"

"A former student." Walt looked puzzled.

"Katya. You remember her?"

"Ekatarina Kalashvili? Are you kidding? The girl from Kazakhstan?"

"That's the one. She's been with you before. On your second trip, I believe." *How did he know that?* Walt wondered.

"Yeah. Christ. She was a big help. Speaks Russian. Smart as a whip. Nice looking, too. She did her master's thesis on *Metalworking in the Culture of the Scyths*, if I remember correctly."

"She's also an expert on oil production. Just at the moment she's at a workshop in Houston put on by the American Petroleum Institute."

"Are we talking about the same woman? My Katya is a horse person."

"She's the same." Paul pushed his chair away from the table and the expression on his face changed. "I hope what I'm going to tell you won't make you angry. Katya works for us."

"Jesus Chri..."

"Hold on. She was working for us when she enrolled in the master's program at JBU. That was just a little sabbatical and she really *was* interested in the Scyths."

"Don't tell me she really comes from Chicago."

"No. She really was born in Kazakhstan. But she came here in her early teens. And she's very bright."

"What else don't I know? Jesus Christ! Katya? You guys checked me out?"

"That's not exactly how I might have chosen to phrase it."

"I bet. Dammit, Paul. Why couldn't you have let me know? Never mind. Don't explain."

"Let you know what? There was nothing to know. She was legit. She took your tests. You're taking this all wrong. Listen to me, Walt. Trust me, and turn this loose. Trust me. OK?"

Walt stood up and walked around the table. When he sat back down he gave Chapman an angelic smile.

"OK! So what's next?"

"That's pretty much it. At least for now. You'll have a very capable group who will appear to be a mixed bag. Actually, they will *be* a mixed bag. You're going to take them on a sweep through the Central Asia corridor of the Silk Road where the New Great Game is likely to play out. That is, if you accept. From the Caspian Sea to the borders of China. It's today's highway for drugs and arms smuggling. And before long it will be the route for gas and oil to reach China. It's where everything is..."

"I'm working to include China."

"Yes, I know. But right now there is a lot going on between Afghanistan and the routes into eastern Europe."

"How much do I need to know about the specific mission of these cats I'll be herding?"

"You don't need to know any more than I've already told you. Look, you have been around the block and you have a soldier's perspective. If things should for any reason turn sour, you can't tell what you don't know. Not that we expect anything to turn sour. You don't need to know any more than you normally know about the students you conduct on trips. Treat these folks like you'd treat your students. Only now they are alums. And don't be surprised if some of them cut the lectures from time to time.

They'll have separate agendas. And they'll probably complain if you get too boring."

"I'm getting into something that I don't understand at all. I'm standing in front of the orchestra without a score. And if I had one, I'm not sure I could read the music."

"It's recorded music. Just wave your arms as convincingly as possible while the sound track is playing. Don't worry about the music. That will take care of itself. Believe me Walt, you are the perfect man for this job. In every way. We need some people who can roam around with a modest degree of freedom. And we think your gang can do it. You can pull it off. Ah! There is one other key point you need to be aware of. Each of your students has expertise in certain areas that may cause him or her to be absent from your standard program. They won't ask for your permission to absent themselves, and they may or may not let you know when they might be absent. You should be aware that this might occur and make your plans accordingly."

"I'd like to say I don't have the slightest idea what the hell you're talking about, but I'm afraid I do know."

"Your job is to run your tour. Sometimes you might need to hold up for a day or two to accommodate any unforeseen schedule hiccups. Other times you should probably hold to your schedule and count on the missing person to catch up."

"Jesus! And how am I supposed to know when and how to make these kinds of decisions?"

"You'll just know. That's why I wanted you. It will be situational, and you'll be able to make the right calls. I'm confident."

"How nice for you. What am I getting into here? This gets worse and worse."

"You're exactly the right man. If I had your talent for this job, I'd go myself, but I couldn't do it."

"I don't even know what you're asking me to do."

"Lead a small group tour of college students, faculty or alums along the great cities of the Silk Road. You've done it before, and done it beautifully. We have a full report from one of your students."

"Katya?"

"Katya."

"I knew something was unusual about her. That little bitch. She took me in."

"So she said. No, not that she took you in. But that she suspected you knew she wasn't exactly who she claimed."

"She was just too good to be true."

"She is good. That's why she's going back. Don't be angry with her. She worries about that. That you'll be angry or resentful. Can I tell her that she's still just a grad student?"

"Tell her. Yes."

"And that it won't come up between you?"

"I think I can manage it. I'll go to work on my head on the flight back."

Paul Chapman laughed. "That's why I insisted we pick you for this job."

"I'm to be the nominal leader? The straw man boss?"

"In a sense, that's it—if you insist on putting it that way."

"Well, Paul, the first thing you should know is that I'll be taking another grad student along. To help with the admin stuff. And it won't be Katya."

"We'll need to check him out, you realize."

"OK. I'll show you mine when you show me yours. She's not a him."

"We'll need details."

That afternoon Walt checked out of the accommodations provided by the Agency and spent the evening walking around the streets of Georgetown. On an impulse he had dinner at an Afghan restaurant where he had to wait thirty minutes to get a tiny table. After dinner, he checked into a Holiday Inn opposite the notorious Watergate complex. He dropped his bag in the room and spent a few minutes walking outside—trying to think clearly.

Herding cats. What the hell have I let myself in for? he asked himself as he climbed the outside stairs to his second-floor room. Herding cats. He unstrapped his leg and placed it beside the bed—within easy reach. For a few moments he considered calling his home number on the off chance that Flo might have come back. But he rejected the idea.

Just as he was falling off to sleep, a poem popped into his head, and—like an earworm—it wriggled around from start to finish several times before he fell asleep. It was by Kipling. He couldn't remember the title of the poem and he wasn't sure that he had all the words right. But it wouldn't let go.

"When you're wounded and left on Afghanistan's plains
And the women come out to cut up what remains,
Just roll to your rifle and blow out your brains,
And go to your god like a soldier."

He remembered that Kipling had written "Gawd."

Fuck! Fuck! Fuck! Katya was working for the Agency when I talked her into going along on my first trip with students. I knew there was something about her. I thought she was too good to be true. These guys have been sizing me up all this time.

And now he would be agreeing to herd cats for the Agency. They had lied to him, were possibly lying to him now. *Possibly?* Probably! But why? What was really going on?

Chapter 29

Dreaming of Somewhere Else

"He says, 'There's nothing left of me.
I'm like a ruby held up to the sunrise.
Is it a stone, or a world
made of redness? It has no resistance
to sunlight.'
This is how Hallaj said I am God.
and told the truth."

FROM "THE SUNRISE RUBY"
THE ESSENTIAL RUMI
TRANSLATED BY COLEMAN BARKS

The Russians, Val and the Mighty Handful, were in the Romanian coastal town of Constanta for the purpose of fixing a leak in their supply chain going up the Danube River into Central Europe. The offender had been dealt with—rather severely as it turned out; he had lost a hand—and the example of his punishment had been communicated to his colleagues. That communication was equally as important as the punishment.

It had taken several days of investigation to ferret the thief out of his hiding place and the Mighty Handful had believed they deserved a few days of recreation. The waterfront bars and hotels around Constanta were teeming with gorgeous whores from Romania, Bulgaria and Russia. The Romanian girls seemed to be uniformly appealing. Yuri licked his lips after bolting his vodka. "Of all the whores in the world, Romanian whores are the best." He was drunk.

Val didn't want to argue with him on that score. He smiled to himself, thinking *Yes, and of all the whores in Romania, Mira is the sweetest.*

He had met her on a prior visit to Constanta and had not been able to forget her easily. She was a curious mix he had not encountered before. Small. Uncommonly pretty and uncommonly strong. He enjoyed her company out of bed almost as much as.... Saint's blood if she was not unforgettable. Like a flame. And so—wet.

While the Mighty Handful used their brief holiday to run up their lifetime scores, Val had sought out Mira and made arrangements to purchase her time for the balance of his stay.

On a warm afternoon in late summer, Val was sitting on the terrace of a small hotel in Constanta with a view of the shingle beach. It was said that this was the place where Ovid, the Roman poet of love, was exiled after displeasing his emperor, Augustus. For the poet, this now pleasant city was a barbarian pest hole at the edge of the civilized world. Val had never read Ovid, but he had learned of him from the American girl who took him to a cottage on Cape Cod one memorable summer while he was at Harvard.

Val was waiting for Mira to come down and when he was with her he preferred to drink little so that he could enjoy her more. The counter at the bar had a tray piled high with ripe pomegranates. Over at the edge of the bar he could see a crate filled with the fruit, probably just arrived from Turkey. While he was waiting for Mira, he asked the barman to make him a glass of freshly squeezed pomegranate juice. As the barman busied himself with the fruit, Val took a small table by a window where sunlight streamed across the tablecloth.

He checked his PDA to see if he owed any phone calls and found that he was clear. The barman approached and set the small tumbler of fresh juice on the table. Rays from the sun gleamed through the ruby liquid in the glass to cast a rosy-colored shadow on the table. He turned the glass, but the beautiful shadow did not change. The startling color triggered some memory in Val that he could not place and for several minutes he fingered the tumbler, trying to recall images that the color had stimulated. His brain was split.

From time to time his memory shifted from the color to the ugly business of the recent past and he wondered if the problem had really been solved permanently or if other members in the chain would become greedy and require another visit. Then he thought about the girl. This was not the first time he had been with Mira, and hopefully, it would not be the last.

This most recent transportation arrangement, he felt, might suffice for two years or so, until his overland route was being managed by a staff in India. Then, he would cancel the arrangements and handle the transportation all the way to buyers in Amsterdam, Marseilles or New York. Baltimore, too, had all the signs of being a good destination. He had only been there once, but it seemed to have all the attributes he was looking for.

Val's mind was beginning to shuffle all the details from the day's business as he turned and moved the small tumbler of pomegranate juice to catch the sun and manipulate the ruby shadow on the table. It was a beautiful color. He was reminded of a poem by Rumi that he remembered reading to a girl he was pursuing in Istanbul. That was years ago. The memory made him smile as he tried to recall the magical lines about the red light reflected through a ruby—and love. But the exact lines would not come to him even though he knew they were there, etched into his subconsciousness—somewhere—elusive and unrecoverable.

As he let his mind drift—playing with the shifting ruby light that pierced the pomegranate's heart blood—he was aware that Mira was in the doorway, looking at him. With the slightest twist of her head, almost imperceptible to all but the most careful observer, she asked wordlessly, *May I join?*

He beckoned to the girl and she came to the table and took a seat beside him. The Romanian girl had been with him twice before, during two brief visits here in Constanta. He had met her in a bar along the waterfront. It wasn't apparent what the hell she was, a gypsy, perhaps? Who could tell in melting pot Constanta? She had never told him anything of her background and he hadn't bothered to ask. The life story of a whore? Who wants to know? Or someone who had been living for a time with a rich man who had died? Or dumped her for another? Who could tell? Who would care?

She was pretty enough, a girlish figure, short curly hair and dark eyes. In a western place she was appealing in western clothing; he had seen her once in a cocktail dress, in a private western club. Her figure was great for clothes although she was not quite so slender as a classic model. Her teeth were dazzling and she knew that her smile had an effect on men. She had been available for the evening when Val had arrived, and he, at loose ends for the next day, decided to use her for the full duration of his stay. "You will be with me twenty-four hours a day," he said. "And when I am away, you will go with no one. Understood?" She had nodded wordlessly, *Yes.* "How much?" he asked. "To do this?" she whispered. She looked him over carefully before giving him an enigmatic smile. "How much do you think I will be worth?"

What enhanced her appeal to him was her ability to dress for the east. She could slip into Muslim clothing and tie her scarf to be at once publicly circumspect and privately flirtatious in a way that made him wonder if maybe she had been born a Muslim.

On his last visit to Constanta he witnessed her chameleon ability on the following day after she spent the night in his room. When he told her where he was heading the next day, she excused herself, slipped out of the room before he noticed and reappeared in twenty-five minutes in entirely different garb. The memory returned with a startling vividness. Moments later, when she had knocked softly on his door he had, at first, not recognized her. She stood with lowered eyes, a Muslim woman. He remembered that moment.

"And then, I may enter?" she shyly asked.

"Mira. Of course. Come in. I hardly heard you leave. And when I saw you were gone, I wasn't sure if you would return."

"So then, I may accompany you today?" she replied.

"If you choose. You understand where I am go…"

"As you see me, so I am," she said.

During that day, walking through the Muslim neighborhoods of the Constanta, this woman became thoroughly a dutiful wife. They barely exchanged a dozen words in ten hours. Back in the room, he had asked her, "Are you Muslim?"

"Only in some ways," she responded enigmatically.

"You are a Muslim. It is okay. Of no matter to me."

"Only in some ways," she persisted. In twenty minutes she was back again, in western dress and looking very stylish. She would turn heads in a room. Without the scarf her short bobbed hair made her look very young, and she smiled to see her effect on him. Moments later he was reminded why he took her in the first place. She was a tireless fuck. Tireless.

And now he was back in Constanta again. And back with Mira. Then he remembered something about the poem by Rumi that had been eluding him. The poem had been about a man in Baghdad thinking about Cairo but when he got to Cairo he was thinking about Baghdad. That's what he had been doing. In Ashkhabad he had been thinking about Constanta; but now, in Constanta, he had been thinking about Ashkhabad. He had been thinking that he would like to take Mira to Ashkhabad. Sunlight through the ruby liquid had been a trigger. He had never had thoughts like this before.

"How would you like to take a walk on the beach?" he asked.

The pair had walked along the beach for over two hours. When the sun began to sink they both realized they were hungry. Val found a hotel that featured Russian *zakuski*, and they each made a complete meal from the variety of hors d'oeuvres that were arranged on the long tables. Then the sated couple made their way back to the hotel at a leisurely pace, neither one wanting to indicate how anxious they were to get naked. They had eaten a considerable variety, but neither one had wanted a full stomach. Val was hoping they'd make it into his room without having to exchange words with any member of The Mighty Handful. If he could spend a couple of days without talking to any of these savages, it would be so much the better. Fortunately, none of them was in sight as the couple made their way to Val's room.

It was much, much later when Val opened his eyes, starving, and saw that she was awake beside him, watching him like a hungry cat.

"You want food," he said, unsmiling.

"I do. And it is late."

"Not too late for food."

"I will go."

"Me," he barked, trying to sound fierce. But she was unimpressed.

"I will go. You can speak only ten words in Romanian. And even those ten sound like shit."

She made him laugh, this girl. They had been conversing mostly in Turkish, which she spoke well and he spoke passably.

"We will go together," he conceded.

"I will pee first," she said, laughing as she jumped from the bed and skipped into the bathroom."

Val lay silent for a moment, listening to her. When the toilet flushed he got up and went to stand behind her at the sink. Together they looked at themselves in the mirror. For several moments they stood, he clasping her as they studied one another closely. It was the first time he had really noticed her eyelashes.

"You are Romanian," he said.

"Of course," she answered, giggling. "This is Romania."

"Yet your Turkish is perfect."

"I lived in Turkey for six years. Actually closer to seven. From eighteen to twenty-four—twenty five."

"Your family worked in Turkey?"

"I was the companion of a wealthy man. He gave me a place to live. In Konya. He owned a brewery. The best beer in Turkey is made in Konya."

"And yet ... Konya does not permit the consumption of alcohol."

"God be praised," she laughed and made a wry face.

He turned her body to face him and kissed her eyelashes, then her mouth.

"You were the companion of a wealthy man?" He decided to play with her. "You taught Romanian to his children?"

"His companion."

"Did shopping for his wife? Cooking perhaps?"

She was an experienced game player and pulled away from him and swagged back into the bedroom, tossing a glance over her shoulder. "His companion."

"But what does this entail, what respon...."

"Companion, companion, companion." She threw a pillow at him.

Suddenly it dawned on Val that Konya, the city where she had lived with her benefactor, had been the home town for Rumi. He held the pillow where she could not get it back. "Konya is the city of Rumi."

"This is well known," she said, struggling to get the pillow from him.

"You lived in the same city as Rumi."

"As I have told you. Yes. He lived there. He is buried there. His tomb sees many visitors."

"You must tell me," he said, tossing her the pillow.

"Only if you treat me gently," she said, hitting him again.

"We will go and find food," he said. "Together."

"I was his companion. He gave me money and a good life. I let him fuck me and I kept him well pleased. We both got what we wanted. Not so different from you, Mister Russian big shot. Not so different."

She went to the window, feigning pique. "And you are lying. It's not food that you want." The game had shifted.

"Why don't you come with me to visit Turkmenistan," he asked, responding to a sudden impulse. The question was not well thought out. It simply popped into his head. Because she did not answer at once, he thought perhaps she might have no knowledge of Turkmenistan. He had not the slightest idea of what she did, what her past had been, where she might be headed. It was an absurd question and he was embarrassed to have asked as soon as the words were out of his mouth."

"I will give an answer. But all in good time."

It was not until the next morning at breakfast that Mira told him that she would go with him to Ashkhabad if he would agree to pay for her return ticket in advance. Then, as soon as she announced her decision she excused herself to visit the lady's room—as if to give him a moment to reflect upon his good fortune.

Now, as she stood in the doorway, smiling at him as if they had been born to the same mother, he felt happy that he had asked and she had accepted. Amazing! She was nothing but a little Romanian whore, whom he had known for less than—what—seven or eight days all together? And yet he felt closer to her than to his own sister. With the least nod of his head he summoned her, and she came toward him proudly, half a dozen heads turning to watch her walk past. He was happy he had asked and happy that she had accepted. How would the savage bastards with him react to her presence in Ashkhabad? He didn't want to think too carefully about that.

Chapter 30

Cats Across Central Asia

> "... but I
> Have never known my grandsire's furrow'd face,
> Nor seen his lofty house in Seistan,
> Nor slaked my thirst at the clear Helmund stream;
> But lodged among my father's foes, and seen
> Afrasiab's cities only, Samarcand,
> Bokhara, and lone Khiva in the waste,
> And the black Toorkmun tents; and only drunk
> The desert rivers, Moorghab and Tejend,
> Kohik, and where the Kalmuks feed their sheep,
> The northern Syr; and this great Oxus stream,
> The yellow Oxus, by whose brink I die."
>
> FROM "SOHRAB AND RUSTUM"
> MATTHEW ARNOLD

From the moment he agreed to the assignment, Walt began to have second thoughts. *Why the hell would they pick me?* he wondered. *They could have chosen anyone in the world. I'm not a spy, not a military expert, and have zero experience in herding a gang of spooks. I don't have the least idea of what these people are looking for, except that it's probably related to drug trafficking on the Silk Road. Weapons, maybe. WMD. And oil. It has to have some connection to oil. But what?*

Walt had asked for more information about each of the members of his group, and Paul Chapman took him to a quiet room to give him a brief verbal rundown on each of the seven.

"The idea is," said Chapman, "to make the group appear like a typical group of American tourists from academia. Professors, faculty members, alumni. A college tour. Mixed ages. A married couple, singles, academics and a wealthy business type, all interested in exotic travel.

Gina Santorini will be one of the people you'll want to work closely with. She'll be your travel agent. Looking for local details in each city you visit so she can book other groups."

"So what does she do in real life, when she's not being a travel agent?"

"You don't need to worry about that. She's a travel agent. Period. She'll probably work with you more closely than any of the others. She can help. Just let her.

Betty and Charles Bismarck. They will be a real estate couple from Oklahoma. Tourists with academic backgrounds. Interested in architecture, museums, all the standard stuff of tourists."

"Shouldn't I be taking all this down?"

"No need. You can study their dossiers before you leave. Anyway, each of your group members will send you specific information in response to your advertisement. They're your clients."

"My advertisement? I never ran any ad. My prior trips were with groups of college students recruited on campus."

"You've run an ad now. It's been run in the last issue of the JBU magazine that goes out to alumni. Some responses should be in your post office box. Remind me to give you the key to your box before you leave."

"An ad? What kind of ad? I don't have a post office box." Walt wanted to get angry but he knew that would just be a waste of time. Whatever they had done, it was whiskey under the bridge.

"Don't get heated up. We had to gamble that you'd take the assignment. I took the big liberty of telling them you were not the kind of man to turn down a request like this. I'll show you the ad before you leave. Let me tell you about the others in your group."

Chapman got up and refilled his cup from the insulated thermos on the table. "This is still good and hot. Want more?" Walt shook his head.

"The Bismarcks. Betty and Charles are one of a handful of husband and wife pairs that are occasionally employed by the Agency in a team role. They're in their early fifties and have been posted to assignments around the world, usually together where marriage is part of their cover. Watching them at work it's hard to discern how much of their banter is intended as part of their act and how much is completely natural. Much of their work has been in the area of drug interdiction.

The others? Kevin McLaughlin is a senior analyst in his early 50's who retired from the Agency after 22 years of service and a bullet wound in the shoulder while posted to Iraq. The bullet appeared to have been intended for someone else. McLaughlin retired to his farm in New York's Finger Lakes region where he raises apples. Since retiring he has studied pomology at Cornell and has become knowledgeable about apples. By including him as part of the team, it has been possible to make contacts with university people in Kazakhstan and Uzbekistan concerning their orchard management practices and apple culture. He brings credibility for contact with academicians in Central Asia, and his interest in fruit and agriculture provides him with legitimate reasons for being afoot in remote areas. This guy is going to look solid. You'll like him.

Personal contacts were used to talk him out of retirement and back into harness for one more crack at a field assignment. One of his chief roles is to provide a sense of the extent to which agriculture has been adapted to produce drugs for consumption in the west. He's been briefed for two weeks—on techniques for estimating field sizes and on things to look for that indicate drugs are being shipped. By the way, each of these individuals will have his own techniques for communicating with key contacts, and that's all you need to know. You'll like Kevin. He's easy to work with.

Keener. Here's a photo. Bill Keener is in his mid-thirties and is relatively new to fieldwork, and to Central Asia. He has a degree from a law school in California, but has never practiced. This is only his fourth assignment in the field and it's not one that seems especially promising for his career. He went to school for Arabic, but unfortunately he appears to lack a natural aptitude for languages and he has retained only enough to exchange a few words and phrases in the dialect spoken in Egypt.

Bill, to put it bluntly, is somewhat pissed by being tagged to accompany a group of nearly over-the-hill geezers on what he sees as little more than a pleasure trip to Asia. He's been coached to collect information on transportation capabilities; trucks, trains and air, to assess possibilities for interception and interdiction. He has something of a reputation with his supervisors as a sharp-eyed observer and a ferret for details. He'll be your tourist with the active camera."

Chapman only knew part of the story on Keener. One other factor in Bill's discontent with this assignment stemmed from the fact that following a recent painful breakup with his fiancée of two years, she recently called him in tears, begging him to forgive her and resume their relationship. She gave a convincing performance and he, remembering the smell and feel of her, would have been only too willing to resume. But he had just been preempted for a week of special high-security training in preparation for Central Asia. Her heart-rending sobs were still ringing in his ears and they only intensified his dissatisfaction with this assignment. But he didn't feel secure enough to turn down the job.

Chapman poured another cup of coffee before continuing. "Paul Kellogg? You'll relate to this guy. Former military with the Special Forces. Came into the Agency after assignments in Afghanistan. He's an expert with various types of weapons and with demolitions. Many of his assignments have been short-duration stints in the Middle East, but he speaks no foreign languages. He's in his early forties and is in good physical shape.

Kellogg and his Vietnamese wife live on Kent Island in Chesapeake Bay and are somewhat reclusive. They have no children and they live aboard a former working skipjack, a kind of oyster boat, that they have converted into a floating residence. Even among his associates at the Agency, Kellogg is something of an unknown quantity, but it's all part of his act. He's intelligent, capable and extremely resourceful. He's the go-to guy in the remote chance that the shit hits the fan and you have to make some tough calls."

"Jesus Christ, Paul, what are you getting me into? Shit hitting the fan? Like what?"

Chapman smiled and leaned forward to pat Walt on the shoulder. "Nothing that you won't be able to handle and I think I can say that with some confidence. Come on, let's get some lunch and then we'll come back and you can learn some more about your clients."

Walt laughed mirthlessly. "My herd of cats, you mean."

Chapter 31

Gina Santorini

> "*It was the Byzantine Emperor Justinian I (AD 527-565) who persuaded two Persian monks to smuggle silkworms hidden in bamboo canes from China to Constantinople. Silk production became a state monopoly, based in Bursa.*"
>
> THE STORY OF SILK
IN "INSIGHT GUIDE—TURKEY"

Chapman was continuing his information dump after lunch. A couple of other spooks were in the conference room, but they were apparently just observers.

"Gina Santorini is an FBI agent who has had nearly 15 years of field experience. Early forties. Her name sounds as if she's of Italian extraction, and in fact her father was a Sicilian. But he married a Turkish woman from Izmir before bringing Gina to the US. Gina grew up in the Chicago area where she was raised in close contact with her Turkish-speaking mother and grandmother. She grew up bilingual and her speaking skills were enhanced by several visits to Turkey and prolonged stays with relatives living there."

Walt held up his hand. "How come she didn't learn Italian from her father?"

"The Sicilian? He was a bad dude. Well known in the Chicago crime world. He was croaked by some competitor when Gina was three or four. No. She definitely grew up part Turkish.

In addition to her language background, she's well versed in the customs of Islam, learned during her visits to western Turkey and the Middle East. Her skin and hair coloring enable her to pass easily as a Turk, Greek, Italian, Palestinian or any other Mediterranean female. These natural attributes were enhanced when Gina attended Georgetown University and studied Arabic. Most of her studies focused on the Arabic spoken in Egypt and, although she can't pass as a native speaker, she easily passes as a

Turkish woman with some limited knowledge of Arabic." Chapman paused, rose and refilled his coffee cup before continuing.

"Her language skills enable Gina to penetrate many communities that would otherwise be closed to westerners, but what makes her valuable as an FBI agent is her ability on the street. Growing up in Chicago gave her a hard edge—sharpened with the special training available at the Bureau.

In the past, on more than one occasion, Gina has operated alone and she's still alive to tell the tale. Most of the agents who have worked with her didn't enjoy the assignment, but they all acknowledge that she is dedicated and very capable. Why don't they like her? She works too close to the edge. Unmarried. She's a risk taker and so far no one who has been in the field with her has ever seen her show fear. It may have something to do with growing up in an ethnic Turkish environment.

Despite her inability to father a child, Gina has more balls than ninety percent of the guys in the FBI. You wouldn't want to get crossways of her."

Walt stood up to stretch his legs. "Somehow, everything you're telling me isn't making me feel better about this. I can't run as fast as I usta."

"Speaking of which," Chapman interrupted, "How do you like your leg? We could get you a new one—or a different one—if you'd like."

"No problem. I'll get back to you on that," Walt said, mildly offended that the matter even came up. He sat down.

Chapman continued his rundown on Santorini's role as the agent-in-charge. "Her role will be invisible to you. You're supposed to be taking the group on an educational tour. Gina's cover will be that she's a language teacher at Georgetown. Actually, she does work as a language instructor from time to time. In Turkish. So she's legit. It might transpire that she has to be away for a day or so, but you don't need to do anything special to track her down."

"Paul, is there any reason that you didn't tell me anything about Katya before now?"

"Katya? No, of course not. But there's not a lot about her that you don't already know. And if you hadn't taken this mission, which you're probably going to be glad you did, there was no reason for you to know more."

"Except that everything I thought I knew is bullshit, and she conned me from the beginning."

"Come on, Walt. How did she con you? She took the classes. Did the work. Got the grades and went on your trips with you. It was part of her training and it has helped make her more valuable. You already know that she is fluent in Ukrainian and she can get the job done in Russian. She's a valuable addition in the field."

"Katya drinks too much. I'd be worried if I was her boyfriend. Or her husband. Or dad."

"Yes, well... we know that, and she has been given a warning. But you probably don't want to know the kind of stress she's been under in the past."

"I like her. If she was my sister I'd give her hell. I'm not worried about her not doing her job. I'm worried about her health."

"Look, Walt. I suspected you might be pissed to learn about Katya. It's understandable. But it's also inappropriate. Katya is solid… and you already know that. She's anxious to know how you'll respond when you find out. So I'm going to tell you a few things about her in strictest confidence. Then, if its OK with you, I'd like to call and have her join us for lunch. I'd like to see you two on good terms before we get started on this little adventure. Sound OK?"

"Who's paying for lunch?"

"Haven't changed much, have you? OK. It's on me. But first, before we go, a bit of confidential information about Katya. Not to leave this room. She's had a rough time."

Paul leaned in close and spoke quietly.

"I'll make it brief. Katya and a senior male were examining an abandoned crack site. Only it wasn't abandoned. Four guys took them captive, tied them up and took them to a barn. She thought they were dead, for sure. They were all going to take turns with her. One of the guys raped her in front of them all. She talked the second guy into taking her into a horse stall. She managed to kill him with a piece of her underwear. Don't ask. She got his weapon, killed the first guy who raped her—self defense, a good shoot—and wounded one of the others. Most of this was witnessed by her senior who was bound. Two dead, one wounded and one captured. And two prisoners—still alive. She was in a different agency—in limbo—when I heard about her and brought her here. She's very bright. But she was a mess when I asked for her. She needed a sabbatical. Surely you understand that, and that's why she went to you."

"Don't tell me any more," Walt said. "This is enough to hold me for a while."

Weeks later, as he was herding the cats along the Silk Road, he had mixed feelings about the Queen of the Spooks, his name for Gina that he only whispered to Tara. Gina was an abrasive person, but his hands were tied. He couldn't punch her and he couldn't walk away. On one of the long, dusty van rides she was seated beside him for a full morning. Her voice was low and confidential, just perfect for a woman spook. *Maybe, like Katya, she's carrying a lot of baggage.*

"How does a guy like you, who seems to like being on the go and has a high energy level, get stuck with some geeky, bookworm, desk job in academia?"

"Geeky, bookworm? Gee, that sounds a bit harsh. Judgmental, too? What made you pick those descriptors?"

"You call this a normal job? Taking people to inspect piles of mud brick rubble? A lot of these places we've visited are less interesting than abandoned construction sites. I grew up in places like these. Ruins? They're boring."

"To you, maybe. But to some people they represent a lot of interesting history. I'm sorry you find it so boring."

He was reluctant to sound defensive, but it was more frustrating to deal with her than with a cranky student, and he had plenty of experience dealing with them. The girls were worst, but even the worst of the students wasn't as much of a pain in the ass as this lady spook.

After a week on the road, the consequences of long hours in vans or buses, unusual meals and toilets that weren't up to the standards of home usually started to hit them about the same time. Even with bottled water, diarrhea from salads or washed fruit was hard to avoid. He toyed with the idea of asking her if she wanted a Compazine suppository, but bit his tongue and stifled the urge.

She always seemed to be spoiling for an argument. He quickly recognized the signs. And yet—something about her complaints failed to ring true. She climbed over ruins with the best of them, listened carefully as he explained what they were seeing, ate whatever was being served, and then disappeared after dinner only to show up in time for breakfast, ready to go again. Where she went and what she did was anybody's guess. Gradually he came to appreciate her qualities of toughness and stamina. By the end of the trip, he would learn to like her. But he wasn't sure if she felt the same way.

Chapter 32

Hong Kong Film Studio

Observe other persons through your own person.
Observe other families through your own family.
Observe other villages through your own village.
Observe other states through your own state.
Observe all under heaven through all under heaven.

How do I know the nature of all under heaven?
Through this.

TAO TE CHING
LAO TZU
(TRANSLATED BY VICTOR H. MAIR)

A team of Chinese film script writers had been struggling for several weeks to come up with a story line that could be built around a noted Mongol chieftain who entered the eastern regions of Central Asia occupied by today's Turkmenistan or Uzbekistan. They were not having a great deal of success.

Kenny Jiao briefed Wendell Cho on the nature of the difficulties when they met to confer in Shanghai.

"It's not that there isn't enough violence, war and rape in the Mongol conquest. It's more that the names of many of the key figures just don't resonate with enough moviegoers in China. Even fewer in the United States and in other parts of the world."

"Everyone has heard of Genghis Khan."

"True. But few people know anything specific about what he did. They may know that his forces conquered Asia from Korea to Vienna, but about his life? As they say at UCLA, Jacko Shitto!"

"But what about all the others? Kublai Khan, Ogodei, Timur, Baibuka…"

Jiao started laughing. "Make a list. They know even less about those names. No American has even heard the name Baibuka. Damn few Chinese."

"Are you certain of this, Kenny?"

"Let's walk out in the street and take a survey. Twenty people. If more than two have ever heard of Timur, I'll buy you dinner and an evening with the girl of your choice."

"No. I won't take you up on it. But what do you recommend? We need to get into Turkmenistan. And I'm starting to feel heat from Mr. Wu. I hope we're not being held up by money."

Kenny Jiao laughed again. "No. Believe me, my friend, you are spending money as we speak. But you just aren't getting much for it."

"So? What to do? Make me a recommendation."

"I think you should make an action romance set on the Silk Road. We can probably find a great story line from a Japanese manga. If it's not great, at least it will be interesting. We just want to make a movie. Something with camel caravans, an exotic oasis town with a sinister emir and a lovely harem girl who sees a handsome camel driver from her window. Desert bandits on horseback. I'll bet we can find a suitable story in less than a week."

"In other words, a piece of shit."

"Ha, ha, ha. Precisely. Look, we don't set out to make a piece of shit. We start with a good story. An interesting plot line that holds together. Maybe it's built around a remarkable garment, made from silk, that's being shipped along the Silk Road. A garment fit for a great princess. The guys that write manga understand story lines as well as—maybe better than—film script writers. Their crafts are much the same.

We want to start with a story that will hold readers. Have you seen Japanese comic books? Manga? Manga artists know how to catch readers and hold them to the end. We find a story that's interesting. We expand the story, fill out the dialog, convert it to film. Wendell, don't make such a face. We can't all be artists. Sometimes we just settle for being good craftsmen. In the process—on occasion—art happens."

"Shit happens."

"Exactly. Shit happens. Art happens. Same thing. Heaven and earth are indifferent."

"Kenny, I am starting to believe you are a philosopher."

"Just so. It has taken you this long to notice?"

"Maybe I should be buying you the dinner. I will talk to Mr. Wu who came up with the idea of the Mongols. I'll try to convince him we should make a story on the Silk Road."

"Give me a week to look, before you try to change him."

"Not a week. By next Wednesday. I see him on Thursday."

"That's not very much time. But OK. I will try. Listen, Wendell. Do you know what one of my famous teachers taught us at UCLA? A man who had directed films and headed a studio? He said, 'everything in film making is in the hands of the gods—the movie gods.'"

"And he gave examples?"

"Many. A great script may make a terrible movie. Or it may become a wonderful screenplay. Come into the hands of a capable director. Only to be spoiled by petulant or demanding actors. Even by simple economics. Dramatic cost overruns. There are too many opportunities for accidents in the process. No one, not even the richest, most talented or most powerful directors have complete control over this process."

"I can understand this."

"But, happily for people like us, some of the accidents happen in the good way and things get better instead of worse. Sometimes..."

"Don't tell me any more. I'll just become confused. Anyway, I see it's starting to rain outside." The streamers were beginning to flow down the tinted glass windows of his luxurious office overlooking Shangai's bustling waterfront. "Let's go find some rice wine."

"In this rain?"

"The weaker the wine, the easier it is to drink two cups."

Jiao laughed. "And you called me the philosopher."

Kenny Jiao called Wendell Cho early on Wednesday morning. He sounded excited. "I was going to call you last night, but I was so excited that I went out and got myself laid."

Wendell laughed. "What could have possibly been that exciting? I definitely seem to remember that you have a low threshold in that direction."

"You are going to be pleased, old friend."

"Don't keep me waiting."

"Very well. Here it is. The script writers I put on the job to look for a manga story? They came up with a killer I think you will love."

"Give it to me."

"Wendell, I'd almost rather make you wait and just fax you the whole script idea. It's only about twenty pages or so, but it's probably better if you read it for yourself."

"Listen, Kenny, I was out late last night with several cost guys and I'm not in a good mood. Don't do anything to make it worse."

"No, certainly not, old pal. Take a couple aspirin. Some ginseng. Hot tea. Listen, I'm also going to have my secretary pull the whole thing apart and send you the manga over the fax. It will only be another twenty pages or so. But the graphics will give you an idea of what we can do with a film treatment. I'm telling you, you're gonna love it."

"What's the name for this classic piece of shit?"

"Oh, that's the best part. It's based on ancient Chinese history..."

"The title..."
"The Silk Princess."
"Ahhhh. I see."
"OK, Wendell, you win. Here's the story line. Straight from the history books. Check it out. Xuanzang, Chinese Buddhist monk, travels across Central Asia sometime around 640 to 645. Silk Road is in full swing. Silk is a commodity then. A Chinese monopoly. Valuable. Plentiful only from China. A state secret. The historians say it was, for a time, fungible, like oil. Or gold. You could trade in bolts of silk."
"So the princess was a trader?"
"Stick with me, Wendell, this really has possibilities. All the countries in the path of the route know of silk, but few know how it is made. In Rome they think it grows on trees. China's near neighbors are first to learn the secret of how it's done. But then, they have no silkworms, no mulberry trees and no technical know-how.

So the ruler of Khotan decides to ask for silkworms, etc., from ruler of China. Emperor says no. So Khotan guy asks for hand of Emperor's daughter. To make strong alliance. Emperor says yes.

Khotan guy sends secret emissary to daughter. When you come to my country, your new home, I can give you no silk. Why don't you bring the stuff?

But Emperor has everyone searched at the border. Silkworms and mulberry seeds can't leave China. Princess wants to please new hubby-to-be. She says him 'No problemo.'

Princess arranges to fix hairdo so that silkworms hidden inside. Border guards can't touch heads of royals.

Mulberry seeds hidden in hairdo. And princess chooses attendants who are all skilled silk workers.

So first place outside China to get silk is Khotan. From there, it just kept going."
"Kenny boy, remind me. I should know, but where the hell is Khotan?"
"Ah, you bad boy. You no do homework."
"Cut the shit."
"Khotan is Chinese wild west. It's at the southern edge of the Takla Makan Desert. North of the Kun Lun Range. Close to Tibet. Colorful. Romantic. Remote as hell. But we can shoot it anywhere."
"Kenny, are you pulling my leg?"
"Can't you picture this, Wendell? No kidding, I'm really excited. Listen, if you don't like this idea once you see the manga drawings, I'll buy you dinner and stuff that comes after. I just gave you a skeleton. Wait 'til you see some meat. And Khotan? Check it out on a map. On the Khotan Darya River. It was an oasis. All the travelers on the southern route around the desert had to stop there. But we don't have to make it in Khotan. We can make it wherever we choose."
"I'll wait to see what you send."

"Oh, man, Wendell. The costumes for this baby are gonna make people's mouths water. I'm already getting excited."

"And who the hell was this Xuanzang guy you started out with?"

"Plus we can use lots of camels and horses. Wait 'til you see these drawings."

"Xuanzang?"

"He was the Chinese monk who wrote the first history telling how silk got out of China."

"But he's not in the story?"

"We could have him start the narration? Yes? Oh! Oh! That's a good touch. Hey, good idea! Start and end. With Xuanzang. Oh! Perfect!"

"I'm going to hang up so you can start sending."

"You're going to owe me big time on this one, Wendell. I think I'll wait 'til we go back to L.A. to collect."

"Bye-bye, Kenny."

Kenny did not exaggerate. The idea was solid and the script writers did a bang-up job in making a remarkable story. They didn't have to stick with the facts, either.

Chapter 33

Mira in Ashkhabad

"I'm twenty-five years old, and that is all the time it took, just one generation, for the water that had been there for millennia to be transformed into dust. Those in charge of the Communist regime decided to divert two rivers, Amu Darya and Syr Darya, so that they could irrigate some cotton plantations. They failed, but by then it was too late—the sea had ceased to exist, and the cultivated land became a desert.

The lack of water affected the whole climate. Nowadays, vast sandstorms scatter 150,000 tons of salt and dust every year. Fifty million people in five countries were affected by the Soviet bureaucrats' irresponsible—and irreversible—decision. The little water that was left is polluted and the source of all kinds of diseases."

THE ZAHIR
PAOLO COELHO

The plane carrying Val, Mira and the Mighty Handful to Ashkhabad landed on schedule and a waiting van whisked them to their hotel. If the Mighty Handful shared any notions that the Romanian girl was to be shared around, they were quickly dispelled when the desk manager provided them with six room keys. Mira and Val went directly to their room while the Mighty Handful reconvened in the lobby before heading for the hotel bar. The bar—in late afternoon—was filled with men, many of them from American or European petrochemical firms, and the Russians soon tired of the loud babble in languages they could not understand. After thirty minutes or so, they called a cab and left in search of a Russian-speaking bar where they could find girls.

Back in their room, Val stretched out on the bed while Mira stood at the window looking out at the city.

"They have many parks here," she said. "Many trees."

"That is because the leader of this country is a madman," Val said. "This country is mostly desert. He takes the water from other countries and lets it piss away into the sand. He is insane."

"Some of the parks look very beautiful."

"But so much water to be sprayed in the air. Only a lunatic would be so wasteful. Anyway, this water is stolen from other countries."

"Why can you say this?"

"Tomorrow I will show you. A canal brings this water from the snow-capped mountains of the Uzbeks, the Tajiks, and from Afghanistan. Turkmenistan is one more reason why the Aral Sea is drying up."

"And you know this how?"

The print dress that Mira was wearing was not opaque to strong sunlight and as she stood in front of the window he could see the silhouette of her legs through the material.

"Tomorrow we will see the canal and you will see water that comes all the way from Central Asia. So, then. Tomorrow. But for now, come here to me."

"But it is not even dark. You can not wait to have me? I am so good?"

"Come now. It will be dark later. When we are done."

"I will bathe first."

"No. Later. I want to smell you."

Mira raised her arms above her head and made a pirouette. "I think I must tell you something, now."

"Tell me something?"

"Yes. Why I came with you on this trip to a country where insane men make beautiful fountains. Far from my home."

"So why did you come?"

"To be with you in the city of love."

"Why do you call it the city of love? This town is a shit hole. The capitol of nowhere."

"It is the city of love."

"Why are you calling it that?"

"That is its name. Ashkhabad. Ashk. Love. It is Turkish, I think."

Val laughed. "Is this true?"

"You didn't know this. And you so smart? Mister Smart. Yes. This is why. I took the chance to come."

"Come here, on this bed, and I will show you why you came."

"No, you can show me later. Now, I will show you. Go back. Close your eyes."

"Like before? What you called it? Melting the candle?"

"No, this is different."

Val closed his eyes, but the late afternoon sunlight was strong and he jumped up to close the blinds.

"Different?"

"You will remember it when I am gone."

She had already slipped out of her dress and was barefoot—in her underwear.

"But your eyes must be closed," she said. "Picture what I am doing with your eyes closed."

Val laughed again. "You must have a name for this, too."

"Yes." A long pause, then a whisper. "I will tell you."

He could hear sounds that were difficult to picture at first.

Then, sometime later, he sensed that her lips were close to his face and he could feel her breathing. Then the soft whisper in his ear. "This is ... Chernobyl."

Chapter 34

Dialogue

*"Don't worry about saving these songs!
and if one of our instruments breaks,
it doesn't matter.
We have fallen into the place
Where everything is music."*

"WHERE EVERYTHING IS MUSIC"
THE ESSENTIAL RUMI
TRANSLATED BY COLEMAN BARKS

Val was playing with two lovely damp curls of Mira's pubic hair. He looked up and her eyes were still open. "Tell me about the old guy," he said.

"'You mean my old Turkish gentleman? I will not say his name to you."

"Your lover, then. Tell me about him."

"My friend."

"As you wish. Your friend."

"I will never say anything ill of him. He was good to me."

"I just want to know about him."

"He was a kind man."

"You fucked him."

"If you say it like that again, I will get up and leave." Her voice did not have the least trace of anger or even determination. And yet, he knew she would do what she said.

"Why won't you say his name to me?"

"Why do you care to know his name?"

"*Tamam*. No name. But tell me why you liked him so much."

"He used to read to me. He really cared for me. Not just for his bed. I can't explain it, but he did."

"What things did he read? Not verses from the Quran, I hope."

"Poems. He read to me from books of poetry. Turkish poets, Persian poets. Hafiz. Rumi. It was lovely to hear him read. It was like being in a dream."

"So what things … ?"

"I can't remember. I do not read well. But one poet he read often was Rumi. You know him, of course. He was for a time in Konya. Lived there. It seemed—when my gentleman read to me—as if Rumi was still there."

"But you don't remember?"

"Not the lines. No. I was never good at that. But they were like stories. The stories seemed almost to be about people I knew."

He put his head on her thigh. The scent they had made together was making him lightheaded and he closed his eyes. "Tell me. One story—that you remember."

"There was a poem by Rumi that he read me. About Baghdad. And Cairo. The name of it was something like, 'In Baghdad, dreaming of Cairo, In Cairo, dreaming of Baghdad.' But don't do that or I can't finish the story.

In the poem a man lives in Baghdad, but he is dissatisfied with his life. He has a dream. The dream says that if he goes to Cairo, to a certain place, he can dig and find a buried treasure. He goes, he digs and there is no treasure. Disappointment. He complains to a native of the city. The man tells him a story. Living in Cairo, he has been dissatisfied with his lot in life. In his unhappiness he dreams, and the dream tells him to go to Baghdad. And he describes the neighborhood and even the exact house of the visitor from Baghdad. But the Egyptian did not go to Baghdad. I stayed, he says, and I am content. You did not stay, and yet, you are not content.

The man from Baghdad understands the message in the dreams. No matter how far you go to seek your treasure, it can always be found right at home. Your treasure is wherever you are."

She dropped her hand onto his head and caressed his ear. "It was very nice for me—the way he read it for me. I wish I could remember the words."

"Perhaps we can find another copy of Rumi."

"One line I remember. It was about passion. *'Either you see the beloved or you lose your head.'*"

"That sounds harsh."

"But it is poetry," she laughed. "And you may yet lose your head."

"When we met I did not think you would be interested in poetry."

"Right now? No. I am just now interested in some food. Do you think we could find food?"

Chapter 35

Chinese Fire Drill

> "A group of mostly strangers has been assembled, often in an inhospitable location, and asked to work in harmony under demanding circumstances. The shooting days are limited, the budget closely monitored, the cast quarrelsome. Each individual is guarding his turf, feeling this is his only line of defense against the absolute monarch of the production, the director."
>
> SHOOT OUT
(SURVIVING FAME AND (MIS)FORTUNE IN HOLLYWOOD)
PETER BART AND PETER GRUBER

The Chinese film team arrived in Turkmenistan a few days before Walt's herd of cats. They quickly sucked up most of the better rooms in Ashkhabad's best hotels and the tourist population immediately felt their presence. Hotel bars and restaurants were full of highly visible Chinese, who tended to be noisy in public spaces. They also brought heavy smokers, and the atmosphere of places with evening entertainment and alcohol reeked of strong Chinese tobacco.

As a rule, most of the regular big spenders were oilmen from major corporations around the globe. Every major gas and oil firm had staff in the City of Love. But there was also a clientele of soldiers of fortune from all corners of the earth, dealing in every commodity from consumer electronics to security services to sophisticated weapons systems.

There were tourists, to be sure, but these visitors did not dominate the scene. In the weeks after they arrived the Chinese gave the inaccurate impression of being the most numerous class of foreigners in the capital.

This impression may have been reinforced by their tendency to flock together, generating lots of raucous laughter and clouds of tobacco smoke. An advance team had been in place for a couple of weeks, making arrangements for hiring horses and camels, renting vehicles and trailers that could be used at the site, and scores of other logistical elements such as tents, catering support, portable toilets, and contract security personnel.

When the Chinese crews hit the hotel bars, more than one amused American—from Texas or Oklahoma—was heard to mutter phrases like "Chinese fire drill!" and "Mongolian cluster fuck!"

Chapter 36

Arkady's Criminal Empire

> 'I was hunted like a wet jackal; but I broke through at Bandakui, where I heard there was a charge against me of murder in the city I had left—of the murder of a boy. They have both the corpse and the witnesses waiting.'
>
> 'But cannot the government protect?'
>
> 'We of the Game are beyond protection. If we die, we die. Our names are blotted from the book. That is all.'
>
> KIM
RUDYARD KIPLING

One measure of the size and complexity of Arkady's crime syndicate was reflected in the fact that he employed seven full-time lobbyists in Washington. These individuals took instructions and handled requests through lawyers, embassy employees and a few soldiers of fortune especially hand-picked by Arkady. The lobbyists worked to influence legislation concerning arms sales to foreign countries, proposed sanctions against foreign arms suppliers, drug enforcement laws and import-export rules, with particular reference to Russia's vodka trade with the U.S., as well as a variety of other topics.

There was good money to be made in the sale of children from former Iron Curtain countries to the U.S. The demand for children to be adopted was a lucrative field. Both males and females—nearing puberty—were good material for the sex trade, which could take many forms. The most profitable, of course, was to place them in brothels or "service bureaus" in places like Romania or Bulgaria where they were available for visitors. It was much harder to get them into the United States. Harder, but not impossible, and very profitable when it could be achieved. Even with "'spillage," the inevitable consequences of losses due to interdiction by law enforcement or breakdowns in the internal organization, it was still lucrative enough to justify a management chain and lobbying support.

Lobbyists were also helpful in briefing members of Arkady's staff on trends in the U.S. Val had cultivated his contact with several key individuals in the Washington firm that was in Arkady's employ. They alerted him to shifting patterns in recreational drug usage, and they did it in such a skillful way that no audit trail was likely to be found. From his Washington contacts, Val learned that the use of methamphetamines was on the rise, and that it was displacing heroin derivatives on the streets.

Val used the Internet to supplement information provided by his contacts in the U.S. After several weeks of study it became clear to him that there was an immense amount of money to be made by supplying a uniform recreational drug product, manufactured in an industrial facility with adequate safety controls. This product, once it existed and could be manufactured inexpensively, would be easy to ship, easy to distribute and easy to market. At least, it would be easier to handle than heroin because it would be easier to conceal. He began to build a file and he took aside a couple of promising young associates and assigned them the task of creating a preliminary business plan for him to discuss with Arkady. *Recreational drugs that can be manufactured without depending on a poppy crop; this is the future.*

"Give me plenty of solid facts," Val instructed them. "I want Arkady to give us enough money to get a pilot operation up and running. We need to be out on the front edge of this trend, and we are already behind."

"Understood!" They were aching to get started and this held the promise of greater responsibilities, including the opportunity to travel. Neither of these young men had been to the United States, but they had studied English and could communicate reasonably well.

"Arkady is hard to sell. But once he sees the money to be made, he is willing to spend it to make it."

Chapter 37

On Location in Turkmenistan

"The Kopet Dag Mountains loomed in the distance like mounds of crumpled purple foil. The city itself seemed perpetually covered with a layer of dust; it never fully came into focus, and the minutiae shifted with each breeze. The streets and houses ran along a precise grid; in true Soviet fashion, all traces of imagination or inventiveness on the part of city planners had been eliminated. 'New city, sir. All new. An earthquake destroyed the true Ashgabat nearly forty years ago.'"

THE GEOGRAPHER'S LIBRARY
JON FASMAN

When the Chinese film crew hit Turkmenistan, six of Ashkhabad's largest and best hotels were booked solid and a dozen luxury apartments were reserved for use by the stars. More than 250 people were included in the film team that came flying in over a six-day period. The surveying team consisted of only nine people, all males, but the film crew was over one-third female.

An advance administrative party had been in the city for over a month, making legal arrangements, coordinating with governmental authorities and agencies, and booking extras to participate in making the film. Drivers and vehicles were hired and contracts were drawn with local food service providers. In two hotels the entire dining rooms were pre-empted in advance and provisions were made for other guests to use nearby dining facilities. All of this work cost money, but the costs incurred were not out of line with those encountered in filming any epic.

An earlier advance crew had been at work on a long list of detailed tasks, charged with hiring 200 horses, half of which had to be sufficiently photogenic to appear in the foreground. About the same number of camels had been hired. Additional horses and camels would, of course, be added by computers in the studio.

In rough terms, the plan was to spend no more than three days in the vicinity of Ashkhabad before moving to the east, toward Mary—ancient Merv. Before reaching the city, the party would split off toward the south, where they would begin filming some desert sequences. The pipeline survey team would take to the road in the direction of the Afghan city of Herat. The route they would take paralleled the highway—which in turn followed the river valley of the Murgap Deryasy. For nearly two hundred years this natural corridor for travel between Russia and Afghanistan had been studied and restudied for its potential as an invasion route. During the era of The Great Game—in which Imperial Russia and Great Britain's Indian Empire eyed one another warily across a harsh expanse—this corridor had been traveled by spies, military engineers and soldiers of fortune, all wearing a variety of disguises to conceal their real purpose. Not much had changed. It had been surveyed many times before—for many purposes.

But despite the large number of secret maps and charts that had been hidden in the clothing of a generation of military spies, the Chinese still lacked reliable maps of distances, contours, elevations and geological obstacles needed to drive a pipeline.

On the Afghan side of the border, the Paropamisus Range rose as a barrier protecting ancient Herat from invasion by enemies to the north. Because of its proximity to Iran and its distance from Kabul, this Afghan city was, in many ways, more Iranian than Afghan. A Chinese team had already been at work on the Afghan side of the border. Money had changed hands and a workable Chinese route had been surveyed across most of the eastern end of Afghanistan. The remaining work to be done was in the south, toward the border with Pakistan.

The route to be covered in Turkmenistan covered only about one-sixth of the estimated total pipeline length. But, to date, it had provided the biggest headache for Chinese planners. Now, the surveying team—fully equipped—was on the ground in Turkmenistan and the work could begin.

Chapter 38

The Mighty Handful Go To The Movies

"Much more than silk traveled the great highway. Paper and porcelain, gunpowder, the crossbow, and the art of printing traveled westward; so did roses, peonies, oranges, peaches and pears, all of which were indigenous to China. China-bound merchants brought glass and wool from Rome, lapis lazuli from Afghanistan, coral from the Indian Ocean, Persian wine and figs, sacred jade from the KunLun mountains, ivory and spices from India, and the powerful Sogdian steeds that the Chinese called 'heavenly horses.' New religions seeped along the caravan routes too; Manicheanism from Persia, Nestorian Christianity from further west, and from India Buddhism...."

CATHAY; A JOURNEY IN SEARCH OF OLD CHINA
FERGUS M. BORDEWICH

Valentin and the Mighty Handful encountered the Chinese film crew in the Turkmen capital of Ashkhabad. They had all been staying for a few days at the same hotel in Ashkhabad, although the Chinese crew was so large that they were put up in several establishments. Some of the key staff and actors had taken apartments and for the duration of their stay it was hard not to notice the Chinese presence in the city.

After the Mighty Handful learned that the Chinese were in Turkmenistan to make a film, they watched the Chinese in hotel bars with increased interest. Many of the young actresses were eye-catching and the Russians made several clumsy attempts to attract their notice. But loutish, middle-aged thugs held little appeal for lissome Chinese females who were used to being the center of attention.

The Russians watched the groups of young people in the hotel with a mixture of desire and jealousy. After three days, in the manner that seems to be common to all bullies, they decided to make an impression on the Chinese film crew by a demonstration of Russian toughness.

It took several large trucks to carry all the equipment the film crew had brought in by chartered flights. The movie equipment was augmented by the modest complement of surveying gear used by the team assigned to begin looking for a pipeline route. They needed only a short length of line that would lead south, across Turkmenistan's Garabil Plateau and into Afghanistan.

The first major technical challenge to construction would be Afghanistan's Paropamisus Range and, to date, the Chinese government still had not received formal approval from Afghanis to enter with their field crew. Mr. Wu believed he could solve this problem with money. There was no intent by the Chinese to ever reveal the presence of their Turkmenistan pipeline survey crew to anyone within any government.

The Mighty Handful spent two days making inquiries about the film crew. The Chinese had six or seven interpreters with them, some fluent in Turkmen and some in Russian. Only one could communicate in Uzbek in case the film crew decided to head north. And there were relatively few bilingual Chinese speakers in Turkmenistan.

Buffet-style meals worked fine for most of the Chinese visitors, but watching the interpreters hustle around to make specific Chinese food requests known was a source of amusement for the Russians. The Chinese affinity for pork products clashed with Islamic aversion to animals that were not approved by the Prophet.

They decided to visit the film crew on location in the desert. This would mean taking a vehicle and they would need to tell Val that they would be gone for part of the day.

"Sightseeing?" Val asked incredulously.

"Why not? These Chinese girls are so pretty, we want to see what they are doing out there in the desert. Our contacts tell us that they are filming just an hour's drive away. Want to come? Can you keep your yap shut?"

"I'll stay here."

By the end of the second day, as the Chinese team was beginning to load equipment in trucks and vans to begin shooting in the desert to the south, the Mighty Handful had devised a bizarre scheme for extorting protection money.

Their plan was to wait until the crew was set up for a film shoot, then to approach them as work was beginning and make their demands. The Chinese would be given twenty-four hours to comply. If they resisted openly, then punishment would be swift, violent and sufficiently gruesome to make repetition highly unappealing. This was the type of activity at which the Mighty Handful excelled. They had no need of money. For them, the plan was simply a way of keeping their coercive skills sharpened to a fine edge.

The Mighty Handful rose early. They ate as they watched the Chinese crew pack equipment and costumes, before heading in a caravan to the site for the day's filming. The column of vans and trucks proceeded to the site of the day's shoot. The Russians were ready to leave as soon as the last vehicle departed.

Unknown to the Mighty Handful, this day's shooting schedule called for action scenes of Mongol horsemen raiding a caravan of traders. There were over a hundred horses and twenty-seven camels in the scenes slated for the day. Most of the exciting action would be provided by a dozen Afghan horsemen and more horses would be added in Hong Kong studios.

The Afghans had been located and hired by an agency in Hong Kong and they had all acted in western movies before. They were relatively inexpensive to hire, and had given convincing performances in the past. They were all daring riders whose skills had been polished in many a Buzkashi contest. In fact, it was rumored that two of them once engaged in a contest in which the headless sheep was replaced by the body of a Russian soldier.

The Afghan riders had been augmented by a large number of Chinese performers and a horde of Turkmen extras hired by the job. The action sequences planned for the day included the footage for a horde of tribesmen to swoop down on the plodding camel caravan transporting the Silk Princess. Standard stuff, made more interesting by the exotic desert locale with mountains in the background—and plenty of motion.

Under the pretext of shopping for the next day's film site, the survey crew had proceeded ahead into the desert. They were absent from the film site when the Russians bounded up in their hired Land Rover. Despite Chinese attempts to wave them off or steer them away, they drove directly toward the largest gathering of people until they reached a temporary security barrier.

At the edge of the shooting site, the film crew had posted two contract security guards to keep visitors out of the area of action. These guards served as a red flag to the Mighty Handful. They drove their vehicle right up to the two men who were standing beside the barrier.

The guards spoke in the Turkmen language that Boris could understand.

"No passage beyond this point. A film is being made here. Please to back up and turn around."

Boris repeated the instructions to his companions who laughed. "Tell them to fuck themselves," Anatoly roared.

Boris got out of the vehicle and all the others followed except for the driver. These men had all begun their criminal careers as 'smash and grab' hoodlums in the cities. For them, violence had become a way of life. They had been practicing since their teens, and any kind of established order prompted them to violence. It was almost a form of recreation. A pair of Russians approached each of the two security guards, staring directly into their faces, intending to intimidate them. The guards, both of whom were wrestlers, were not easily cowed but, even though armed, they hesitated drawing their weapons, and they still had not seen any signs of overt hostility from the Russians.

Without any attempts to prearrange their actions or coordinate their assaults on the guards, the four thugs acted as a single unit. In the blink of an eye they threw hammer blows into the abdomens of both guards and followed instantly with vicious kicks to the shins and the back of the knees.

Immediately, both guards were disabled, still conscious, now on the ground. Another second and they had both been relieved of their weapons, ancient revolvers that seemed to be relics from another era. Then, in a move that he had employed numerous times in the past, Boris approached each of the stunned men on the ground and viciously stomped on each of their feet, effectively crippling them by crushing bones and ensuring they would be unable to walk. The older of the two guards fainted from pain, but the younger man just whimpered pitiably. Boris gave him a half-hearted kick to the neck to shut him up and the four Russians, laughing, returned to the van.

They proceeded to drive in the direction of the crowd of people and vehicles where the action would be taking place. Amid all the noise and turmoil, it took several moments to determine which Chinese were interpreters.

The whole action was like a game for the Mighty Handful. Schooled in violent, irrational acts, they depended upon the periodic infusion of adrenaline that sex or alcohol could never provide. They laughed uncontrollably as they drove toward the gathering in the distance.

At the temporary corrals where the horses and camels had been held for several days, the wranglers responsible for the livestock had been camping out for most of the week. They had been up since before daylight, saddling and costuming animals in preparation for the day's action shoot. Today was the big scene for the Afghan riders and the mounted extras. Makeup people had been working to get the riders into appropriate Mongol gear. Members of the Chinese caravan were dressed in flowing garb suitable for desert travel, and if the costumes were not historically accurate, who would know?

Today's filming was intended to concentrate on the action sequences in which the raiders swoop down on the armed caravan bearing the Silk Princess. The caravan would attempt a futile defense, the desert equivalent of circling the wagons, but the wild riding of the Afghan horsemen would make resistance futile as they would encircle the panicked camels and quickly dispatch most of the men. They would leave a few younger boys and all of the females to be carried away as slaves.

The Mighty Handful, whose object was simply to create mayhem, drove up to within ten yards of the camera crews and the administrative team supporting the director. Three men in canvas bush jackets walked over to intercept them. As they drew nearer, Boris called out, "Who speaks Russian?" One of the men turned and called for an interpreter and a Chinese woman left the cluster of film workers.

"They send us a woman?" Boris said for the benefit of his companions.

The Mighty Handful had begun the morning with no specific plan, but for each of them the opportunity to bully a group into submission was second nature. Even in prison they had found this technique to work for them; to satisfy some internal urge. Now, almost as if they were thinking with one mind, they decided to ratchet the confrontation up a notch.

Boris faced the interpreter. "Tell this group we are here to collect the fees for the Turkmen government."

The interpreter was puzzled. As far as she was aware all arrangements with the government had been completed and all legal papers were in order. "I don't understand what you are asking," she stammered.

"Money. We want money. Just tell everyone we want their money." Anatoly was grinning. "And watches. Tell everyone to take off their watches. I will collect."

The young woman, astonished, was reluctant to relay this bizarre message, but everyone in the film crew now had their eyes on the Russians and shouts from a distance indicated that the injured guards had been discovered.

Over near the corrals where handlers were just finishing saddling the animals and adding the necessary elements of costuming, the Afghan riders were standing in their Mongol armor, smoking Chinese cigarettes. Half a hundred Turkmen horsemen—also in costume—were being inspected by a wardrobe manager. The Afghans were waiting for instructions to mount up. The first scenes would be close-ups of them in a sequence intended to indicate preparation for the attack.

Wendell Cho had gone to the corral directly after reaching the site in order to watch the camels being prepared. He had always been interested in camels and he had no concept of how they were packed for caravan journeys. When the commotion broke out over in the direction of the camera crews, he turned to see what was happening and recognized the coarse-looking Russians as the same group of troublemakers that had been harassing several of the young actresses in the hotel bar.

His instinct for detecting bullies was well developed, as was his willingness to make quick decisions when the need arose. Part of this instinct had been honed during the years he spent at Rice. Several visits to bars in Houston and Galveston had resulted in altercations where his companions had either shed blood because they hesitated too long before reacting, or else they drew blood by getting the drop on the bad guys. It was a wild-west kind of thing, and in preparation for this movie Wendell had watched a lot of westerns.

He saw the Afghan riders turning in the direction of the commotion to see what was happening and he ran over to them. In his haste to take action, he forgot that the Afghans didn't speak Chinese and when they failed to respond to his directions, he realized that he wasn't even sure what language they did speak. The wardrobe coordinator who had helped them into their costumes was able to communicate in their Tajik language. He relayed Wendell's brief message.

"Those men. Russians. Five. Come to stop filming. You take horses. Drive them away. Buzkashi? Buzkashi. Play Buzkashi with those men. Drive away." Wendell remembered a film from Afghanistan, depicting their national game, a fiercely violent form of polo played with the headless carcass of a dead sheep. The word *Buzkashi* did the trick.

The Afghans looked at him and then looked at one another. Their faces had puzzled expressions. They pointed to themselves and then they pointed to the Russians and raised their eyebrows to indicate questioning. Wendell had no idea what they were saying, but the wardrobe man was bobbing up and down. "Yes, yes. You go. Quick."

The Afghans began laughing. In their Mongol costumes they looked terrifying but they were laughing as they clambered over the corral fence, found their waiting mounts, and signaled for the gate to the corral to be opened.

For the film sequence they would have been armed with short bows and long lances, but these were not readily at hand when the Mongol raiders thundered out of the corral. Twelve men in leather armor were mounted on twelve leather-protected horses with the Mongol's small, circular shields hanging from the pommels.

When the Mighty Handful turned in response to the sound, they were welcomed by the frightening spectacle of twelve Mongol warriors charging them with their shields up. Boris, first to realize the danger, reached into his jacket pocket for the little Vektor automatic that Val had given him. He pulled it out and fired in the direction of the charging horsemen. The nearest horse staggered and went down, throwing his rider.

Instantly, the Afghan riders were seized with a new determination; there is no love lost between Afghans and Russians. A second later they thundered over the Mighty Handful, pounding them to the ground with blows from the leather-covered wooden shields. Turning their mounts they doubled back and the horses milled through the Russians who had been taken completely off guard.

When the Mongols struck, Yuri, who had been the driver, was halfway between the vehicle and his companions. His first reaction was to turn and make a dash for protection behind the van, but one of the Afghans split out of the formation and gave him a slam with the flat of the Mongol shield. The force of the blow landed mostly on his shoulders, but it knocked him into the hood of the van where he hit on his left hip. Fortunately he remained conscious and scrambled into the vehicle, behind the wheel, managing to close the door as the horsemen wheeled and rocked against the driver's door.

As the Russian looked through the windshield, several members of the film crew who had been costuming the Mongols were running with long lances to provide the horsemen with weapons. Yuri was listening for the sound of gunfire, but when he looked, all of his companions were on the ground and several had rolled into a tight ball, probably to prevent themselves from being trampled by milling horses—or seized by riders.

Yuri's back was throbbing from the blow, and he was briefly aware that if he had taken the hit on his head his skull might have been cracked. Pain in his hip made pressure on the gas pedal excruciating, but he had dealt with pain before and he pressed harder, steering the van into the throng of milling horses. His mates scrambled into the safety provided by the van. All except Boris. He was lying stretched out on the ground. Yuri drove to within a few feet and the two men—bleeding in the back seat—jumped out, stuffed Boris in the van and tumbled in behind him.

"Get us out of here," Anatoly yelled. Yuri swung the van around and headed back the way they had come. Horses and riders were milling around the vehicle and the Mongol horsemen were now armed with lances that they jabbed into the sides of the vehicle, yelling and screaming like demons. For reasons The Handful would later find hard to explain, no one was motivated to open a window and shoot at the horsemen. One possible reason could have been a desire to avoid a lance thrust through an open window.

The total encounter had probably taken less than twenty-five minutes. Excluding the horse, who was grievously injured and had to be put down by a veterinarian, the two Turkmen security guards—hired from a local service provider—had suffered the worst injuries. Several broken metatarsals would require time to heal slowly and painfully.

Boris was still unconscious when the van returned to the hotel. He recovered in the parking lot and was able to walk into the hotel lobby where he headed for the bar—closed at this hour of the day—and raised such a racket that the manager came and opened the cabinets to give the Russians a bottle of vodka. *Afiyet olsun, you goat-fucking son of a whore*, he swore under his breath.

Although he had probably suffered a moderate concussion, Boris did not seek medical attention and his headache lasted for the next two weeks. The spot where he was struck remained tender for another two weeks. Yuri had a row of dark bruises across his back, caused by studs on the front of a Mongol shield. His hip, on the side that had slammed into the hood of the car, turned an ugly blue-black color over an area the size of a dinner plate. Gradually it turned green and then yellow in a process that took over a month. Anatoly and the other two members of the Mighty Handful had various cuts and bruises. Ferenc had a broken nose and two chipped teeth. No one suffered any thrusts from Mongol lances, but after Boris fired his pistol, it was probably a good thing that the horsemen had not been handed lances as they left the enclosure. It could have been much worse on both sides of the encounter.

At the first blow from the Afghan horseman, Boris had lost his Vektor. It flew several feet away and he never saw it again. His eyes were closed. The little pistol was picked up by a Turkmen extra who was part of the camel-handling team. Since no one seemed to be overly concerned when he picked it up, he slipped it inside his costume and it became his property.

One interesting aspect of this bizarre encounter never came to the attention of the Mighty Handful. After the Afghan horsemen began to mill around the corral gate, the camera crews, who had been making preparations all morning, swung their cameras toward the site of the attack and captured it all on film. Two different cameras were ready to go when the action broke out, so the footage of the tussle was actually very interesting. The skill of the horsemen was apparent.

Weeks later, back in Shanghai, Wendell Cho used the edited film sequence on several occasions for audiences of CHOCO managers, and for a few of his close personal friends. The Chinese enjoyed watching the utter defeat of the thuggish-looking band of Russian bullies.

At the time, it had taken Wendell Cho several moments to figure out what was happening. Once it was clear that the Russians had come to execute some type of amateurish shakedown, he laughed to see their quick defeat by the Afghans.

Back at the hotel, none of the Handful seemed anxious to fill in the day's details for Valentin. He knew something had happened to bloody their noses and dampen their spirits, but he held back from asking too many questions. Privately, he was pleased to see the injuries they had sustained, and he waited for them to speak up. Gradually he pieced together the main elements of the day and it was clear that they had been bested—and severely embarrassed—in a physical confrontation.

The upshot of their encounter was to make them even more vicious and sadistic, and their venom would soon poison and destroy the relationship between Val and Mira.

Chapter 39

Valentin's Unexpected Orders

"All his early years Genghis Khan spent in obtaining first the control of his own tribe, and then in establishing the absolute supremacy of this tribe over all his neighbors. In the first decade of the thirteenth century this work was accomplished. His supremacy over the wild mounted herdsmen was absolute and unquestioned. Every formidable competitor, every man who would not bow with unquestioning obedience to his will, had been ruthlessly slain, and he had developed a number of able men who were willing to be his devoted slaves...."

THE MONGOLS; A HISTORY
JEREMIAH CURTIN

From Ashkhabad in Turkmenistan, Valentin and his crew were scheduled to fly to Samarkand. There was a slight problem there that required correction. Their next stop was Tashkent, a trip that was scheduled to be made in two hired vans. Val planned to take Mira on the trip. Besides being uncommonly good in bed she was a clever and undemanding travel companion. He found himself growing fond of her. He had never heard her complain—about anything. Unlike some of the women he had known, she could eat anything set before her.

"How far am I supposed to go with you?" she asked. "And when do I get to go back home?"

"Then you are already homesick?" he replied. "You find traveling with me that unappealing?"

"Traveling with you is fine. But I don't think I would like it if you went away and left me with those pigs you travel with."

"Then... are they bothering you?" He knew the answer.

"Only when your back is turned. And now that someone has whipped them, they are worse than ever."

This brought Val up short. True, he knew they were savage and violent, but they had never expressed any particular interest in Mira from the first time they had seen her. And he had just assumed.... But that, he realized now, was a mistake.

"They have approached you to...."

"Approached? That is an interesting word. They have talked to me, yes. But I don't think I will tell you some of the things they have said they would like to do with me. You would not like to hear it. In case you do not know it—but I suspect you are unwilling to admit what you must know—you are traveling with animals."

His brain was whirling as he tried to think of a solution that would keep his sand castle from toppling.

"Mira, I will speak to them."

"Don't think of it now. Tomorrow will be soon enough. Sleep on it. Even better. I have a suggestion."

It was just as well Val didn't attempt to find a solution to a problem that had been building for some time. Pavel and Yuri had already made separate calls to Arkady and spoken to him about Mira.

"He's becoming a slave to this clever little whore from Romania," they told him. "She is trash. From what we could learn she was a whore in Turkey for several years before ending up near the waterfront in Constanta. But he seems to be fond of her. Already he is too soft for this job. She is only making him rotten and soon he may be too weak for the work we do."

"How old is this girl?"

"We don't know for sure. She looks young. Like a girl. But she may be as much as thirty. Even older."

"Leave it to me. I will take care of her from here. She will never arrive in Samarkand. I will make him kill her. Tomorrow. Only this. Do not kill her yourselves. When he does it, make sure that he finishes the job. If he does not, then you kill him. Is that clear?"

"It is clear."

"You sound too eager. Remember this. I need him just now. He is important. Don't be too eager because that would make me angry."

"He is to kill her? Or else we are to kill him? If he refuses? Correct?"

"Correct. Call me tomorrow. No! Call at midnight, Moscow time."

"Da!"

"Make it a short call. I will be busy all evening. Then you can tell me everything when we meet in Almaty after a few days. Oh, yes, one more thing. Have this call transferred to his room. No! Better yet, give me his room number. I plan to be with Ludmila all evening. Let him have one more night with his little whore. I'll call him in the morning."

The call in the morning came shortly after breakfast. Their hotel had a large buffet which included four different types of melon and eight kinds of bread. Val was starving after another interesting night.

Arkady's message caused him to lose the breakfast he had enjoyed. When the cell phone rang, Mira had left the table to go back to their room for something, and he was glad she was not there to see his discomfort.

Arkady was blunt. "Valentin, my lad. It will be good to see you in Almaty. But our boys tell me that you are being led around by your dick."

"Who told you that? And what did they say? Arkady, that is bullshit."

"Don't talk, Valentin. Just listen to me. Lose the girl. Today. This girl must never come to Samarkand or Almaty or anywhere else because she must . . . ."

"I will put her on the next plane to Istanbul and ship her back where I found . . . ."

"Shut up, you stupid cocksucker—and just listen to me."

"I will listen."

"Lose the girl. Lose her. Lose. Do you understand? Or must I spell it for you? Yes, you obstinate fool, I must. You must kill this girl."

He paused, but Valentin, stunned, could not think of the right response. When Arkady began again, his voice was soft and insinuating.

"You must kill her yourself, and you must do it today, Valentin. You want to become one of us? You want to continue in our organization? Enjoy its benefits? Reap its rewards? Enjoy its pleasures? Then you must pull your share of the load. And. You must obey every order you are given. This is fundamental." Stunned, Val was unable to answer.

"Look, Valentin. I am not asking you to kill your mother. Of course, if I did I would expect you to obey. Or to pay the price. But this woman is a whore. And already she has seen everyone who is traveling with you. She could identify every one of you. And unless she is a fool, she knows what you do.

You must kill her. With your own hands, or by your own hands. Otherwise—well, do not compel me to draw the picture again."

Val remained silent.

"Are you still there, Valentin? I hope you have heard everything because I am not repeating."

"I'm still here."

"Do it today. Then everything is fine. Fail to do it and—well, my lad—we had a nice relationship for a while. Hello, still there?"

"Still here."

"Valentin, comrade, do not be downcast. She is just a whore. When you get to Almaty I will give you your choice of ten young girls. Any of them. Or all of them. Even a couple of Mongolian virgins, fresh from the high plains. You will like them."

"I'm still here."

"I must go now. Ludmila is calling me. But Valentin, one more thing to remember. Yuri and Pavel know about this conversation. So you don't need to discuss it with them."

For the first time, Val realized the full significance of the trap he had constructed for himself with his cleverness. The line went dead. He went into the toilet and puked up his breakfast. When he washed his face and came back to the table, Mira had returned. Her face was glowing and she looked very young.

But—he knew—there was no way out. *Unless...*

The plane to Samarkand was scheduled to leave at 2 p.m. Everyone was packed and ready to go by ten o'clock. As they loaded their bags into the van, Yuri took Val aside. "You have a chore to do first? Where would you like us to go to do it?" Val's chess player mind had been working in high gear. All of the men carried automatics, but Mikhail, he remembered, also carried a small police-style revolver, American made, that he had sent home when he worked for a time in New York.

"Take us out east of town. Then, when the road begins to parallel the Kara Kum canal, take us north into the cotton fields. Turn off anywhere where we'll be out of sight."

"You'll make it fast?" Yuri asked. "We will have time to eat lunch at the airport?"

"Fast. Don't worry, fuckhead."

When Mikhail came to the back of the van to stuff in his bags, Val pulled him aside. "Can I borrow your revolver for an hour?" he whispered.

Mikhail opened the side pocket on his day pack and pulled out the revolver from its oily foil traveling envelope. "What happened to your automatic?" he asked.

Val ignored the question. "You'll have it back by lunch." He checked the cylinder. It was fully loaded. He made sure Mikhail saw him and he said the words loudly. "Good! Six rounds!" So far, so good. His plan might just work. If not, then he might have to risk taking on the whole bunch of them. And that was not likely to have a good outcome.

The travelers piled their baggage into the van. Mira, the smallest, got into the back seat and Val sat next to her, in the middle. In thirty minutes they were across the canal, headed north into open fields; once desert, now irrigated by water that had originated far away, as snow melt from the sides of the distant Tien Shan Mountains.

Yuri was in the front seat, next to the driver. "How far you want to go, chief?" Val was looking for a place where a short walk could take them over a rise with enough height to get them out of sight.

Mira had been silent for the entire ride. After several minutes, Val picked a spot he thought would do the job. "OK. Stop here," he said. Mira gave him a puzzled look, but she remained silent. Even as she was stepping out of the van, she never protested. "Why are we getting out here?" she asked meekly, after they were standing by the side of the road.

Yuri rolled the window down all the way. "Don't be all day. Lunchtime. Remember?"

Val took the girl by the arm. His pulse was racing, and now, for the first time, he saw fear in her eyes. It was a look he would always remember.

Leading her by the arm, he walked a distance from the van and looked back to see if they were out of sight. Just ten yards further and the top of the van disappeared. Mira's eyes were wide with fear. Wide. dark. Lovely.

She could sense at once that she was doomed, even though it had come on her unexpectedly. Still, she never pleaded. Never begged. Never asked him why.

"Kneel down," he commanded as he took the revolver from his jacket pocket. The girl kneeled and for the first time he saw a large tear roll down the side of her cheek. Her mouth turned down as if she might be about to cry. She still had not said a word to him since they first got out of the van. Her eyes held all the questions. He had to act swiftly if anything was to be done.

Without a word he clipped her above the right ear with the butt of the revolver. It was hard to gauge the blow, but he didn't want to fracture her skull. The girl fell forward, unconscious.

Moving quickly he rolled her on her side, pulled up her skirt and ripped off her panties. Then, taking a sharp pen knife from his pocket, he sliced off her right ear. Using the ear as a blotter, he made a blood stain on her blouse, between her breasts. More blood needed. Two times. Three. That looked convincing. Then he turned her head to the side so that her ghastly, bleeding wound was visible. Her ear canal had filled with blood and he managed to turn her head so that blood dripped down her cheek. It looked as if she had been shot in the ear. Using her ear as a paintbrush, he smeared blood across her thigh. *Make it visible.*

Racing to complete the plan he had conceived, he stuck the equivalent of about a thousand U.S. dollars into her brassiere. In three currencies: U.S., Russian rubles and Turkmen manats.

Next, he turned her exposed pelvis toward the road, in the direction of the van. He spat on her thigh to make a conspicuous wet streak. Three times. Four. He swished his mouth to aereate his saliva. Spat again. Stood back to survey the scene he had created. Satisfied that she might pass inspection as a violated corpse, he fired the revolver into ground. Once, twice, then three times in rapid succession. Counting the seconds, he waited for three minutes, keeping one eye open for anyone from the van. After the terribly long interval, he fired the last shot. And walked back to the van.

"You need practice," Mikhail laughed as Val handed him the revolver. "What took so long?"

"I never fucked a dying girl before, you moron."

"Let's see," said Yuri, stepping out of the van. "You might have missed every time. Or lost your nerve."

"Don't do her yourself," Val snarled. "You can still catch the clap from a dead girl. And believe me, the last one didn't miss." Val's pulse was still racing but he strove to appear calm. This was the all-important test. Both their lives hung in the balance. Hopefully she would recover and walk back to Ashkhabad to find help—if Yuri didn't decide to shoot her himself. Val's plan hinged on the hope that the girl wouldn't come to or cry out before the van left and they were gone.

It seemed to take forever for Yuri to return and Val waited in agonized suspense, fearing the sound of an automatic. But when the suspense was unbearable and Val feared the man might call out, Yuri's head appeared over the rise and he was back at the van.

As the van turned to go back, Yuri said, to no one in particular. "No kidding, he fucked her corpse." Turning his head slightly, he added, "How did you like her best, Valentin? Alive or dead?"

Val laughed and it was a laugh that contained relief as well as a silent pledge that someday he would even the score. He kept laughing until Yuri repeated the question. "Alive or dead?"

"Dead she reminded me of your mother, moron. Just get us to the airport, so that little Mitya won't miss his lunch."

Chapter 40

Mira Finds Help

"*Then I washed thee with water; yea, I thoroughly washed away thy blood from thee, and I anointed thee with oil.*

I clothed thee also with broidered work, and shod thee with badgers' skin, and I girded thee about with fine linen, and I covered thee with silk."

EZEKIEL 16:10-11

When Mira regained consciousness, she thought she was dead. It was pitch black, her head throbbed, and there was a stinging pain engulfing her face that she could not identify. Val had arranged her unconscious body to produce a particular effect for viewers, and her torso had been twisted so that her upper body was on her left arm which now felt as if it was paralyzed. Her lower body, exposed from the waist down except for shoes, was freezing.

When she opened her eyes, everything was black. If she had been lying face up, she might have seen stars and been able to take stock of her surroundings, but in the cold darkness, racked with diffuse pain, she believed that she had died and was at some unidentified way station between earth and hell. She closed her eyes and drifted off into a painful semi-consciousness.

Sometime around sunup she regained consciousness again. This time she lay for a long while without opening her eyes. When she did open them, somewhere in her field of vision a small lizard was darting between straggling blades of grass. The lizard stopped and looked at her before it disappeared. It helped her to recall what she had experienced. The little reptile reminded her that she was alive. Lizards could not survive in hell—and hell would not be so cold.

In her wildest imagination, she could not have guessed that Val had struck her to save her life. Or that the mutilation of her head had been the price of continued existence. Despite her pain, it was several minutes before she became aware that her ear had been severed. The bleeding had stopped, but her ear canal was full of clotted blood. The blockage affected her sense of balance, and when she tried to stand, she fell. Blood had run down the side of her face and neck and stiffened the top of her blouse.

Her exposed bottom was cold and she wondered if she had been raped, but she was too numbed and confused to be sure. It didn't feel like rape had felt in the past. Slowly she began to move her aching body, working her arms and legs.

When she felt her ear she experienced an electric shock. Her head was stinging. The side of her face was sticky with blood and there was blood at a couple of other places on her upper body. But she found no trace of wounds on her body. But her ear! He had cut off her ear. Why? It was incomprehensible. As she gradually began to move and regain circulation, she found herself crying softly.

Somehow she had expected more from Val. *My ear? Why my ear?* What had she done to deserve this kind of treatment? She had tried to please him in the only ways she knew. And he had never given her any indication of the cruel streak she had seen in his companions. Her underpants were hanging on a prickly cotton plant several feet away.

After several minutes she began to try to think of a plan for survival. After all, she thought, *I am still alive.* She stood up, tried to arrange her bloody, dirty clothing. In the process of brushing away dirt and plant debris, she discovered the wads of currency that Val had jammed into her brassiere. She removed the bills and counted the money briefly before folding it and replacing it in her underpants, recovered from the cotton plant. Her ear hurt now. It was throbbing like a pulse as she began to move.

Gradually the whole experience came back to her. They had been on their way to the airport when Val had decided to get rid of her. Why hadn't he just left her behind? In her life she had experienced much cruelty and indifference, but never such an act of senseless violence. Val was no better than the brutes he traveled with. No! He was much worse. And she had cared for him!

Her ear seemed to throb worse when she was standing so she sat back down on the ground trying to form a plan of action. In the distance she heard voices. They sounded like women's voices.

She stood up to see where the voices originated but the road wasn't visible behind the shallow swale Val had chosen. Slowly she began to walk in the direction of the voices.

Three Turkmen women were walking slowly beside a tiny mule-drawn cart driven by an ancient man clad in ragged trousers and a tattered, pin-striped suit coat. The women wore long dresses of flowered print material and headscarves of solid colors. The group was traveling south in the direction of the city. When they saw Mira, they stopped and looked at her with fear and astonishment.

She walked directly toward them. The Turkmen language was close enough to Turkish that she felt they would be able to understand some of what she asked.

Lutfen. Bahnah beer doctor chahrir missiniz? Lutfen. After asking for a doctor without giving any details, she asked for a ride to town. She asked again where she could find a doctor, but women seemed reluctant, or afraid, to speak to her. She felt certain that they wouldn't ask questions. Despite their reluctance to talk to her, the women were kind and helpful, insisting that she take a seat on the back of the cart. It was so low at the back that her feet would have dragged on the ground, so they moved her further back and placed her sideways so that her legs could fit inside.

It took them nearly an hour to hike back across the Kara Kum Irrigation Canal and into the fringe of the city. As they walked along the dusty road, they were passed by a steady flow of northbound trucks carrying people to work in the fields. Without asking questions the women demonstrated remarkable empathy, taking turns walking beside the jogging cart and holding Mira's hand. She was grateful for these signs of human kindness.

As they came into the limits of the city she again asked the women where she could find medical help. *Doctor, nerede? Burada doctor var mi?*

Yok. The answer came back, no. Or perhaps they just didn't know. But as they encountered paved roads and multistory buildings Mira knew that she would be able to find medical help. Then she remembered that there had been a suite of medical offices next door to the hotel where she had stayed with Val.

The old man driving the mule cart had looked at Mira with amazement when she came out of the cotton fields, but during the walk to town he neither spoke to her nor did he turn to look at her though she sat but a few feet behind him. The procession crossed a main east-west thoroughfare leading back to town, but the group seemed to want to continue heading to the south—toward the distant purple mountains.

As soon as Mira saw a vehicle with the markings of a taxi, she swung her legs out of the cart and hopped off. This triggered a hasty conversation among the three women. Mira thanked them repeatedly and each one took her hand in both of theirs, then touched their hearts and wished her well.

The exhausted girl found a driver for the dusty cab and gave him the name for the hotel where she had been registered just one day earlier. She had pushed her hair to cover the missing ear but, bloody and dirty, she still looked ghastly. She should have tried to talk one of the women into parting with a head scarf.

Her world had changed in twenty-four hours. As she rode to the hotel she moved forward, against the front seat, as close as possible, and discreetly removed the folded bills from her underwear. She pulled out several bills in Turkmen manats. She knew the address for the hotel but she didn't know the address for the medical building.

At the hotel, she paid the driver and walked a few paces to the garden adjacent to the hotel entrance. She was feeling faint and light-headed. Mira sat down on a bench bordered by marigolds and calendulas. *Just for a few moments, to clear my head.* In addition to her injuries, which included a mild concussion, she had taken no food or water for twenty-four hours. It had happened to her a score of times in her young life, but this time was different. This time, minutes after she sat down, she fainted.

She was slumped on the bench when Walt's party found her. Gina noticed the blood at once and went to help the injured girl. "Jesus Christ!" she snarled. "Some SOB has cut off this girl's ear."

Chapter 41

Gina Follows a Hunch

"After welcoming him and his Cossack companion, they decided to announce the following morning that two Russian merchants had arrived in Merv hoping to establish regular caravan traffic between Ashkhabad, the nearest Russian settlement, and the Turcoman traders of the bazaars."

THE GREAT GAME
(THE STRUGGLE FOR EMPIRE IN CENTRAL ASIA)
PETER HOPKIRK

Between Gina, Walt and a couple of doormen from the hotel, Mira was lifted into one of the waiting vans and driven next door to the complex of doctor's offices. There they found an English-speaking Turkmen surgeon who had interned at Lankenau Hospital in Philadelphia. He offered the opinion that the ear had been severed with a very sharp blade, possibly a straight razor. There was little he could do except to treat the wound with a view toward keeping it from becoming infected.

"You may know," he told Gina after taking her aside, "that in your country they can fashion prosthetic ears that are attached by a subcutaneous magnet. It is not inexpensive. And we have little call for such measures here. This was obviously a deliberate mutilation."

"We found her outside our hotel," Gina countered, defensively. "This girl is a total stranger to us. We are here as part of a cultural tour." She had no interest in any involvement with local law enforcement. The doctor likewise had no interest in notifying police. He was simply letting someone know that other alternatives were possible.

"Fortunately she is a woman, and her hair and her scarf will prevent the injury from being too noticeable."

"Yeah, she's a lucky girl," Gina snarled sarcastically.

Gina and Walt waited until the girl's injuries were treated. She had a large hematoma on her temple where she had been struck. She had no idea what had hit her and she was deliberately evasive with the doctor. When her head was bandaged, the doctor led her by the arm to the waiting room where Walt and Gina were talking quietly by an open window. Outside, a road crew was resurfacing a parking lot and it was being compacted by a roller. For Walt, the smell of hot asphalt would be linked to his memories of the injured Romanian woman.

"This seems like a curious crime to me," Gina had told him. "Her face wasn't mutilated. Or any of her sexual parts. I may be crazy, but I want to talk to her a little. Try to find out what happened. She hasn't said a word about going to the police. Maybe she was raped and just can't talk about it. Something is bizarre about this. Put everything on hold for a day. I'll take full responsibility."

"She speaks Turkish," Walt said. "But she doesn't sound like a Turkmen. Close. But no cigar."

"I know all that. I talked to her a little bit when we found her."

"So what is it you think you'll find out now? And what difference does it make?"

"Maybe nothing. But I've just got a feeling. Did you know that a Russian did her ear?"

"No. I didn't hear that."

"Look, I can't explain it. It's a hunch. But she's just too weird. She's not from here. She says she had a Romanian passport. I'm going to work on it. What the hell is she even doing here? By herself? Something is strange about this and I have a feeling. I get paid to have hunches. Especially if they turn out to be right."

Gina and Walt escorted Mira back to the hotel. The first thing they did was to feed her. At the buffet table she loaded a plate with yoghurt, melon slices, bread and cheese. Her new friends noted that she drank nearly half a liter of tea. After she ate they could see that she was pale and exhausted, so they booked a room and helped her to get settled.

After Mira was settled in bed, Gina offered to take care of having her bloody clothes laundered, or replaced. Mira, grateful not to have to worry about details, was happy to acquiesce, and too tired to protest or question. She slept until nearly five p.m. and when she woke, Gina was in her room with fresh clothes. Her skirt had been washed and the bloodstained blouse had been replaced with one from the Americans.

She also had fresh underwear and a new head scarf. Mira sat up in bed and drew up her knees. "Who are you? Why are you helping me?" They spoke in Turkish.

"My name is Gina and I'm trying to be your friend. You looked as if you could use some help when we found you."

"I was treated badly by a man I thought was my friend."

"Do you mind if I ask your name? My name is Gina. And as you may have guessed, I am from the United States. I am a visitor here."

"As am I. My name is Mira. I am Romanian. I am grateful for your help. When I feel better—perhaps tomorrow—I must try to arrange transportation so that I can return home. All of my papers, passport, visa, have been stolen."

"Who stole them? And why did they harm you? Did you try to put up a struggle?"

"Not like that. I came here as the guest of a man I thought was my friend. He invited me. He was Russian. With a group of five men. All of them, I think, bad men. Him, I thought was not a bad man."

"Where did you meet them?"

For over an hour Gina talked to Mira, but as the room grew shadowed and the afternoon wore on, she could see the girl was tired.

"Would you like to go down and eat? Or could I have some food brought up?"

"Just now I would prefer to sleep again. And maybe take one of these tablets from the doctor. My ear is hurting."

"Can I look in on you in a few hours? Maybe at eight? Eight-thirty?"

"If you wish."

"Mira, do you think you can trust me?"

"How could I be sure? Maybe I can never trust anyone. I just want to go home. Home to Romania."

"I can help you. Go to sleep for a spell. I am your friend. Even if you never trust me, I am still your friend. Lock this door when I am gone." And Gina slipped out the door. She went straight to Walt's room. "Let's take a walk."

Outside the hotel, they walked to one of Ashkhabad's many water parks with fountains and statues of the nation's self-proclaimed Sun King, Turkmenbashi.

"You've been with the woman all this time?"

"We're still not done with her. Here's what I learned. She's from Romania. Met this Russian guy in a bar. She's a working girl. A whore. Had lived in Turkey for several years with a wealthy beer baron. The old guy died and his son picked her up for a little while. Just like part of the business. In Konya. That's why her Turkish is so good."

"So? It sounds as if she's had a tough life. So what?"

"The Russian guy was kinda youngish-looking and generous, with lots of money. Nothing much like the old Turk she had lived with. Or his young son who kept her for a while after the old guy died. She never really took a liking to him. The young one. His old Turkish father she was fond of."

"Help me out here, Gina. Why do we care about the romantic relations of a one-eared Romanian whore? Even a very pretty one? It's a sad case, I'll admit. But why should it affect us?"

"Stick with me. The good-looking Russian guy is traveling with five goons. Real thugs according to her description. She was afraid of them and she doesn't seem like the type that scares easily. She said they made her blood cold; she said she knew they were killers. But the younger one. No. And, get this. He traveled everywhere with his laptop. Between his laptop and his satellite phone she said he was talking to someone for much of his time. Also there were a lot of big lists, like inventory sheets."

"So … ? I still don't get it."

"Well, it's still just a gut feel. I don't know what the Russians might have been up to. Arms, oil, drugs, women. But it has the feel and smell of a ringleader traveling with a squad of hit men. Either for protection, or to carry out some wet work. As enforcers. She said she guessed there was some bad blood between the younger one and the goons. But they had to work together."

"Still, it sounds like long odds that it could be related to anything we're … "

"Yeah, I know, I know. What a weird coincidence. Even so, I have this feeling … "

"I changed everything by two days. Do whatever you think you need to do. I can flex. Our drivers and guides will still have to be paid, but that's peanuts." Walt hesitated. He was still not satisfied.

"One thing bothers me about what you've said. She told you that the Russian guys were criminals and killers. But what did she see? How did she know?"

"She looked at their hands. They all had fresh cuts on the back of their knuckles. Wait. Don't give me the look. She said that the first time she saw them they had just come in with blood spatter on their pants legs and shoes. And believe me, Walt, when you grow up in Romania, you can recognize blood spatter. I'm giving her the benefit of the doubt. Hey, her ear didn't fucking *fall* off."

Chapter 42

Mira's Debriefing

> "... the nomadic Xiongnu, Mongols and Turks were above all cavalrymen and archers, avoiding pitched battles and hand-to-hand combat, preferring quick raids, constant harassment and kidnapping. They withdrew behind a cloud of arrows rather than drawing their swords; they were elusive, but helpless when facing fortifications. Their skill resided in the speed of their horses and their skill at shooting."
>
> THE SILK ROAD (MONKS, WARRIORS & MERCHANTS)
> LUCE BOULNOIS
> TRANSLATED BY HELEN LOVEDAY

Encouraged by her new American friends, and still suffering from a mild state of shock, Mira stayed in bed for two days. The American women brought food every day, so she could eat when she felt like it. But her appetite was gone, and when she was awake, in bed, she tried every trick she had ever developed to induce sleep. Excluding sex. She tried not to think of Val and the way she had allowed herself to be pulled along into this nightmare.

While she was inactive, she lost a couple of pounds, making her already pretty face and neck even more beautiful. Her cheeks became flushed and feverish, giving her a wind-burned look that went well with her short, tousled haircut. Everyone who visited her in her room was struck by the change in her appearance since they found her.

Gina arranged for the doctor to visit and change the dressing on her ear. The pills from her first visit to the clinic seemed to be doing a good job in managing pain. The girl appeared grateful for the unsolicited help, but at no time did she seem to want to talk much about her experience. Gina waited for her to show signs of restlessness before resuming the questions.

On the third day, Mira showed up in the hotel dining room as the Americans were having breakfast. Gina got up and met her at the buffet table and escorted her to the table where the group was gathered. The girl was introduced to members of the group she had not already met. Everyone was amused by the sight of a rather small, very pretty female putting away a breakfast that might have stuffed a lumberjack.

After breakfast, Gina asked her to go for a walk. Mira couldn't help noticing that they were followed at a discreet distance by two of the men from breakfast.

"So you're planning to return home? To Romania?"

"That is my plan. I will make some phone calls today."

"You may need some time to obtain a passport. Perhaps I can help. Perhaps I could persuade you to stay for a few more days."

"There is nothing here for me. And my memories are not pleasant."

"I understand. But that is in the past and you might enjoy a few days with us. We are tourists out to see the country of Turkmenistan, and you might join us while you continue to recover from your ordeal. Is anyone expecting you in Romania?" The last question caught Mira off guard and she was silent for a long moment. The two women were passing a bench at one of Ashkhabad's numerous water parks. A fountain with an unlikely pair of dolphins was spurting two thin streams about ten feet into the air. Gina walked a few steps before she realized the girl was not beside her. Mira had stopped to sit on the bench.

When Gina sat down, Mira looked her in the face as if trying to gauge something about her character before she spoke.

"In Romania, I have nothing. And I have only few friends. No family. When I go back, I will be nobody. I have been several things in my life, including whore. It is what I know. It is what I do. I drifted into this ugly place because a man wanted me. Or seemed to. I wanted to be wanted. Now, I feel lost. I am a face on a Romanian passport. Nothing more. My friends in Romania would scarcely miss me if the Russian bastard had killed me." She spoke with emotion, but there was no trace of self pity.

When she finished speaking she looked away. Gina gave her a few moments to regain her composure.

"With us you could feel yourself among new friends. We are here for an outing. We will visit Mary and see the ancient ruins. Then we will go to the north into Uzbekistan and visit Khiva. Near Urgench. You could come with us. You could be our guest for a few days. Until you are feeling stronger."

"I feel strong now. Anyway, why would you offer this to me? What do you want from me?"

Gina knew she must tread softly now, or she could easily lose the girl and any information she might have. And chances were good that she had nothing useful anyway. It was just a hunch. Just a feeling.

"Mira, you are a small bird. If you want to fly, then take off and disappear and we will just be happy that we saw you. But if you choose to stay with us for a short spell, we would be pleased. You are a very pretty bird—as you know well—and your mere presence can make people smile. It is a gift you were given. Even if you may not have wanted it." Gina paused. Perhaps she had said too much already.

The girl was thinking. "I have only a little money," she said. "Perhaps enough to get back to Constanta."

"If you join our group for a few days, you would be our guest. You would not have to worry about money."

"And so the Russian bastard told me. Just the same thing." She hung her head. Gina watched her face closely, loved seeing the expressions flit across her wounded face as the Romanian girl weighed the risks, considered the downsides and finally rolled the dice. She was a brave young woman. Gina could recognize it.

"I will join you and be a bird with your group for a few days."

"Wonderful. And to make you comfortable about returning to Romania, I will give you..."

"No. Give me nothing. No guarantees. You have offered me... as your guest. I will choose to trust you. Meanwhile, I must try to replace the passport."

The two women looked at one another for a long interval without speaking.

"And I must find a headscarf."

The next day, the group, augmented by one, squeezed into a van and got an early morning start for the oasis town of Mary. Mira conversed easily with Walt and Gina in Turkish, but to others in the vehicle she could say enough words in English to make her a pleasant traveling companion. On the whole, everyone in the group was content to have a new, pretty female among them. But nobody had a clue why she was there, and Gina would have been hard pressed to explain Mira's presence.

When the party made rest stops along the way, for tea or for toilet breaks, she chatted with Walt and Gina, smiled, stretched herself, and integrated quietly, seamlessly into the group. To make it easy for the girl to buy refreshments during their occasional stops, Gina pushed her to accept a handful of Turkmen currency.

"No! No money! I have money," the girl said with an expression that was close to tears.

On the ride between the Turkmen capital and Mary, the ancient oasis town once known as Merv before the Soviets renamed it, Walt provided a running commentary. He had, long ago, made an accommodation with their Turkmen guide who was required by law to accompany them.

"The ancient city existed as early as the 6th century B.C. when it was occupied by Persian fire worshippers known as Zoroastrians. Some practitioners of this religion still live quietly among their Muslim neighbors in Turkmenistan and bordering Iran."

He talked about Merv as the place once known as Margiana that was visited by the Macedonian army under Alexander the Great in the 3rd century BC.

Merv had not escaped the wrath of Mongol hordes in their sweep from the high plateaus to the east all the way to the borders of Europe. The region's long history had been one of conquest and reconquest. The city had fallen to the Russians not long after the American Civil War had ended, and it had been strongly influenced by Russian culture since before the Revolution. It had fallen to the Bolsheviks in 1919, and became part of the autonomous Turkmen SSR in 1924.

Soviet planners built the Kara Kum Canal, 660 miles of irrigation ditch, expressly to support the introduction of cotton culture along the arid margins of the desert. The canal was successful in enabling cotton farming, and also the cultivation of melons—and other crops—in a desert environment. But irrigation came at the cost of starving the Aral Sea to the north, now steadily shrinking with alarming consequences for the environment.

Chunks of this lore were translated selectively by Gina as the two women sat side by side in the back of the van. Gina held off asking Mira the series of questions that had been taking shape over the past days.

The Cat Herd spent the morning roving the ruins outside ancient Merv—while Gina looked for an opening when she could be alone with Mira. Gina was waiting for the right quiet pauses that would permit her to ask more questions concerning the Russians who had brought her to Turkmenistan. That opportunity never came.

As they wandered among the archaeological sites in Merv, Walt kept the group moving. He maintained a steady flow of information on the history of the ancient oasis town. Gina realized, belatedly, that she would probably have to wait for another opportunity—unless she wanted to disrupt the planned day. Some members of the group were clearly restless, especially since each person had specific areas of interest which, by now, they would have preferred to have pursued in vehicles with drivers of their own.

Gina sensed that a small revolution was in the making. She was also aware that she had gummed up the timetable with the addition of Mira to their small party, and—while no one had complained about the girl—Gina was getting bad vibes.

Back in Ashkhabad, they stopped at lunch in an open bazaar near the train station and had shashlik; mutton grilled on skewers, accompanied by a selection of vegetable dishes including carrots, eggplant and rice. During the meal, which was served with gallons of tea, Katya ordered a bottle of wine and Walt noticed that, while it was shared with the group, Katya drank about half just by herself and seemed none the worse.

In two days, Walt had planned a scenic drive across the forbidding Kara Kum desert for a visit to the ancient Silk Road oasis town of Khiva. This site was located across the border in Uzbekistan, a country only slightly less bizarre than Turkmenistan. Gina would have been willing to pay for Mira to accompany them, despite the fact of her missing Romanian passport and the likely expenditure of bribe money to get her into the country without wasting a lot of time. But Mira had already made it clear that she didn't want to risk going into another country.

That evening, back at the hotel, Gina intercepted Mira in the lobby. She had a fresh dressing on her ear and her short hairstyle had been artfully arranged to take attention away from the dressing. All covered with an unobtrusive kerchief. During the day, as they had walked around Merv, Mira had worn a headscarf and it had been possible to forget that she had been injured.

"Mira, I need to talk with you in private. Can we walk outside for a few minutes?" In the dry air, heavy with the smell of dust, they headed in the direction of the water park where they had talked earlier. Gina came right to the point.

"Mira, we'll be leaving the day after tomorrow. Like I told you earlier, we're going to Urgench, in Uzbekistan—and you made it clear that you don't want to come. But the truth is that it's probably not safe for you to stay here."

"I can take care of myself." *Yeah, sure Mira. I can see that.*

"Yes, I don't doubt that you know how to survive. But already men in the hotel have been looking at you. When they see you alone, you will be vulnerable. And you know how cruel some men can be."

"I do know."

"We—my friends and I—would like to help you. And our circumstances are such that we can help you quite a lot. I believe that the men who brought you here were very bad men. That they were members of the Russian Mafia."

"They were bad men. Yes, maybe Russian Mafia. I have thought this myself. But I did not want to say."

"And they deserve to be punished."

"Yes, of course. Bad men always deserve to be punished. But who can punish them? They are armed. And they know no law."

"Mira, we have friends in the United States government who would like to know about these men. If you could go to them and help them identify the men who brought you here, you would be well paid. Enough to travel back to Romania if you insist on going back there. Or to anywhere else in the world where you wanted to make a new start. Back to Konya, perhaps? Or to Antalya? You said you were happy there."

"Yes. But that was long ago." Gina was encouraged. The girl had not rejected the proposal out of hand. Perhaps she was thinking it over.

"Mira, this is my proposal. If you agree, tomorrow we will make arrangements for you to fly out of here to Moscow. On an American military flight where no passport will be needed. Someone from the American Embassy will meet your plane and take you to a safe house. From there we will book you on a flight to Rome. In Rome you will be picked up by our friends who would like to talk with you. They would provide comfortable accommodations. Comfortable and safe. It might take two days. Three at most. They would show you many photographs to see if you recognized any faces. You could recognize these men."

"In Rome? All the way to Italy? So far?"

"It's not so far. By next week this time you would be back in Romania. Or wherever else you might choose. My friends are placed to help you with entry visas and any other documentation to take you wherever you want to go."

"This is a lot to think about."

"And there is not a lot of time."

"You can do all this?"

"Yes."

"You are with the American government? You and your friends? You are military? CIA, perhaps?"

"Mira, you just spent a whole day with us. Do we seem like CIA to you? We are tourists, here to see the land of the ancient Silk Road. But we have friends in the government, and we have connections with many people who have an interest in the story you have told us. Not many women are invited into countries of Central Asia by men who subsequently mutilate them and leave them alive. Your experience is unusual and unique. You must know that."

"Unusual. Yes." The girl had a faraway look in her eyes, almost as if her mind was somewhere else. Gina was beginning to feel slightly frustrated.

"So what do you say? Will you go to Rome for us? I need to know so I can make several phone calls and have the arrangements put in place."

"And what will you be able to do, Miss Gina, when those men come back to find me and hurt me? What will *you* say then?" Gina was trying to think fast. How could she answer this legitimate concern? Her face must have betrayed her sudden consternation, for Mira reached out and touched the back of her hand.

"Do not give me an answer. You do not have an answer. I understand your request. Can we eat our dinner first? Then, afterwards, I will decide what I will do."

Gina stood up. "Let's go eat."

Later that evening Gina began making the series of calls that would smooth Mira's passage from Ashkhabad to Rome. She was making calls until well after midnight. Mira flew—undocumented—out of the Ashkhabad terminal shortly before noon the next day. Gina's arrangements went smoothly and Mira was met in Moscow by a woman from the Embassy in Moscow who spoke passable Turkish. The girl had been accompanied by a junior officer from the Embassy in Turkmenistan.

Things happened quickly. Before she had a chance to think through any possible downsides to her accession to Gina's request, she found herself in the air again and shortly afterward she was placed in comfortable lodgings in Rome. A car and driver whisked her to a walled compound somewhere in Rome where several men and a few women asked her to repeat the story she had told to the Americans with Gina and Walt.

A doctor came and examined her ear. The doctor could not speak any language she understood, so they spoke little, but he handled her gently. When he looked at the wound he said under his breath, "Something very sharp." He gave her some additional medication for pain and changed the dressing.

Then men in suits began asking her to look at a very large number of photographs. They would stop every few hours and walk around, take coffee or tea, or sometimes, carbonated drinks. Then they would resume. It was very boring and tiring, but on the afternoon of the second day, suddenly, she was looking at Val. Valentin Kuriatin. It might have been taken five years ago because he looked slightly younger, but he was still the same. Dark mustache still trimmed in the same way. Still handsome, with fine, close teeth and dark, intelligent eyes. *Still a cruel bastard.*

Within an hour of spotting Val, she had also picked out the faces of two of his companions. The two were former KGB. She looked at photographs until noon on the third day, but she did not see any more familiar faces. The Americans had paraded a veritable library of photos in front of the girl and she had been able to identify three of the men. Neither she nor her interrogators had a clear picture of what had happened to her in the cotton fields of Turkmenistan.

She was scheduled to return to the American compound to make detailed arrangements for her next move when she disappeared. At the time she was believed to have had the equivalent of less than a thousand dollars U.S. in her possession. A check at air and rail terminals never turned up any trace of the vivacious young woman who simply dropped out of sight.

Chapter 43

Visiting Khiva

"Love
Is the great work
Though every heart is first an
Apprentice."

FROM "THE GREAT WORK"
THE GIFT; POEMS BY HAFIZ
HAFIZ (1320-1389)
TRANSLATED BY DANIEL LADINSKY

The Cat Herd was staying in Urgench while they were visiting Khiva. Walt's plans called for them to continue on to Bukhara. On their first night at the hotel in Urgench, Bill Keener and Paul Kellogg, the two scariest members of the Cat Herd, had failed to show up for dinner and Walt could only wonder where they might be prowling.

Before breakfast, Gina took Walt aside. "This is a bullshit plan," she said.

"Why so?" he replied, determining not to take offense.

"Well, for one thing, it's so much off the beaten path that people are still carrying shit on camels. The main route from Ashkhabad is through Mary to Bukhara. Jeez, you know that. That's where all the heavy truck traffic is found. This may be a great place for students, but it doesn't cut it for us."

Walt had to admit she was right. But he had, after all, been told to treat this group just like his students. And Khiva was too good to be missed.

"Look," said Gina, "There's gonna be a slight adjustment to the plan. I'm gonna try to fly out of here today. There's a light plane I can take out of Urgench, so I'm going up to Tashkent for a day. I'll take Chuck Bismarck with me. Just go ahead with your cruise today. When I get back, it's possible we'll need to head back to Ashkhabad. Across that goddamn desert again. Then, from there we'll go through

Mary to Bukhara. I know this wrecks your plans. But I'm giving you a heads up."

"If that's the plan, I'll go to work as soon as we finish talking."

That evening, the place where they were staying brought in a local trio to play in their restaurant and bar. Keener and Kellogg showed up in time for dinner. The musicians had a guitar and bass, together with a curious drum set that didn't resemble those normally seen in the west. In addition, the guitar player had a second instrument called a saz, rarely seen in the U.S. Paul Kellogg, who claimed to play a little jazz guitar, was intrigued by the instruments, but even more by the music the group was playing. "This is great stuff," he said, his eyes fastened on the saz player. "How come we never hear anything like this back home?" It was the most animation Walt could remember seeing from this guy who had appeared to be totally bored as they drove around the sites of Khiva. Members of the Herd had stayed through the first set and appeared to want to stick around for the second set. Walt excused himself and left to go to his room.

Tara had come tapping at his door shortly after midnight and he had let her in.

"I need to be held," she said.

He had let her in without protest, but she read the look on his face.

"Don't look at me that way, professor. I'm not a bad person. I won't bug you. Promise."

"Jesus, Tara. What am I going to with you?"

"You really don't want me to answer that."

He woke her early the next morning to send her back to her room. He watched her put on her clothes with feelings of tenderness for which he could not find words. In the black and white early morning light he wished he could watch her forever. Just look at her. When she was ready to leave he held her tight and kissed the top of her head.

"Listen, Tara, I don't want this group to know *anything* about us. No good can come of it. On the other hand, I want the world to know. I want to shout about you. But not until this job is completed. I don't know what these guys are supposed to be doing. And we shouldn't even be talking about this. So. Don't spill the beans about us. We can come out after this job is finished."

The girl's eyes grew wide and filled with tears.

"You didn't need to tell me that. I'm not a child."

"Tara, Tara, no, you're not. But it's hard for me to keep my eyes off you. So I can't help but think it could be something like that for you. And it's important that we keep things cool until after we're back."

"I've got it figured out, professor. You better start trusting me."

He opened the door and pushed her out.

The group was fed, seated in the van and on the road shortly before ten a.m. He planned to take them on a circuit of the city that had been ancient Khiva, the city that had once been envisioned as the marshaling point for an Imperial Russian Army that might invade India—by way of the Khyber Pass. The drive was around a wide loop, much of which was through desert fringe or irrigated fields of cotton and cereal crops. Walt avoided running comments at the beginning and listened in on several of the conversations to try to gauge the mood of his group.

Kellogg, the former Special Forces guy, was the quietest member of the entourage and so far he had seemed to be the one least interested in any of the comments Walt made as they traveled. He was also the one who had the most unexplained absences. Even this morning, he had arrived after breakfast, apparently having eaten somewhere else. But he was always ready to go on time.

So it came as something of a surprise to Walt when Kellogg spoke up. "I have to admit, Walt, that Khiva is really interesting. The buildings, the architecture. That tile work is really something. It must have cost a fortune. It's hard to imagine the cost of doing something like that in Baltimore. And it seems pretty clear that this place could never have existed but for the river."

Kellogg's comments got the group talking about the things they had seen on the previous day—crossing the desert.

Kevin McLaughlin gave Walt an opening he needed. "You told us that Khiva was ruled by a Khan. That it was one of several khanates that survived in Central Asia up until the time of the Russian Revolution. But that place looks like a frigging movie set. How did it survive through all the destruction of two world wars? You probably told us yesterday."

"One of the reasons we're seeing crops out the window is because of the near presence of the Amu Darya River. This is the river that Alexander the Great knew as the Oxus. It flows from the mountains of Central Asia to the Aral Sea and it has made this region habitable since the dawn of time. But for Khanates of Central Asia, we can thank Genghis Khan. Want to hear?"

There was a murmur of approval from most of the members.

"During the days of the Roman Empire, the Silk Road was in operation and caravans traveled over this general route heading in the direction of Istanbul. Eventually the trade extended to other cities of Rum—that was the Turkic name for all of western Turkey that was once ruled by Rome. Actually, Khiva wasn't on the main route, but it benefited from proximity to the trade.

Rome, and later Constantinople, were population centers where merchants could find their best markets. The natural oases along the routes across Central Asia gradually developed into caravansarais and market towns that could support the merchant caravans. The cities developed naturally at places like Khiva, Bukhara, Samarkand, Tashkent. The oasis closest to modern-day Tashkent was known as Kokhand. Unless something else comes up, we'll plan on going there in a few days.

After Mohammed began the Islamic religion, waves of Arab invaders introduced Islam by the sword. The first waves weren't spreading religion. They were just looting. These caravan towns were prosperous. Eventually, however, the religion caught on. We already talked about that. This region fell under the sway of the Islamic religion. We know this was sometime in the 8th century. Now, fast forward to the 13th century, when Genghis Khan and his Mongol hordes sweep out of Mongolia and overrun the lands to the west.

His empire grew to extend from Korea and the Sea of Japan all the way west to the Ukraine, Poland, Bohemia and the valley of the Danube. Hard to imagine all this being overrun by Mongolians. But that's what happened. Much like Hitler rolling into Belgium or France. It was blitzkrieg. His whole Mongol nation consisted of nomads who could live on horseback and shoot accurately over their horse's backs.

But their empire grew too big to be manageable. And Genghis died. His sons and grandsons carried on his work. Still, Mongol Asia was just too big and unwieldy. Then sometime in the 1200's, I think around 1260, one of the grandsons, Kublai Khan, divided up the great Khan's empire. Kublai Khan. You've all heard that name?"

"From Coleridge's poem," Katya spoke up. "'*In Xanadu, did Kublai Khan, a stately pleasure dome decree. Where Alph the sacred river ran. Down to a sunless sea.*' But I never knew where Xanadu was located. Or Alph."

"Or the caverns measureless to man," laughed Walt. "But, yes Kat, you got it. That's the guy. Kublai Khan. His empire was just too big and unwieldy. Also he had the same kind of problem that King Saud has in Arabia today. Too many brothers and sisters competing for the empire. And cousins. It gets to be unsafe and you never know who's behind the curtain.

Kublai Khan broke up his empire into four separate Khanates. The Khanate of the Great Khan was, basically, the original empire extending from Mongolia, east to the ocean and south to Tibet. A second Khanate, Chagatai, covered Afghanistan and most of the other "stans," as well as the southern margin of today's Kazakhstan.

A third Khanate was that of Persia, embracing Iran, Iraq, and the southern Caucasus.

Finally, the Khanate of the Kipchak included Western Asia, Russia and the Ukraine. These tribes were also known as the Golden Horde."

"So we're travelling through the Khanate of Chagatai?" Betty Bismarck asked.

"Right. Except that over time it kept breaking up into smaller pieces. It fragmented because of the sheer size of it—coupled with the inability to communicate and the difficulties of ruling. The same thing happened to the Roman Empire. It just grew too big to be controlled from Rome."

The van was moving through irrigated fields separated by the ever-present rows of poplars used as boundary markers. Occasionally they would pass small groves of pistachios, plums or apricot trees, then the vast fields of cotton, made colorful by patches of wheat and barley.

Walt noticed that the woman he knew as Betty—God only knows what her real name might be—was making notes. "I can make you a copy of everything I've just said," he offered pleasantly.

"Thanks," she said. "I'm just kinda interested in these trucks we've been passing. Haven't you noticed?"

Walt had no idea what she was talking about. "Since we left town, ever since around ten-thirty, we have passed nine westbound trucks, all red, all Mitsubishis. Not in a convoy. Spaced about fifteen or twenty minutes apart. What an interesting coincidence. Don't you think? I've got the name off the trucks. Looks like a family name. Shishkin. What does *kardesler* mean?"

"Kardeshler. It just means 'brothers.'"

"Go ahead with your story," Betty said. "I'm just killing time."

"Did you notice?" Paul Kellogg said. "Two men in every truck. Driver. And a shotgun?"

Chapter 44

Feedback From Mira's Trip

> "...a maintenance worker walking home along the track of the Transcaspian railway was startled to hear a train approaching from the direction of Krasnovodsk. For he knew that no trains were due at this remote spot on the single-track line at such an hour. As it got closer he could see that it carried no lights, something unheard of even in those disordered times. Mystified, he scrambled up the embankment and hid behind a clump of camel-thorn to watch this ghost train pass. Instead it glided silently to a halt close to where he crouched in the darkness."
>
> LIKE HIDDEN FIRE
(THE PLOT TO BRING DOWN THE BRITISH EMPIRE)
PETER HOPKIRK

Flying out of Urgench in Uzbekistan, Gina and Charles Bismarck left the group for two days to visit the American Embassy in Tashkent. They chartered a flight with a Russian pilot who occasionally flew tourists over the desert to view Khiva from the air. In Tashkent, using secure communications technology, they were able to establish a voice link with agency people in Rome who had debriefed the Romanian woman. The agent in charge at Rome had good news and bad news.

"It took us three days of slogging before she found faces she recognized. But all indications are that she made a positive identification. Out of the six men she was traveling with, she picked out three."

"What about the guy who cut off her ear?"

"She got him on the second day. The one she calls Val. Valentin Mihailovich

Kuriatin. He was an engineer-mathematician type trained at Moscow University. Went in the army and was assigned for a time at the Russian's Baikonur Cosmodrome in Kazakhstan. Some sort of a computer whiz for the Russians."

"Mira said he traveled with a couple of laptops. One for a backup, maybe?"

"He also studied in the U.S. At Harvard. They tell us that he didn't seem to care about getting a degree, but he took all the killer courses and scored high. Breezed to an MBA. Before that he had an assignment in India. We don't know much about that."

"So why do I have the wind up?"

"We think you're on the money. He definitely has ties to the Russian Mafia. We just don't know exactly what they are. Most likely it's drugs or weapons. We don't think he's linked to gas or oil."

"Why do you say drugs?"

"Let me skip to the other two guys and we'll come back to Valentin. The other two guys she ID'd are definitely Russian KGB muscle. She nailed them spot on. But she also helped us a lot with the ones whose pix weren't on file. They're heavily tattooed. Almost certain to be ex-convicts—from Russian prisons."

"Enforcers?"

"They're probably the strong-arm guys. Apparently, something goes wrong or they have somebody who sticks their hands in the till, these bad boys go out and break legs or remove fingers. That's if you're lucky."

"Are you going to send me pix of the ones she got?"

"Later today. Pix and a written summary. But let me tell you about these two she nailed—the former KGB killer types. These guys were also known as hit men, torturers, borderline psychopaths. After the KGB meltdown, they found work with criminal networks. Actually, Mira found the ones we thought would be hardest to spot."

"Explain."

"The other three? She said they were so heavily tattooed we could never miss them, and she described a lot of the tattoos that were visible. This means they are most likely convicted criminals. Almost certainly for violent crimes. So even though we can't put names on them, they should be uniquely identifiable. They're wearing their fingerprints on their arms and legs. Some on their necks, even. Our guess is that these guys are just as deadly as their KGB counterparts. Maybe even more so.

Wherever they turn up for a few days, the body count is likely to rise. She says they are very sadistic with members of the opposite sex. They hurt three of her girl friends in Romania. They use young women like Kleenex. Mira is probably lucky to be alive. She told us they didn't like her. Although she couldn't say why, because she had no dealings with them."

"Did you ask Mira what she thought Val might be doing?"

"She didn't really know exactly what he was doing. Except that he spent several hours a day on his laptop. Also, she says that he did a lot of talking on his cell phone.

Sometimes she couldn't understand what he was saying. It sounded like some kind of business: shipments, deliveries, pickups, that kinda stuff. But she couldn't be sure about the product. We didn't want to lead her with too many questions about drugs. Yes, we interrogated her thoroughly."

"And you gave her money to travel on?"

"Sure. Of course. She said she wanted to go back to Romania. We helped her with the passport. I suspect that's where she is right now. She disappeared on us just before we were going to take her to the airport."

"So you aren't sure if she actually went home?"

"Did I say she went home? No. Like I say, she ditched us. And we didn't have her under surveillance. She came in voluntarily. No reason to think she'd skip on us. I think she just got tired of us. We worked her kind of hard."

"So we couldn't find her if I wanted her?"

"Why would you want her? It doesn't seem likely that she's involved with these guys in any way. It looks like she was involved with the brainy one in a gang of bad boys and something went haywire. She was in the wrong place at the wrong time."

Gina was slightly pissed but she pressed her lips together and tried not to say anything sharp or sarcastic. She didn't know this agent personally and she didn't want to come across as a hardass, but one of her pet peeves was someone who answered her questions with a question. She was working to control her responses whenever this happened; this time she was successful.

"Did she tell you why she went to Turkmenistan with men she had just met?"

"Well—after all—she is a whore. The Russian guy gave her money. She wasn't at all clear about the reason for the trip. Especially since she was frightened by the five guys. I think she might have been a little sweet on the good-looking one. Val. Although—considering her profession one has to be a bit skeptical."

"She said she was afraid of the five guys?"

"Definitely. They scared her, but she felt secure when the Valentin guy was around. Oh, yeah. I forgot without my notes in front of me. She said that Val called them the Mighty Handful. She didn't know why. Yeah. She said she was afraid of them. They talked to her when Val was away for any reason. She tried to work it so she was never alone with any of them. And twice, she says she saw blood spatter on their shoes and pants leg."

"How do you think she would she know it was blood spatter?" Gina wanted to hear him say it.

"Listen, Agent Santorini, you grow up in Romania and you've seen blood spatter. You know how old this girl is?"

"You know, I never asked her that. Not old. I'd guess about twenty-five."

"She just turned thirty-four. You wouldn't guess it, would you? Especially considering what she does for a living. She looks younger. This little girl has been around the block."

"If I wanted to get in touch with her, do you think you could find her?"

"Why would you want to get in touch with her? I can send you a transcript."

Fuck! Gina had compressed her lips more than once in this conversation. If she kept talking to this fucking guy any longer she was gonna lose it and tell him where to stick his transcript.

"Agent Donnelly, excuse me. I'm just getting a sign that I'm needed. We'll have to break it off for now. I'll look forward to the material you'll be sending. Thanks very much for your assistance." *Asshole!*

"You're welcome. If we can help in the future be..."

She broke the connection. JoJo the dogfaced agent—her private name for Agent Charles Bismarck who had a faint resemblance to Walter Matthau—laughed. "That went rather well, I thought," he barked. "You lasted a whole ten minutes without telling him to kiss your ass. So why do you want to talk to Mira again?"

"Actually, I don't really need to talk to her. I'd just like to come up with a way to keep her from getting killed."

PART 4

CONFUSION

Chapter 45

Trouble in River City

*"Someone
Will steal you if you don't
Stay near,
And sell you as a slave in the
Market.
I sing
To the nightingale's hearts
Hoping they will learn
My verse
So that no one will ever imprison
Your brilliant angel
Feathers."*

FROM "SPICED MANNA"
THE GIFT—POEMS BY HAFIZ
HAFIZ (C. 1320—1389)
TRANSLATED BY DANIEL LADINSKY

Two psychopaths from the Mighty Handful had traveled to Tashkent to deal with a logistics problem. It hardly matters which two took the assignment, which was intended to be brief. Members of Kuchka are virtually interchangeable. Whatever conditions exist within the human gene for twisting or warping the moral compass—they all share it.

The unanticipated disclosure of Mira's survival that was revealed in Tashkent occurred because a truck driver from Ashkhabad got sick on the day that he was scheduled to drive his normal route. Without telling anyone, he asked his brother-in-law—a recent arrival from Ukraine who had emigrated east against the current—to fill in for him. The brother-in-law, who had a criminal record in Europe, failed to understand Valentin's tracking system and he poked around into part of the cargo, leading him to make some unplanned diversions of the drugs he discovered.

A few phone calls quickly pinpointed the problem and targeted both men for punishment that was swift and severe. Actually, about as severe as punishment can get.

The Kuchkans were in a busy truck park on the outskirts of Tashkent when they were spotted by a driver they had employed before during several of their visits to Ashkhabad. They had drunk vodka together at a roadside caravansarai that had been converted into a truck stop between Ashkhabad and Khiva.

"Ya, friends, and imagine seeing you here in Tashkent. This is a coincidence, yes? When will we have time to drink vodka together again?"

"Ya, Nevzat. You should be in Ashkhabad, polishing up your van for our return."

"In three days, my friends. My wife is waiting by the clock. But when will I see you again?"

"Who can tell, Nevzat. We go where we are sent. But maybe you will not be much older when you see us next."

"And your other companions? Will you bring them again? And the dark man and his handsome little woman?"

"Before you have aged too much."

"But why did you give that girl to the Americans? This has made me wonder."

"Speak plainly, Nevzat."

"The little dark-haired one, like a jewel from a Pasha's harem? Why did you give her to the Americans?"

"That was before we left, Nevzat. We gave no one to Americans. We sent the girl home. We will never see her again."

"The Americans sent her home. After they fixed the injury to her head."

"You are mistaken, Nevzat."

"No. Truly. The Americans. I spoke with my friend who drove for them—around the region."

The Kuchkans looked at one another as various scenarios raced through their minds. Neither of them could reconcile what Nevzat was telling them with what they thought they knew.

The Kuchkans were back in Almaty before the bodies of their two victims were found, and within a few hours of their arrival they were talking to Yuri, the only one of the Kutchkans who had seen Mira's body.

"Your Turkmen friend must have been mistaken," Yuri snarled. "I saw her myself. He shot her several times in the body. Then one shot to the head. I saw for myself. And he said he fucked her before she died. Or maybe she was dead. That I did not see. But his semen was running out of her body. That I saw. Your friend had been drinking."

"Yes, perhaps he is insane. Or he confused the girl with another. But no!—he had not been drinking. He was steady." Both men were certain that the Turkmen driver had been sober.

Yuri was rewinding his tapes; then a fast forward and a desperate rewind. This was not good. Arkady would not be pleased. And he was the only one who had gone to look at the girl, had seen the bloody wound where she had been shot in the head.

He was furious at the thoughts that were forming in his brain. *What if that smooth-talking child of an ulcerated whore had played a trick?* The Turkmen driver would have had no reason to lie. No! He had seen the girl after they had left Ashkhabad. The girl was still alive. Valentin had managed to fool them all. And if the hint of this reached Arkady? His displeasure was ugly to contemplate. Unless, perhaps, it came from Yuri himself. *Immediately. Directly. Now. From me.*

"Listen, brothers, if the girl is alive—let us assume your friend tells the truth—then she and that fucking Valentin Mihailovich have deceived us. Let us take this for the truth and report it as such to Arkady. Otherwise…."

There was general agreement that Arkady must be told and that he was certain to be furious.

"Better that I tell him at once," Yuri said. "By phone will be better." The others nodded in general agreement.

"Come, my brothers, and let me share with you some memorable vodka that will make your hearts leap and your eyes water. And I will need it before I speak with Arkady."

When Arkady learned that the girl had been seen alive after Valentin had reported her dead, he was apoplectic. "Bring that son of a bitch to me," he roared.

But Val was in India working on some concepts for improving his tracking system and its ability to minimize fraud or deception in collecting payment at time of delivery. He was also working on managing border transits for diverse types of packaging concealing his drugs.

He had been studying this problem for some time and wanted to talk it over with some of his Indian friends. A part of him was also anxious to see how Neela might look to him after the passage of several months.

Arkady's first reaction was to send a pair from the Mighty Handful to India to guarantee that Valentin never returned. He toyed with the idea of having him brought back alive so he could kill him personally. After all, it was his honor that had been sullied by the deliberate disobedience.

But this, he knew, was not reasonable. If he had known capable, dependable men in Bangalore he would have placed the contract there, but his knowledge of reliable Indian contractors was lacking. At some level he blamed himself for allowing Val so much latitude.

He called Val's office in Almaty to learn when he would be returning. By the end of the week. He would make sure a greeting committee would be waiting when Val returned. In his rage at being deceived, Arkady did not stop to think about the damage that might be done to his drug empire with Val out of the way. He was aware of the revenue stream that flowed into his vast network based on the system Val had set up, but he had little understanding of its true complexity and sophistication. The business of arms sales and arms smuggling was comprehensible to him, but the maze of relationships being managed by people who worked at desks—this was beyond his comprehension.

Before leaving Bangalore, Val checked in with his office to see if any important calls had come in or if he was scheduled for any appointments. He was not surprised to learn that Arkady's office had called. He was, however, put on guard upon learning that the man, himself, had placed the call. That was something Arkady rarely did.

"He sounded angry," said Anastasia. "Like something had irritated him. I don't think we're late with any reports."

For reasons he would have been hard pressed to explain, Val sensed that something was wrong. Some alarm went off in a corner of his brain.

"Listen, Anastasia. We know the hotels where the Mighty Handful put up when they come to Almaty. Look at your records. Find the last places where they have stayed. It may be the same place every time. Check at the front desk and find out if they have booked anyone we know from The Mighty Handful—or booked anyone else from Astana for this weekend. Get the names and see who else might work for Arkady."

"For this weekend?"

"Yes. I need to know who is coming that does not regularly visit. And Anastasia Nicolaievna. Go in person. Take cash with you. Get this information even if you have to pay for it. And don't mention this to anyone."

"Are you in trouble?"

"Anya, I am always in trouble. But you shouldn't be concerned. I'm looking out for you. Only one more thing. Do not tell anyone when my flight is arriving. Destroy any records of my recent trips."

"But they know you will be here before Monday for your scheduled activities."

"But not exactly when I return. Move quickly and I will call you before I take the plane."

"I will go after we finish talking."

"And Anya?"

"Yes?"

"Spaseeba."

Val's next call from the airport confirmed what he had suspected. Two members of the Mighty Handful would be in Almaty when he returned. He had not discussed their visit with Arkady and now his suspicions had been aroused. Possibly their arrival in Almaty meant nothing. But somehow, Arkady might have learned the secret Val had tried to conceal.

The entire drug tracking network operating from Almaty was designed and managed by Val. He had deputies who understood parts of the system, and a few bright young analysts probably even understood the entire operational concept. But they lacked the contacts or the experience to put an entire system together on their own.

A couple of the most talented could, no doubt, have surpassed him in their systems skills, but they lacked his experience from the U.S. and from arduous hours in the cubicles of Bangalore. It would take any of them years to duplicate his accomplishments.

It was satisfying to look at the setup he had created. His successes had given him a comfortable lifestyle but it was beginning to move him in directions that were unforeseen and unsatisfying. His dissatisfaction with Arkady's control had been building for some time but had been tempered by the work.

Earlier, when he committed himself to life as a criminal, he knew that he had closed himself off from certain activities. He had been willing to give up these activities, but he had not troubled himself to consider exactly what these 'give ups' would entail. Or the demands that would be made of him by his employer—in this case, Arkady. He knew—had known for some time—that he was displeasing Arkady, but he had naively thought that the excellence of his management of the drug network would more than compensate for any perceived deficiencies. But. This. Is. Not. So. He said the words aloud as the Tupolev's pilot made the announcement that he was beginning his descent for a landing at Astana. The woman in the seat next to him thought for a moment that he was talking to her.

Val had asked Anastasia to schedule a car and driver to meet him at the terminal one day later than he was actually arriving. No need to broadcast his plans to the entire world. He would make his own arrangements for transportation. After reaching the terminal, he checked his bags in two lockers, together with his laptop and briefcase. He took a couple of ATM cards and withdrew everything to make sure he had enough cash for a few days. Then he took a cab to the outskirts of town toward the south and stopped after spotting a small, unostentatious hotel. He had the driver drop him at a quiet corner and walked the quarter of a mile back to the hotel.

As he ate in a nearby restaurant, Val wondered if perhaps he was being paranoid. After all, he had no concrete evidence that Arkady had decided to remove him as a thorn in his side. But he knew that some river had been crossed. He had defied the Khan and now the Khan had sent his emissaries; and they would arrive bearing a silken cord. A silken cord with knots—if he was lucky. He knew that Arkady would send men who already despised him, and they would want to take their time killing him.

Unfortunately he traveled without a handgun, but he usually made arrangements to have weapons shipped in advance and stored in a secure location. He had guns at several locations in Almaty, but now he wasn't anxious to go back into the city. If he had become a marked man, perhaps it had always been inevitable, and he knew that the blame was his alone; but whatever the cause, his life—from this moment —had changed forever. The question now was, simply, how long could he stay alive.

Chapter 46

Off the Beaten Path

"It is due to these architectural complexes that the medieval towns of Central Asia have acquired their inimitable appearance. The most noteworthy of the surviving complexes are those in Bukhara and, particularly, in Khiva, with their slender minarets, which are cutting the skyline of densely built-up blocks with a network of narrow streets."

**THE ART OF CENTRAL ASIA
GALINA PUGACHENKOVA AND AKBAR KHAKIMOV
TRANSLATED BY SERGEI GITMAN**

On the drive across the desert they had passed few trucks—but three camel caravans. The largest contained thirty camels. At soon as they reached Urgench, Gina had chartered a Russian pilot to fly her to Tashkent. She took Charles Bismarck with her. "Back in a day or two," she explained to Walt. "Don't leave without me."

The former Khanate of Khiva was one of the three major buffer states between Imperial Russia and Colonial India. Khiva survived the Russian Revolution and the wrath of the Bolsheviks better than the sister khanates of Bukhara and Kokhand. A key factor may have been Khiva's willingness to surrender before Bolshevik artillery had time to blow her mud walls to smithereens.

As a result of the minimal damage inflicted by war—and subsequent reconstruction that took place during the Soviet era—the Khiva of today looks like a movie set for a Disney production of the Arabian Nights. Walt had led his charges through a very full day, which included visits to most of the important tourist destinations.

In Khiva there are dozens of handsome madrassahs, mosques, minarets, palaces and caravanserais to dazzle western visitors. It is a particularly appealing destination for those who have never seen the stunning patterns of Islamic tilework.

They walked the deserted streets of Ichan-Kala and hiked around much of the ancient mud wall enclosing the old fortress. Next, he had taken them to the gates of the citadel and they had photographed the walls, gates and minarets at the Kunya-ark, mud bricks dating from the 1800's.

His group had been interested to see the tile work at the Muhammad-Rahim-Khan Madrassah built around the same time that the American Civil War was winding down. It was hard for Walt not to throw in the same kind of information he liked to provide for his students. And the Herd of Cats had been impressed by the versatility of mud brick construction exhibited at the Pahlavan Mahmud architectural complex.

They ate at a restaurant within walking distance of the guesthouse where they were staying. The dinner menu was dominated by Russian dishes and there was plenty of wine and vodka to go around. Walt held off alcohol, as did Tara, who gave him several sideways glances across the table. He hoped the others would not notice. He left the group at the table, with the excuse that he needed to make several phone calls before turning in.

Nearly an hour had gone by when the light tapping came at his door. Tara slipped in like a cat, through the door and into his arms.

"What a lovely day, professor. Is it always this nice on your trips?"

"Only when you're along. What else can I say? You put me on the spot."

"Come on. Show me something."

"Jesus, Tara. I know you're not an animal."

"Sometimes." She laughed. "No. Never. It's just you."

"How does that line go over on campus?"

"Oh, come on, professor. Don't hurt my feelings. I know, down deep, you really believe me."

"Who wouldn't want to?"

"Come on. Tell me another story. No, don't look at me like that. Just the story. Honest. Just the story."

He thought of an interesting tale from the history of ancient Khiva, but then he got sidetracked. There were no stories. There was no history of ancient Khiva, no tales from the Arabian Nights. Maybe the reenactments of a few scenes from the Arabian nights. Sometime in the small hours of the night, she opened swollen eyes and wriggled close against him.

"I love you, Walt," she said.

He pulled her close to whisper in her ear. "Call me pegleg."

"I was just dreaming about us; about the places we went today."

"And … ?" He was still half asleep.

"I dreamed that after the tour we were in bed together and we were watching a late night movie. Casablanca." She snuggled closer. "After today and tonight, why would we ever want to watch Casablanca?"

"It's a good movie…?"

She snuggled into his neck and bit him gently. Her voice was pouty. "But the ending is so sad. And I'm not Ilsa." There it was. Baby shampoo.

"And I'm not Rick," he said grasping the small of her back roughly. "And now I'm awake."

On the morning of the third day, before breakfast, Gina—back from Tashkent—knocked at Walt's door.

"Walt, look—I'm sorry to bother you, but I wanted to catch you before breakfast to give you a heads up. I know we're supposed to be on the road to Bukhara tomorrow morning. But I've just been thinking about your itinerary and I think we need to make a change of plans." Tara slipped into the bathroom and shut the door.

Walt was in no mood to dissemble. "What's up? Come in. Don't stand in the hall." *She asked for it. She knocked at the door. If it couldn't wait, she'll just have to deal with it.* "That's just Tara in the bathroom," he said. "She's taking a shower."

Gina didn't bat an eye.

"Remember crossing all the sand, when we were driving across the Kara Kum? Remember the Bismarcks making a few comment about the camels—and the relative absence of trucks?"

"I seem to recall."

"Well, they've been out this morning, scouting traffic. They got up early this a.m.—doing their transportation thing. They counted a few trucks that look suspicious but they're all headed up north, toward Kazakhstan. Nothing like the traffic they saw when we were over by Mary. They think the regular route leads southwest from Bukhara and goes though Mashad in Iran. Somehow they're pretty sure that drugs are involved. Otherwise…." She hesitated, possibly because she was still uncertain herself.

"But the key thing for you is—they want to go back to Ashkhabad. They want a couple more days in that city to watch the trucks come in, see where they stop, where the drivers hang out. They want some data. They think drugs are involved. They don't think it's weapons or any other contraband. And they are basically drug sniffers. That's where their expertise lies."

"We can go back. Yeah, I had planned to head for Bukhara tomorrow. But we can go back today if you like. I'll get on the phone as soon as everyone is in their offices."

"Tomorrow seems like a better plan. And we want to go to Bukhara by way of Mary. That's where the traffic is. Let's go ahead with your program for the day. We're certain to be under surveillance by the Turkmens although I gotta admit, they're doing a pretty good job of staying out of sight. So let's act normal. Spend the day. Make the tours, and then head back tomorrow. Make up some kind of bullshit stories to tell the drivers."

"That's why I make the big bucks."

"We can compare later," she said with a harsh laugh. Walt was getting to like this hard-faced woman.

Gina started to leave. "I just thought I'd give you a heads-up before breakfast. So you can start making calls and jiggering arrangements."

"Don't worry about any details. I'm on it."

"The Bismarcks tell me they'll probably need a couple days there to figure out what's going on," Gina said.

The shower was running in the bathroom, but Tara had been listening at the door and she heard the whole story. She decided that since their cat was out of the bag, she might as well have some fun out of it and it wasn't in her nature to seem sneaky.

She stepped into the shower long enough to get wet, wrapped herself in a towel and stepped back into the room.

"Oh, hi, Gina! I thought I recognized your voice. Did I hear you say we're going back to Ashkhabad?"

"Good morning, Tara. Something like that." Gina didn't blink. "Walt can fill you in on the details. I'll see you guys at breakfast. We'll have plenty of time to talk later today." *She's bulletproof. Bulletproof* was the word Walt was thinking.

The Herd of Cats had finished touring the attractions of Khiva. Gina and Charles Bismarck had shared information from their brief detour to Tashkent. By dinner time on the third day, the group had reassembled to discuss the new plan to return to Ashkhabad, back across the desert; this time by a shorter, but rougher, road.

They had driven north from Ashkhabad across the Kara Kum desert by a western route that was better maintained. Now, they wanted to return quickly. Walt had managed to book them back into the same hotel. Then, from Ashhkabad, Walt's revised plan would take them back through Mary and on to Bukhara.

Chapter 47

In Vino Veritas

"*To abstain from action is well—except to acquire merit.*"

"*At the Gates of Learning we were taught that to abstain from action was unbefitting a Sahib. And I am a Sahib.*"

"*Friend of all the World,*" *the lama looked directly at Kim,—"I am an old man—pleased with shows as are children. To those who follow the Way there is neither black nor white, Hind nor Bhotiyal. We be all souls seeking escape. No matter what thy wisdom learned among Sahibs, when we come to my River thou will be freed of all illusion…*

KIM
RUDYARD KIPLING

Val was drunk. He hadn't planned to get drunk, and he had begun with just a few glasses of Ukrainskaya to relax. But one thing had led to another and he had been in a melancholy mood. Now he was definitely drunk and he didn't care. He was thinking about possible places he might go, in Russia or in India or Bukhara. Or the United States. Or possibly even Central Asia. *Iceland?* He was thinking about places he could go to be beyond Arkady's reach. In a corner of his alcohol-fogged brain he could picture Mira as he had left her. Bloody. In an obscenely exposed posture. Unconscious, possibly even dead. He had used her. Discarded her.

As far back as he could see, some group had always relied on the exploitation of some other group in order to succeed. In Imperial Russia, before the Bolsheviks, the ruling classes relied on serfs to run their estates. Across the vast plains of Asia the Mongol hordes subjugated the occupants of the territory they overran and made them slaves, or laborers—or taxpayers. Even after the empire of the Great Khan was fractured into pieces, the lesser Khans continued to exploit the original inhabitants.

In Bukhara, the Emir captured slaves from Russia and other surrounding territories. And what of him? What of Arkady? They had no slaves but they had a virtually inexhaustible source of inexpensive labor ready to do their bidding. Wasn't this akin to slavery? Actually, it was better than slavery, because they didn't have to support their workers.

The U.S., like Russia, had abandoned slavery around the same time Russia freed her serfs. But they maintained—still maintain—an underclass to do the bidding of the rich and powerful.

He knew that he was making a crazy mistake to get drunk in this tiny hotel. There were only six stools at the bar and about the same number of tables, but he didn't feel like turning around to count the fucking tables. The bartender had set the bottle of flavored vodka in front of him and left the room.

Right this moment, if someone had burst in on him he would have resisted with anything at hand, most probably this bottle, and hoped that his resistance would compel his assailant to kill him in self-defense. That would be an acceptable outcome. Some of the other alternatives were horrible to contemplate.

Even as drunk as he was he realized that he was trying to think about three things at the same time. His thoughts were whirling. Part of his brain was trying to plan a good escape. Another corner was contemplating an appropriate revenge against Arkady. And there was a buried segment that was attempting to deal with his great crime against Mira, a totally blameless person who had given him nothing but pleasure. How could he atone for this wrong? His thoughts were totally tangled and as he poured another drink he knew that he needed to find a different way to shut down the chaos that was going on inside his head.

PART 5

FLIGHT

Chapter 48

Flight

"According to the tradition of the steppes—which is known as Tengri—in order to live fully, it is necessary to be in constant movement; only then can each day be different from the last. When they passed through cities, the nomads would think: The poor people who live here, for them everything is always the same. The people in the cities probably looked at the nomads and thought: Poor things, they have nowhere to live. The nomads had no past, only the present, and that is why they were always happy, until the Communist governors made them stop traveling and forced them to live on collective farms."

THE ZAHIR
PAOLO COELHO

Val spent a restless night in a cold, drafty hotel outside Almaty. He gave the owner a fictitious name and went directly to his room. He lay in the darkened room and tried to formulate a clear plan of action. Through the unpleasant scenarios that kept suggesting themselves, he cursed himself for not planning a solid escape route for this situation. In retrospect, his fall from grace—if that's what it could be called—appeared to have been inevitable.

His room was cold. He went down to the hotel's tiny bar and drank for another hour, until the bartender wanted to go home. In an alcoholic fog he returned to his room. For some reason his key would not turn in the lock and it took three attempts to open his door. His problems with the door reminded him of his weakness relative to Arkady.

At each move, he could see how Arkady might anticipate him and take precautions to make sure that he could not escape. He had learned that Arkady's vindictiveness would not allow anyone to avoid his wrath. If only he had spent less time in building such a strong, capable infrastructure for the business and more time in planning for a contingency such as this.

The truly ironic part was that he had saved a substantial amount of money which was securely placed where it would be hard to find; but, unfortunately, it would be almost equally difficult for him to get at it under the present circumstances.

His records at the Almaty office complex would probably point directly to his properties in other countries. His head was spinning, trying to plan a reasonable course of action that would allow him to escape with his life, but it's hard to make clever plans when one part of your brain keeps shouting that you are a fool, and the other part is drunk.

Arkady would bring in a team of ex-KGB professionals; all old men now, but wily and experienced in the evasive tricks he was likely to use. And all of them would be killers. Gray-haired, rheumatic and possibly suffering from the full range of age-related ailments, these cruel old bastards would nevertheless jump at the chance for one last hunt. And these men would receive a good fee for hunting him down.

Try as he would, Val could not keep his mind focused on the danger he was now facing. The thoughts that kept returning over and over had to do with the plans he would now be forced to abandon. All his dreams for creating a powerful crime network utilizing the immense capabilities of computers would never come to fruition. Once he had conceived of industrializing the process for manufacturing methamphetamines and introducing them into the vast, unserved markets of the world. His research had indicated that most impromptu labs were located away from population centers, in rural regions where detection was more difficult. And even under these conditions, the production of relatively small quantities was dangerous. It was a business designed for Central Asia. The techniques employed in his distribution networks were ideally suited for this far-less-bulky product.

In the past he had developed several schemes for transferring large quantities of cash using techniques that were safe, reliable and difficult to track. Now, there was no way he could see these plans through to implementation.

After an hour or so, with his brain whirling, he went down into the lobby and asked the night clerk where he could find vodka. The hotel bar was closed and the streets outside were quiet. The youthful clerk, muttering under his breath, went behind the bar and sold Val a bottle of Stoli. Ten minutes later he was back in his room where, despite the internal voices warning him to stay focused on his escape, he proceeded to get even drunker. The whole time he was drinking himself into a stupor, his brain continued to whirl, out of control, recognizing the danger but apparently powerless to make concrete plans that might save his life.

He woke at the first light of day, still dressed, stiff and chilled from sleeping atop the bed and badly hung over. Somehow, inexplicably, his mind was able to stay focused on the problem of paramount importance: staying alive. He knew that Arkady would start his search slowly at first, trusting that the first batch of killers would succeed. He would only widen the dragnet after—and if—the first attempts were unsuccessful. He knew he needed to move. He also knew that Almaty's airport could be easily watched.

His mustache was a distinguishing feature that he could lose. He considered taking it off at once, but held off when he reminded himself that someone at the desk might recall that he had come in with it.

Hastily jamming his belongings into his pack, he checked out of the hotel, found a cab after several blocks on foot, and headed for the train station. There, taking care not to draw attention to himself, he slipped into a toilet and managed to shave off his mustache.

At a kiosk in Almaty's train station he purchased an inexpensive astrakhan hat and took a third-class ticket on the next passenger train for Shymkent. Before boarding, he purchased a couple of boiled eggs from a vendor on the platform.

On the train he talked with the conductor, an iron-haired Ukrainian who had come east as a child with Stalin's New Lands program, and considered extending his ticket from Shymkent to the small town of Arys. From there the line extended south to Tashkent in Uzbekistan. But upon reflection, he felt that Tashkent might be too obvious. Arkady knew that Val had been to Tashkent many times in the past and might have contacts there. Shymkent seemed like a better bet and they had an airport with reasonable connections.

Leaving the train at Shymkent, he went directly to the airport and purchased a ticket on the earliest flight to Ashkhabad. Ashkhabad was a bad choice; he knew that. But he had a cache there, security against a run-in with some members of the Mighty Handful. It wasn't all he might have wished, but it included a small, semi-automatic pistol, several passports with different names, several blocks of cash in American dollars, British pounds and Russian rubles. It was probably enough to take him anywhere in the world.

On the afternoon of the following day, he visited the leased lock-up and retrieved part of his cache. With a groan, he realized that he had given the pistol to one of the Mighty Five who had lost his weapon during their unfortunate encounter with the Chinese film crew. *Damn!* He had intended to replace it, but.... *Damn! What's happening to me?*

The records for his lock-up were in the Almaty office, but it would probably take a few days for his pursuers to check out all the promising leads. He found another hotel, checked in, and slept for ten hours. When he woke up, some time before midnight, he was hungry. He found a place that was still cooking and ate his first big meal in 72 hours.

Next morning he checked out early and was in the train station before there was much activity. He purchased a train ticket west-bound for Turkmenbashi. From there he could take the ferry across to Baku.

In the passenger car he took a window seat, expecting to be alone, and he began the uncharacteristic chore of sucking the juice from an unusually large pomegranate purchased from a fruit vendor outside the station. At some unconscious level he might have been attempting to remake his persona. Although he frequently asked for pomegranate juice to be squeezed, he had not eaten the fruit with his hands since he was a boy. He started to spit the seeds into his handkerchief, then thought better of it and put them on the floor under his seat.

Minutes before the train pulled out, the seat next to him was taken by an elderly Englishman who spoke reasonably passable Russian. Val considered moving his seat; the car was far from full. But he considered that move might make him stand out, so he determined to put up with the Englishman.

His seat companion seemed to want to engage in conversation, but it took very little in the way of responses from Val to keep him chattering away. The English was a retired academic, so he claimed, touring Turkmenistan on his own, possibly with the intent of writing a magazine article or two. From Ashkhabad he had driven out to Gök-depe, the town they would be passing through in about thirty minutes.

Val had intended to put his head against the window, close his eyes and try to think clearly about the moves he would make once he reached Turkmenbashi. It was unlikely that Arkady would have men searching for him there, at least not until they had checked out some of his haunts that were known from the past. But his plans for a serious thinking session were disturbed by this nattering Englishman who seemed oblivious to his listener's body language.

"Have you visited Gök-depe before, sir?" The English's Russian was actually very good.

"No. Never."

"But you are a Russian? Correct? You know the story of the famous battle that took place there? Why it is famous in the history of Turkmenistan?"

"No. I do not know." He wanted to add, *But I suspect you are going to tell me.*

"The city was once the site of a substantial fort. Located more or less along the route of the ancient Silk Road. But it had fallen into the hands of the Mongols, and during the last decades of Imperial Russia it was part of the Khanate of Persia. The Russians wanted to gain control of Central Asia with the ultimate aim of driving Great Britain out of India. Their easiest route into Central Asia was along the line we're traveling today. This is where they built a rail line intended to carry troops and supplies in the direction of India. The fort at Gök-depe was an obstacle in their way. They sent one of their most aggressive generals to take the fort."

"General Skobolev?"

"Aha. Then you know the story. Exactly. General Skobolev. But the first time Skobolev attempted to capture Gök-depe he was repulsed by the more numerous

Turkmens."

"A version of the story has been running on Turkmen TV for some time."

"Yes, they plan to hold an impressive ceremony at the mosque in the future. It is one of the projects favored by President Niyazov."

"The madman."

"Not so loud, my friend. We don't know who might be eavesdropping on us."

Val gave a short, bitter laugh. "It could happen."

The English would just not stop chattering. "I spent yesterday walking around Gök-depe. An interesting historic site that the western world has largely forgotten. And yet, it is a place where countless thousands were slaughtered."

"The same can be said of half the cities of Central Asia. There is little difference today. We call them prime ministers or presidents. They called them Khans. Or Emirs. But they are all the same. Wealth. Power. Women. Weapons. And frequently drugs of some type. Nothing changes."

"You are a pessimist, my young friend. But there is truth in what you say. May I ask? What do you do for a living?"

"Computers. Business applications." It was hardly a lie.

"And where do you have your headquarters? If I may be so bold. I hope you will not take the question to be rude."

"It is OK. I operate across all of Kazakhstan." That was a big enough area to dissuade him from further questions."

"I should have guessed you would know about General Skobolev."

It occurred to Val that if he got up and moved, the English would be more apt to remember him than if he encouraged him to just keep rattling away about his visit to Gök-depe.

"Actually, I know very little about Skobolev, other than his name and that he was resposible for killing a lot of Turkmens."

"A fascinating story, " the English said. By the way, my name is James. James Huffington." He extended his hand. Val gave him the name from the passport that was in his pocket. The others were concealed in a compartment in the bottom of his pack.

"Skobolev's army of Russians was repulsed by Turkmens on their first attempt to take the ancient fort. It happened in 1879 and was a humiliating defeat for the Russians who had superior weapons. They fled in disarray back to Krasnovodsk on the Caspian. Krasnovodsk, today's Turkmenbashi—where we are currently heading."

Val smiled again. "Honoring their beloved president." Huffington ignored the response and continued talking. He leaned back in his seat, eyes closed, and seemed to address the ceiling.

"Skobolev returned with about 7,000 soldiers, infantry, cavalry and some artillery, and camped outside the walls. The artillery, which included rockets, was able to create havoc in the city, but the thick walls were not falling before the guns. Inside, the walls there were at least 10,000 Turkmen soldiers and probably 40,000 civilians.

The general decided to blow up the walls with a giant mine. He had his men tunnel under the wall to place a huge explosive charge. The Americans once did the same thing in their Civil War. At a place called Petersburg. The American Yankees blew an enormous crater in a fortified line. Skobolev's miners placed two tons of explosives in their tunnel beneath the mud walls. The explosion opened an enormous gap in the walls and killed several hundred defenders outright."

"And so, Skobolev was able to capture the city? Even though he was outnumbered by the defenders?"

"Skobolev was not interested in capturing the city. He wanted to obliterate the city. Like Hitler at St. Peters… at Leningrad. He turned his men loose with orders to spare no one. Not children, not women, not old people. Everyone was put to the sword. He believed that a durable peace resulted from a dramatically violent suppression. Skobolev told his troops, 'The harder you hit them, the longer they remain quiet.' The number of Turkmens killed will never be known with any certainty, but it was probably somewhere in the range of ten to fifteen thousand. His own losses were fewer than 500. It was truly a bloodbath. Rape, plunder and slaughter. An American newsman at the scene reported that babies were bayoneted."

"But Skobolev became a great hero?"

"Oddly, no. Not even in Russia. When news of the slaughter spread across Europe, the Imperial Court was embarrassed by the reports of Russian savagery and Skobolev's actions were repudiated. A year later, after having been shunted aside, he was dead of a heart attack, said to have been experienced in a brothel."

Val laughed. He was thinking of Arkady. How long would this evil son of a bitch remain alive? His liver must be the size of a soccer ball. And he spent enough time atop whores for a heart attack to be a distinct possibility. *The sooner the better.*

The train slowed, they were coming into Gök-depe. "I think we should be able to see the mosque from the other side," said the English Huffington.

All that was visible across the rooftops were the four impressively tall minarets at the Turkmenbashi mosque Huffington had visited. It occurred to Val that for the last decade of his life he had been living at a frantic pace set by his quest to build an empire based on technology that was employed for crime. In his pursuit of wealth and gratification, including a substantial dose of sex, he had neglected many other important dimensions of life.

At some level he found it embarrassing and annoying that this Englishman knew more of the history of this Central Asian country than he—born and raised in this vast land—had understood. And he had only scratched the surface of the Englishman's knowledge. As he crouched on the seat, peering out the window at the distant minarets, he considered moving to another car and leaving the talkative Englishman to enlighten someone else. But something led him back to his former seat.

Chapter 49

Train Ride Across Turkmenistan

"About 100 miles south-east of Krasnovodsk (Turkmenbashi) the railway passes two huge outcroppings of rock rising from the desert floor—the Great and Little Balkhan mountains. For me this grotesque chaos of rock, shaped over the centuries by elements, was—even more than Ashkhabad—the "gateway to the desert", a forbidding foretaste of the wilderness to come."

SOVIET DESERTS AND MOUNTAINS
GEORGE ST. GEORGE

A few passengers boarded at Gök-depe and the train began to move out of the station. The elderly gentleman put his head back and closed his eyes. Perhaps he would go to sleep. But, no! He began a monologue. It was as if he was talking to himself.

"Nothing changes. In the days of the Assyrian Empire monomaniacal rulers exploited this land because it is watered and supports agriculture. Horse country. Good horses and sufficient forage to support them. Alexander came through here. Why? Because water, grass and food made it possible. The Medians extended an empire that spread to the east and west. To the west until they butted up against mighty Rome. Rum. To the east it was probably geography that stopped them. Always it was a handful of individuals who left traces of their passage." Now the Englishman turned toward the window, but his eyes still appeared to be closed.

"The Mongols came. Led by Genghis Khan, they crushed everything in their path. But they grew too big—no different from Rome—and they had to split up so vast an enterprise."

He paused, and when Val looked his eyes were still closed and he seemed to be oblivious to whether Val was listening or not. Val said nothing. After several moments, the old gentleman continued where he had left off.

"The remnants of Genghis Khan survived in the form of the several Khanates of Central Asia. For a time this was part of Persia, then part of the Khanate of Khiva. A single man usually held everything together. Then, when Great Britain and Russia differed over who should take control, Imperial Russia won. The simple explanation for the Russian victory was probably—geographical proximity. It was easier for the Tsar and his generals to send their army.

General Skobolev could bring his men and horses and cannons more easily than the English from their distant island. And so, we now have the interesting example of a Turkic language written in Cyrillic characters. Interesting, don't you think?" His eyes were still closed.

Val had never actually thought about it.

"Until Ataturk took over the reins of the former Ottoman empire, the spoken Turkish language was written in Arabic letters. He killed off the entire written language and replaced it with Roman characters. With only a few minor changes. By the way, did you know, my friend, that in parts of western Turkey the spoken Turkish was occasionally written in Greek characters? Arabic, Roman, Greek, Cyrillic. They have all been used to write the spoken Turkish language. Think about it. If it had always been written the same way, what might the world know about Central Asia? H'mmm. I wonder what the Uighurs might have done in the past to write? Surely not Chinese. Interesting."

He pulled a small notebook from his jacket pocket and scribbled a couple of notes to himself. Then he returned the notebook to his pocket, closed his eyes, and continued as before.

"Now, today, after the breakup of the Soviet Socialist Republics, we have a nominally independent republic that has again come into the hands of a monomaniacal despot. How does this happen time and time again? Nothing changes. Life goes on. But nothing changes. Well, we are riding on a train and not on a camel. But human nature—that remains the same. Some people are mostly good. Some are mostly evil. And a small handful always dominates the masses. Nothing really changes." He opened his eyes, but he was looking straight ahead. "Nothing has changed since the time before the Mongols came. Except that now the Mongols are here."

"Now there are Turkmens. And Russians. No Mongols in these days," Val said.

The Englishman began to laugh even though Val had not said anything funny. "*Au contraire*, my friend," the Englishman said when his laughter subsided. "Wait until the scientists come in and analyze the DNA from your Turkmen colleagues. Then you will have a clearer picture of what happened to the women after the Mongols killed all the men and boys. There is probably as much Mongol DNA in Turkmenistan as there is in Mongolia." And he resumed laughing until he choked himself and had a brief coughing fit.

The train track was paralleling the Kara Kum canal. Fields of cotton, barley and wheat stretched away to the north. The fields were divided by rows of poplars, receding into the distance. Occasionally, small plots had been planted as orchards. Val could not recognize the trees by their shapes to distinguish among peaches, plums or apricots. Workers were in the fields and judging by the head scarves there were as many women workers as men. He wondered if hashish was a major crop here, but he was unaware of any major suppliers in this entire country.

Now the Englishman was looking at him. He had opened the pack between his feet and pulled out a small plastic sack of chickpeas. He offered the opened sack to Val. "Leblebi? " He used the Turkish word.

Val considered making a polite refusal, but his hand was already moving toward the bag.

"Thank you," he said in English.

Sometime in mid-afternoon, English Huffington fell asleep and his head tipped forward, making his breathing noisy. Val tried to think about the steps that would carry him westward from Turkmenbashi, across the Caspian Sea to Baku. From Baku he might risk a plane to Istanbul where he would be more difficult to find. He could rest for a few days while he plotted his next move.

He closed his eyes and rested his head against the window. A month ago all his energy was devoted to his work, building and operating a drug network like the world had never seen. In the process it was his hope to rise in the world he had chosen to inhabit. Now—largely because of his brief involvement with a woman he barely knew—he was a wanted man, pursued by the most determined and ruthless killers on the planet. How had this happened? So quickly? So unexpectedly?

It was those bastards, the Mighty Handful; they were the ones who had done him in with Arkady. Arkady had never really liked him. That much was true. That much he knew. But he had come to believe that Arkady valued him for the work he had done, and for the promise of better things to come. That's how Val had seen their relationship.

He realized now that he had deluded himself. Arkady was exactly what he projected, nothing more. He was as he described himself. A criminal. Unpredictable, amoral and vicious when it suited his whims. He was no different than the ancient Emirs and Khans from the days of the Mongol conquests.

Because he had allied himself with this leader of the Russian crime world he was now a hunted man, and his life, if he could preserve it, would need to take an entirely different direction. How had this happened to him? How had he allowed it to happen?

His mind raced through a score of scenarios. Most were ugly. While his traveling companion slept, he tried to think of all the places in the world where he could seek refuge, begin again, and have some expectation of avoiding Arkady's wrath. Soon he might have a score of former KGB men on his tracks. They were probably already in motion. Then—in an attempt to talk himself out of becoming paranoid—he tried to downplay his importance in Arkady's criminal empire. Arkady had many enterprises besides drugs: weapons, vodka, prostitution. The drug network was but one source of the money that flowed in his direction. *Yes, but face it, man, nothing else is so well organized, so profitable and so seamlessly managed.* The weapons trade, for example, was a complex mess, requiring constant personal attention. And travel. As he aged, Arkady had less and less interest in visiting remote corners of the world to make deals, kill competitors, or punish those who had attempted to cheat him.

Arkady was aging and, thought Val, it was only a question of time until his health began to fail. The drinking! That would exacerbate any of the ailments associated with aging even if it alone was not sufficient to kill him. But this was just wishful thinking. The ugly brute was still alive. And he was eager to punish Val to the limits of what his cruel mind could devise. Ugh! An involuntary shudder ran through his body. But the Englishman Huffington was still sleeping soundly.

He looked closely at the face of the sleeping man. He was not young. In his late sixties at least. Maybe older. Not eighty, certainly, but possibly as old as seventy-five. Now he was traveling the world; and, no doubt, living comfortably in the process. Not a bad way to live. Of course, in Val's own case he would prefer to travel with a female companion. Someone to fuck. Someone to talk to before fucking. During fucking. After fucking.

He thought about Mira and wondered how she might have survived, what she must have thought about him; and he wondered what else he might have done. It was possible, of course, that he could have killed all of the Mighty Handful by himself. Perhaps that's what he should have attempted. It's what he would like to have done. But then, in all probability, he, Valentin Mihailovich, would be dead now. And an ugly death it would have been if Arkady had his way.

Now, he was condemned to run. He thought about the sea voyage from Turkmenbashi to Baku. Then, from there to Istanbul. Flying was the only way. The land route—he smiled to think about it—the old Silk Road across Asia Minor—would require him to cross Azerbaijan and Georgia before reaching Turkey. It would have been an interesting trip. But too many borders. Too uncomfortable. He would fly from Baku and take the risk. It was unlikely that Arkady's arm was so long—or so quick to react.

His thoughts skittered back to Huffington whose mouth had fallen open. Traveling alone. No one was pursuing him, of course. What kind of a life had he led? Val could not know, but he guessed his most recent work must have been in academia. A teacher of some sort? History? Political Science? *I should have asked him a few questions*, he thought. One thing was certain. The old gentleman knew a bit about history. Valentin had not known the story of the mine and explosion used to breach the walls of Gök-depe. It was interesting. He would not have minded a life like this. Traveling with a compliant female, of course. But traveling to interesting places, amassing interesting facts, meeting new people, talking with strangers ...

Now, that might never happen. And all because that son of a bitch Arkady. And those assholes he had foisted off on him. The Mighty Handful. What misbegotten sons of whores to have to travel with. Ugh! How had he been able to tolerate it?

A life on the run. Would he be able to handle the uncertainty? Of never knowing when the end might come? And of being powerless to act? His desire to create something memorable had come to an end. The world might never come to see him a figure as powerful and wealthy as Arkady. He could accept that. And what if Arkady found someone who could step into his shoes. What then? The work of his mature lifetime would go to benefit someone else.

Of course, he had been bringing a few promising replacements along. Slowly. Step by step. He had been training several younger men. In the process, he had gained a faint glimmer of Arkady's insistence that he involve himself in the enforcement aspects of the trade. Otherwise, the business was not substantially different from the bakery trade. Or dairy products. Milk, butter, yoghurt. *Or, as Arkady said, banking.*

All of the potential replacements were still too soft to be involved in enforcement. And those of his workers who were adept at enforcement weren't bright enough to comprehend the system required for the work.

Turn it loose! Turn it loose! He would not be going back there again. Ever! That phase of his life was over. Now, Arkady's empire—assuming the bastard could find someone capable of managing it—would continue to pump vast quantities of money into that ugly bastard's hands for as long as he was able to remain alive.

The injustice of it struck at Valentin's soul. Unless...!

The train was passing through Kum-Dag, Sand Mountain, and it slowed in preparation to stop briefly to pick up and discharge passengers. On the platform he saw three young girls, possibly Europeans but more likely Americans or even Canadians. Two brunettes and a blond, judging by the hair he could see at the side of their headscarves. They were wearing tight jeans and zippered sweatshirts that covered their bare arms, but the scoop neck blouses indicated that they were foreigners in an Islamic country. For the first time in the past few days he opened his mind to let in thoughts about Mira, thoughts that had been swirling—uncontrolled—for days, and he recalled that when he had first met her in Romania she had been wearing a small cross. It was embossed on a circular silver disk about two centimeters in diameter. Like a coin. St. Basil's cross, and it had been concealed under her clothing. He had meant to ask her about it, but after she took off her clothes for that first time, the cross had disappeared and he never saw it again. Until Ashkhabad. One night, while she was sitting astride him—slick with sweat—he noticed she was wearing it again, and she, noticing his attention on the medal, slipped it off without a word and placed it around his neck. He had never taken it off. As the thought formed in his mind, he reached automatically to feel its shape under his shirt. They had never discussed it.

She had never asked for it to be returned.

The girls on the platform reminded him of his crime against Mira. For the first time he thought back on all the other crimes he had committed since throwing in with Arkady.

Arkady was dedicated to maintaining his self-image as a criminal, someone not only beyond the law but outside the norms of human behavior. And he insisted on surrounding himself with like-minded individuals. The Mighty Handful were simply reflections of his own persona, the man he had been in the past. They reinforced his belief in himself. Arkady was a monster and he had converted Val into a grotesque imitation of himself. In his desire to achieve his dream of wealth and power, Val had allowed himself to be corrupted even more—even more than he had corrupted himself. He had corrupted himself in his quest for money, but he had permitted Arkady to take him a step beyond—into the dark realms of pure evil.

What explanation could ever be offered to Mira, a warm-hearted woman who had been generous with her body and had been a memorable companion?

Now, the life he had chosen to pursue had collapsed utterly and he could expect to live forever in constant peril of death. And not simply death. He could expect something considerably uglier.

And who to blame? He had only himself to accuse. The network he had created was generating millions and the money flowed straight into accounts tied to Arkady's empire. He had foolishly neglected to build himself an escape route. His head was spinning back into its endless loop.

Despite his signal success in building a complex distribution system that paralleled many of those operating successfully in the western world, he had failed to descend to the level of depravity and cruelty required by Arkady. It should have been apparent to him from the beginning, but enamored of the technical challenges of building his system, and lulled into heedlessness by the easy availability of money, alcohol and an abundance of willing young flesh, he had failed to see what had now become obvious. Now…? It was too late and his life had changed forever.

Assuming he could get to Istanbul and find a *pansiyon*, a lodging house where he could gather his wits, what then? Where could he go that Arkady would not look? He had seen the man in his rage and he understood his capacity for vindictiveness.

The American girls had left the platform and the train was pulling out. Val had come to a conclusion. If he had to live in constant fear that his life might end at any moment, he would not wait passively. He would work to destroy the network he had created. True, he could not reach Arkady, and he could not impact Arkady's vast network of criminal enterprise. But the drug network that was channeling heroin and hashish into Europe and beyond; that, he might be able to cripple.

The poppies and the hashish would still grow. But let it be carried out on camels. The bar codes, scanners and computer networks used to track drugs from Central Asia around the world; those he could do something about.

Chapter 50

Val Changes Direction

> "*The good news is that one part of Afghanistan's economy is booming. The bad news: It's the opium business, which, by United Nations estimates accounts for more than half the nation's gross domestic product. Cultivation of opium poppies, which produce the raw material for heroin, is a record 379,650 acres this year, up 44 percent from 257,000 in 2005, according to preliminary crop projections. That indicates a major failure for U.S.-backed eradication efforts. Afghanistan last year provided nearly 90 percent of the world's heroin supply.*"

THE LAND OF THE OPIUM POPPIES
FROM "U.S. NEWS & WORLD REPORT"
AUGUST 28, 2006

The English gentleman was still asleep. Val managed to slip out of his seat without waking him and moved to the other side of the car. He sat by the window and looked at the fields under cultivation, watered by the canal that was slowly—steadily—draining the Aral Sea. He felt like the Aral Sea. Doomed. Condemned by forces beyond his control. For the first time in months, maybe years, he thought about himself, his life and the motives that had been driving him for the last two decades. Avid for wealth and power, he had allowed himself to be corrupted even beyond that which had been born into him.

And now, with so much within his grasp, with such a powerful vision for the future, it had suddenly been taken away, placed beyond his reach. Part of his brain had been thinking of escape routes and the methods he would employ to build a new life and a new identity. He had considered living in France, or possibly Spain. But the United States also offered attractions. Florida. A distinct possibility. The weather was better than New England and for hurricane season he could always go abroad.

But somehow—and he could not understand exactly how—this train ride, the conversation with the English, and the sight of three girls on the station platform had served to turn his mind in a different direction. Probably it was the prospect of a life on the run.

He would defy Arkady. It was not likely that he could bring down so powerful an enterprise and it would be foolish to believe that he could exact any type of revenge on the Mighty Handful. But the complex system that he had put in place, the system that was funneling wealth in a steady stream to Arkady's criminal empire, that system he could disrupt. And it was just possible that with a bit of luck he might be able to dismantle it in its entirety. Arkady would be compelled to acknowledge the contribution he had made.

It might cost him his life, but at least he would have taken the initiative. The thought of a life on the run had been appalling to his true nature. He liked to face his problems, confront his challengers and show that by using his wits and his cleverness he could solve complex problems and confront difficulties. That he could prevail in adversity.

Fuck Arkady and his gang of criminals. He would attempt the seemingly impossible. He would not flee. He would return and he would find a way to be revenged for the wrong they had done him. He would pay them back for the wrong they had compelled him to inflict upon Mira. And many others.

Arkady had been correct about one thing. He had called Val a criminal and that was beyond dispute. He had chosen a life of crime, and that choice had been made freely. But he had selected a type of crime that was suited to his own temperament. It was a type of criminality that was willing to profit from the personal weaknesses of others. He profited from the self-indulgence or greed of others. Arkady and his ilk were criminals of a different breed. They were driven by their own brutal natures and misanthropic tendencies to employ torture and other violent methods to take what they wanted for the pleasure of creating misery. They were like the Mongols.

Perhaps Arkady had been correct to compare Val to a businessman, to a banker. But enough of this! Would he turn around? Should he retrace his steps? Confront those who would be sent to kill him? He knew that the men sent by Arkady would not be content to simply end his life. They would want to do more. That, hopefully, he could deny them but it would take careful planning and constant vigilance. And perhaps he could make them pay a price.

The train was slowing. They were coming into the city of Nebitdag. It was unlikely they would be looking for him in this corner of the world. For that matter they would probably not begin looking for him in Ashkhabad. The English Huffington was awake. He was beginning to fumble in his day pack for a bottle of water.

"Well, Mr. Huffington, I have enjoyed your companionship on this ride," Val said.

"You're leaving us here? Somehow I had gathered the impression that you were continuing on to Turkmenbashi."

NEW SILK ROAD

"Change of plans. I just remembered some unfinished business back in Ashkhabad."

The Englishman reached into his jacket pocket and pulled out a small plastic envelope containing business cards. "If you're ever in the vicinity of London, please give me a call. Perhaps we could get together and continue our discussion about Central Asia." Val glanced at the card which had Huffington's name, address and telephone number, but no title, no company affiliation, no e-mail, fax or cell phone number. The address was for Greenwich, not London.

Val offered him a card in return. It was a card with the fictional name he had chosen. Val's card contained all of the information that Huffington's card lacked. The old gentleman looked at it with an amused smile. "So. You have an import-export business. You must be a very busy man."

"Sometimes." Val stood up to go. The train was slowing.

"One brief question before you go, Mr. Chernov. It's of a personal nature. I hope you won't be offended."

"Yes?"

"Are you carrying any kind of weapon?"

Val laughed with surprise. "I don't understan…"

"Because if you are not, I suggest that you obtain one in Nebitdag."

"I still don't know what you are getting at."

"Time is short, Mr. Chernov." He took the card Val had just given him and scrawled something on the reverse side. "Go to the Central Market in Nebitdag. Look for the tea house called The Crescent Moon. Ask for Sevkiyet and show him this card. Very important he sees this mark. He will help you."

Val glanced at the card. It bore several curious marks that resembled those on the monuments found in Mongolia. They were not unlike the runic characters encountered in the Scandinavian world.

The train had stopped. This was all very mysterious—and totally unexpected. Huffington extended his hand for a brief handshake. "You should be armed if you return," he said. "Good luck." And he moved to the far end of the compartment. The car gave a brief shudder, followed by a hiss of steam and squeal of steel on steel. They had stopped at the platform. Huffington was already seated at the far end of the car, looking out the window.

Val left the car with his bag, found a bench and sat down to examine the card. In plain block Roman letters the Englishman had printed the name SEVKIYET and written several characters. Symbols. The first looked like a stem with thorn projecting. The second resembled the fletching on an arrow. Or a flechette. The third resembled a crude pitchfork with three tines.

Val was completely puzzled and he tried to recall details of his conversation with Mr. Huffington during the ride. What had he failed to observe? How had the

Englishman concluded that he might need a weapon? It was beyond his capability to understand the meaning of this seemingly chance encounter. But it made him worry. A station master with a dark uniform and an old fashioned railroad cap was passing.

"Pardon me, Memur Bey. Which way to the Central Market?"

The Crescent Moon Tea Room was located on one of the streets facing the Central Market Square. Since it was not a regular market day the crowds were down and pedestrian traffic was concentrated around the shops and stalls in the enclosed portion of the market. The Tea Room was about half full of patrons, mostly older men in traditional clothing and caps. Val went in and took a table near the window where he could watch the inside and outside simultaneously. He wasn't sure where this mysterious recommendation would lead, but he was curious, and recent events had made him more reckless. He laughed inwardly—but the laugh was accompanied by an involuntary shudder. A week ago he would have tossed the card and forgotten the whole encounter with the eccentric Englishman.

A waiter approached and Val requested tea and a roll with sesame seeds. When the waiter returned with a small tray, Val waited until he was leaning over the table with the tea before asking—in as casual a voice as he could manage—"Where can I find Sevkiyet?" The waiter straightened up and looked him over carefully. Then, without speaking or acknowledging the question, he turned and walked behind the curtain.

A few moments later a large, Turkic-looking man came out and approached his table. The man had the appearance of a grease-wrestler: heavy mustache, thick-set build and hairy arms that looked more like tree limbs. The man stood at the table and held out his hand to receive something. It took Val a second or two to realize that he might want to see the business card that the English Huffington had marked. The Turk took the card and examined both sides briefly. Then he turned and returned to the kitchen room behind the curtain. A few moments later he came back with a box of the type used by bakeries to contain squares of baklava.

He placed the box in front of Val and stood so that he was between the table and other patrons in the tea room. His glance was inviting Val to open the box. Val lifted the lid and a saw a piece of flannel cloth. The distinct smell of gun cleaning solvent was unmistakable. He folded the flannel back to see a pistol. It was a 9-mm Taurus semi-automatic. Model 908. Small and handy. It looked as if it would hold eight or nine rounds, but there was no clip loaded.

Val moved his hand as if to pick up the weapon, but the Turk stopped him with a hairy paw. Then, the hairy paw lifted the cloth to show that there were three full clips in the box. "I hope you may enjoy," the big man said.

"Kaç para? What do I owe you?" Val asked in a low voice.

"No charge to you. Go with God. And go now." Then in a lower voice he added, "There is no one named Sevkiyet. Do not come here again."

Sitting on a bench in the train station, Val was completely puzzled. What had just happened? Sevkiyet or sevkiyat meant something like "a consignment of goods." Maybe the Englishman meant something else, and was a bad speller in Cyrillic. And what to make of the Mongol runes?

Was this some type of game in which he was an unwitting pawn? He needed a weapon and it had been his intent to seek one in Nebitdag. Now, through circumstances that were implausible and incomprehensible, he found himself in possession of a weapon, which—presumably—was in good working order.

On the train ride back to Ashkhabad, Val carried his pack onto the outside platform. He needed to be sure that the pistol was in working order, that the firing pin wasn't defective. That could prove embarrassing, possibly fatally so. He waited until they were passing a wide expanse where there were no villages, no roads, no signs of workers in the field, and when he thought it would be safe, he fired a single round, quickly checking to see that a new round had been chambered. Then he replaced the pistol, safety on, in the pastry box, closed the pack and entered a different car after first putting his pack in the overhead rack. He walked to the end of the car, empty handed, and stepped outside, careful to keep his pack's location in sight. After twenty minutes it appeared that there was no response to the sound from the pistol so he reentered the car, recovered his pack and returned to his seat.

It was after dark when the train arrived in the station at Ashkhabad. He ate Russian food from a vendor in the station. *Kapustnie Kotlety*. Cabbage cutlets. Somehow plain food tasted better now that he was taking matters into his own hands. From the station he took a cab to the hotel where he had stayed with Mira. The girl was on his mind. When he checked in, the young man at the front desk remembered him from his recent visit. "Yes, of course I remember you. Good evening, Mr. Kuriatin, sir. Good to have you with us again."

"Have there been any messages for me?" Val asked. "Has anyone been asking for me." Happily, the answer was no. Val carried his bag containing the items he had with him when he fled Almaty and the pastry box with the pistol. He put the pistol under his bed and threw the bag on a chair. Then he headed down to the bar.

People were still streaming into the dining room but the bar was full of patrons and there were only a few empty tables. The hotel seemed to be packed with foreign oil men. There was an empty seat at the bar, next to a couple that appeared to be American or possibly European. Val slid into the seat by the good-looking blonde woman and said in English, "Mind if I join you?"

Katya turned and took in Val's dark good looks. He had the look of a Turk, either from this country or from Turkey, but his clothes looked more like he was from Istanbul. She answered in Turkish. "Lutfen. Iyi geceler."

Val was slightly surprised by her response. Noting that her accent was not good, he answered in English. "You are Turkish? Pardon me, my mistake. A thousand pardons. I did not realize." And then in Turkish he repeated the same apology. But Katya, who commanded only a few word of Turkish, couldn't understand what he was saying.

She laughed, and replied in English. "My mistake. I thought *you* were Turkish. You look as if you might be Turkish. Forgive me. I didn't know you were an American."

Now it was Val's turn to laugh. Still in English he added, "I am Russian. We may have the makings of a comedy routine here."

Two seats over, Paul Kellogg muttered into his drink. "Move over, David Letterman."

In Russian Katya came back, "You are Russian? No? Then why are you speaking to me in English and Turkish?"

Val took the small tumbler of vodka the bartender had set before him and knocked it back. Then he rubbed his mouth with the back of his hand. The girl was very pretty and she had made him laugh.

"You claim to be American and yet you are speaking to me in decent Russian? What part of America are you from? And may I get a drink for you and your friend? This has already been more fun than I have had in many days."

Paul Kellogg was slowly sipping a glass of raki and water at Katya's elbow. He turned his head to look directly at Val but he was talking to Katya. "This guy has got a pretty good line of shit, Katya. Maybe you should be buying him a drink."

Val had lived in the Boston area long enough to know how to read the tea leaves. "Excuse me for interrupting you," he said, addressing Kellogg. "Let me introduce myself. My name is Valentin, but everyone calls me Val. I have studied in your country, so it is nice for me to have someone from the U.S. to talk with. And I am very tired just now from travelling. I hope I did not seem rude." And he extended his hand. Kellogg, tense as a rattler but managing to look calm, took the proffered handshake.

A few minutes later the trio was joined by Kevin McLaughlin followed almost immediately by Gina Santorini.

Gina had just come from the American Embassy by a roundabout route that had her change cars twice, arriving finally in a local taxi. She had been looking at photos sent by wire from Rome. She was astonished to see that one of the faces she had just been studying was sitting on a barstool in front of her, apparently trying to chat up Katya. With Kellogg nearby there wasn't much chance of him getting on any base, but go figure the odds of this happening. Val was introduced as a Russian businessman who had studied at Harvard.

The mustache was gone, yes, but she was certain this was the same man. She studied his face carefully. *That mustache has just come off recently*, she thought.

Gina waited a moment or two, tried to arrange her thoughts before taking any action and finally made a show of fumbling in her shoulder bag like she had lost something. "Katya, could I interrupt your conversation for a moment and ask you to join me in the ladies room? I seem to have forgotten something." Katya slipped off the stool and the two women proceeded to the ladies.

Inside, Gina pushed her to the far wall, against the outside window. "Katya, I can't believe this. Tell me the details later. That guy? Val. It's him. He's the one who was with Mira when her ear was cut off. She believes he did it. It's him. This is really incredible."

"Maybe it's a mistake?" Katya suggested. "You've just spent a lot of time looking, but couldn't you be wrong?"

"Not a chance. Look, he hasn't even bothered to change his name. Mira told us the guy's name was Valentin. Val. She wasn't sure of his last name but the guys in Rome said that he was Valentin Something Kuriatin. It's the same guy. It's him. I need to think fast about what to do next. This came up kind of suddenly."

"He doesn't seem like a criminal type. He told us he was a businessman. He said he studied business at Harvard."

"Neither did John Gotti. Katya, he's high up in the Russian Mafia. Jeez! Go figure the odds! They aren't exactly sure what he does, but he's high tech. This bastard was once assigned to the Russian space center in Kazakhstan. Ya, ya, ya! I can't believe this is happening!"

"So what are we gonna do about him?"

"What has he talked about? What drew him to the two of you?"

"Honestly? I think it was my ass on the barstool. Shit, I don't know. He acts exactly like most assholes at a bar. He just seems to be sniffing me."

"Look, I don't want us to stay in here too long. We'll play this by ear. Cozy up to him a little. Not too much, but enough so I can ask him to join us for dinner. If he says yes, we'll figure the next step from there. If he says no, I'll have Paul follow him. This guy has got some connection with the Russian crime net and we need a handle on what it is."

"Cozy up, huh? Nobody told me I'd be bait."

"Cut the shit, Katya. Just make nice. You can do it. Nobody's asking you to spread your legs. Come on. Let's get back."

The group, joined by Walt and Tara, had moved their drinks to a table and Val had joined them. He was chatting amiably with Walt about some remote place they had both visited in Kazakhstan. Val had already accepted an offer to join the Americans for dinner and as soon as Katya and Gina came back, the group moved into the dining room. Gina was still trying to figure out a way to get into a long conversation with Val.

Their waiter asked them if they might prefer dining outside and, since the night was mild, they moved to a poolside table where there were fewer people to listen in on their conversations. Gina arranged to sit across from Valentin.

Betty and Charles Bismarck were off on some caper and would not be joining them until tomorrow. Keener had been with them at the bar, but had left to dine at another hotel.

The dinner was pleasant enough and Gina learned that Valentin had visited Cape Cod and Nantucket while he was studying at Harvard. He was a pleasant companion at dinner and he seemed to be well traveled, but she carefully avoided asking him any direct questions about his business. All the time her brain was spinning. She was certain he was the one who had injured the Romanian girl. What had been his motive, and what had brought him back to the place where the two of them had stayed? Was he really some type of psychopathic sadist as his actions seemed to confirm? More important was… what was he doing in Turkmenistan? It was clear from the information provided by Rome that he was highly placed in organized Russian crime but what she had been given to look at was, unfortunately, vague.

The group enjoyed a slow, leisurely dinner as the moon rose in the east. The scent of roses from gardens surrounding the pool perfumed the air. Val seemed to be enjoying himself like a man who has just been released from prison. He was attentive to everyone who was speaking. He participated appropriately, but not excessively, ate and drank modestly, and purchased four bottles of wine for the group on his card. Gina was finding it hard to get a handle on him. After coffee, and more coffee, Walt and Tara were the first to excuse themselves and slip away. *Yep, we can guess what they'll be doing*, Gina thought wickedly. *Honeymooners*.

Gina had already made a bet with herself about Katya, too; that she'd be paired off with someone before the trip ended. But so far she hadn't seen any evidence.

Kevin was next to leave. But not before making enough eye contact with Gina to be assured that it was OK to leave. That left just the four of them at the table: Katya, Paul Kellogg, Val and herself.

The waiter came around to see if they wanted more coffee, more anything. But they had already overdosed on coffee. Valentin came up with an offer. "Well, my friends, this has been an interesting evening for me. And I thank you for inviting me into your group. Not often that I am invited to dine with a group of traveling scholars." Privately he was saying to himself, *If you are whom you claim to be.*

"But you are traveling in what was once the mighty Soviet Empire. And even though times have changed, the influence of Russia is still strong here. So let me introduce you to something that you might not have experienced. If you will allow me. We might all have an evening toast with Ukrainskaya. You know this drink?"

Katya was smiling, but none of the others had ever heard of this vodka with the distinctive aroma of lime-blossom honey. "I will get it. They have it here," and saying this Val stood up and headed for the bar. Gina feared that he might be leaving, and she considered sending Paul after him. A few minutes later the Russian was back with an unopened bottle.

Ninety minutes later, the bottle was substantially lighter and the four had their elbows on the table. They were talking like old friends. Conversation at the table was flitting around without any apparent motivation, like a shuttlecock in a senior's badminton game. Kellogg had ceased drinking long ago and Gina was trying to stay clear while she put together as many details as possible on this man. Most of the Ukrainskaya had been consumed by Valentin and Katya.

Valentin had crossed some kind of Rubicon; or more appropriately, some kind of Oxus. He had decided to pull apart the system he had created which had never been recognized or appreciated by Arkady. Now, he was just taking a little time to figure out the best way to do it and these Americans were giving him a few new ideas. Out of the blue he inserted his little bomb.

"And you all tell me that you are American academics." It was not inflected as a question. Gina's warning bells went off, but she was ready. "We're not all in teaching. Some of us are in administration, and the couple you didn't meet yet are supportive members of the alumni association. Walt is the teacher. An assistant professor. He's widely known as an authority on Central Asia. And the young woman, Tara, is his administrative assistant."

"Yes, so you say. And that disappoints me. I had been hoping to meet someone who could introduce me at the American embassy."

Gina sat up. Paul pushed his chair back. Katya, who had been leaning with elbows on the table, head in hands, shook her head as if trying to wake up.

"American embassy?" Gina said. "Why would you need to be introduced there?"

"Well, my academic friends, I might have some information they would be interested to pass along."

"Why would you need someone to introduce you? You could just inquire at the gate."

Val laughed. "Of course, of course. But academic support always lends one such credibility. Don't you think?"

Kellogg appeared to be borderline angry. "What the fuck is he talking about?" he said quietly.

Katya might have been slightly drunk, but she was starting to transform herself into her Wonder Woman persona.

Gina emptied her small tumbler and turned it upside down on the table the way she had seen other Russian drinkers do it. She repeated the question. "Why do you need an introduction at the embassy?"

Val leaned forward on his elbows and spoke in a low voice. "I have information. They may find this information useful."

"Information on what?" Gina repeated.

"Are you from the embassy?"

"Is it about weapons or terrorists?"

"You represent your country?"

"It is of interest only to governments? Not ordinary people?"

Val laughed. Katya noticed that his teeth were perfect. Like a movie star's. *Could they be capped*, she wondered. "We seem to be caught in a loop," Val said.

Gina's head was clearing rapidly. *We don't want to lose this guy.* She didn't want to lose him, but neither did she want him to get so pissed off with them that he stopped talking.

"Well, Val of the deep, dark secrets—I don't have any friends at the embassy, and none of us is connected with the government, but I am a citizen in good standing, and they should be willing to talk to me there, so... I could go with you." She hesitated, but he was looking at Katya. "If you think it would be helpful."

"Not one American woman alone with a Russian man," Val replied. "That might not look so good. But with two women? That might be better. Don't you think?" Katya straightened up and brushed the hair back from her eyes in a gesture that Val had seen and interpreted a hundred times within a half-mile circle of Harvard Yard.

Over the next quarter hour they discussed arrangements for the two women to accompany him—vehicle and driver to be provided by them—in a morning visit to the American embassy. It was agreed that no calls would be made in advance, and that they would simply show up at the gate and take it from there. Gina, of course, had no intention of abiding by this agreement, but she tried to be as accommodating as possible to ensure his participation.

It was agreed that they would meet at ten a.m. in the lobby and go from there. Back in her room, Gina used her cell phone to send a long, coded text message to her agency representatives at the embassy explaining the plans for tomorrow, and confirming that they would be prepared to record whatever information Val was ready to divulge. She was uncertain whether it would pertain to terrorism, weapons trade, or even, possibly, drugs. But she ID'd him as the man who had been responsible for the problems with the Romanian girl.

After spending nearly an hour keying in the long text message, Gina walked down to Walt's room. It was after midnight when she tapped on his door. "Open up!" she said. "Chop, chop. It's me." She heard the sound of voices inside and then he opened the door in his underwear. Boxers. Briefly she told him that the plans for tomorrow would have to be altered. He asked her to come in from the hall.

"No. Thanks anyway," she said. " I can fill you in on the details tomorrow at breakfast. But I'm afraid I may have to upset your apple cart again."

"I can't say it wasn't expected."

She looked down before saying good night and noticed his prosthesis. *My God*, she thought. *This guy has lost a leg below the knee. And I never twigged to this before? What can be wrong with me?* And from that moment she began to think of Walt in a completely different light. Gradually it would begin to dawn on her why Paul Chapman might have chosen him. She made a mental note to try to learn more about their connection after they returned home. *I've been walking beside this guy six or eight hours a day? And I never had the slightest idea? Gina, you're slipping. How did I miss this?*

Walt's Herd of Cats assembled for breakfast at quarter past seven. While they were eating, Gina expected to see Val in the dining room, but he never showed up. She filled Walt in on details of their conversation with Val. Ever the agent sniffing for details, she couldn't help examining Tara's face carefully. Armed with her new knowledge she was filled with respect for the pair—and with admiration for Tara's puffy eyes. *Good girl!* she thought. Now several things fell into place and she was kicking herself for being so obtuse.

After the group reassembled in the lobby, she tapped Paul Kellogg to ride shotgun with the driver, Rajiv, who had been provided earlier by the embassy. That was the only difference in the arrangements that she had made with Val. She was fairly confident he wouldn't balk with Kellogg's presence in the vehicle on the ride over, just as long as he didn't accompany them inside. But where was Valentin? It was after ten and she had expected him to be on time since he had seemed anxious. At 10:15 she inquired at the desk to see whether he had paid his bill and checked out. No, he was still here. Ten-thirty. She had the wind up. Something was wrong. The desk rang his room. No answer! Bad news. He had flown the coop. Dammit. It was her fault. She should have assigned Keener or Kellogg—one of those guys—to watch his room overnight.

In the lobby she signaled to Kellogg, who followed her outside. They walked in the direction of the circle of rose bushes around the drive. "You can get in his room without being noticed?"

"Easily." He didn't bother to look at her.

"He's in 617. Facing south. Six-seventeen! Take a look around. It seems he's flown the coop. Look and see if there are signs of a struggle. Or if he just bugged out."

Kellogg was back in just under a half hour. This time they walked past the end of the drive and out along the park with the fountains, to the bench where they had first found Mira.

"A struggle," he said.

"Really?"

"Yep. It reads like a nosebleed, but that's just a wild ass guess."

"Take anything with him?"

"Nope, his little bag is all there. Just the stuff he was wearing. This looks like a simple snatch and grab. By the way, he's traveling light."

"Maybe somebody knew he was planning to go to the embassy today."

"Possibly. Oh yeah, Taurus 9-mil under his bed. Loaded. I left it."

Gina was starting to feel bad. She was examining all the ways she could have screwed things up. "Do you think our table could have been bugged last night?"

"That, or somebody could have had a listening device trained on us. Lots of ways we could have fucked up. We just got sloppy."

Ouch! That hurt, coming from Kellogg. By 'we' he meant her. She had been making all the key calls.

"I think I may have screwed the pooch," she admitted. "But that's under the bridge now. So what do you think we should do next? Any ideas where we might look for him?"

"You shitting me?" said Kellogg unsympathetically. "And we're in fucking Turkmenistan?"

But Gina wasn't really expecting an answer. She was thinking about her own problems. *What am I going to tell our guys at the embassy?*

Chapter 51

Snatch and Grab, Russian Style

> "The region was overrun by the Mongols under Genghis Khan in 1220. In the 14th century, Uzbekistan became the center of a native empire, that of the Timurids. In later centuries, Muslim feudal states emerged. Russian military conquest began in the 19th century."
>
> UZBEKISTAN
WORLD ALMANAC AND BOOK OF FACTS, 2004

After the drinking session with the American professors, Val had returned to his room. He checked his new gift pistol and placed it under his bed, just out of sight but within easy reach. One round chambered. Safety off. Then he undressed and brushed his teeth. For the past several days his mind had been totally occupied with the notion of flight, but since resolving to pull down the network he had worked so hard to create, his concern with escaping Arkady's wrath had been pushed into the corner. And part of his brain was occupied with thoughts of that pretty American girl, Katya. *What a healthy mare.* She had the look of a wild ride and he had seen the way she looked at him earlier. *Maybe tomorrow? We will see.* For Val, any slender, attractive woman under fifty was a girl.

He had been down for about three hours when he was awakened by a rattle at his door.

After Val failed to show up in Almaty, Arkady had sent two members of Kutchka to search for him in several of his usual haunts. The other members were at loose ends awaiting other assignments. Yuri and Anatoly decided to make a short trip back to

Ashkhabad on "personal business." Their real motive for returning to the Turkmen capital was to take revenge on the Chinese film crew at whose hands they had been bloodied and embarrassed.

Yuri and Anatoly had been in the lobby of the hotel collecting information on goings and comings of the Chinese when Val had arrived at the front desk. They had both spotted him at the same time and taken refuge behind newspapers.

Now, as Val reached across the bed and leaned down to recover his pistol, the two men burst into the room. The first man through the door drove his knee into Val's face at the edge of the bed. The blow smashed his nose causing profuse bleeding, but it failed to knock him out. That was accomplished by the second man who clipped him on the temple with the butt of the little Vektor automatic that Val had given him. In addition to knocking him out, the blow gouged out a square flap of flesh about one and a half centimeters on each side. That, too, bled freely.

His assailants mopped up the blood with a couple of towels before wrestling him into his pants and shirt, followed by socks and shoes. Then, after checking the hall for traffic, they each took one of Val's arms over their shoulders and manhandled him into the elevator. In the lobby the night clerk had his head down and he never looked up as they walked Val out the door. Their van was waiting a few yards beyond the entrance and they dumped him in through the side door. Anatoly climbed in beside him and began tying him with rope and tape they had brought for the Chinese.

The only people moving were members of the night staff—janitors, cleaning crews—whose duties rarely allowed them much time to pay close attention to what goes on around them. But for the past several days one exception to this generalization would have been provided by Bill Keener. The young agent—driven by the twin spurs of fitness and romance— liked to keep in shape by running at least two or three miles every day. He had found that the best time to do this was in the small hours of the morning, depending on the neighborhood. In this part of Ashkhabad, with its broad, tree-lined avenues and multiple public parks, he considered it was relatively safe to run alone. He had returned from his run a few minutes before the members of the Mighty Handful dragged Val out of the lobby and threw him into the back. Cooling briefly in a shadowed corner, Keener watched the abduction with interest.

One of the men climbed in the back with the unconscious form Bill recognized as Valentin, the Russian businessman he had met briefly in the bar. Gina would be interested in this.

A courier from a local bakery had just ridden up to the lobby on a bicycle, parked it under the marquee and disappeared inside. As the van doors closed and vehicle pulled away from the curb, Bill sprinted to the bike, climbed on and began pedaling after the vehicle. Even as he saw the van make the first turn and pull onto the broad thoroughfare, he was laughing at himself. *Keystone Kops. How long do I think this is gonna last?*

Within a quarter mile the van turned several times and moved into an area where several construction sites seemed to have been abandoned, left unfinished for a time until funds could be found to continue the work. In one of the unfinished buildings of six or seven stories, the bottom floor had been partially enclosed. It was into this labyrinth of blocks, bricks, scaffolding material and construction junk that the Russians had dragged their still-unconscious prisoner. Keener approached close enough to form an opinion that this was probably the end of the line. The place had the look and feel of a kill site. He only lingered long enough to form a general idea of how to get back to the exact spot, then he retraced his route and pedaled back to the hotel as fast as he could. He left the bicycle where he had found it. It was possible that it hadn't even been missed. Now he had to wonder how Gina was going to like being wakened in the small hours.

What the hell, he thought, *If I don't wake her, it'll just be the call to prayer. But I think I better tell her.*

Chapter 52

Arkady's Punishment For Val

> "The scourge of the Mongol conquests was terrible beyond belief, so that even where a land was flooded but for a moment, the memory long remained. It is not long since in certain churches in Eastern Europe the litany still contained the prayer, 'From the fury of the Mongols, good Lord deliver us.' The Mongol armies developed a certain ant-like or bee-like power of joint action which enabled them to win without much regard to the personality of the leader…"
>
> **FOREWORD TO THE MONGOLS—A HISTORY (JEREMIAH CURTIN)**
> **THEODORE ROOSEVELT**

When Keener told Gina that he had seen Val being kidnapped, she was reluctant to believe him. "Let me get some clothes on and meet you in the lobby," she told him. It was after six a.m. when she came down. Val had been invited to join her shortly after seven for breakfast.

"This is getting too weird," she told Keener. "Are you sure it was him. Did you get a good look?" Keener was slightly intimidated by her and he hesitated.

Gina was adamant. "I'm gonna wait 'til seven-thirty or eight," she said. "Give him a chance to show. If somebody grabbed him to off him, it's just as well we're not involved. And you could have been mistaken."

Keener started to protest, but Gina silenced him with a gesture. "Let's find some coffee," she said. We're waiting."

At seven-thirty the remaining Cat Herd was assembled in the lobby, as Walt had made preparations for the day's tour around Ashkhabad. He knew nothing about developments during the night. And he never knew from one day to the next who would be going with him and who would be off on some secret mission. His group for the day was slim.

Val had never joined Gina for breakfast, but that wasn't her biggest worry. They had agreed that he would join her at 10 for the drive to the embassy.

By eleven, Gina knew the bad news. Paul Kellogg had been in Val's room and Gina trusted every word he said. Val was gone and his room didn't look good. She should have listened to Keener and taken action sooner. She had made a bad call and gotten a bad outcome. Now it was time to call in the cavalry.

Gina summoned Paul Kellogg to one side. "I want you to get the Russian guy. Valentin. Do you think you can find him? If he can talk, I want you to find him and bring him back. Can you do it?"

"I have no idea. Keener was the one who followed him. He tells me he's pretty sure where they are. But that was... what? Three, four hours ago? Five? Six? Who knows where the hell they are now. Could be long gone. The guy is probably dead and dumped. Finding him alive sounds pretty optimistic, you ask me."

"That's true. But if he's alive, I want him. I want to get him to the embassy. He had something he wanted to spill. And we know he's highly placed. I should have put someone to watch him. I screwed the pooch."

"You want me to grab him?"

"Correct."

"All by myself? Why the hell did you wait so long?" She ignored the rebuke.

"You don't think you can handle it?"

"I'm glad you have such a high opinion of me. Or is it that I'm disposable?"

"Take Keener. He's gotta show you where they are. This has got to go down fast. And clean."

"Yeah! We hope! I'd rather go in with McLaughlin."

"Do you think he's up to it?"

"More than Keener. Mac has been there. Keener still wants to go there." He paused. "Keener can drive and get us in and out."

"That sounds like a plan."

"One more thing. You want him? Right? The Val guy? No matter what? You want him? Have I got that straight?"

"I can't make it clearer. I want him."

"Just checking to make sure. Don't let me hang out on this. 'Coz I don't come back with him, I might not come back."

"Bullshit. Come back. Take Mac. Take the blue van. It's just around the corner on the right. Unmarked. The embassy driver just dropped it off." She handed him the keys. "There's plenty of heat in the tire compartment under the floor. Pick out what you like. But move the van away from the entrance. Park some place over beyond the statue of their fat president, across from the fountain—to pick out your weapons. There's not a lot of foot traffic on that side. Just old women feeding the pigeons."

"Where do you want me to bring him? Assuming, one, I find him, and, two, he's still alive."

"Have Keener call me on his cell. Call when you have him and I'll tell you where we can meet. Maybe the embassy, or maybe we'll change vehicles. Depends on what you find—and what the embassy people recommend."

"Anything else I should know?"

At the construction site where Val had been taken there were only three men present. Val was supine on a couple of planks that were supported on concrete blocks. The half-finished room was filled with piles of sand, several stacks of bricks and some random timbers scattered around. Val's hands were taped together in front of him and clamped to his body by a rope. His ankles had been place on a board placed athwart the planks supporting him and secured so they were about two feet apart. His shoes and socks had been removed.

He was dimly aware of pain in the area of his face and head. As consciousness returned he sensed that someone was slapping his face in a perfunctory manner. His whole body was just one dull ache. It was hard to breathe. His mouth tasted like blood and there was blood in his nose, but he couldn't spit. He had to swallow the stuff in his throat and he had to concentrate on breathing because his nose was stoppered with blood. When he tried to move his head he couldn't turn in either direction. His head was taped to the plank like an accident victim on a backboard.

"Valya, Valya, wake up! We need to talk to you. We need you to be with us."

Slowly he opened his eyes and saw Yuri and Anatoly. He should have fled when he had the chance. Now it was all over for him and he had only himself to blame. He felt fear at a level he had never known before. He couldn't breathe. He was suffocating. They weren't even aware.

These men were known by him. Cruelty and sadism were meat and drink to them. Many of their evil practices were familiar, and some of their worst deeds he had avoided watching. It had not been to his credit that he had been present.

"Valentin Mihailovich. You are awake, I see. Do you know that we have been waiting for you to wake up for several hours? So now we have no more vodka. Also now it has become light so we can see your face clearly. You know why we are here, of course. Do you not? Blink your eyes when I speak to you, you intelligent bastard."

Val blinked.

"You know, don't you, that you have offended Arkady. By deceiving him. And he is very angry with you. Yes? Answer me, cocksucker!"

Val blinked again.

"And you know that he has begun to send people looking for you. But Yuri Andropovich and I came back to Ashkhabad to teach a lesson to those Chinese monkeys making their fucking film in the desert. Happily for Arkady, we walked into you quite without intention. Answer me! Show that you understand!" He slapped Val again.

Another blink.

"When we called Arkady he was very glad to hear from us. He was happy to learn that we had found you."

"Tell him what Arkady has promised us," Yuri interrupted, like a child with a secret that can't wait.

"You tell him."

"He is giving us each a new girl. Flying them in from Romania. He says they will be young and very pretty."

Val blinked again. Despite his fear, he thought about Mira. He pictured her in the hands of one of Arkady's brothel managers in Almaty.

Yuri stepped forward and gave him another half-hearted slap. Val found himself wishing they would just step up and slash his throat and be done.

"You know that Arkady wishes you dead? Of course you do. But more. He wishes for you to suffer great pain. He is angry that you disobeyed him and deceived him. He brought you along, supported you, developed you, and he is disappointed that you have repaid his generosity with treachery. So he wants you to pay. Dearly."

Val blinked. He did not want more slaps even though they were easily borne—relative to what he knew he could expect.

"So then, Valentin Mihailovich, this is what it comes down to. We must make you suffer great pain in order to win our little prizes. You understand, do you not?" He did not wait for Val to blink. "You arrogant cocksucker. All the time with us, thinking yourself better. Yuri Andropovich and I, for years in the KGB, working in the field, all hours, constant danger, wounds, a hellish life in many countries with risks you could never imagine, and you, you arrogant bastard, lording it over us—as if you knew something." He had run out of steam. That was as far as he could go without a pause to reformulate his complaints against a man he scarcely knew and could not understand.

"Yuri and I are going to hurt you. But we are curious to see what things will hurt the most, and we must watch carefully to see what we can learn from your pain. You will be of considerable help to us in the work we are sometimes called on to perform." As he was talking, Yuri had unfolded a pair of mechanics coveralls—of the kind occasionally seen for sale in open bazaars—and was putting them on over his clothes.

"So, Valentin Mihailovich, arrogant cocksucker that you are, you find us without many of the tools we might have preferred. So we will just have to make do. Are you listening? Paying attention? You are coming apart. Bit by bit." He slapped Val twice, but Val was concentrating on getting enough air in his lungs to stay alive. The blood in his nose made it difficult to breathe and he had to work on inhaling and exhaling. As the CO_2 built up in his bloodstream, panic took over and he could feel control slipping away. He was becoming a different person. At the same time the pressure in his bladder increased uncontrollably. He was losing the ability to think clearly; wild panic was causing every muscle to scream.

"Yuri Andropovich and I have always wondered which is the most painful: to be cut with a sharp knife, or with a dull knife. Perhaps you can help us to solve this little dilemma. I have a sharp knife, but Yuri has only this cheap plastic object that is disposable. So you will let us know by the best means you can think of."

Anatoly handed his knife to Yuri who was standing between Valentin's two bare feet. With a quick swipe of the knife, Yuri severed the small toe of Val's right foot. His body went into a series of jerks and spasms against the restraining ropes, and his eyes grew wide with pain and horror. Under the tape, his bleeding lips were beginning to exhibit the bluish cast of cyanosis. Oxygen deprivation. His eyes rolled back in his head until only the whites appeared, making him look dead.

"Don't try to fool us, Valentin Mihailovich. That can't have hurt much. I told Yuri that the sharper the blade, the less the pain. But he won't believe me. You can decide for yourself."

Yuri fumbled under the coveralls and found the plastic knife, possibly picked up at the hotel's buffet table. He began to saw off the little toe on Valentin's left foot. Val's body strained against the rope, five-six times and then his chest began to labor. He was slowly suffocating from the tape and his own blood. His tormentors hardly seemed aware; instead they were obsessed with differences in the way his feet were bleeding.

"Try again, Yurochka. That is interesting. Perhaps you are just becoming too skillful. Perhaps if you take the teeth off the plastic. Maybe a butter knife next time. Or just take half."

Yuri took off the next toe from the right foot and watched as Val's leg spasmed from the hip down. It was not possible for them to know whether or not he was still conscious. When the fourth toe was sawed off the left foot, Val's leg seemed to elongate and retract, but his eyes remained half-closed with only the whites were showing. He was no longer responding to Yuri's slaps by blinking.

The vehicle containing the three Americans pulled off the avenue and entered the construction site. In one corner of the complex—which appeared to be apartment blocks—workmen were stirring, but the end where Keener led them was abandoned, still littered with construction debris. "There's their van. That's where they parked when I followed them. It doesn't look like it's been moved."

"And you say there's just two of them besides the Russian guy?"

"There were just two in the van. I got no idea how many guys they might have met up with."

"So we really don't know what we're walking in on?"

"Hey, this wasn't my idea. I'm just trying to be helpful."

"Whaddaya say, Kevin. Are you cool with busting in with me?"

"I think we should go in by different routes."

"I'd rather not do any shooting."

"We might not have a choice."

"What kind of sticker are you carrying?" Paul asked.

"I took a new Sting out of the trunk."

"Are you comfortable with these Uzis? These fuckers were manufactured in Croatia. Disposable. We can just toss them when we're done. They'll lead straight back to Croatia."

"Which one of us goes around the back?" Kevin McLaughlin asked. *I'm glad I picked this son of a bitch instead of Keener,* Kellogg thought. *He's got what it takes.* "I'll take the back way," Kellogg answered. "There'll be doors or windows back there somewhere. There's so much shit around here I'll probably have plenty of stuff to duck behind."

"One minute," Mac whispered. "This has got all the hallmarks of a potential goat fuck. We may be compelled to shoot. Understood?"

"Of course," said Kellogg. "Just use your judgement. That's why we're here. Us. And not somebody else. Let's go." He checked the Uzi again and, crouching, began moving swiftly toward the rear of the building shell where Keener said the Russians had taken Val. The Uzi was in his left hand, safety off, and his right hand was free.

A few seconds later he was rounding the corner of the concrete structure. The forms still had not been stripped from the columns of the upper floors. As he rounded the corner he could hear voices. They seemed to be talking in Russian. *Sounds like we're in the right place.* The door in the back wall was in the far corner. There were two windows intervening, so he ducked below them and crawled over to the door opening.

At the open doorway, which lacked a frame, he was unable to see the men in the center of the unfinished concrete floor, but a stack of construction blocks provided him with an opportunity to approach closer while remaining unseen. By a stroke of luck, arrangements at the far end of the building enabled him to get a glimpse of Mac in the doorway. Mac's door at the opposite end of the floor had no pile of blocks placed like the one shielding Paul, but it gave Mac a clearer shot at the men inside.

Paul entered the open space, still without interior walls, and silently worked his way to the rear of the block pile. From the tone of the men's voices he could tell that neither he nor Mac had been detected. It appeared that the Russian man, Val, was tied to some planks, but it wasn't clear exactly how they were torturing him. One of the men had blood on his clothing, so it was likely that they were dishing out some major pain.

In addition to the Uzi, Paul had brought a pistol with a silencer. Feverishly, he tried to think of an approach that would prevent the torturers from quickly killing the man on the board, if that was their ultimate mission. He feared a shot might kill or wound their captive.

Glancing around, he saw a small cluster of steel reinforcing bars, *rebar*, about a half-inch in diameter and twelve feet long. He had stepped over them to get in close behind the blocks.

Quietly he lifted one bar at the edge of the stack and slowly balanced it at its center. Then he looked at the far doorway and motioned to attract Mac's attention. *Come in*, he motioned with his hands. *Make a noise*, he signaled by opening his mouth and pointing. But he no sooner made the signal to Mac than he realized his mistake. If Mac created a distraction and drew their fire and was hit, the fault would lie with him. He had made a snap decision and, immediately, he knew that it was wrong. Now, only he could correct his stupid blunder. Picking up the bar with his right hand, he stepped from behind the stack, with the pistol in his left hand.

A moment before Paul made his move, Mac yelled from the doorway and stepped inside the partially completed block wall. The two Russians turned to face Mac, oblivious to Paul who was now approaching them from behind. When he was about twenty feet or so from the Russians, Paul hurled the rebar at the man who was drawing his pistol at Mac.

Just as Anatoly was crouching to aim and fire, the bar speared him from behind. *At about the level of his third or fourth thoracic vertebra*, thought Paul, whose wife, Nyugen, was a nurse. *In the back*. Despite its weight and penetrating power, the crude spear failed to pass through his body. It did, however, penetrate his scapula and continued on through his upper rib cage to lodge halfway into his lung.

Anatoly dropped his pistol and fell to the floor with a groan. Before he hit the deck, Paul Kellogg had reached Yuri, whose pistol had been slow to emerge from beneath his coveralls. Yuri wasn't sure what was happening. The only weapon in his hand was a bloody plastic knife, somewhat dulled now by use. His brain, absorbed in torturing Valentin, was still in first gear. They were being attacked from two directions, and their assailants didn't appear to be Turkmen police or soldiers. But before he could do much more thinking than that, Kellogg had clipped him above the ear and he dropped to his knees, stunned, but still conscious.

Yuri was furious at being struck, and in a blink he thought of ways he would punish his assailants once they fell into his hands. That brief image was the last that would stimulate his reptilian brain, for in the next second Kellogg had dropped the Uzi, drawn his razor-sharp, double-edged fighting knife and made one quick swipe across Yuri's throat. The Russian criminal fell forward like a stone.

Another two steps and Paul was beside Anatoly who was coughing up bloody foam and trying to say something in Russian. *Probably cursing me*, Paul thought, as he drew back Anatoly's head by his hair and ran the blade across his throat with enough pressure to sever the windpipe and the jugular. Then he pushed his body forward to the floor. Both men were finished by the time McLaughlin had crossed the room.

"Jesus Christ, Paul. That was fast. Good job."

"How is our man...? Holy fuck! Look what these bastards have done to him."

"Sadistic bastards. They were cutting off his toes. Jesus. And look, I think he's already dead."

Val's lips were blue despite the blood. His eyes were closed and there was no perceptible movement of his chest.

"Fuck!" snarled Kellogg.

"They already killed him?" queried McLaughlin. "From the toes?"

"Look at this bush jacket. Fuck! Fuck! Fuck! Nguyen just got it for me. She looked everywhere. Finally ordered it from a catalog. Now look!" It had a smear of blood on the right arm, and a spurting artery had left a line of drops across the front.

"Fuck!" He peeled off the jacket and threw it on the floor. "Mac. Make me secure. Make sure we have a perimeter here. Take a quick look around. Don't shoot anyone if you don't have to. Then hightail it and get Keener in here to give us a hand."

"Is the guy dead?"

"Fuck the guy for now. Just do what I said! Go! Go!"

McLaughlin headed for the exit; Uzi down by his leg.

Kellogg turned his attention to the man on the board. A few quick slashes and Val was freed from the board. His feet were a mess. He appeared to be dead.

Paul felt for a pulse at his wrist, but could find none. Then he checked at Val's carotid. *Faint.* He was still alive, but judging by his color he was nearly gone. Paul wrestled him onto the floor and ripped the tape from his mouth.

Paul's mind was racing. *He's still alive. How important is this guy? Do I want to do CPR on him? If he's got AIDS and I get it, what have I done to the rest of my life? And Nguyen's? Fuck. Somebody. Give me some guidance.* He looked at Val's face, pulled his eyelids back. The pupils still looked normal. Then he noticed the small silver chain around Val's neck and pulled it out. On the chain there was a curious circular medallion, small, with an embossed cross of some weird type; three cross arms. Seeing the cross, he thought about Nyugen and he knew what she would tell him to do.

"Fuck, fuck, fuck," he groaned aloud, tipping back Val's head to open his airway and pinching the Russian's nose, already clogged with drying blood. "I gotta do it. God help me," he whispered to no one.

Paul began performing CPR on the injured Russian, whose hands were still taped together at his waist, until he could hear Mac and Bill Keener returning. By the time they were back, Val had begun to breathe on his own. Despite the pain from his injured feet, the threat to life had been the result of having his mouth taped shut with his nostrils partially closed by blood.

The three men carried the groaning Russian to their van. Keener was turning around, ready to leave the site, when Paul remembered his bush jacket. "Hold up," he yelled, jumping from the van and dashing back to the spot where he had abandoned the bloody garment. With the same knife that had killed Val's torturers, he cut his khaki jacket into ribbons and recovered the label that clearly identified its American origin. On his sprint back to the van he noticed a burn barrel to one side of the rutted track leading from the site and he dashed to the barrel to dump the cloth fragments, retaining only the label.

Twenty minutes later they had picked up Gina and were on their way to the American embassy. In less than an hour, Val was receiving medical attention from an embassy doctor.

A hasty exchange of messages with headquarters in Washington followed, reinforced by the recommendations of embassy personnel in Ashkhabad. It was generally agreed that the three men who had visited the construction site to recover a Russian national alleged to be Valentin Mihailovich Kuriatin should leave the country on the first available military flight out. They never left the embassy compound except to go to the airport. Gina and Tara took care of collecting their stuff and checking them out of the hotel. Accordingly, by six in the evening, Paul Kellogg, Kevin McLaughlin and Bill Keener were on the same plane with Valentin Kuriatin, a major Russian crime figure, bound for Germany where the mutilated feet received a higher level of professional attention. From Germany, Kevin and Bill went home a few hours later by commercial air, while Paul hung back to be aboard the military flight that carried Val back to the Washington area. At this stage of a rapidly changing scenario, Val was still very much of an unknown quantity, and he made the flight to the U.S. in cuffs and leg restraints. As Val's painkillers wore off, Paul found him to be an interesting conversationalist with a professed interest in visiting the Chesapeake Bay region. "If you ever get out of this jam and get your shit together," Paul told him, "…just look me up. I shouldn't be hard to find. You can come over and Nyugen will show you what real crabcakes are. You aren't going to find them in Central Asia."

After three members of the Herd of Cats were returned to the U.S., the brain trust in the Washington Office felt that Walt's educational mission might be starting to lose any residual credibility as cover. The Herd was now composed of four females and only two males, Charles Bismarck and Walt. It seemed to be an appropriate time to call a halt to this year's field trip to the Silk Road. Accordingly, Gina was instructed to wrap it up. Walt began calling to shut everything down.

While Val was being processed through Germany on his way to D.C., the remaining Cats had continued on to Bukhara, passing through briefly on their way to

Samarkand. From Walt's perspective, the trip was probably laid bare to any one who was paying attention. He could see no useful purpose to continue the deception of behaving like a group of tourists. As they bounced over the route to Bukhara, he quit talking and listened to the quiet conversation between the Bismarcks.

"Thirteen Mitsubishi trucks spaced about eight to ten minutes apart? Same logo. This has got to be one hell of a well-oiled machine. What do you think those trucks are carrying?" The Bismarcks were taking notes and talking in low voices.

The Bismarcks had more than a dozen years of drug interception work as a team. They looked like younger versions of Ma and Pa Kettle, or perhaps an Iowa farm couple, taking a vacation away from the pigs, but, stateside, the facts they dug up almost always held up in court. They just didn't seem to fit the part.

It was this deceptive appearance that had made them effective in the past, and they had a good record of racking up convictions. This assignment was a bit unusual but they really fit the role of middle-class American tourists on the journey of a lifetime. They could have been chosen by central casting. Even their clothing seemed to have been selected to project an image of middle-class America. But instead of coming off like prototypical ugly Americans, they came across like a couple of quiet, well-behaved, goggle-eyed Quakers.

Walt noticed that everywhere the Bismarcks went they were quick to take notice of the bus terminals, railway stations and vehicle parks, and they had a knack for approaching people and finding locals who would speak with them. It was uncanny how they could find English-speaking truck drivers or mechanics who would talk to them for an hour as they sat drinking endless cups of tea.

Walt had planned to continue on to Tashkent, but when the whistle was blown on the trip the remnants of the Herd departed from Samarkand for Moscow. "Too bad for the educational aspects," he told Gina, smiling wryly. "You guys are missing the best part."

"Next time," Gina said, but she didn't smile.

The phone call summoning him to the capitol came to his hotel in Moscow from a staffer. It was a short, businesslike call—unclassified—during which he learned that Chapman regretted that he couldn't call personally; he was in the hospital for a couple of days due to complications from bypass surgery.

Their flight back took them from Moscow to JFK. Uneventful. Everyone got together again in Washington.

After Walt and Gina herded their cats back to the United States, all of the cats had reports to make to their individual agencies. Walt and the Herd were also summoned to a debriefing session outside Washington that lasted for three days.

To Walt, the Washington visit seemed like much ado about nothing. They had brought back little information of importance; nothing that was new. Nevertheless, he was summoned and he responded.

On the plane from Moscow he talked the situation over with Tara and they considered the possibility that she would join him there for as long as he was needed. But her presence with him in a Washington hotel seemed to be an invitation to unspecified headaches they would prefer to avoid. Wisely—reluctantly—they decided that she would return directly to her off-campus apartment and their future would be revealed to them.

"If you weren't so interesting in other ways," he told her, "I would just like to keep you for a sister."

Though disappointed, she treasured the compliment and kissed him on the ear. "There's a name for that." Halfway through the flight, he changed his mind. "Come with me to Washington," he said abruptly. "To hell with what anyone thinks."

Even though she was half-asleep, she smiled. "I was hoping you'd change your mind."

The people who had begun to interrogate Valentin were elated by the information he divulged. The drug operations coming out of growing fields in Afghanistan and Kazakhstan were so sophisticated that they were creating a market for growers in other countries where conditions were better.

Paul Chapman and his colleagues were amazed to learn that the culture of cannabis and opium had become so profitable in parts of several regions in Central Asia that scores of Kubota tractor dealerships had sprung up to serve communities that had used animals for cultivation since the days of Genghis Khan. The Bismarcks had a lot of solid data on the expansion in farm machinery sales, but it was hard to find a way to link it specifically to drugs.

After Valentin got down to work with some of the talented people at the CIA, it was just a matter of time before the network he had built was taken down. Unfortunately, he had not been able to leave with his laptop computer. The Mighty Handful had taken his cell phone and PDA. But his personal contacts in India still responded to his calls. Apparently no one in Arkady's office had explained to them that Val was no longer in the organization. The simple truth was that Val was largely irreplaceable; not by design, but just as a result of his intense personal involvement in every aspect of the work. There were staffers in the Almaty office who understood many of the details, but no one who understood the big picture.

Within a week, CIA agents in India had visited the Bangalore software firm and service bureau handling Val's tracking system. Using the tried-and-true technique of preclusive buying, they had put the Indian technicians to work on a handful of bogus assignments that provided them the identical revenue stream with the understanding that the contract, negotiated with Val, was to be voided. This was confirmed by calls from Val to his Indian contacts. The legality of this arrangement was questionable, but nevertheless it was done, and there was little Arkady could do to prevent it. Indeed, he only knew the details after the fact, and even when briefed he did not fully understand how the changes would impact his operation.

He learned fast enough a few weeks later when it became clear that the flow of drugs was severely compromised and the revenue stream flowing back into Kazakhstan basically began drying up. It took some time to get a handle on the extent of breakage and to assign a small army of people to fixing the problems.

After Valentin was examined and treated at Walter Reed, he was released into the custody of people in the same branch as Paul Chapman and whisked away to a safe house in northern Virginia. It was generally felt that he would not be a flight risk and so, after a few weeks, no one was assigned to watch him around the clock. In any case, he had no passport. He was picked up every day and taken to the Operations Center to provide information on his network and to help with its dismantlement.

In the course of this work he met with Bill Keener and Paul Kellogg from time to time. Paul Chapman was, of course, in constant touch with what was going on.

Val underwent an identity change at the recommendation of the CIA and he is now a government employee; an independent contractor with office space in an undisclosed location. He lives modestly in government supplied housing in a community where—it is hoped—he will be hard to find. Actually, since the death of Arkady no one is continuing the search and, of the three surviving members of The Mighty Five, two will probably be dead within a few years, from advanced liver disease.

Val uses a cane, but whether he needs it to walk or just likes to have something in his hands to use as a weapon is a question. He works for a unit involved with drug interdiction, but he considers most of the men he works with to be unimaginative buffoons. They are, of course, much easier to work around than The Mighty Five. If he had any leaning toward philosophy, he might be inclined to think that he had made a mess of his life. But years of working on the dark side have taught him to think like a criminal and he can see that millions are to be made in the area of pirated CDs with music and movies. He thinks of starting anew. Once or twice he has wondered how and where he lost the little medallion that Mira gave him.

Surprise! Not long ago he met an interesting woman.

The two Bismarcks, Charles and Betty, were sent back to somewhere in the Midwest where they resumed their efforts at tracking marijuana and cocaine coming in through Mexico and Central America. They brought back much more information than anyone suspected they had collected. Their notebooks contained coded details of shipping companies in Kazakhstan, Uzbekistan and Turkmenistan, even to the point of providing the names of individual drivers, dispatchers and office managers. Even Gina, who had been with them the whole time, was astonished by the amount of hard data they had collected. Unfortunately, none of the people involved in criminal activity was vulnerable to prosecution in an American court, but if that day should ever arrive.... In many cases they concluded that individual drivers, shippers or operators facilitating drug shipments were unaware of what was going on. They were simply cogs in the giant enterprise that had been growing slowly for several years.

One of the more interesting facts they uncovered was that a large quantity of hashish had crossed all the way from Kirghizstan into Turkey and across the Bosporus to Istanbul in a shipment of 750 frozen sheep carcasses. The shipment started with 1200 carcasses, but at least 250 were split off at Trabzon and sent by ship to a port on the Black Sea. The destination was never determined because the carcasses were shipped in a refrigerated cargo container and they were lost in the transit through Trabzon's container port. Another 200 were simply unaccounted for.

The techniques used by the Bismarcks to obtain such details continually mystified their superiors. Charles, who had a trucker's knowledge of vehicles and engines, together with a wife who was quiet and modestly dressed, simply hung around the coffee shops and tea houses where westerners were tolerated; and people told them things. They both seemed to be possessed of photographic memories.

There has been some sort of weird chemistry between Valentin and Katya. Strange, isn't it? He is quite a bit older, but there's a definite attraction. Could they share Mongol DNA? It's understandable on Val's side; he, after all, is clearly a hound. But handsome, shapely Katya? There are half a dozen guys—inside the government and out—who have been salivating over her for years.

Valentin was being debriefed by Chapman and half a dozen analysts from the Operations Center. Katya was sitting in on the meeting when they broke for coffee. Val cut her off at the coffee pot.

"Today you will go with me to the cafeteria?" he asked.

She laughed. "You don't know the way yet?" He smiled, showing her his perfect teeth. His top lip has a scar where Yuri had kneed him in the hotel room . "I am forgetful. Sometimes more than others." And in a low, purring voice he added, "Around you."

"Where do they teach you this kind of stuff in Russia?" she said.

"I learned it in Boston." His teeth were just about perfect, and even though she knew he was a very bad boy, Katya wondered how they would feel if she ran her tongue over them.

Chapter 53

The Movie

*"We all
Sit in His orchestra.
Some play their Fiddles.
Some wield their Clubs.
Tonight is worthy of music."*

FROM "THE AMBIENCE OF LOVE"
THE GIFT; POEMS BY HAFIZ
HAFIZ (1320-1389)
TRANSLATED BY DANIEL LADINSKY

Mr. Wu's movie shoot in Turkmenistan was finally wrapped up—in the can, as they say—and the Chinese survey of a route across the eastern end of Turkmenistan was also completed.

After the brief unpleasant experience with a gang of psychopathic Russian thugs, no further problems were encountered with criminals, terrorists, religious fundamentalists, industrial saboteurs or the government of Turkmenistan. Several Turkmen officials learned of the pipeline survey, but they were skillfully paid off by members of Wendell Cho's intelligence gathering team, not all of whom were Asiatics. You might be surprised to know that several of them were Americans, traveling on American passports. More than one had lobbied in the halls of Congress, but that's another story.

The survey was completed and the movie was ultimately released for audiences in China where it did surprisingly well. Take a look at it when it is released in the U.S. *Silk and Blood*. It did better than expected in China and was a good career move for little-known Chinese actress Li Ju Zhang. The star actress they had considered using, Zhi Shu-Bian, stormed off after four days in Turkmenistan. Li was a brick.

Everyone loved her.

Kenny Jiao's suggestion proved to be right on the money. Writers hired with CHOCO money had gone to work diligently, searching the vast literature of China and Japan for a Silk Road story, and they found several that had strong possibilities. A couple of stories were written around oasis caravanserais in which a wild local girl would become enamored of a young man in the caravan and would run away to follow him on his adventure. On the way to the next oasis town, their caravan was attacked by raiders and the girl was carried away as a slave.

Some of the better stories centered around the way in which the young man separated himself from the caravan and found his way into the camp of the raiders to recapture his sweetheart. On the way he had to enlist the support of unlikely allies, mostly locals who had suffered at the hands of the raiders. It was a thin story line, but it was standard boy-girl stuff with plenty of violence and bloodshed. No firearms, but plenty of swords, scimitars and Chinese bombs, including smoke pots and rockets. Best of all about these stories was that they were able to completely avoid overt conflicts with Islam and other religions found along the Silk Road: Buddhism, Zoroastrianism, Manichaeism, Nestorian Christianity, or Catholicism. Islamic zealots might object to the amount of bare skin or exposed hair, but the Prophet and his teachings were never mentioned.

The writers were starting to make progress when Kenny Jiao came up with the Manga story about the Silk Princess that he described to Wendell Cho. Once everyone had seen it, the idea took off like a scalded hog.

For a time, the writers toyed with the insertion of martial arts combat, but that idea never caught on. They did manage to work in more camels than *Lawrence of Arabia*. Some of the camel scenes were much more exciting than they had planned or expected. A few camels turned in notable performances.

The standard movie disclaimer, "No animals were killed or injured during the filming of this work," was appended to the version slated for release in the United States. But it's a lie. Six camels died during the filming process. Also one horse.

By setting the film story in oasis towns they enjoyed the advantages of filming in the vicinity of ancient Merv. Mr. Wu's simplistic notion of sending in plenty of pretty Chinese actresses proved to be a sound one and these young women did provide an effective distraction. By using second and third tier players he was able to hold down costs, and he was willing to spend money in order to provide more girls rather than fewer.

Permit a slight digression. During the filming of the sequences in Turkmenistan, Wendell Cho made arrangements for Mr. Wen Wu and several of his closest friends to visit the shooting site. Mr. Wu's party arrived in Ashkhabad in CHOCO's Lear Jet. Kenny Jiao was present at the time. Wendell Cho arranged a couple of lavish dinners during the visit. Wu brought along several cases of rice wine.

The guest list for these dinners included several stunning young actresses from the cast, and a party atmosphere prevailed. Late on the evening of the second dinner, Mr. Wu, prodded by Kenny Jiao, initiated a poetry contest. After several of the guests contributed poems, Wendell suggested that the group focus on any poems that included the mention of silk. This made things much more difficult, but Mr. Wu was delighted.

Cast members present at the table were intrigued to hear businessmen reciting lines with such emotion. Mr. Wu was enjoying himself immensely and he waited for several moments of silence before he coughed to get the attention of everyone at the table.

"I can recall a fragment if that will be acceptable." There was a general slapping of the table, so Wu cleared his throat.

"It is by Yen Chi Tao. Period unknown.
I remember the first time I set eyes on her:
'Heart' had been embroidered on the silks she wore;
The strings of her guitar sang of the thoughts we shared.
The moon that shone so bright, that's still up there,
Made rainbows of her dress as she appeared."

The group applauded warmly and a smiling Mr. Wu rose to make a modest bow. After the murmur at the table subsided there was another long pause, suggesting that maybe the silk contest was at an end. But then the Chinese actress Li Ju Zhang—who was at Mr. Wu's right—raised her hand for attention. Li was wearing a dress of emerald green silk that looked as if it had been sewed to her lissome body. After Kenny Jiao motioned everyone to silence, Li spoke.

"May I offer a poem which includes silk? Or is this a contest for men only?" No. No. Of course not. Proceed.

The young woman rose, stretched her arms, shrugged her shoulders, and hearts beat faster.

"I think this one will satisfy the criteria, but you must judge. It may surprise you. It is by Li Yü. Tenth century." She recited slowly, with emotion—and gestures.

"*Her morning toilet done she stood*
And in the censer lightly sprinkled sandalwood.
Then with a glimpse of pearly teeth she turns her head
Towards him, singing sweet and clear
From lips of cherry red.
Stains on her silken sleeve rich depths of color spread

From cups filled and refilled with fragrant wine.
Provocative and with careless grace

She leans across the embroidered bed,
Chews at a scrap of scarlet wool,
Smiles and then spits it in her lover's face."

When Li finished the poem everyone at the table stood to applaud. It was a triumphal close to an entertaining dinner. Mr. Wu was ecstatic—Li was a favorite guest in the Wu home. Kenny Jiao was delighted. He had played a hand in getting Li to accept the role. The film's director, T.Y. Soong—whose box office hits include *Kung Fu Harlots*—was beaming. *That's my girl.* He had directed the young actress in three films previously and had a special fondness for her. Wendell Cho was grinning from ear to ear. To him, this was a sign that the expected budget overrun of fifteen percent would probably not be a problem.

Li's performance was capped by several toasts. The evening was a huge success and Mr. Wu's party flew home the following day.

Weather proved to be a friend to the moviemakers. Only three shooting days were lost due to sandstorms and the toll on equipment proved to be within the limits predicted by Jiao's cost wizards.

The completed film was screened for Mr. Wu privately, then shared with members of the board. They declared themselves satisfied. By this time the data from the survey team had already been processed.

The film is currently being adapted for release in the United States where it is not expected to do especially well. Kenny Jiao's business team expects that it will attract the same audience that was drawn to *Seven Years in Tibet*: viewers who will accept a thin story line in return for an exotic location and pretty faces.

The pipeline survey results? That has turned out to be a big disappointment for Mr. Wu and all the members of the CHOCO board. Not that the team didn't do an excellent job. No. No problem there. It was that damn Turkmen president. *Unpredictable son of a bitch.* At the same time the surveyors were loading all their data into CHOCO's computers, Turkmenbashi, the modern-day Khan of the Turkmens, was opening the door for a conglomerate from Argentina. It appears that this South American alliance might be successful in getting approval from the Russian government and officials of Russia's petroleum colossus, GAZPROM, to put in an east-west line leading across the Caucasus to the Black Sea. This route was preferred over the Chinese plan to run the line to the Indian Ocean ending at the Pakistani port city of Ormara.

The jury is still out on the ultimate success of the Argentineans. For the time being, however, CHOCO's pipeline plans are on hold.

Chapter 54

Mira

"But he is so young, Mahbub—not more than sixteen—is he?"

"When I was fifteen, I had shot my man and begot my man."

KIM
RUDYARD KIPLING

Despite the hours she spent with American intelligence experts, no one ever learned very much about Mira's background. One reason was because she didn't know her own parents. Her earliest memories were of an old woman she called grandmother. They lived with gypsies, although it wasn't clear that grandmother was, herself, a gypsy. Mira just never knew her origin—and she accepted this lack of information as a natural condition. In the same way, she never knew her exact age or her true birthday. As a small child she was part of an extended community of gypsies who occupied substantial neighborhoods in several Romanian cities. She traveled a lot as a child and before she tried to read she was schooled to commit petty thefts for which she was rewarded.

The sexual abuse began when she was around ten or eleven and she early learned to watch for certain signs in males who were likely to cause her pain. At age thirteen she had an opportunity to join a circus troupe. Her granny had recently died from a disease that seemed to be pneumonia—some kind of respiratory illness—so there was nothing to keep Mira from going on the road.

The years she was with the circus provided her with most of her education. A family of acrobats looked at her compact figure and saw possibilities. After two weeks of intensive training it was clear that she had the potential to become a better flyer than Olga who was coming up on her thirty-fifth birthday and wanted to have a baby. In the air, at fifteen, the girl appeared to be fearless. Mira spent several years as a flyer, thrilling audiences from Bucharest to Berlin and as far east as Moscow.

It was an exciting period in her life, during which time one of the old men in the troop took an honest liking to her and taught her to read. Other men in the troop were not as considerate and at seventeen she had her first abortion, performed by a Jewish doctor in Poland. Despite the language barrier, the doctor took time to make sure that the girl understood the all details of birth control. He was a good teacher.

Pressure from males in the troupe eventually forced her to leave the circus and she was on her own for a couple of miserable, hardscrabble years before she found her way to the Black Sea coast town of Constanta. She had only been in Constanta a few months, working at a waterfront tavern, when she was "discovered" by the old Turkish gentleman, a wealthy brewery owner who took a fancy to her.

There is a curious, indefinable quality about Mira, even though she is a whore, that makes intelligent men—who have enough money to support her—want to take her out of circulation. There is a sweetness in her disposition that is pleasing, and although her knockabout life has made her into a skillful sex partner it is not these abilities alone that make men want to keep her. She has seen much of the world, but it has not made her outwardly harsh or bitter. Her experience with men inured her to their hardness and brutality, until the old Turk took her to Konya and put her in a small apartment.

His Muslim wife knew of Mira and would have taken violent steps to have her removed—perhaps even killed—but the old man, in a uncharacteristic fit of rage, let it be known to members of his family that if any harm came to the girl the consequences would be dire. His threats were very graphic and no one had expected him to be capable of such fury.

In truth, he was more like a father than lover. In winter she lived in smoky Konya, and in the long, hot summers he put her in a small, breezy place near the beach in Antalya. He provided her with enough money to live, and she found a daytime job in a restaurant beside Antalya's picturesque harborfront. This money she could save or spend upon herself. She became a very capable cook with a comprehensive knowledge of Turkish food.

For two of the summers that she occupied the apartment, she took a job with the captain of a distinctive caique used to carry charter parties along the Mediterranean coast. She had met the Muslim captain at the restaurant and, as he had a daughter about the same age, he was not constantly trying to take her to his bed. The charters were typically for a week and often their clients were Germans. Sometimes the charter parties were interested in scuba diving, and there were several wreck sites that were popular destinations for recreational divers.

The coast was beautiful. Every day was a joy, filled with the blue skies, turquoise bays and the rocky beaches of southern Turkey, broken by tiny, stunning harbors that were snug and lovely for those who knew how to enter safely.

Mira was hired to cook, but in shorts and a skimpy blouse she was usually a welcome addition to the crew, and her quiet, adaptive demeanor made her as acceptable to female clients as the males. Actually, she only wore shorts a few times because the boat's captain, a Muslim, gave her disapproving looks. He never came out and said anything, but she could tell he was displeased and she wasn't eager to have him dissatisfied. She shopped about in the public market to find some baggy harem pants and loose blouses that were comfortable, airy and well suited to her job—which was to make delicious meals and be an unobtrusive sailor, a man-of-all-work. But her experience in the circus as a featured performer was hard to shake. She was always aware of how she looked to her audience. When one has been lifted up to a trapeze on the trunk of an elephant, one is never quite the same again. She was used to having all eyes on her.

Occasionally the charter boat encountered a group made up of couples from northern Europe: Sweden, Denmark, Holland. And on more than one occasion, these people wanted to perform sex acts on the boat. This led to some problems with the captain and on one occasion the charter was terminated after three days. But Mira learned a lot. About Turkish culture, European behavior and life aboard a boat. Her work on the caique was a valuable part of her education. Every time she went, she discussed matters—in advance—with her old patron who was always supportive and agreeable.

One summer she had a brief sexual adventure with a handsome young German doctor, traveling with four comrades, all physicians. They were avid divers—from Hamburg—and their week on the coast was uneventful and relaxing. But the youthful surgeon was smitten with Mira and he returned two weeks later for another week's vacation, during which time he tracked her down and. in broken Turkish, pursued her convincingly. He introduced her to scuba diving. He instructed her in the fundamentals and made certain that she understood the basics before taking her down to one of the popular wrecks. They made love on four occasions. Twice in his hotel and twice in her apartment. It was the only time she brought a man there in order to sleep with him, and later, in tears, she told the old Turk. He never said a word, but simply held her until her tears subsided, and from the way he stroked her hair and held her back, she knew that he had forgiven her.

The doctor wrote her two long letters, but they were in German and she could never find anyone she trusted to translate them. She kept them with her personal things until the day she left Turkey.

Another thing she kept was a small, silver charm given to her by the boat skipper when she made her last trip of the season before she quit. It was a tiny dolphin. That had been the name of his caique. *Yunusbalagi*. Dolphin.

In truth, her old Turkish benefactor was more like the father she never knew. Sometimes he made demands on her, but they were always gentle and he was always so generous. In the years she was with him, she never refused—never wished to refuse him—anything. An observer of their relationship might have described it as one based on mutual respect. It was as close to love as anything gets in this difficult world.

As he aged, the Turkish gent visited her less often but he stayed in contact by telephone and hardly a week went by that he didn't call her, ask after her health and financial status. During this time she saved the U.S. equivalent of about ten thousand dollars. This gave her a feeling of security and independence that might almost have been guessed from the spring in her step. On any given day when she left her apartment, she could look either thoroughly European and stylish, or Islamic to the degree suggested by her planned destination. In the market, she usually became Islamic.

She cried when she was informed that he had died, and wondered if she would be punished by his family members. She was making arrangements to travel back to Romania when the son appeared and made a proposition.

The old man's son was also married and he had three young boys. Mira was not attracted to him. But he offered to let her remain in the apartment in Antalya on a permanent basis. There would be no return to Konya. He would expect to visit her, from time to time in Antalya, and it was to be understood that she would entertain him. She was, after all, a whore. This new relationship was quite different from the previous one, and it did not last much more than a year.

What has she been up to since she escaped from Turkmenistan with her life? It is perhaps a bit surprising that she has never quite put the real story together; that she has her life at the cost of her ear, and that Valentin had no real choice in the matter. This has never penetrated her consciousness. But her wound healed and she has found a way to style her hair so that it is not readily noticed. And she wears a ruby stud in the other ear.

She went back to Romania after leaving Rome and took up with her old friends. She moved into a small apartment with Andrea. The two women lived next to Milla and Monica. A stunning quartet! They all worked in restaurants and bars, only occasionally working as prostitutes to supplement their meager incomes. By sticking together and comparing notes they avoided the need for a pimp. In fact, when threatened by a thug who wanted to take them over, they pooled their resources to hire a muscle man to remove their tormentor.

Mira quickly saved enough money to return to Turkey. She has gone back to Antalya, a pleasant city with a mild climate where she had enjoyed several worry-free years and where she feels comfortable. It was easy for her to find work in the hotels or hotel restaurants that cater to Europeans: many Germans and Scandinavians, but occasionally some Dutch, English and a few French. She has made arrangements to take another job with a charter boat captain carrying parties for cruises on the

Mediterranean. In the back of her mind, she hopes she might attract another man like the German physician who was once smitten with her. If she should be that fortunate again, she believes she will have the skills and the patience to hang on to him and she would like to try living in Germany. It's easy to believe that she can succeed.

PART 6

THE CARAVAN RETURNS

Chapter 55

Florence Returns

"Think, in this batter'd Caravanserai
Whose Portals are alternate Night and Day,
How Sultán after Sultán with his Pomp
Abode his destined Hours, and went his way."

THE RUBÁIYÁT OF OMAR KHAYYÁM
EDWARD FITZGERALD

Tara was permitted to attend day one as a courtesy, but after that the meetings were closed to her. She and Walt stayed at the Willard Hotel.

The agency thanked Walt for his services and sent a confidential letter to the president of his university thanking him "for supporting" Walt's participation in an important government activity.

All of the members of The Cat Herd acknowledged that the experience had been interesting. In the team debriefing, Walt didn't hear all of the details that individual specialists gave to their respective organizations. But he did get to see the big picture. He was surprised at what his group had accomplished.

While Walt and Tara were in Washington, Paul Chapman—out of the hospital and getting around—invited them to dinner. They ate at an upscale seafood restaurant with a view over the Potomac. There were only half a dozen small groups in the large, upstairs room. Chapman thanked them for their support and he noted that every member of the Herd of Cats had nothing but good words to say about Tara's role during the trip. The group had learned of Walt's nickname for them and they had adopted it to refer to themselves.

As the after-dinner coffee was being poured, Chapman reached into his jacket pocket and pulled out an evil eye. The blue string was rusty and stiff with dark blood and Walt recognized it immediately.

"You asked me to keep this for you a while back," he said, handing the object to Walt.

"Tell me," said Tara, grabbing Walt's arm like a teenage girl.

"It's a story for later," Walt said.

"Let him tell you the story after I've gone," Chapman laughed. "I wouldn't want to have to correct him if he made any mistakes. Maybe this is a good place for me to bow out," he said, pushing back his chair to stand. "You two puppies stay and have a drink. I've got to be up early tomorrow to go to New York. And I'm still not a hundred percent. I'll send a car to carry you back to your hotel. Oh! One more thing. I'm authorized to give you a bonus for the successful completion of your assignment."

"I've already been paid," Walt said.

"This is a bonus. For a job well done. We considered giving you a certificate of achievement, but this might be just as good." He handed Walt a business envelope.

"Open it now?"

"If you like."

Tara was squirming so hard it was all Walt could do to keep from laughing at her.

The check was for twenty-five thousand dollars.

"I'm assuming this isn't a mistake," Walt said, handing it back. Chapman looked puzzled.

"Tara, don't you need to powder your nose?" Walt said.

The girl smiled, touched his shoulder and left immediately.

Chapman knew something was coming.

"Look, Paul. No more contacts with me. Or my employer concerning me. OK? I'm in a new line of work. All that other stuff was in the past."

"Now, Walt, don't be hasty. You have skills that are..."

"Paul. Keep the check. And lose my phone number. Forget me. I don't want any more jobs. No more cats to herd. No contacts. Get out of my life."

"Take some time to think about it, Walt. Don't be too..."

"Paul, are you listening? It's done. Over. I have paid my dues."

Chapman put the envelope beside Walt's plate.

"You earned this bonus. But I can respect your decision. If you should change your mind in..."

"No changes. I'm moving in a new direction."

"I can only wish you well."

Tara was back at the table, but she stood, looking for a sign from Walt before she sat.

"Good timing," Chapman said, standing. "I was just about to say goodnight."

Chapman leaned to shake hands with Tara and she sprang up to kiss him on the cheek. Then he turned and left.

It had been less than a month since Walt and Tara left Pennsylvania, but it seemed much longer. Chapman's office offered to provide a government car and driver to take them home, but Walt declined in favor of booking on commercial air. Back at home, his empty house had a closed, musty smell. By agreement, Tara went straight to her apartment.

"We can cool it for one night," he said. "There'll be loose ends for each of us to pick up, and if we're together not much will get done. And I'm not ready for you to start washing my elastic bandages."

"You're right, of course," she said with a laugh. "But get ready."

In the empty house, Walt's first reaction was to pick up the phone and call Tara at home, but he resisted that urge. There were no messages on the phone because he had disconnected the answering machine before leaving. He moved through the quiet rooms like a ghost, wondering if he wanted to keep the house, considering the advantages of getting a smaller place—closer to the campus, a row house maybe with no yard—within walking distance of shopping and restaurants. Smaller might be a lot better.

Later in the evening, after he had unpacked, he went to the post office and picked up the mail in his box. The mail took the balance of the late evening and he worked at his desk for a couple of hours. To keep himself company, he loaded a couple of symphonies by Prokofiev and listened as he opened envelopes. But somehow, at the end of an hour, the music was unsatisfying and he had no interest in playing it again. Looking through his collection, he spotted Tchaikovsky's *Eugene Onegin* which he hadn't played in a long time.

He put on the first disk and found that, even though he couldn't understand the Russian, the sounds were familiar and seemed to match the music. The opera fitted his mood. He was halfway through the second side when the phone rang. His heart skipped. Tara. Perfect.

"Hi! It's just me." It was Flo. "I wasn't sure if I'd find you at home or not. I called earlier in the day. How was your trip?"

"OK. It was fine. It's good to be home."

"I'm glad you're back. I'm coming over. I want to see you. I need to see you." *Huh? What the hell was all this?*

"How about tomorrow, Flo? I just got in not long ago."

"No. Tonight. It's important. I'll be right over. Don't go anywhere. Twenty minutes, max."

"Flo, listen..."

"Love you. Bye!"

He was baffled. *Love you, bye? What the hell is going on?* What had gone wrong with her romance? And now, he was going to have to talk to her tonight. What would she want? What would she need? He couldn't guess. Well, yes, he could guess, and he didn't like the way it came out.

On the CD, a deep baritone voice was singing and it sounded interesting. He reached for the booklet and checked the player to see which track was playing. Track nine on side two. He flipped through the pages that hadn't been turned for a couple of years and the spine cracked on the little booklet that accompanied the CDs. *Damn. Loose pages. Here it is. Prince Gremin is talking to Onegin.* Gremin, of course, has married Tatiana, the woman Eugene now loves but spurned years ago. He read Gremin's words to Onegin and was surprised at how they matched his mood.

> "Love is no respecter of age.
> Its transports bless alike
> those in the bloom of youth
> yet unacquainted with the world
> and the gray-headed warrior
> Tempered by experience!"

Amazing. He got up from his desk, walked to the liquor cabinet and poured himself a drink. What else? Vodka! But he didn't drink it. He carried it back to the desk and continued reading.

> "…
> And the gray-headed warrior
> tempered by experience!
> Onegin, I shan't disguise the fact
> that I love Tatiana to distraction!
> My life was slipping drearily away;
> She appeared and brightened it
> like a ray of sunshine in a stormy sky,
> And brought me life and youth, yes, youth and happiness!"

He read as he listened to Prince Gremin's aria to the end before drinking the vodka. Then he hit the return back to track nine and listened to the words again. From then on he listened intently until the opera played to its final, typically Russian end, when Onegin—rejected by Tatiana despite her admission of love for him—sings his final words.

Pozor!… Toska!…
O zhalki, zhrebi moi!

Ignominy! Anguish! Oh, my pitiable fate!

Onegin, you dumb, pathetic bastard! What a knucklehead!

When the opera ended, Walt, mechanically, hit the replay button for side two and the music resumed. Half an hour later, the doorbell rang—kind of a courtesy warning—and the front door opened.

"Hello! It's me," Flo called as she entered. She could have been returning from a trip to the convenience store. *So cheerful.*

"In the study. I'm in here."

She came into the room where he was slouched in the sulkiest position he knew how to assume and kissed him on the cheek.

"You don't seem very happy to see me." She did look very good. Dressed summer casual. Right out of the L.L. Bean catalog. Not too much. Not too little. Just right. He was embarrassed by his churlish failure to rise or to make a better response. He felt slightly ashamed but he hardened himself.

"I had no reason to expect you tonight, Flo."

"I know. I know. But I had no idea when you'd be back. I called more than once. It was good to find you at home. I needed to talk to you. Aren't you even going to ask me to sit down?"

"It's still your home, Flo. Yes, please. And if you want a drink, you still know where everything is." She sat on the sofa's edge, knees drawn up, legs together, perfect.

"How was your trip, Walt?"

"Look, Flo, I don't want to seem rude, but we both know that you don't give a damn about my trip. You've made that abundantly clear. Everyone came back safely and that's the big thing. So why don't you tell me what really brought you over here this late at night."

"Walt, this thing with Waasdorp. It won't work between us. It was a mistake for which I am equally to blame, and for which I sincerely beg your forgiveness. I want to come home, Walt. I want to be your wife. I want to be a help to you and to make a good home for you."

"You guys didn't give it much of a chance. Maybe you should work at it a while longer."

"No, I know already. It won't work. He's not like you, Walt. He's a different kind of man."

"I have no idea what that might mean."

"Anyway, he's married. And has kids. He loves his kids. He misses being with his kids every day."

"That part, I can understand."

"And anyway, it's you, Walt. I want to come back. I want you to take me back. To forgive me." She was trying to squeeze out a few tears but it was proving to be harder than she thought. The opera in the background had just reached Gremin's speech to Onegin. Track nine. The part about the gray-headed warrior—tempered by experience.

"Can we turn that thing off while we're talking?"

He tried to make his voice as gentle as possible but it came out sounding harsher than he intended. "No, Flo. I've been listening to this. This is the best part."

"But I'm talking to you."

"I can listen to two things at once."

"So you always say. But I just wish you would pay attention to me."

"I have paid attention to you, Flo. And I'm listening to you now. Look, if you want to come back, you're back. A lot of your stuff is still here. Come back. You can have it. You can have it all. You can have everything if that's what you want."

"No, Walt." Her voice took on a harsh, angry tone that was all too familiar. "It's not the goddamn house. Don't you get it? It's you. It's you who must forgive me. No wait. Not must. It's you who I'm begging to forgive me. I said must, because you must do it if I am to be happy again."

"What the hell went wrong?" *Jesus, she's not going to work up a cry on me?*

"Oh, everything. And my father tells me that I'm a fool."

The opera was moving to its dark ending with the gloomy dialogue between Onegin and Tatiana. Eugene is about to get the final, painful kiss-off from the woman who loves him, but is now married to another man. *Yes, I love you, goodbye forever! Yep, there's that high note. Eugene is history.*

Walt removed the CD and returned it to its case. The pages of the booklet fell on the floor and he let them stay. "I'll get that," she said. When she kneeled to pick up the pieces, she was textbook; right out of modeling school. *Knees together, back straight. Perfection*, he thought. *If Tara bent over to pick up those pages any guy in the room would stop to look. So what's wrong?*

Just let it go, he said to himself, immediately regretting his churlish behavior.

"Look, Flo. I'm tired. You take the bedroom tonight. I'll sleep in the guestroom. We can talk in the morning."

The morning was no better. When he woke and showered, she had already been up for some time, fixing breakfast, as if nothing had ever happened. He was forcing himself to eat something and trying to figure out the right thing to do—when the phone rang.

"I'll get it," Flo said. And before he could get up from the table she had the receiver.

"Hello. Yes. Yes, he's here. Whom shall I say is calling?" She handed him the phone and rolled her eyes.

"Yeah. Hi! Yeah, me, too. I just picked up the mail, washed all my dirty shirts and stuff. No, it went OK. No problems. No. No. No. Everything's fine. It's OK. Not this morning. Listen, how about if I call you back around lunchtime. Sure, that would be good. Yes, me too. Later. I'll call you."

"That was the little blond girl, wasn't it? Tara. I knew it. That little whore. She's had her eye on you from the first week she showed up. That little foreign slut. I can't believe this."

"Tara is American. Like you. Like me. American." He started to say *She's not a whore*, but he couldn't bring himself to think that Tara needed to be defended.

Things might have been less acrimonious if Flo had held off calling Tara a whore and a slut. But something in that mindless evaluation—especially in light of her own behavior—hardened his heart and strengthened his resolve.

I'll leave, he thought. *Just walk away. Across the steppes. All the way to Kazakhstan if need be. I can't live with this woman who can't stand to see me with my clothes off. Tara might choose to come with me. Or she might not.* In his heart he was sure of her answer. *It's all just a great adventure anyway. Let's see what the future might bring.*

A short time later, the university upgraded Walt's status to full professor, making a considerable change in his salary and retirement benefits.

Chapter 56

End of the Line

"Security was essential to maintain and expand the trade routes that became known as the Silk Road. Fortresslike way stations called caravansaries acted as havens against the wrath of weather and the plots of thieves. Without them, the deserts and wastelands would have been impassable barriers."

THE ROOT OF THE WILD MADDER
BRIAN MURPHY

The drug team had been able to determine that the traffic in hashish and marijuana was increasing dramatically as increasing acreage was devoted to production. Opium cultivation was continuing to expand but was showing signs of leveling off. The most astonishing advances had been made in the development of packaging and shipping methods which made the drugs harder—and more expensive—to detect. The number of ways in which drug products could be packaged for concealment was astonishing. The methods were so clever and so pervasive that observers believed interdiction of a substantial volume would never be practicable and that drug seizures were, in fact, little more than sampling techniques to confirm that, *yes*, we're seeing drugs.

The big breakthrough in understanding, however, came not from the work of individual Cats, but from the information obtained from the man they brought in, Valentin Mihailovich Kuriatin, a highly placed member of the Russian Mafia. Kuriatin spilled the beans on techniques used to ship vast quantities of drugs into Asia, Europe and North America. He had masterminded an astonishingly sophisticated network that was now in the process of being dismantled. People within the Agency were thankful that Kuriatin's talent had been employed in the drug end of the business and not in the weapons trade.

Valentin—ever the sly fox—considered alerting his new masters to the possibility of recovering his laptop from the place he had left it. But, upon reflection, he decided he could do enough damage to Arkady without it, and he didn't want to be too compliant.

On that day in Ashkhabad, when most of her companions had been involved with getting Valentin Kuriatin out of Turkmenistan and en route to the U.S., Katya had taken a walk. The broad, park-lined avenue was sunny and inviting. She walked for over a half-mile, lost in thoughts of her own. Sometime around noon she felt the need to sit down on a barstool, and she headed for the nearest large hotel that looked as if it catered to westerners.

She was sitting at the bar slowly nursing a vodka and tonic when Kenny Jiao wandered in and sat a few seats away. The bar was mostly empty and Kenny, educated in Texas and California, was accustomed to checking out attractive females on bar stools. To top it off, Katya was wearing a sweatshirt that said RICE.

"Pardon me, miss, but I couldn't help noticing your sweat. Did you attend Rice?"

"The shirt is from Rice. I got it at the student union last time I was in Houston," Tara answered. She turned long enough to get a look at Kenny, but most of her answer was directed at the backbar mirror.

Kenny moved one seat closer. "Then you are from Houston? I don't want to seem rude, but..."

"Nope. There to see about getting in their grad program," she lied.

Kenny moved another seat closer. "No kidding? Small world. I went to Rice. Got my B.A. there before moving to California to attend UCLA. So you're in their grad program? Taking what?"

Katya turned to look at Kenny more closely. *Chinese? Japanese? Hard to tell. His English is unaccented. Not bad looking. What the hell. It's just conversation.*

She turned to face him and crossed her legs on the stool. That was all it took. Kenny moved across the next three seats to sit beside her. "Hi. I'm Kenny. Kenny Jiao. Gee, small world. I never expected to meet anyone who's been to Rice."

"That's not me. I still haven't been admitted."

"Yeah, but you've been there. You know the school. I love Houston. Had a great time there. And Galveston. Some of my best memories are from Galveston."

"I can hear your seabirds calling," Katya said.

"This is a treat. Let me buy you a drink. Bartender, another for the lady." Katya looked at her glass. Half full.

"Don't tell me," she said. "You're an oilman. You can always tell an oilman."

Kenny Jiao laughed. "Would you believe me if I told you I'm in the movie business?" he said, putting both elbows on the bar and trying to get her to look straight at him.

"Sure I would. And you'd probably like to make me a star. You see something. Something indefinable. Maybe I'd like a screen test."

"OK, OK," he laughed. "Let's erase everything and start over. My name is Kenny. And you are ... ?"

"Kat."

"Cat? Just Cat? That's all?"

"It's not enough?"

Oops! Kenny was getting vibes that were not good. But they weren't bad either. They were neutral. No, actually if he read them more carefully they were on the playful side of neutral. This woman wasn't mean. She was just tough.

"Cat is fine. It's great. Really. It's just that ... " he pretended to cough.

"What's wrong?"

"I've always been allergic to cats." Now it was Katya's turn to laugh, and she turned to look at Kenny more closely.

"OK," she said. "My name is Katerina. People call me Katya. Or Kat. So! Thank you for the drink, Mr. Movie Mogul. What are some of your blockbuster hits?"

"I wasn't bullshitting you, Katya. Kat. I really am in the movie business. But I'm a small fish. I'm what's called a production assistant. I'm a flunkey. A well-paid go-fer."

"So you work in Hollywood?"

"In Hong Kong. Actually, all over. I go wherever the film crews are working. I work for several Chinese film companies. Kind of a floater to wherever they have problems I can solve."

"A trouble shooter?" she asked.

"Something like that."

Katya had started on the drink ordered by Kenny Jiao. She swiveled on the stool and took a slow look that covered everything; head to toe.

"So what's happening in Turkmenistan that requires you to come all the way from Hong Kong?"

"You'd be surprised. But I'm afraid to tell you the truth. If I say I'm making a movie, you'll laugh at me. Or even worse. Get up and leave."

"You did hang out in Galveston," she laughed.

"But what about you, Kat? Why are you in this corner of the world? It's a long way from Houston."

"Art and architecture. Central Asia. Stuff of the intellect. I'm here on an educational tour. I'm improving my mind."

"On a barstool? Only an American could say that and be convincing."

Kenny squared himself at the bar and quit staring at the region between Katya's cheekbones and the front of her sweatshirt. "I'm really here with a film crew. They're on location over near Mary and I had enough dust yesterday. Anyway, I'm not in the movie. I just coordinate a lot of the logistics and prep work. My work is mostly over. This part is mostly boondoggle. Unless there's a problem, I can just screw off until the damn thing is in the can."

"Sounds like the gravy train."

"Unless they have a problem. If there's a sandstorm and some equipment gets damaged, that's when I have to go in high gear. Twenty-four seven until the problems are fixed. I pray to the weather gods."

He nodded toward her empty glass but she shook her head. "I better get walking. Walk off these calories."

"Trust me, Kat," Kenny said. "Leave 'em on. Look … you like Chinese food? Right? I know where there's a Chinese restaurant that's pretty good. Have lunch with me. Yes? You can tell me about art and stuff."

"Can we walk there from here?" she said.

At lunch, Kenny ordered a small bottle of rice wine which they shared over the meal. Kenny was beginning to show signs that the alcohol was taking hold. Katya, who matched him in body weight, was in her zone. By now, the gentleman from Hong Kong had taken the opportunity to look at her carefully, and he liked what he saw. *She could almost pass for Chinese in some places*, he thought.

"I'm glad you agreed to have lunch with me," he said.

"But you're kinda disappointed that I'm not going to go back to your hotel room with you. I've heard all about you movie guys and how you try to seduce girls over lunch. With Chinese dumplings. And wine."

Kenny laughed. This American girl was a lot of fun. It was almost like being back in Houston.

"You're reading me all wrong, Katya. It's just a treat for … ."

"Save it, Kenny. There's no line I haven't heard. More than once. So just finish telling me about the movie. Better yet, why don't we leave and walk back to the hotel. We can have something to drink while we talk."

"Sure, that sounds fine." They got up to leave. "But aren't you afraid I'll try to get you drunk—so I can have my way with you?"

"Oh sure," she said. "I'm terrified—you being a Rice guy and all. I've heard about you guys and your prowess. But I'm trying to learn to overcome fear."

On the walk back, she put her arm through his, in a friendly kind of way, as if they had been pals for years. They were walking past one of Ashkhabad's ubiquitous water parks, where a quartet of bronze fish were spurting streams of water high in the air. "This is a crazy place," she said, cheerfully. "Nothing is as you would expect it to be. You're probably a secret agent from the Chinese CIA. So let me tell you right now, you're wasting your time on me. And I don't even want to know your secret mission." She gave his arm a yank.

"I'm just pulling your arm."

Back at the bar they took a table near the corner and ordered vodka. After two more drinks Kenny's thoughts were starting to run in what Katya described as the "two-vodka groove."

"If I tell you something, will you promise not to get angry? Or take it the wrong way?"

"That's asking for a lot," she said. It was after two p.m. She was only planning to spend another hour with this guy.

"OK. Here goes. You are very pretty. In parts of China—even in Hong Kong, I think—you could pass for Chinese if you wanted."

"Well, thank you very much, Kenny. That's very sweet of you. But I can't reveal all my beauty secrets."

"Why not? What could I do with them? You'll never see me again."

"Let's have one more drink," she said. "Maybe I'll tell you mine after you tell me yours."

It was after five when Katya returned to her own hotel. She had to wait an hour for Gina to get back from the embassy where she had been arranging for Val and three male Cats to get out of the country.

"The Chinese have smuggled in a pipeline survey crew as part of their movie-making contingent."

"Oh yeah? Sez who? Where'd this come from?"

"I have it on good authority."

"Do I detect vodka?"

"Do I detect chicken shit? They're surveying a line from the fields at Dauletabad down to Gwadar in Pakistan."

"And you know this how?"

"Fucking crystal ball. And fuck you, Gina!"

Once they knew what to look for—and where to find it—investigators in Washington readily confirmed that the Chinese film crew visiting Turkmenistan had been intended as cover for a survey team. It was also easy to ascertain that they were looking for an optimum route out of that country—across Afghanistan heading for the Indian Ocean. This move, long suspected, had been relatively transparent, but the Chinese film crew actually appeared to be on track to produce some kind of action or adventure film. The organization behind the film activity was CHOCO, the China Oil Corporation, whose central offices were in Shanghai. Not a lot the Feds could do about it. China is big!

Katya didn't even get a pat on the back.

What happened to Arkady? Happily for the world, Arkady has left us. It happened about six weeks after Val left Almaty, intending to flee from his death sentence. After a late night drinking session, Arkady developed what doctors later described as "an esophageal bleed." It began with vomiting which contained a volume of black material that could only be old blood. Distended veins in his esophagus had begun leaking into his stomach and it was the old blood that came up first. The vomiting exacerbated his damaged esophageal tract and soon he was hemorrhaging fresh blood. If he had sought medical attention immediately he might have survived, but the bleed occurred after he was in Ludmila's apartment and the only ones there were Ludmila, his mistress, and one totally incompetent housekeeper who was terrified by the sight of blood. They waited for several hours to seek help. By then he had lost a lot of blood, and the delays at the hospital where he was carried proved to be the icing on the cake. Who can say for certain? Maybe Ludmila knew exactly what she was doing and she didn't think too many people would be saddened by his passing. In any case, she had taken good care of herself and her living standard won't change appreciably with Arkady's departure.

He did attract a big funeral, and it would be interesting to interview all the attendees to obtain their feelings about the man.

After Arkady's death the pressure to find and kill Valentin Kuriatin lessened steadily since no one was throwing money at the problem. Within the boss's circle of business colleagues, a successor was quickly found for the vodka distilleries. The new manager was well-versed in marketing techniques and he immediately moved to increase the export side of the business.

The trade in illegal arms split off and became a separate business. Some of those closest to Arkady had anticipated that an internal war would take place as individuals competed for the job of filling his shoes. But the conglomerate he had held together by the force of his will had grown too big for one man to manage and the partners were able to come to reasonably amicable agreements on how the business should be split. The arms portion of the business went to a former KGB deputy secretary.

That's not to say there weren't a few problems. Other colleagues resented his approach to the weapons trade and the new boss died within three months in a mysterious car accident. His replacement may find life to be a chancy proposition, as well.

Weapons are still being manufactured in many parts of the world and they find their way to other parts of the world. There is money to be made, but this trade seems to attract a particular type of man—very few women—who enjoy danger mixed with the aroma of cleaning solvent and the smell of powder. Such men tend to be fatalistic about life and view everything—possibly correctly, depending on the roll of the dice—as beyond their personal control.

What about the drugs? The empire that Valentin had believed he could someday mold into a world-class business worthy of a case study at the Harvard Business

School? It fell into the lap of an ex-Army colonel of Buriat origins, who probably still worships the blue sky like some of his Mongol ancestors. Like Arkady, he is a brute and the business is unlikely to attain the level of efficiency attained under Valentin, but people—everywhere—continue to demand drugs. The colonel will do well with his drug empire.

The split-up following Arkady's death didn't take place without a price. So far, at least three deaths have resulted from power struggles as lesser chiefs fight for key roles.

Katya? What of this interesting female? She has been given a desk assignment after several years of field work, but she chafes under managers who don't approve of her lifestyle even though they are not permitted to admit as much. It is not easy to work for the agency at a desk job when your administrative boss is a born-again Christian, but at the same time, this isn't something that you can easily complain about. She wants to make a career move, but meanwhile she is drinking more than she should. She doesn't do well singing *Kumbaya*. Katya belongs in the field.

Last month she visited Cape Cod where she met a salty oceanographer at a breakfast joint. They went out several times and clicked, and Katya wouldn't mind taking things to the next level. Unfortunately, she has not been completely honest with him concerning the nature of her work, and that may be a problem. She knows that she needs to cut back on the drinking and she plans to do it, but right now she is under a lot of stress.

Some readers of this account may find it curious to come up against so many interesting females with two-syllable names, but such coincidences happen all the time. Keep in mind that Katya's real name is Ekaterina. Gina, too, uses her nickname in preference to the five-syllable handle on her birth certificate. She doesn't want anyone—even close friends—to call her by the name she was born with.

The best thing that could have happened to Walt came from taking Tara on the trip with the Herd of Cats. Because they were all adults instead of college students, he and Tara began to travel as a couple. She had inserted herself into his life with no encouragement on his part. In the broadest sense, she was a gift—out of the blue. How do such things happen? It's a question he'll think about as long as he lives. With no effort on his part at all, this girl just walked into his life, loving him from day one.

She loved everything about him. She shared his interests without wanting to get into the limelight, she respected his scholarship and she knew enough to be able to help whenever he needed her. At the same time she knew better than to try to involve herself before she was invited. Best of all, his leg didn't bother her at all. Flo had never been able to accept the leg. With Tara, it was never a problem.

Flo never talked much about it, but it mattered to her. When he was naked with

Tara she would call him pegleg, but it always came out as a private expression between them. They whispered to each other when they were in bed and sometimes they said outrageous things to make one another laugh. Nothing was off limits, nothing was sacred, and she was always, always on his side.

In private she was crude and ready for anything, but in public she was a model. Faculty teas and all the other crap that is part of university life wasn't a problem for her. If she didn't like this aspect of his work she never said a word, and as a research assistant she was a gem.

For a time, Walt had trouble determining whether he loved this woman, or if he was just responding to her attraction to him. But every move she makes is so sincere, so selfless and so supportive that it is impossible not to love her. She is, quite literally, too good to be true.

After the Herd of Cats returned from Central Asia, Walt went to work in earnest on untying the knot with Florence. His lawyer recommended that he and Tara live apart until the divorce was final. In the strongest possible language the attorney emphasized that the cost penalty of living together with Tara would probably be substantial.

Walt talked it over with Tara, who laughed. "As if that would matter to me. What matters to me is whether or not you need me in your life. The rest is bullshit. That's why you hire lawyers in the first place."

"You want to move in, then?"

"I want you to want me to move in. I want you to need me to move in. I want you to beg me to move in. Otherwise, I'm comfortable in my apartment."

"Tara, you know that I wan...."

"My god, you are fuzzy-brained to be such a smart man. Look. It's very simple. You have triggered something in my brain. You are stimulating some chemicals in my body that make me wild for you. You can't help it. And neither can I. It may even have something to do with Central Asia.

"I'm trying to follow you but...."

"Just be quiet and let me finish. Whatever is happening to me because of you is wonderful. Even if we split tomorrow, I'll never be the same after you. I could still have a wonderful life without you in it. Maybe. But it would never be the same. But what I feel when you are around is not going to last. It can't. It's too intense, and it's too chemical. It's going to fade. What would be nice would be, by the time it does fade, if we've got something else. Something that will keep us together so I can spend the rest of my life with..." and her voice rose by an octave, "your fuzzy-brained, one-legged, occasionally wishy-washy ass."

"Tara, I hardly know what to say. Sometimes I think you are so much smarter than me."

"I know. Me, too."

"Move in with me. I'm telling the lawyer not to bring it up again."
"Just shut up for a bit."
"Don't be mad at…"
"Just shut up. And take off your pants."
"We can go in the den."
"Just do what I say. Forget the leg."
"The den will be more comfortable."

"Will you just do what I tell you?" Despite her words, she wasn't angry and her eyes were as wide as a hunting cat's. Her pupils were dilated and she looked as if she was going into a trance. "I need to sit on your lap," she whispered.

Walt is going to be surprised at how easy it will be to divorce Florence, and how good it will feel to marry Tara shortly afterward. It will be a good many years before her infatuation for him wears off and by then they will be as comfortable as old shoes.

Next year they are going back to visit the Silk Road. Walt is hoping to expand the trip to three weeks and he hopes the increased cost will not be a barrier to participation. There are still a lot of details to be worked out with the Chinese, but he is hoping that he can link up with universities in Shanghai or Beijing and use those connections to get approval to extend his tour to Urumchi on the northern edge of the Takla Makan. *From the Takla Makan to the Kara Kum. Wow! What a trip!* Tara is as excited as he is, because if he gets approval the two of them will make an advance scouting trip to work out details for accommodations and transportation.

There is, of course, a secret place in Walt that he rarely visits. That private *terra incognita* lies somewhere at the intersection of his own physical defect and what he perceives as Tara's perfection. In the weeks after his return from Herding Cats, he has taken a decision to write a book about silk. He believes that its title will be simply that, *Silk*, and in it he will collect interesting facts about silk in the history of the world.

"Do you think there's enough material for you to do a whole book just about silk?" Tara asked.

He laughed. "The problem will be what to leave out."

"Don't get all porky. I was just curious."

"There's a lot of material that could be used to tell the story in a way that's different and possibly unique. For sure there won't be much that's original. Except my own perspective."

"But you can do it? Right?"

"OK, you tell me. What cloth material is mentioned in the Bible's opening book, Genesis, and then shows up again in Revelations?"

"Are you kidding me? Silk is in the Bible?" He smiled because he knew that really had surprised her.

"Of course, like a lot of things from the past there are still a couple of mysteries to be solved."

"Now you're making me curious."

"Actually, it's sometimes translated as silk, and sometimes as linen. Silk had a bad name for a time. Too luxurious."

His own personal library contains much useful research material and the departmental library at the university holds even more. JBU is close enough to Washington that he can take advantage of the Library of Congress whenever the need arises.

In the process of his reading and preparation for tackling this new project, he had been reading widely, and one of the works that passed through his hands was a piece of fiction by Turkish author Orhan Pamuk. The novel was titled *Snow*, and it was set in the Turkish city of Kars.

Walt had been in Kars during his boyhood days. He visited the city with his childhood pal, Ekrem, on their way to visit the ruins of the ruined Armenian town of Ani. Because the place seemed so familiar, Walt took the story in slowly, picturing the scenes of his boyhood and wondering why he had not made more of an effort to preserve his friendship with Ekrem.

So it came as a jolt when he hit a single line by the Turkish author that rang like some kind of universal truth. *"Immersing oneself in the problems of a book is a good way to keep from thinking of love."*

Early on, he knew himself to be totally ensnared by Tara. She had told him as much. *Ensorcelled* was the word she had used, and he felt that it was true. But what of her? How could he hope to hold this creature, given his defects? Physical *and* mental? Coming out of his experiences as a Cat Herder he felt as if he had allowed himself to be used. This, in his mind, qualified as a defect, a character flaw. Even his material success, stemming as it undoubtedly did from his work for the government, felt somehow tainted.

With Tara he was always happy, always in the moment, because he knew that it might end at any time. It could last forever, or burst like a bubble tomorrow. After the time she showed him the photos of them together in bed, the subject had never come up again. Some time into their "couplehood" he screwed up his courage and asked her about the photos.

"I still have them," she said. "Don't worry. They're safe."

"Yeah, OK. But the thing that's always puzzled me…was…why. Why did you take them in the first place?"

"I can't explain it," she said, moving in close to offset—with physical contact—anything she might say to upset him. "I was unhappy because I could see you were unhappy. Plus I really wanted you. I wanted to *get* you. I wanted you to want me. I don't really know. I was kinda *desperate*. You might have noticed."

"Well, it worked; what you did."

"Was it so bad of me? Do you condemn me for it? Am I a disappointment to you?"

"Come here," he said, ready to move on. "A disappointment? Well, you didn't take my good side."

So the topic was put to rest for another interval, but still, somewhere deep inside his skull, near the place where remembered aromas and tastes are stored, something about that episode still itches.

Ah, yes, just one more loose end that you may be wondering about: that strange English gentleman that Valentin met on the train between Ashkhabad and Turkmenbashi. Huffington was his name? After Val was interrogated—or perhaps we should use the term 'debriefed', he spilled the beans on every aspect of Arkady's enterprise. Of course, Val never understood the full scope and range of Arkady's arms network, but for the drug business, he worked hard to give up details, contacts and names. He dealt Arkady a blow which, had the vicious bastard lived, would have driven him to apoplexy.

But—although it was frequently in his mind—he never told his handlers a single word about the Englishman he met on the train to Turkmenbashi. He never mentioned the source for the Taurus pistol—one round missing—that Paul Kellogg later recovered from beneath his bed in the hotel room at Ashkhabad. They never asked. He never told. The whole experience was too bizarre. Like much of his life. Strange. Unpredictable. Like the details in some fantastic fairy tale. Like his being in America. He thought—correctly—that the Huffington episode, fantastical as it was, would have put his whole credibility in jeopardy.

He liked working with Americans. Part of it was being disconnected from the stresses of working for Arkady. He had been in the country long enough to be comfortable with the language, a fact he confirmed by having several dreams totally in English. Naturally they were dreams about women.

Anyway, getting back to the Englishman—what is there to tell? What did he know? The whole encounter was a mystery. Something out of a dream.

Could Huffington have been some type of English spy? Sent to Central Asia to gather intelligence to be used by Britain's spy agencies? That was the most plausible explanation. But how had he sensed that Val needed a weapon? And the curious business with the symbols on the card? And the tea room? It was all baffling. Every time Val thought back on the details of the train ride, it seemed as if some critical element of the puzzle was eluding him. If he had told that unbelievable story to the Americans, everything else they had accepted would have been called into question. He toyed with the notion that one day he would visit England and look up the Greenwich address of the Englishman. Any attempt to make contact was out of the question. Val knew he was still being watched and would probably be under suspicion for some time to come.

There are plenty of unresolved questions remaining in this story. Katya's background, for example. She has a history that Walt glimpsed momentarily during his Washington briefing by Paul Chapman. It was to be kept confidential. Or the interesting story of why Paul Kellogg and his Vietnamese wife live aboard a skipjack in Chesapeake Bay. There just isn't time enough for all these loose ends. Especially since we began with the truly vast topic of the Silk Road. Like the Silk Road itself, the story just runs along, branching and threading in many directions; stretching without apparent end, into the hazy distance.

Think of the route—simplistically—as stretching all the way from Xi'an in Central China, across Asia into Europe ending in Rome. Then consider the sea routes to make the same trip as it would have been made at the beginning of the Christian Era. Finally, think of all the places where you have encountered silk during your lifetime. It's in the Bible, just as Walt told us. Silk. Thrice in the Old Testament: Genesis, Ezekiel and Proverbs; once in the New. In Revelations. Silk. The Silk Road. The ancient route has enjoyed a fascinating history. Just like our players.

Speaking of players—Paul Kellogg: He gave his wife a little medallion with a cross that he brought back from Turkmenistan. He never told her the details of how he took it from around the neck of a man to whom he gave CPR at the possible risk to his own life. He did, however, have a blood test performed as soon as he was back in the states. Valentin's mouth was, indeed, bloody. So Paul felt like he had earned whatever protection the cross might provide. Nguyen wears it constantly.

He has tried to describe Turkmenistan to her.

"Remember how weird Iraq seemed when I was there before? With all the statues and posters of Saddam? Turkmenistan is much weirder. You can't go anywhere without seeing gilded statue of Turkmenbashi. The guy must be nuts. It's just a matter of time before he really goes off the deep end." She seemed to listen attentively, but her hands were busy and she was actually focusing on what she was doing. Making crabcakes.

EPILOGUE

Epilogue

> "I am a naked man standing inside a mine of rubies,
> clothed in red silk.
> I absorb the shining and now I see the ocean,
> billions of simultaneous motions
> moving in me."
>
> FROM "I HAVE SUCH A TEACHER"
> THE ESSENTIAL RUMI
> TRANSLATED BY COLEMAN BARKS

One night in their Mercersburg apartment, Walt told Tara about his dreams in the hospital in Germany. She knew that he had spent several boyhood years in Turkey, but she had never heard the story of the trip he made with Ekrem to the abandoned Armenian city of Ani. In the process of telling the story, he mentioned the Silk Road Bridge; and while saying its name in Turkish, he also told her the bit about Ekrem's little sister, Ipek, whose name, he had suddenly realized, meant "silk."

"That was her name? Silk? What else about her do you remember?"

"That was all I ever knew. Ipek. Silk. I never knew if she even had a middle name. You know—before Ataturk it was common for many Turks to just have one-word names. No family name. Ataturk was the one who Europeanized Turkish names. Their family name was Ispahani."

"And you remembered her name after so many years? You had a crush on her. I bet."

"Come on, Tara. She was just a little girl. She was five years younger...."

"Yeah, OK. Oh, yes. Almost as young as little me. You pervert."

"Good grief. Why did I bring this up?"

Tara pulled in close, and they were talking in whispers.

"Pervert. Pervert," she breathed in his ear. "I'll bet you want to do all kinds of things … to me."

"Why? Why? Why is this happening?"

"Because you want to tell me everything. You want to tell me the secrets you never told anyone else. But there's no hurry."

"I don't really have any … ."

"And you want to take me to Turkey some time. Back to the places you visited as a boy. So I will know everything about you, and gradually I'll absorb all of you and you will no longer exist—except as part of me. And I can walk around after your total absorption lit up like a light bulb. A walking big O."

"Were you drinking while you were in the bathroom?"

"You know you want to take me to Turkey. You know you are dying to do me in Turkey. You already said."

"True."

"Maybe even on that mountain. At sunrise."

"Possibly."

"Maybe a knee trembler?"

"Not likely."

"How about with snow on the ground?"

"Unlikely. But I wouldn't rule it out completely."

"And we can look up your friend. See if we can find him."

"That would be interesting. I never thought of it."

"And Ipek. We could see what she turned into. That would be fun, too."

"I was never friends with Ipek. She probably wouldn't even remember me."

"She was how old? Eleven? Twelve? Her brother's pal? She'll remember."

"It might be interesting to see what happened to Ipek and Ekrem. Really. They probably live at opposite ends of the country. I doubt we could find them."

"Don't give me that crap, professor. I know I could find them if you turned me loose."

"Maybe I will. Turn you loose. But I don't know if you should be turned loose. That's a scary thought."

"What's scary is that your Ipek—your beautiful *silky little boyhood crush*—is now all *growed* up and more appealing than me. You might see her again. Fall in love and dump me."

"Are you worried about that?"

"Maybe. Maybe I should be."

"Are you really worried?"

"Yes!" *Tiny, pouty voice.*

"Still worried?"

"A lot less, now."

"Please don't be worried."

"Um!"

His lips were against her ear and his voice was barely audible. She could feel his words as much as she could hear them.

"Her name was 'silk.' Just her name. But you, Tara. You *are* silk."

"Um! With you."

Walt remembered Eugen's words from the opera. "Lyublyu tebya," he said.

Tara pulled back and looked at him, her cat's eyes wide with surprise.

"Lyublyu tebya," he repeated.

"Oh," she said. "You sweet man. You will make me melt."

"Yes," he said. "Go ahead. Keep melting."

To be continued.

ISBN 1425118364